PRAISE FOR EMILY COLIN

PRAISE FOR THE SEVEN SINS SERIES

- WINNER, 2022 Gold Moonbeam Award for Best Book Series
- WINNER, 2022 Silver IPPY Award for Young Adult Fiction
- WINNER, 2021 North Carolina Indie Author Award in Young Adult Fiction
- FINALIST, 2021 and 2022 Foreword INDIES Award in Young Adult Fiction
- SHORTLISTED for The Manly Wade Wellman Award for Science Fiction and Fantasy

PRAISE FOR SIEGE OF THE SEVEN SINS

This is easily one of the best books I've ever read. *Siege of the Seven Sins* has it all—heart-stopping action, breathtaking characters, high stakes, and a thrilling story, all wrapped up in beautiful prose.

— MADELINE DYER, SIBA-AWARD-WINNING
AUTHOR OF THE *UNTAMED* SERIES

Thrilling, heart-wrenching, and blood-pumping.

KARISSA LAUREL, AUTHOR OF *THE
STORMBOURNE CHRONICLES*

With an intriguing world, an impossible love story, and characters I both loved and loved to hate, the stakes are high. What if love was a death sentence? ... A series everyone should know about.

— M. LYNN, *USA TODAY* BESTSELLING AUTHOR
OF THE *QUEENS OF THE FAE* SERIES

PRAISE FOR SWORD OF THE SEVEN SINS

This book is absolutely unputdownable. It's all my favorite things about high-stakes fantasy and dystopian: a world close enough to ours to satirize our own flaws. Badass, rebellious characters. DEEPLY forbidden love. Swords, hand to hand combat fight scenes. Secret societies, escapes, withstanding torture... I didn't even realize how much I'd missed books like this until I fell into this one.

— MICHELLE HAZEN, AUTHOR OF *BREATHE*
THE SKY

A romantic dystopian with a fantastic—and unexpected—twist ... *Seven Sins* is powerful, sexy, hopeful, and unsettling.

— HEIDI AYARBE, AWARD-WINNING AUTHOR
OF *FREEZE FRAME*

A rollicking ride through forbidden love and deadly adventure. ... I haven't ached for love like this to conquer all since Tris and Four. Eva and Ari forever.

—LEIGH STATHAM, AUTHOR OF THE
DAUGHTER TRILOGY

Amazing characters and a fast plot that will keep you on the edge of your seat!

—S.E. ANDERSON, AUTHOR OF *THE
STARSTRUCK SAGA*

A beautifully crafted story with so many intense moments I couldn't stop reading. This is the best book I've read in a long time.

—MICHELLE MACQUEEN, AUTHOR OF *WE
THOUGHT WE WERE INVINCIBLE*, FOR YA
BOOKS CENTRAL

Sword of the Seven Sins ... offers a new take on the dystopian genre. Colin's characters push the plot forward, while her writing immerses the reader in a rigid world on the brink of change.

—BOOKSTACKED

An absolutely mind-blowing, spine-tingling, action-packed extravaganza ... an electrifying, imaginative, phenomenally well written book. The tension, banter and angst blazes.

— EMERALD BOOK REVIEWS

Much of the fun here is watching Colin build her world ... The chapters move swiftly... The book should prove a hit with fans of *The Hunger Games.*

— WILMINGTON *STAR NEWS*

Sizzling hot and exploding with tension.

— LISA AMOWITZ, AUTHOR OF *BREAKING GLASS*

An absolutely wild ride ... I couldn't stop reading.

— THE WORD TRAVELER

PRAISE FOR THE DREAM KEEPER'S DAUGHTER

A splendid mix of time travel, romantic yearning, and moving on after grief.

— *PUBLISHERS WEEKLY*

A passionate and sweeping tale of a woman haunted by a loss she can't explain, and a future she can't yet choose.

— ERIKA MARKS, AUTHOR OF THE LAST TREASURE

This story immerses you in a time that should not be forgotten and explores the infinite rippling effect of decisions, guilt, accountability, and love.

—SAMANTHA SOTTO, AUTHOR OF LOVE AND GRAVITY

PRAISE FOR THE MEMORY THIEF

This absorbing first effort brings to mind the mountaineers of a Jon Krakauer read, the tenderness of a Nicholas Sparks novel, and the enduring love story of Charles Martin's The Mountain between Us, all sprinkled with a heady dose of passion.

— BOOKLIST

Mesmerizing . . . dazzlingly original and as haunting as a dream.

— CAROLINE LEAVITT, NEW YORK TIMES BESTSELLING AUTHOR OF PICTURES OF YOU

[A] richly emotional tale . . . a writer to watch.

—JOSHILYN JACKSON, *NEW YORK TIMES*
BESTSELLING AUTHOR OF *A GROWN-UP KIND
OF PRETTY*

STORM

OF THE

SEVEN

SINS

STORM OF THE SEVEN SINS

BOOK THREE IN THE SEVEN SINS SERIES

EMILY COLIN

Colin, Emily. 1975-.
Siege of the Seven Sins: A Novel / Emily Colin
ISBN (Pbk.) 978-1-961469-07-5
(Ebook) 978-1-961469-06-8
1. Science Fiction. 2. Young Adult Fiction. 3. Fantasy Fiction. I. Title.
813'.6
v.230611

BLACK ORCHID
BOOKS

Published by Black Orchid Books
A division of Emily Colin Consulting
Wilmington, NC
Cover Design by Lisa Amowitz

To my readers, who have stuck with me through this series and made Ari and Eva's world come to life.

You know who you are.

EPIGRAPH

"Some rise by sin, and some by virtue fall."
—William Shakespeare, *Measure for Measure*

"Freely we serve,
Because we freely love, as in our will
To love or not; in this we stand or fall."
—John Milton, *Paradise Lost*

CHAPTER 1
EVA

"You should have let me kill him," I say to Ari, staring at the bed where the Executor—my *father*—ought to be. I pace to the mattress, put my hand on it. It is cold.

The man was stitched together like an Architect Day turkey. There's no way he escaped on his own. He had help from someone familiar with the rhythms of the infirmary, who knew how to drug the guards' kaffi. Who could keep a badly injured man alive while on the run.

Mei.

What did she say, the night of the battle in the Hall? *Maybe I should've mixed in some valerian and poppy, too. Enough of that, and you'll sleep right through the ceremony.* She gave me everything I needed to see through her façade, and I didn't have a clue.

I want to scream. But instead, as Ari sprints down the hall to check on Kilían and Karsten, I force myself to focus. To ignore the angry rumbles of my panther and my wolf, furious at the loss of our prey.

Fade and Adrien lie sprawled on the floor, unmoving. Ronan crouches next to them, shaking Adrien's shoulder, his expression grim. Two of his best guards are unconscious. His prisoner is gone. In the Commonwealth, Efraím would have had his head for less.

Lifting the mug that lies next to Fade's hand, I inhale. Beneath the aroma of kaffi lurks the woody odor of lavender, along with two foreign scents. I'd wager my sverd that if we tested the cups' contents, we'd find valerian and poppy in the dregs.

I close my eyes and let my panther come forward, sampling the air. Sure enough, I can pick out Mei's scent: the distinctive aroma of anise, undergirded by rose petal oil. Leaving Ronan to rouse Adrien and Fade, I follow the trail down the hall, but it dissipates as I round the corner, near a sink. She must have changed and washed to make herself harder to track, then fled through the door at the end of the corridor.

I drop my gaze to the floor. Sure enough, there's a pile of clothes.

Why would she help the Executor escape? He held nothing over Mei. She had no ties to him, no feelings for his cause.

But she knows how much I hate him. She's furious with me for killing Riis, even though he only wanted to use her. And helping the Executor is the surest way to undermine all I've fought to achieve—maybe to assure my death.

Everything ugly in my life can be laid at his feet.

Ari materializes next to me. "Karsten's gone." Though his voice is even, I can feel his fury pulsing down the bond. "Kilían's here, but barely conscious. He must have tried to stop them. One of them bashed him over the head with a tray table, got him pretty good."

"We'll get him help," I say. "But first..."

His gaze flickers down to the pile of clothes. "Mei's?"

"She was more dangerous than we gave her credit for." I think of the girl who rode with me in the woods, who told me she was tired of being useless, of everyone thinking she was just a pretty ornament who was good with plants. Who told me there was no recipe to assure the dissolution of love or friendship.

Sure, the Executor probably used every tool at his disposal to convince her to help him. But she was fallow ground, ripe for the seeds he planted. I may not know much about friendship, but whatever Mei and I are now, 'friends' doesn't make the list.

Grimly, I push my thoughts of Mei out of my mind. There will be time enough to rage at her later. "The Executor must have left something," I tell Ari. "A clue."

"What are you talking about? This isn't a game—"

"Of course it is," I say impatiently. "That's exactly what it is to him."

Turning, I stride back down the corridor, past Adrien and Fade, who have begun to stir, past the healers who are bustling up and down the hallway. I shove my way into the room that used to belong to the Executor, looking everywhere: at the small side table, the stool on which the healers sit, the bed.

And then I see what I missed before, in my anger and my haste. Propped against the Executor's pillow is a single white bandage. On it, printed in spiky black capital letters, is this:

GOOD HUNTING, EVA.

Incandescent with fury, I run my fingers over the bandage. And then I close my eyes and make a vow to my mother and my father. I swear it five-fold, on behalf of myself and the four shadow-beasts roiling within me.

I will find you.

CHAPTER 2
EVA

The wind gusts, sending an icy breath of air snaking through Ari's room in the guards' quarters. It smells like smoke, from the fire in the Great Hall, and the remnants of burning flesh.

Ari and I stand at the open window, watching the trackers disappear down Ash Avenue. Jaxon, my former familiar-to-be, is with them, as is Riley, skúmaskot of House Minneska. In wolf form, he can track the Executor, Karsten, and Mei to the city's edge. He won't go further; the danger is too great. But he can show the trackers where to start hunting.

I ache to accompany them. But Councilor-in-Chief Adelman forbade it, and Ronan backed him up. The Executor's disappearance could be a trick, they said. A ploy to isolate, capture, or kill the Brotherhood's most valuable weapon. So I'm stuck here, as useful in determining the Executor's whereabouts as a lump of coal.

The wolf inside me paces, hackles raised in fury, and Ari clenches his hands on the sill. The wind rummages through his dark hair, plastering his black gear to his body. There are smudges of exhaustion under his green eyes.

"By the Sins, Eva, I'm so sorry." His guilt rolls through our bond in waves, tasting of sour ashes. "I give you my word I won't rest until that cockroach of a man lies dead at our feet."

The last of the trackers disappear from view as I turn from the window. "It's not your fault. I knew Mei was a traitor, and I let her live. She's a Mage; who knows what she's capable of? I was a fool to show her mercy. If not for me, none of this would have happened."

His eyes narrow. "Don't you dare take this on yourself. If it's not my fault, then it's not yours either. Any more than it's Fade or Adrien's, for not realizing she'd drugged their kaffi. You heard Ronan when he questioned them. They're furious with themselves. So is the healer who worked the desk. She fooled them all."

I shake my head, misery twisting through me. "I should have—"

"No. This isn't on you, Eva. I won't let you carry this burden alone, like you did when you..." He breaks off, but I know what he's thinking of: the time I surrendered myself to the Executor and the bellators so he could walk free. I nearly died, and he risked his life to save me.

I don't care that he made me promise never to endanger myself like that again. I would do it a thousand times if it meant Ari would live.

His hand drops to his dagur, caressing the hilt. The Houses pray to the many-headed gods; Ari places his faith in his blades.

"And you," he says softly. "I have faith in you."

I jerk back, surprised. The familiar-skúma bond between us is new, and I have no clue how much either of us can sense through it when I'm in human form. If he can hear my thoughts when I'm making no effort to project them, then that's... disturbing. But also, somehow, beautiful.

The corners of his lips rise in wry acknowledgment of our

connection. "Believe me," he says, his voice hoarse, and opens himself to me.

I sense his anger. His determination. The steel-cable strength of his love. And his sincerity. He truly doesn't hold me responsible for what's happened.

If he can forgive me, maybe I can try to forgive myself.

He takes one step closer, then another, and when I don't retreat, he wraps his arms around me, holding me tight. He smells of smoke and soap and home.

I should probably push him away, tell him this is the time for hunting, not holding. But the moment our bodies touch, the tension flows out of me. Part of that is just being close to the person who knows me better than anyone else in the world, even my worst, most brutal parts, and accepts me anyhow. Part of it is relief that I didn't lose him at Karsten's hands, that he's still here with me. And part of it, I know, is the bond.

It doesn't matter. All I care about is that I can hear his heart beating, strong and steady and *mine*. On this, my beasts and I are in agreement. He belongs to us. Others will harm him at their peril.

He draws back, looking down at me. "If you want to hunt the Executor down, little warrior, then we will. I belong at your side; you know that. My fight is yours. When I raise my blade, I do so in your service."

"You'd defy Ronan?" I say, scanning his face. "And the Council?"

"The hell with these Brotherhood bastards. They need *us*, not the other way around." His voice deepens, taking on the eager edge it always does before battle. "How fast can he be moving, wounded like he is? We'll find him, and we'll kill him."

A shudder runs through my body and into his, a perfect circuit. I breathe and he exhales, his fingers tightening in my hair. "We'll wait until nightfall," he says, his voice low. "That way, we won't be missed. If the trackers haven't brought him back, we'll go after him."

I glance around the bare room, sighing. "What are we supposed to do until then?"

Ari arches a dark eyebrow. "Oh, I can think of a few things."

His burnt-sugar scent deepens, the bond making our connection uncanny. I can feel the callused pressure of his fingertips on my bare upper arms, but also the softness and heat of my skin, and the way he holds himself back from gripping me tighter. When our bodies touch, I feel not only the warmth that coils deep in my belly, but the desire that sparks within him.

"The door isn't locked," I say feebly.

"Easily remedied." His hand cups my cheek.

"Someone could come looking for us."

"Conveniently, we'll be right here." His fingers slide lower, tracing their way down my neck, and I shiver.

"We might lose track of time."

"Luckily for us, the sun comes with a built-in dimmer." His lips ghost their way along my throat to my collarbone, his breath hot on my skin. "I asked you once if you'd have me, Eva. I know you were frightened, then; I was frightened, too. And there were secrets between us—your secrets, and others' lies. But now there's nothing between us but these damnable clothes"—his fingers grip my hips—"and I'm asking you, again."

I want to say yes, with every fiber of my being. But now, with the Executor missing and the Houses still far from united on their decision to invade the Commonwealth, there's a question that needs to be asked. "What about Sebastían?"

Ari freezes. Then he steps back, his lips pressed into a hard line. "You're not still considering marrying him." His voice is cold. "Not after we..."

Wedding the panther prince in order to solidify the alliance between the Houses is the last thing I want. But now, more than ever, I can't dismiss the possibility. "Little as I care to, I have to consider it. With everything that's happened, we need that alliance, Ari. I can't be the reason we don't find the Executor and take the Commonwealths down. How could I live with myself?"

The connection between us severs, as if Ari's slammed a door in my face. I'm alone in my own skin, and it's both a relief and horribly unsettling. "By the nine hells, Eva, I gave you my *soul*," he says, shoving a hand through his hair. "If that's not enough, what is? Will I never be enough for you, no matter what I do?"

"How many times do I need to tell you that *this is not about you?*" My voice rises. "It's not even about me! It's about doing whatever we need to do to destroy the place that murdered your mother—and captured and abused mine—and made us stand in a public square and watch people's heads get chopped off to teach us a lesson. Now, with the Executor compromised, this is our chance."

Ari's jaw clenches. "You told Ronan you hoped finding out Cordelia was alive would unite the Houses, so that we could be together. Was that just a lie?"

"Of course not! But that was before the Executor vanished. And until we know for sure what the Council decides, we'd be fools to do something we can't take back."

He looks livid. "Really, Eva? Because from what you're saying, this would be the perfect time. By the Architect, it might well be the *only* time. Tell me, what do you envision? You, all curled up in bed nice and cozy with your panther prince, while I pace the door outside your chamber, waiting for a crumb of your attention?"

I feel my wolf stir, pacing up the path that leads to the surface of my body. "Of course not!"

"You said you loved me." The words are an agonized whisper. Damn him. "I do."

"Then how can you even think about marrying him? By the Sins, you're alone with me, in my *room*. For the first time since we found out who you are—what you can do—it won't hurt me to kiss you, to touch you. Do you know how long I've waited for that, Eva?" His eyes bore into mine. "How much I've thought about it, dreamed about it? And here you are, talking about marrying another man. How is that supposed to make me feel?"

The closed door of the bond creaks open, and I feel everything he does: rage and pain, in equal measure. I open my mouth to reply, desperate to make him understand, just as I hear footsteps in the hallway.

Someone's coming, just as I'd warned Ari they would.

Inside the guards' quarters, with armed warriors stationed at every entrance and two more flanking Ari's door, we should be safe. But that doesn't stop him from palming a knife and moving in front of me, even though of the two of us, I am arguably far more dangerous.

Even furious, his first instinct is to protect me.

Whoever it is doesn't knock. Instead, they wrench the door open, so hard it smashes into the wall. Ari's knife leaves his hand, but as it does, I hear his grunt of surprise.

He's pulled his throw at the last minute, and a good thing, too. Because there in my doorway, his prematurely white hair standing on end and his navy-blue eyes wild, is Councilor-in-Chief Adelman. Gone is his usual cold self-possession. In its place is restless energy, thrumming through him with such strength, I can almost see it. He smells like a slow-burning fire, a scent I associate with a predator on the hunt.

Ari's blade thunks into the doorframe next to his head as the Councilor steps into the room, his midnight-blue eyes fixed on mine. The knuckles on his right hand are bloody.

His gaze lingers on me. Shifts to Ari. Then back to me again.

"Sir?" Ari's voice is low, filled with warning. Whoever stands before us isn't Councilor Adelman, the cool-eyed diplomat. This is someone else, crazed and undone.

"Your eyes," he says to me, his voice trembling. There's an odd note to it: pain, tinged with longing. "They're hers. I should've known. Why didn't I see?"

Hers. There's only one person he can possibly mean.

My mother. The skúma the Executor kidnapped twenty years ago.

CHAPTER 3
ARI

I could have killed the Councilor-in-Chief. If I hadn't pulled my throw at the last moment, I would have. Only instinct and training buried that blade in the doorframe rather than in his throat.

But the man doesn't notice or care. His gaze is pinned on Eva, and he looks...decimated. Like a razed city, the remains smoking as they crumble to dust. He's shaking, and from the looks of his right hand, it's endured an encounter with an object that failed to yield. Gone are the crimson dress robes he normally wears. He's clad in the black gear of the guards—the gear I'm wearing myself—and it's as wrinkled as if he slept in it. Except, judging by the dark circles under his eyes, he hasn't slept at all.

"Cordelia," he says. "That bastard told you she's alive?" When Eva steps from behind me and nods, he barrels on: "What did he do to her? And how the hell did he escape?"

His voice cracks on the last word, and the intensity boils off him, adrenaline blowing his pupils wide. When Eva doesn't reply, he closes his fingers on her wrist. "Answer me."

"Take your hand off her," I say, before I think better of it. He is, after all, my superior. In the Bellatorum, insolence like this would've gotten me whipped, or worse.

But Adelman doesn't seem to hear me. He's still staring at Eva, who bites her lip. "I don't know. Mei was more cunning than we realized. But last night, when I went to see him... He told me the bellators found Cordelia, in the wreckage of the bombing. He took her back to the Commonwealth and kept her there. And then he—he—"

"He *what?*" The man's grip tightens, his knuckles whitening. I tense, roused at seeing him manhandle her this way. No matter our disagreement about Sebastían, she's mine, and I am hers. No one will touch her against her will, not when I stand beside her.

Eva could twist free of his grip; it's a simple matter of leverage. But she doesn't. Instead, her gaze flicks sideways, toward me. "It's okay, Ari," she says, her voice soft. And then, to the Councilor, "He—he used her. Her body. He claimed he loved her, but what does a man like that know of love? And when she didn't feel the same, he blamed her for putting a spell on him. He said, *I will burn the city you loved, and stand laughing in the ashes.* I think...he meant Vik."

Councilor Adelman drops Eva's wrist like it's on fire. "He... hurt her?" he says, as if he hasn't heard a word of the Executor's threat to the city for which he's responsible. Rage darkens his eyes, and he runs a hand through his hair, which has seen better days. When he speaks again, his voice is limned with iron. "He *violated* her?"

Eva swallows hard. "He took her against her will." Her misery runs down the bond to me, an ice-cold current. "And I am the result."

The words land hard, pebbles that send ripples spilling outward into the room. For a moment, the three of us stand there, Adelman's face blank with shock. And then he moves, snatching the ceramic pitcher from my dresser and hurling it against the wall. It smashes to bits, sliding to the floor in a cascade of blue-and-white crockery and tepid water, and when I glance at the Councilor-in-Chief, I see the reflection of the wreckage in his eyes.

He's breathing hard, his chest heaving. For the first time, I notice a silver chain around his neck. It's hung with a charm of a wolf, the symbol of House Minneska, that rises and falls with the stutter-stop of his breath. His wounded hand rises, clenching the charm so hard, the scabs on his bruised knuckles burst. Blood runs down his fingers in slow-seeping rivulets.

"I see," he says, biting out the words between clenched teeth. And then he turns and leaves, closing the door behind him with a click that's as emphatic as if he's slammed it.

CHAPTER 4
EVA

An hour later, Ari and I find ourselves sitting around the huge wooden table in the Council of Nine's chambers, planning what I hope will become an invasion.

Councilor-in-Chief Adelman sits at the table's head, in possession of himself once more. The fierce anger and desolation that marked him earlier are gone. But though he conceals his bruised hand beneath his crimson robes, I haven't forgotten the sight of it.

Who is Cordelia to him? She's more than a lost skúmaskot, a fallen soldier in the conflict between the Commonwealths and the Houses. I'd stake my life on that.

The surviving councilors—Trina, Elijah, and Peder—are here too, clad in their black robes patterned with a crimson wolf. Ronan is in his usual seat at the far end of the table, wearing his crimson-and-black guard's gear, his graying braids tied back with a blood-red ribbon. But the seats where my skúma trainer, Gertrud, and the former Council members used to sit, before they were slaughtered in the Battle of the Great Hall, are filled with strangers.

Well, almost-strangers, anyway. Sebastían's blue-green

eyes fix on me as I take the seat across from him, the only one that's still available. Behind him stands his familiar, a tall girl with yellow-gold hair that tumbles to her waist. I last saw her in the Hall, using a metal platter to deflect the bellators' blades. Her face is expressionless, her fingers laced at the small of her back.

Sebastían stands as I take my seat. He's clad in a cream linen shirt and pants, tied with a turquoise sash—Satrizona's signature colors. "Eva," he says, ignoring Ari completely. "Lovely to see you again, though I wish the circumstances were better. It was a pleasure fighting beside you, though. Second only to dancing with you."

I sink into my chair, feeling Ari's wordless irritation. We're the last to come in; the skúma representatives from all four houses are already seated, their familiars standing behind them. Sure, every seat at the table is taken, but we could always bring in more chairs. No, this arrangement is meant to illustrate our superior status, the fact that familiars' significance lies only in their relationship to their skúma.

The inequality of it makes me uncomfortable, as does my complicity, and I struggle not to get to my feet in protest. If I want to persuade the Council to let me hunt down the Executor, getting on their bad sides so soon is a poor course of action.

"Introductions, I believe, are needed," Councilor-in-Chief Adelman says, gracing me with a small smile. "This, of course, is Eva Marteinn and her newly bonded familiar, Ari Westergaard, both formerly of the Commonwealth of Ashes. Eva, you'll know the wolf Layla Edevane of House Minneska and her familiar, Zion Morais."

Layla and I have just shared a few words, all of them after the recent battle. Her son, Erdahl, was the sole skúma in Vik when I arrived, and at first I thought he was an orphan. In fact, when Councilor Adelman told me Sebastían was the only other living mature skúma, I thought all the skúma children had been deprived of their parents through battle or plain bad luck. But no; he'd meant Sebastían was the only mature skúma without a mate. Lucky me.

Along with Zion and her husband, Riley, Layla was on a diplomatic mission to San Fraesco when I got here. The first time I saw her, she was tearing out Bellator Espen's throat in the Great Hall, her familiar by her side. She's slim, with a coil of burnished brown hair and eyes that match its shade almost exactly. In wolf form, she's massive and gray, but now, other than a hint of watchfulness in her eyes, there's no outward sign of her beast.

Zion's skin is even darker than Ronan's, a gleaming ebony. He gives me a reassuring smile as Layla inclines her head in acknowledgment.

"And, of course, you've met Sebastían, panther of House Satrizona." The Councilor-in-Chief gestures across the table. "Behind him is his familiar, Ilsa Croce."

"Pleased to meet you," Ilsa says. *Now* she wears an expression, but it's calculating, assessing. I think I liked her better before.

"Next to Ronan," the Councilor-in-Chief continues, "is Eldrina Alinsky, falcon of House Montyorke. And behind her stands her familiar, Danica Smythe."

Eldrina is exactly like I'd expect a falcon to look in human form. Above the purple caftan that indicates her allegiance to House Montyorke, she boasts beady dark eyes, a hooked nose, and a suspicious, intent expression. Her familiar isn't much better: thin as a whippet, and as tense as if she expects a clash to erupt in the next five minutes.

"You fought well," Eldrina says by way of a greeting, but by her tone, she might as well be saying, *You've tracked filth all over this floor, and by filth, I mean yourself.*

I return her frigid salutation with an innocuous smile. "My familiar and I thank you for the compliment."

Her cold gaze solidifies into ice. "Indeed," she says, a world of distaste in each syllable. She doesn't trust us, and I understand why. When Ari and I bonded, our natural gifts were amplified to an extraordinary degree. Together, we're more powerful than any skúma-familiar pair I've ever heard of. No wonder she's wary.

"And across from Eldrina," Councilor-in-Chief Adelman says, clearing his throat to dispel the tension, "is the selkie Tristan Segel and his familiar, Gael Abano."

Tristan, too, reminds me of his beast. Though he can't be more than twenty-five, his sleek, chin-length fall of prematurely silver hair shines in the firelight that flickers from the wall-mounted torches. When he half-stands to greet me, his gold-and-green robes rippling, the movement is as smooth as if he's gliding through water.

"So," the Councilor-in-Chief says briskly, "to business. We have several urgent items to discuss, beginning with the planned capture of the Commonwealth's Executor and the retrieval of the skúmaskot Cordelia, long thought dead."

Try as he might—and I can tell he's trying; he flattens his good hand on the table in an effort to steady himself—he can't quite keep his voice neutral when he says Cordelia's name. But if the murmurs that echo throughout the room are any indication, he's not alone.

"How do we truly know she's alive?" Tristan says. "Are we simply taking the word of a man known to be a dictator and a deceiver?"

"That's a fair assessment of him," I say, "but the Executor told the truth. He did it because he knew it would hurt me. And because he had nothing left to lose."

"We'll get him back," Trina says, speaking for the first time.

"Even now, our scouts are searching for him. And when we find him—we will have answers."

"It's not enough." Councilor-in-Chief Adelman grips the edge of the table. "We need to make a plan to retrieve Cordelia, now."

Elijah, who's sitting next to him, places a hand on his arm. "Deveraux, I know what she meant to you. We don't take this lightly. If she's out there, we'll bring her home. But don't let your emotions cloud what must be done."

The Councilor-in-Chief turns, his dark blue gaze pinning Elijah to his seat. "My feelings have nothing to do with it. I know my duty. Right now, that entails capturing a threat to our way of life and bringing one of our most valuable assets back to Vik, where she belongs."

Elijah doesn't look convinced, nor does he look happy. But he sits back, heaving a sigh. "Very well. Proceed."

Councilor-in-Chief Adelman takes a deep breath. I can smell the frustration and grief emanating from him in waves, and from the way Sebastían's nostrils flare, I'm sure he can, too. His eyes meet mine, unexpected sympathy in their depths, and I resolve to press him about the connection between my mother and the Councilor-in-Chief. He knows something, I'm sure of it.

"To retrieve Cordelia," Councilor-in-Chief Adelman says, "we must take the Commonwealth of Ashes. But to do that, we need to unify our forces."

Sebastían's gaze slides from mine. "If you want the support of House Satrizona," he says, his voice chill as the wind off the Silber, "you know my conditions. Marriage to Eva Marteinn of House Minneska, or no deal."

The bond heats with the conflagration that Sebastían's words spark in Ari, banked only by his tightly-leashed control. *Arrogant bastard,* my familiar hisses inside my head. From the feel of it, he's about two seconds from pinning the Panther of the West to the wall.

"You don't see everything that's transpired in the past twenty-four hours as enough fodder to unite with Minneska?" I demand, in an effort to avert disaster. "Are you that stubborn?"

Sebastían's lips quirk, as if my anger amuses him. "It's not stubbornness, Eva. It's my responsibility...and I'd like to think it would be your pleasure, as well. Certainly, I've never suffered any complaints."

A red-hot blush heats my cheeks and, seeing it, Sebastían's lips curve. As if his smile's evoked it, I remember how I called for aid when the Executor cornered me, and how his panther answered, charging up the stairs to protect me. A tie that I don't understand binds us, an uncomfortable intimacy not born of what I want but who I am...and who he is, as well.

At the sight of my blush, Ari steps forward, palming the hilt of his dagur. "That," he says, the edge of each word as sharp as his blade, "is over the line."

A low rumble rises in Sebastían's chest: his panther's warning growl. "Hold your tongue, familiar, lest you lose it."

My embarrassment fades, replaced by indignation. "Don't speak to him that—" I begin, but Ari cuts me off, his tone smooth and deadly.

"Are you threatening me, Sebastían Pardúr, in front of witnesses? Because I don't need Eva to fight my battles for me. And nothing would please me more than to prove it."

Sebastían braces his hands on the table and pushes to his feet. "How dare you!"

"Enough!" The command comes from Councilor-in-Chief Adelman. "While we held the Executor, we had the advantage in any negotiation. Now, he's on the loose, with intimate knowledge of our logistics and capacity. We must plan a concerted strike against the Commonwealth, and yet the two of you are squabbling like children and wasting our time."

Setting his jaw, Sebastían sits back down. The movement is fluid, catlike, as if his beast lurks just beneath the surface of his skin. "My apologies, Councilor-in-Chief."

"May I point out," I say, my tone dry, "that I am a person, not a disputed territory. I am not an asset to be won nor a bone to be fought over."

Sebastían leans forward, his expression earnest. "I understand that, Eva. But *you* must understand that I have a duty to carry on my bloodline. Though wolfblood may be your rightful inheritance, the Commonwealth's genetic manipulations have gifted you four times over. Would you deny our shared species the opportunity to survive?"

"I—" I begin, just as the double doors to the Council's chambers creak open and Kilían limps in.

His eye is blackened, a line of stitches stands out against the pale skin of his throat, and he's holding his left arm as if it hurts, but he moves steadily enough. I suck in my breath as his eyes flick to Ari, then to me. "Westergaard," he says in greeting. "Marteinn."

I hadn't thought I missed anything or anyone from the Commonwealth. But hearing Kilían say our names, the way he did so many times during my training, sends a rush of unexpected nostalgia through me. To my surprise, I have to fight back tears.

Ari's hand comes down on my shoulder, gripping tight. "Lead Interrogator Bryndísarson," he says, using Kilían's full title to emphasize what he's capable of—and the respect he should be accorded. "Commander of the Thirty."

Kilían comes to attention. Though the movement must hurt him, he gives no sign. "I apologize for my lateness, Councilor-in-Chief Adelman. Your healers refused to release me until they determined I was fit to venture out on my own."

The Councilor-in-Chief's brows quirk upward. "If you'll forgive my saying so, Bellator Bryndísarson, I can hardly blame them. You look like you ought to be in the infirmary."

"With all due respect, sir, you can't afford that." He shifts his weight, then winces. "As Westergaard pointed out, I led the Bellatorum's elite force and reported directly to the Executor. I was privy to his plans to invade your territory. If you're having a strategic discussion about retrieving him and marching on the Commonwealths, then you need to have me at this table."

No matter how stoic Kilían might be, it's clear he's suffering. I push my chair back, getting to my feet, and at the other end of the table, Eldrina scoffs. "You'll give up your seat for this one, skúma? How do we know he's not a spy left behind to witness our most sensitive negotiations? I say we show him the door and keep him in the infirmary under guard until he's well enough to be imprisoned."

"He isn't a spy," Ari retorts. "This is the man who first told me the Brotherhood of the Wolf existed. Who gave us the information we needed to escape the Commonwealth. Without him, you wouldn't have your precious four-beast skúma. You owe him a great deal."

"And why should we believe you?" Eldrina's tone is laced with scorn. "Who are you but someone who has contravened our old ways? Your abilities are unnatural. For all we know, you seek to turn Eva Marteinn against us."

Ari's rage simmers through the bond. Behind me, I hear the clink of metal as his hand drops to his weapons belt. Before he can draw a blade, I fix Eldrina with a glare. "He's my familiar. And he's right: Kilían's backed your cause from the beginning, at great personal risk. If you want my support in this fight, you'll accept them both. Do I make myself clear?"

Falcons are powerful birds of prey, but panthers will hunt birds, if need be—and Eldrina knows it. After a brief battle of wills, her dark eyes drop from mine and she sits back in her chair, every line of her lean body projecting displeasure.

"Ari Westergaard's motives aside, who will vouch for the bellator?" Tristan's upper lip rises in a sneer. "Other than his brainwashed sycophants?"

Sebastían turns to look at him, a growl rising in his throat. "That's my future mate you speak of. If she respects him, then that's good enough for me. It should be good enough for you too…no?"

Ari laughs, a sardonic chuckle that fills the room. "At last," he says. "Something we agree on."

I want to argue with Sebastían about the 'future mate' comment, but how can I, when he's advocating for me and, by proxy, for Kilían? And it's working. The selkie is terrified; I can smell the fear baking off him, acrid and sour. "I—I meant no disrespect," he stammers.

"Really. And yet, you spoke so clearly, with such disdain." Sebastían's voice drops to a threatening purr as his claws slide from their sheaths. "One can hardly help but wonder what you *did* intend, then. For surely it wasn't your intention to insult the honor of the Panther of the West, royalty of House Satrizona. Such a thing would be tantamount to idiocy, and you, Tristan of San Fraesco, are not an idiot. Or so I have always believed."

He bends closer, his voice light, considering. "But if not a calculated insult, then what, Tristan of the Waters? Are you an idiot, a conniver…or just a coward? Because there's no place for a fool at this table, and connivers or cowards must be punished."

His gaze drifts to me, as if he thinks he's doing me a favor by meting out Tristan's just deserts. But I glance away, my own gaze roaming to each of the skúma and Council members in turn. Which do they think I am—a fool, a conniver, or a coward? Or their last, best hope?

My eyes fall at last on Tristan. Sebastían hasn't even touched him, and he's shaking so hard, it's moving the entire table. But when I spare a glance for the Panther of the West, he shows no sign of backing down. Instead, his lips rise in a smile, as if Tristan's terror pleases him.

We need to put a stop to this. But how? Instinctively, I look to Kilían for guidance and find him looking right back at me. The expression in his blue eyes is inscrutable as always, but he tilts his head ever so slightly toward the panther. *Intervene,* that gesture means. *You are the cause; you must be the solution as well.*

"Sebastían," I say, putting a hint of my own panther's growl into my voice, "enough."

I feel his energy flare, the same way I did when he charged up the steps the night of the battle in the Great Hall. His beast recognizes mine, but her presence does nothing to calm him. Instead, he growls back, as if she's only spurred him on. And around the table, one by one, the Council members and other skúma bow their heads in respect. Clearly, all they value is power, and my link to Sebastían provides it. They couldn't care less if Tristan suffers as a result.

I want nothing more than to slit all their throats, but that would hardly help my cause: to rescue Tristan and prevent blood from being shed, so that we can move on to what really matters. In desperation, I reach for Ari and feel him opening the bond, lending me that delicate touch that worked so well for him in the interrogation chamber, the gift that made him Kilían's favorite when it came to worming secrets out of even the most recalcitrant citizens.

"Come now," I say to Sebastían, my voice gentle, cajoling. "You threaten Tristan for failing to trust my judgment, yet here you are, refusing to back off when I say my honor has been sufficiently avenged. Surely you don't hold the leader of House San Fraesco to a lower standard than yourself. Or have I misunderstood what you're made of?"

My words sink home; I can see it in the depths of his eyes, see the human behind the panther swim to the surface. "As my lady wishes," he says at last, retracting his claws.

Relief sweeps over me, reflected in the faces of almost everyone around the table. Sebastían is the exception; he's examining his nails, as if to make sure they're as pristine as before. But I see something else on their faces, too: respect that I was strong enough to make the Panther of the West back down. Recognition of how powerful the two of us could be, together.

Much as I hate to admit it, I can feel the pull of Sebastían's beast, calling to mine. *You could be his queen,* my panther whispers to me. *Who would dare stand against you then?*

CHAPTER 5

ARI

As Sebastían straightens, a self-satisfied look on his smug face, I have to resist the urge to let the air out of his inflated ego with my blade. He sinks back in his chair, steepling his hands on the table's polished surface and eyeing Eva with a proprietary confidence that enrages me. How she can even consider marrying him after all we've been through is beyond me.

It's ironic, really. Here we are, bound tighter than any marriage contract could offer. But I've never felt further away from her.

Through the bond, I feel some type of turmoil—guilt, maybe? Shame?—as she turns to Kilían. He's still standing across from the room's cavernous fireplace, just inside the doors. The light from the flames sets his red hair aglow, in sharp contrast to his pitch-black gear. "Take my seat," she tells him, loud enough for everyone to hear. "I offer it freely. And you deserve it, no matter who will vouch for you."

"That's not nec—" Kilían begins, just as the double doors to the Council's chambers slam open and a man bursts through. The evening's theme, apparently.

My hand goes to my weapons belt—at least these Architect-forsaken fools allow me to carry my blades in here now. Ronan draws his gun. Every skúma comes to attention, and Layla growls, her wolf's voice emerging from her human throat. There are guards posted outside the Council's chamber, but as recent events demonstrated all too clearly, guards can be killed.

The newcomer stands in the doorway, panting. He's tall and lean, with dark hair that brushes his collar and bright green eyes. He's also covered in blood.

"I will vouch for the bellator," he gasps. Sweat gleams on his brow. "And if Councilwoman Bridgette were here, she'd do the same. For he once saved not only my life, but hers as well."

Kilían goes dead white, blue eyes blazing in his pale face. His right hand falls to his hip, where his weapons belt would normally hang, as if he's seeking the comfort of a blade. Ulrich and Madsen haven't let *him* in here armed, and I can't say I blame them.

But Kilían doesn't look like he wants to harm the intruder. In fact, he looks like a single word from this man could bring him to his knees.

"How much of that is yours?" He steps closer, then freezes. His hand hovers above the man's gore-soaked jacket, as if he's afraid to touch him, which makes no sense at all. Kilían's spent most of his life around men drenched in blood.

Does he *know* this stranger? The others seem to. Ronan's holstered his gun, and Layla's stopped growling. But how would Kilían—

The man shakes his head, his chest heaving. "None of it. That's what I came here to tell you. Councilor-in-Chief"—his gaze finds Adelman's—"the scouts you sent were attacked. I found them on my way back from Banabrekkur. Three of them were already dead. The other two were badly hurt. All of this blood," he says, gesturing at his clothing, "is theirs. And the blood of the men they killed."

Banabrekkur. The word snags in my mind. I've heard it before, but where?

A murmur of distress rises around the table. Sebastían growls, and Ronan's face sets in rigid lines of fury. As captain of the guard, the scouts are his to command. Now he's lost three of his best guards in a recon-and-retrieval mission of two injured men and an unskilled traitor.

Jaxon, I think, my heart picking up speed. He was on that mission. And the Architect knows he's got a self-destructive streak a mile wide. Is he lying dead in the woods, having taken a stupid, thoughtless risk to save his companions?

The Councilor-in-Chief rises to his feet, his chair scraping the marble, and voices what all of us are thinking. "What the hell happened?"

The newcomer shrugs one shoulder, a movement that's strangely familiar. "The surviving scouts were unconscious. I was able to rouse them enough to learn the gist of the battle in the Hall and the Executor's escape." His voice squeezes tight around the Executor's title, as if he has particular reason to hate him. "I dragged one of them back here. Jessamine. The other—Jaxon Fjeri—was able to walk on his own, though he was in considerable pain. He—"

"Jaxon's alive?" Eva interrupts. "Will he be all right?"

"He'll heal." The man's voice is surprisingly gentle. "He took a bullet to the shoulder, but it didn't hit anything vital." He looks over Eva's head, at Ronan. "He said to tell you the scouts tracked the fugitives into the woods beyond Minneska, but then the trail evaporated. When they tried to pick it up again, they were attacked by a band of rogue exiles."

"Exiles, so close to Vik?" Adelman's gaze darkens.

"The scouts killed four of them; I saw the bodies. I can take you there."

"I'll speak with Jaxon." Ronan's voice is gruff. "Then, with your permission," he says, turning to what remains of the Council, "we'll send a party to bring back our dead, and hunt down the bastards who killed them."

"Let us go with you," Eva says at once. "You'll be focused on retrieving the scouts and hunting the exiles. Ari and I can concentrate on finding the Executor."

At the sound of my name, the newcomer's eyes widen. He scans the room, as if searching for me. Discomfited, I clear my throat. "I'm with Eva. It's impossible for Karsten and the Executor to vanish into thin air, like some kind of Architect-cursed magic. They're out there, and we'll find them. But we can't afford to waste any more time."

"Risking yourselves is unwise," Peder begins, but Adelman cuts him off.

"All right. The two of you can go. But you'll wait for Ronan to return from the infirmary after he's gathered intelligence from Fjeri. The Executor's disappearance and this attack may well be connected, and I won't have you tearing off without a plan." His deep-blue gaze bores into Eva, like he knows we planned to hunt the Executor down, with or without permission.

Sebastían glares at me, as if he thinks I planned to kidnap his so-called *future mate* and drag her into the woods by her hair. What a joke. If he thinks I have a prayer of telling Eva what to do, he's lost his mind. But thank Lady Luck for small favors, he doesn't speak.

"I'll be back as soon as I can. Be ready." Ronan stands, dropping a hand on the newcomer's bloodstained shoulder in acknowledgment before pushing through the double doors.

Adelman follows. Not a moment too soon, the accursed meeting's over.

As people begin to file out behind Adelman, the newcomer's gaze flicks to Kilían. To me. Back to Kilían again. And then, to my bewilderment, the Lead Interrogator gives a small but definitive nod.

What in the nine hells?

I stalk toward Kilían, wanting answers. But the Lead Interrogator, who's always hyperaware of every movement in his vicinity—a raised eyebrow, a cynical tilt of the head, far less a six-foot-two armed warrior heading straight for him—isn't looking at me. His eyes are fixed on the newcomer, and the expression in them is unmistakable: a fierce, shining joy.

And then I know. The first time I entered this room and stood before the Council of Nine, I'd asked them just one question, the one that mattered most to me. And Adelman had replied, *He's stationed to the north, in Banabrekkur.*

Realization breaks over me like a rogue wave, a moment before Kilían speaks. "Kennett," he says, his voice hoarse.

"Hello, Kilían," my father says, his lips curving in a rueful half-smile. *My* smile. "It's been a long time."

CHAPTER 6
ARI

My father. Here. In this room. After all this time.

I don't know what to say. To do. And from the looks of it, he doesn't, either.

Kennett opens his mouth and shuts it again, looking like one of the goldfish that bobs in the stone-rimmed pond behind the House of Echoes. His gaze lingers on me, flicking from my face to my body to my blades and back again, like he's trying to drink me in and can't do it fast enough. I force myself to stand as steadily as I would for inspection, aware of the roomful of witnesses. The Council already mistrusts me. The last thing I need is to hand them a vulnerability to exploit.

"You have my eyes," my father says at last, his voice breaking. "But just from looking at you, I can see you have your mother's heart." And then, to my consternation, he throws his arms around me.

I stand frozen in his embrace, bewildered. For one thing, we're of a height, and though I'm more muscular and he's whipcord-thin, otherwise it's eerily like hugging myself. For another, when I envisioned our reunion, I didn't imagine we'd have an audience. Though a few people have left the room, most of them remain, transfixed. I can feel Sebastían's eyes burning a hole in my back, just waiting for me to crack.

My eyes meet Kilían's over Kennett's shoulder. And to my relief, despite the months we've spent apart, he and I share a moment of perfect understanding. "Kennett," he says, the words coming slowly, as if they pain him, "this isn't the time."

My father drops his arms at once and steps back. Dried blood flakes from his clothes onto the marble floor, and when I glance down, I see it stains my gear as well. Surely there's a metaphor here, but I'm too exhausted to exploit it.

"I'm sorry," Kennett stammers. "I shouldn't have done that. I just—Ronan sent word, but I never expected—and then after Miriam—" His voice catches, his Adam's apple moving as he swallows. "I'm sorry," he manages again, before subsiding into silence.

"Don't apologize. I'm grateful that you're happy to see me. I thought you might blame me for—well." By the Architect, now I'm the one stumbling over my words. Me, who once spent an entire night kneeling in the Commonwealth's sanctuary under the gimlet eye of High Priest Erlich, a bar of soap between my teeth, to cleanse me of the sin of being silver-tongued.

I force myself to quit babbling and meet the green eyes that are so much like my own. "I'm glad you're alive. And that you don't hate me."

"Hate you?" Kennett's eyes widen, and now they don't look like mine at all. There's a guilelessness in them I could never possess unless I worked to put it there, to convince someone I was as innocent as they needed to believe. "Why would you think that?"

By the Virtues, I don't want to have this conversation here. Or really, at all. "Because of Miriam," I say, pointing out the obvious. "If it wasn't for me, she might still be alive."

My father's expression solidifies into an expression I recognize: resolve. "Don't you think that for a second. Do you hear me? She died doing what she dreamed would happen one day, what she prayed for when she lay down to sleep, each night since we left the Commonwealth. She prayed to the many-headed gods, to the Architect, to anyone she hoped might listen. And when Ronan sent me word of her death, he told me the last face she saw was yours." He blinks, his eyes glossy with unshed tears. "Her prayers were answered, Ari—may I call you that? She could ask for no better end. And neither could I."

My throat is suddenly tight. Behind us, I'm conscious of the remaining members of the Council rising from the table, of the murmur of conversation as they leave. Sebastían goes last—big surprise—his gaze lingering on me as he passes through the doors, his watchful familiar right behind him. After a moment, Eva and Kilían follow, looking equally thunderstruck, leaving me alone with my father. We have the privacy I wished for, but I don't know what to say to Kennett any more than I did when we had an audience of sixteen.

I could tell him of the instant connection I felt with Miriam, of the longing in her gaze when it met mine, right before the bomb blew her apart. About how we never got to exchange a word before I watched her die. But perhaps such a confession would only make things worse.

So I say nothing, and my father fills the silence. "It's you who should be angry with us, for leaving you behind." His tone is bleak. "We had little choice. Kilían can attest to that. If there were any other path, believe me when I tell you we would've taken it. Kilían swore he would look after you, but even still... abandoning you tore your mother's heart in two."

Kilían did *what?* It takes all my training to school my features so the shock I feel at this revelation doesn't show. I've never understood why the Lead Interrogator was willing to help me, why he risked so much to defy the Commonwealth. Now I know: he swore an oath to my parents. What I don't understand is why. And remembering the unguarded expression on his face when Kennett appeared in the doorway, I can't help but think the two are connected.

I don't like things I don't understand. What you can't comprehend, you can't control.

My father searches my face, desperate for absolution. "I understand if you can't forgive me. But Miriam...it would mean a great deal if you could find it in your heart to believe she always meant to come back for you." He runs a hand through his hair, ruffling the blood-flecked strands. With a start, I recognize the gesture I make when I'm struggling to contain my feelings, or frustrated beyond what words can convey.

"It broke my heart, as well." His voice shakes. "I held your mother in my arms as she fought to go back for you. There's not a day I don't think of that moment and wonder if I made a terrible mistake, even if the cost was all our lives. If it wouldn't have been better to have died together than to have left you. Kilían's promise or no, we abandoned you, Ari. And I"—he blinks, reining himself in with an effort—"I am sorrier than I can say."

Through the gap between the crimson curtains that line the chamber's windows, I can see the shadows lengthening. If we're going to retrieve the fallen scouts and hunt the Executor before nightfall, we'll have to leave soon. Anything could await us in the woods. For all I know, we might not survive it. And so I turn to my father and speak my heart.

"No forgiveness is needed. A lesser man and woman would've yielded to the Commonwealth, would've been too terrified to brave the Borderlands. But you escaped. You fought to make the world a better place, a place fit for your son."

The last word feels foreign, impossible and wonderful at once. I see the echo of my own wonder on Kennett's face, in the way his lips part and the blood rises to heat his skin. His hand lifts, as if to reach for me, but then he thinks better of the gesture and lets it fall.

The clock is ticking; Ronan will be back at any moment. With an effort, I force the words past the lump that's formed in my throat. "I hold no grudge toward either of you. My only regrets are that I may have brought my mother's death upon her, and that I had no chance to speak to her before those bastards took her life. No matter her intentions, I hold myself responsible. So if you wish me to forgive you, Kennett...then I only ask that you do the same."

Tears shine in my father's eyes, and he bows his head. "Thank you," he whispers. "Your understanding is more than I expected. More than I deserve. You're not to blame for the Commonwealth's sins, Ari. If Miriam were here, she'd tell you the same. You survived; you're here with me now. And that is the greatest gift I've ever been given."

Slowly, warily, as if he's afraid I might push him away, he lifts a hand to cup my face. His touch is warm, and unmistakably tender. "Your mother named you Lucien when you were born. Because you brought her light. But Ari...it means 'lion.'" His lips curve in that achingly familiar smile. "You are fierce, my son. You are brave. Together with those who fight beside us, you are the warrior who will bring light to the world."

I stare at him, stunned. He looks back, his eyes glinting with pride. Pride in who I am—what I've become—that he can express without fear of punishment, because we both fought free of the chains that bound us.

And suddenly, I know just what to say.

"With fire and iron," I tell him, the bellators' battle cry. "I'm proud to claim your blood as my own."

I watch as a single tear breaks free, carving a path down my father's cheek. And this time, when he wraps his arms around me, I let them stay.

CHAPTER 7

EVA

When Ronan comes back, his expression grim, we make our way to the stables. We'll need horses to retrieve the scouts' bodies and give them a decent burial.

Ronan, Riley, and I take the lead, with Kennett, Kilían, and Ari on our heels, exchanging cautious conversation. His father is Ari's mirror—the tone of his voice, the small gestures he makes. It's uncanny, as is the raw, unguarded way Kilían stared at Kennett when he burst into the room. The latter is a mystery to be solved...but a mystery for another time, after we've reclaimed our dead. And, hopefully, gathered a clue as to where Mei's taken the Executor.

Erdahl, the young wolf skúma, comes too. As Riley and Layla's only son, he's been in training since he can walk, and Riley's seized on this as an opportunity to give the young skúma some real-world tracking experience. The two of them will stay behind when we reach the edge of the city, but Erdahl's excited anyway. Undaunted by the death of the scouts, he skips along beside Noe, his father's familiar, talking a mile a minute until Riley tells him to hush.

When Ronan shepherds us into the barn, we find Mateo Nord, one of the weapons experts we traveled with from the Commonwealth, grooming a pregnant mare. The stalls that held Frost and Iris, the horses Mei and I rode together, stand empty. She must have taken them with her, to carry Karsten and the Executor. The thought infuriates me, and I inhale, letting the scents of hay, horses, and apples settle me, calming my beasts.

"Sir." Mateo comes to attention, the curry brush stilling in his hand. His blue eyes are red-rimmed. Though Mei never returned the favor, he loved her. And now she's gone, under the worst circumstances imaginable. I don't blame him for crying.

"Nord," Ronan says. "I was expecting a groomsman."

"I finished my duties for the day. And occasionally, I pass the time here." Mateo strokes the horse's neck. "This mare's due soon, and as you might recall, I apprenticed in husbandry before joining the guard. Perhaps I can be of service to you."

Erdahl crowds into the stall, wanting to see the pregnant mare up close, and Mateo smiles at him, a tender lift of his lips I've only seen him bestow on Mae. He rests a hand on the boy's dark hair, guiding his small palm along the mare's flank while he waits for Ronan's reply. Erdahl's eyes widen in wonder, and he croons softly to the mare, who whickers in response.

Mateo can say what he wants about his husbandry apprenticeship, but it's obvious why he's here: he's grieving. He lost the girl he cared for, two of his friends are wounded, and three more lie dead in the woods. But when Ronan speaks, he does Mateo the kindness of pretending the weapons specialist's presence in the stables is nothing but a convenient accident.

"We need three horses that'll put up with carrying the dead. I intended to ask a groom, but"—he looks up and down the straw-coated aisle, flanked by half-doors—"they all seem to be absent."

The mare nudges Mateo, and the weapons specialist reaches into his pocket and hands Erdahl an apple. The young skúma holds his hand out, and I watch as the mare dips her head, taking the fruit from him with a gentleness that belies her size. Erdahl pets her lowered neck as Mateo steps out of the stall.

"There are two geldings and a mare I'd trust to carry a corpse," he says. "We had two other horses that wouldn't spook, but they vanished when Mei did." There's a slight catch in his voice when he says her name.

"Fine." Ronan's lips thin. "Point us toward the ones that remain, and we'll be on our way."

"Of course, sir. But you're going hunting," Mateo says, his gaze roving between Ronan and the rest of us: Ari and I, studded with weapons; Kilían, who looks exactly like what he is; Riley, Noe, and Erdahl, radiating eagerness to be off; Kennett, who found the bodies. "I respectfully request to accompany you."

Ronan's eyebrows twitch. "We're retrieving our fallen comrades."

"So you'll be distracted," Mateo argues. "With your permission, I'll stand lookout for you and keep an eye out for the band of exiles. And our escaped prisoners. Sir," he adds hurriedly, when Ronan's eyebrows quit twitching and rise.

I spare a glance for Kilían, who looks amused despite his injuries. Discipline by expressive eyebrow is usually his domain. Perhaps he and Ronan will get along, although both of them are used to being in charge. If they don't manage to work out who's the alpha here, things will get ugly.

"We'll catch whoever's responsible," Mateo vows. "I swear it on the white stag that roams our woods."

Ronan looks him up and down—his red-rimmed eyes, the way his hands tremble where they hold the brush, the too-firm set of his shoulders. And then he sighs. "All right, Nord," he says. "You're with us. Don't make me regret it."

RILEY SHIFTS into his wolf as we make our way down Ash Avenue. He tracks, nose to the ground, then sniffs the air, leading us unerringly along Mei's trail. In human form, I can barely smell her—a hint of rose petals riding the icy breeze, laced with the faint tang of star anise—but Riley has no such problem. He trots along, glancing back at us over his shoulder to urge us to hurry.

The rest of us are all on horseback, except for Noe and Erdahl, who walk alongside Riley, and Kilían, who eyes the large animals with a narrow-eyed suspicion that would make me laugh if I weren't afraid he'd lop off my head. Kennett hangs back with Ari; I can hear their voices rising and falling in an eerily similar cadence. It would be easy to catch their conversation, but I don't want to invade their privacy. So instead I focus on the scents that crisscross the trail, letting the occasional phrase waft toward me on the breeze: *your mother, one day I'll tell you the whole story, could never have imagined.*

The red-roofed houses grow further and further apart, scattered in wide-open fields, until finally the woods loom before us. Though winter is on the horizon, there are enough evergreen trees here to form a leafy barrier, blocking our way so that we can't see what lies beyond. Riley comes to a halt and paws the ground at the trailhead of a narrow path, just wide enough to accommodate a horse and rider, with a gesture that clearly means: *She entered here.*

I can smell blood now, rust-sharp and drying. Even before Kennett speaks, I can tell this is the way he came with

Jessamine and Jaxon. There are multiple routes in and out of these woods. Why this one? What does it mean?

Something nibbles at my consciousness, there and then gone. It's the voice of my wolf, saying, *Think for the pack, Eva. What endangers us most? What could save us?* But whatever she intends me to notice, my human brain can't get hold of it. The thought sinks back into my subconscious, a half-hooked fish escaping a line.

Kilían steps back, in line with Riley, Noe, and Erdahl. Wounded as he is, he won't accompany us further. "May the blessings of the Architect be with your hunt," he says.

"Let's go," I reply, and nudge my horse in front of Ronan's, into the woods.

WITH EVERY STEP my horse takes, I can smell death. Worse still, there's an odd, lingering presence weighting the breeze, as if the air's molecules have been infused with it.

We ride heavily armed and ready for an ambush, with Ronan admonishing me to speak up if I hear or smell the slightest thing out of the ordinary. But the woods are quiet, as if the creatures who live here are hiding, and not from us, either. I don't like it at all. When I breathe deep, though, I smell nothing but the sharpening reek of blood, the hidden-in-plain-sight scent of forest, and that strange, intensifying weight.

We ride up, into the foothills. It's steeper here, but the horses find their way. We're heading toward the mountains, toward the invisible boundary line that Mei, as a Mage, was able to cross, bringing Ari and me into the Brotherhood's stronghold. The first time I looked down into Vik, the city's lights glittering against the press of darkness, Jaxon told me that if Mei wasn't with us, I wouldn't be able to see a thing. It was one of the city's main defenses: if enemies managed to reach it, without one of Vik's Mages by their side, they couldn't enter. But Mei didn't see this ability as the gift it was.

Mages used to be able to do more, she told me, on one of our walks in the forest. *We could speak with nature, and She would reply. We could harness the sky. But that was taken from us long ago. Now, all that's left to us is to guard the borders of the land we protect, and coax it into yielding the plants that will heal our charges.*

The city's magic has turned on her now. As a traitor who's brought shame on her family, she can no longer enter Vik, let alone bring anyone with her. When she took the Executor and Karsten out of the city, she left for good. But that's little consolation.

"We're almost there," Kennett says, distracting me from my thoughts. "Just outside the boundary line. It worries me that the attackers were so close. Like they were trying to get inside."

Ronan makes an uneasy sound, low in his throat. "When I talked with Jaxon, he said the exiles seemed to come from nowhere. That he'd never seen anything like it." His gaze scans the woods. "There's only one place where the boundary dips. Where the line is in the foothills. That's where you found the bodies?"

Kennett's horse tosses her head, like she too is growing uneasy at the smell of blood, and he steadies her. "Yes. I was almost home. I...I was hurrying." His back stiffens, as if he's said too much, and I realize he must have wanted to reach Vik as fast as he could, after getting word of Ari's presence. "It was dawn when I came across them, and their bodies...they were still fresh." His voice cracks on the last word. "I thought I heard something as I was making my way down the slopes. But in the forest, sound travels, and I—"

His shoulders slump. "I thought perhaps...a cracking branch, a falling tree, the screech of a panther, hunting close to dawn...but it must have been gunshots I heard. And the screaming was Annika, when they—before she—" He scrubs a hand across his face. "If I'd been earlier, maybe I could have helped. Maybe I could have saved them."

Silence falls, broken only by the small noises of the forest and the crushing of leaves beneath the horses' hooves. To my surprise, Ari is the one who breaks it.

"If you'd been there," he says, "you would have died along with them. It's as the warrior Sun Tzu says: 'If equally matched, we can offer battle; if slightly inferior in numbers, we can avoid the enemy; if quite unequal in every way, we can flee from him.' You had no choice but to flee, intentional or no."

The tense set of Kennett's shoulders relaxes, as if he worried that his warrior son would judge him and find him wanting. But all he says is, "The path veers left, up here. The clearing lies to the right. We'll have to tie up the horses and go on foot."

His directions are unnecessary. I'm almost choking on the stench of blood and offal now, weighed down by the unpleasant heaviness of the air. I haven't been across the boundary line since I came to Vik. Maybe this is an odd side effect of being so close to it, a warning.

I'm just about to ask Ronan about this when, as Kennett said it would, the path curves. When I raise my head, scenting the air, sure enough, death lies to the right, through a patch of trees and briars we'll have to hack through. They've been disturbed already; bits of fabric cling to the branches. Kennett and Jaxon must have forged their way here through sheer force of will, with the aid of a knife too small for the job. It must have taken terrible determination, what with Jaxon wounded and the other scout, Jessamine, unable to help.

There's just enough room off the path to tie up the horses. Then Ronan pulls a hatchet from his belt, Mateo does the same, and we make our way through the path they carve for us. With each step, that sense of *wrongness* grows stronger.

I feel the moment when we break through the boundary: as if a bubble has popped, giving way to the unprotected space on the other side. There's resistance, like the protective ward is struggling to hold me. Then it's gone, leaving me exposed and disoriented. That same odd heaviness still weights the air. It's worse now, harder to breathe through.

Next to me, Ari shudders. "Thanks for the warning," he mutters to Ronan as Mateo hacks through a clump of poplin-berry bushes, revealing the clearing.

If it wasn't the scene of a massacre, it would be beautiful: hemmed by evergreens with deep, glossy leaves, dotted with scarlet berries. Light sifts from the sky, filtering through the trees and dappling the earth, falling full across the scattered bodies.

Four are the rogue exiles'. The rest are ours: Annika, one of the guards Ari trained; Xavier, a man whose hulking bulk concealed surprising speed and grace; and Simeon, one of Ronan's best scouts and an excellent tracker. Their bodies are contorted, blood pooled beneath them and streaking their clothes, their weapons missing. Annika's mouth is stretched open in horror, a rictus that death has frozen in place. Three feet from her lies Simeon, his eyes wide and blank. A raven takes flight from one of the trees and lands on the ground beside him. It hops closer, its beak lowering to Simeon's face, and I let out an instinctive growl.

The raven turns its head to glare at me, sharp intelligence gleaming in its midnight-black eyes. It's ridiculous, but I could swear the bird looks familiar. It reminds me of the one that roosted on the cornice below my windowsill the night after that disastrous, accidental shift in the library. I regard it, narrowing my eyes, and it tilts its head, as if assessing whether I'm a threat. Then it takes flight, retreating to the branches above.

Ari bows his head. "Integer vitae sclerisque purus," he whispers. *Unimpaired by life and clean of wickedness.* The bellators' blessing for the dead.

I open my mouth to give the expected reply, but Kennett gets there first. "Transit umbra, lux permanent," he says, staring down at the crumpled bodies. *Shadows pass, light remains.*

Such is the hold of the Commonwealth, I think, listening to the ease with which the words pass his lips. *All these years, and he hasn't forgotten our ways.*

"May the many-headed gods welcome you with open arms," Ronan says, kneeling beside the scouts and touching two fingers to their foreheads in turn. "May the wolf call you home, into the pack."

Within me, my own wolf raises her head. She howls, a sound that vibrates through me and clenches my hands into fists. But then she freezes. The hackles rise on her neck, and anxiety thrums through her, chased by fury. *Danger,* she growls within me. *Do not linger here.*

I take a deep breath, then another, trying to fight through her voice and hear my own. Trying to breathe through the air's strange heaviness. The sense of *wrongness* that nagged me at the edge of the woods, that pursued me through the boundary line and beyond, blooms into something far more tangible. "It smells..." I say, my eyebrows knitting.

"Like what?" Ronan says, his voice uncharacteristically sharp.

Drawing another breath, this one to steady myself, I close my eyes. I can feel Ari next to me, a column of energy that flickers red against the darkness behind my lids. *Mine,* my wolf thinks with disturbing avidity. *All mine.*

The wolf's voice is greedy. I don't care for it, but this is no time to quibble. Right now, I need her heightened senses. I wait for Ari's consent to pulse down the bond, for him to tell me that it's all right to shift. And then I tug, and feel his energy, his essence, flow toward me.

Now that I can see the exchange so clearly, I understand why I hurt him, before. I was only *taking* from him. But now, it's different. His energy mingles with mine, red particles combining with a strange blue aura that must belong to me. The bond pulses, expanding effortlessly, his red and my blue interweaving to form a vivid violet. His energy flows toward me and mine flows back again, strengthening him even as I feed myself. It's a heady feeling, tingling and warm. My skin threatens to burst with it.

"By the Sins," I hear Ari whisper, his voice hoarse, a moment before the tingles erupt into sparks and the change breaks over me, leaving me in wolf form, panting on all fours. His hand comes to rest on my back, grounding me as I ground him. The energy courses back and forth between us, waiting to be used.

I get my bearings and inhale again, carefully scenting the air. Beneath the reek of blood and the cloying odor of rot, there it is: the unmistakable scent of star anise.

Could Mei have done this? Helped to slaughter these guards —people she'd grown up with, had likely helped to heal? Nearly killed *Jaxon,* who she'd traversed the Empire with?

More unlikely still, could the Executor have taken shelter with a band of exiles? People he reviled and had perhaps personally condemned to wander the Borderlands? Why would they take him in? Why wouldn't they finish the job I started?

That sense of wrongness grows, stronger in wolf form, threatening to choke me. Huffing out a growl, I force myself to prowl over to Annika, Xavier, and Simeon's prone bodies. I lower my head, snuffling along their ruined flesh and shattered bones.

The scent of star anise is strongest on Annika, who died of multiple stab wounds. This makes sense; the killers had to get closer to her than they did to Xavier and Simeon, who were shot multiple times. The smell is familiar, like Mei, but not. And beneath their bodies, the earth seems invisibly disturbed, thrumming with an energy that vibrates through me.

I pace to the bodies of the fallen exiles, their torsos riddled with bullets. The ground beneath them is just leaves and dirt. There's no sense of that strange energy I felt near Annika, Xavier, and Simeon.

"What does she smell?" Ronan's voice vibrates with impatience. I lift my head and growl over my shoulder at him, but he ignores me. "There's no sign of the Executor. And every moment we spend out here is another moment we're exposed. We need to get the bodies up on horses and back inside the city, so the deadwardens can examine them before we give them decent burial. I'm not leaving them out here overnight."

My wolf agrees, but the rest of me isn't satisfied yet. I back away from the bodies and pace the clearing, following the disturbing scent to the edge, where the bracken is crushed and the branches are broken. This is the way the attackers retreated, but I'm hesitant to follow the trail. There are only a few of us, and I could be tracking my way straight into an ambush. I don't smell Mei, precisely, nor do I smell the Executor or Karsten. But I smell something *like* her, and that scent of wrongness thrums through my bones.

I finish my circuit, then trot back to sit at Ari's feet. Sending my worries and half-formed conclusions down the bond toward him, I see him stiffen.

"She says it smells like Mei, but not. And not her old trail. This is fresh. The scent is strong, as if there were multiple

people here that held Mei's scent. She says they went that way.
" He gestures toward the crushed patch of bracken, leading away from Vik.

With every word Ari speaks, Ronan looks more alarmed. "Are you sure, Eva?"

I huff at him in disgust. My nose doesn't lie.

"By the gods," Mateo mutters. "She really—she—"

Ronan shoots him a sharp look, and he falls silent. I glance between the two of them, becoming unhappier by the second, until Ari speaks for both of us. "What does this mean?"

"Nothing good," Ronan predicts, gathering his graying braids into a tight fist.

In bitter agreement, my wolf raises her head and howls. Above us, the raven takes flight, soaring upward until it's no more than a dark blot against the forbidding arch of the sky.

CHAPTER 8
ARI

With those scouts murdered and Ronan's reaction to whatever Eva smelled in the woods, there's no way I'm tearing off after the Executor alone tonight. On the ride back, I pressed Ronan to explain himself, but he told me he wasn't at liberty to say more until he spoke with the Council. Being kept in the dark infuriates me, but not nearly as much as what I'm doing now: marching off to a formal dinner, because apparently even when a vicious dictator is on the run, friends lie moldering in the woods, and the future of the Empire is on the line, these virtueless fools feel the need to stand on ceremony.

The meal's being held at the Ash Tree Inn, where the other skúma have been staying since the fire destroyed their quarters in the House of Echoes. It's a four-story building crafted from stacked stone, with a roof of red tile. The front entrance is a portico supported by four massive columns, and as I turn off of Spruce Street to approach it, I see every window ablaze with candlelight. Idiots. They might as well be saying, *Look! Our most valuable assets are all right here, illuminated for your murderous convenience. Kindly come in and slaughter us.*

Grinding my teeth in frustration, I step inside. I have to admit it's beautiful: vaulted ceiling, massive (if poorly defensible) windows, stone hearth boasting a crackling fire. The Houses' banners drape the walls: crimson and black for Minneska, turquoise and cream for Satrizona, purple for Montyorke, and gold and green for San Fraesco. At the room's far end is a profligate display of food, enough to feed the Commonwealth of Ashes for a month.

A pig reclines on a silver platter, a shiny red apple stuffed in its mouth and its hindquarters skewered with a silver arrow. Heaped around the carcass are more apples, baked and dusted with cinnamon. On a table by itself is a towering chocolate cake, slathered in icing and topped by tiny figurines: a falcon in flight, a panther on the hunt, a seal arrested mid dive, and a wolf, surrounded by its pack.

Eva stands alone by the pig, inspecting it. Her black hair gleams in the candlelight, and the velvet, crimson dress she wears clings to every curve. The dress dips low in the back, and my eyes travel over the slits that bare her legs to mid-thigh. She looks just as dangerous as she did in the woods, when she took the form of her wolf, but for entirely different reasons. Mesmerized despite my frustrations over this mess with Sebastían, I carve a path to her side.

"Dare I ask where you've concealed a blade this time?"

She turns at the sound of my voice, eyes bright with amusement. "Hello to you, too."

I raise an inquiring brow, and her hand creeps to one of the slits in the dress, baring it so I can see the pale expanse of her thigh, the black edge of the leather sheath, and the silver glint of a knife. At the sight, I think my heart actually stops.

A smile lifts her lips. "I take it you like—"

"Eva," Sebastían says from behind us. "You look lovely."

Speak of the sins-damned devil.

The warmth building between me and Eva evaporates, replaced by tension of a different kind, as we turn to face him. And there he stands: turquoise tunic studded with tiny beads that glimmer as he shifts his weight, sleek black pants, brown hair tied back with a cream-colored ribbon. Every bit the pompous, glorified prince.

Eva's smile fades. I feel that now-familiar, unpleasant mixture of guilt and shame roil through the bond a moment before she speaks. "Sebastían. What can I do for you?"

"So formal, Eva. I was hoping you and your familiar"—there's a moment of deliberate hesitation before he says the word—"would give us the pleasure of your company for dinner." He gestures at his table, where Ilsa sits, eyes on the three of us.

Eva's eyes flick to me, conflict clear in their depths. "I don't think—"

"Come, Eva." He lifts his palms in a gesture of supplication. "Perhaps we've gotten off on the wrong foot. I just wish for us to get to know each other...all of us," he says, with a grudging nod in my direction.

Her eyes are still on my face, and with an internal sigh, I dip my head. The last thing I want is to spend more time with him, especially because of the claim he thinks he has on Eva—the one she won't renounce. The guilt that travels through the bond whenever she's around him makes me want to punch something, starting with his face. But my feelings aren't all that matters here. Maybe I can pick his brain about what happened in the woods. Perhaps he'll know something that can be useful to us—something about why that simple phrase, *like Mei but not,* sent Ronan into a frenzy.

It's fine, I tell her through the bond. *I'll behave.*

Eva's gaze travels between us. "All right," she says, her tone doubtful.

"Look at you, so afraid the next battle in this war is going to erupt at our dining table. I'll be on my best behavior, I promise." He tilts his chin at me. "If, of course, everyone concerned does the same."

I straighten to my full height, hand resting on the hilt of my dagur, and glare down my nose at him. "I think I can contain myself. Provided that I'm not provoked."

Eva looks between the two of us, makes a noise that sounds like *ugh*, and stomps off toward Sebastían's table. With one final glance over his shoulder—he's reluctant to turn his back on me, and I can't say I blame him—the Panther of the West follows.

Annoyed, I survey the food, trying to figure out if anything looks good enough to surmount the appetite-suppressing effects of Sebastían's presence. Perhaps I should pluck the miniature panther confection from atop the cake and devour it. The notion entertains me so much, I've taken a step in the cake's direction when I hear footsteps behind me.

If it's Sebastían, come to see why I haven't obeyed his princely summons, I'm going to shove him right into this cake, face-first. Gripping the hilt of my blade, I spin, a scathing remark on the tip of my tongue.

It isn't Sebastían. It's a group of four boys: Erdahl and three others, clad in the colors of their Houses. One of them has Tristan's silvery hair and sleek body; a second has a narrow face and a slim, aerodynamic form; and the last shares Sebastían's blue-green eyes, except they're curious rather than arrogant. Only a matter of time, I suppose.

"Can I help you?"

Erdahl edges closer, peeking up at me from under his thick lashes, his expression almost shy. "Forgive us for staring, Master Westergaard," he says. "It's just...it's only..."

His voice trails off, and I'm hard-pressed to keep my mouth

from curling up in a smile. *Master Westergaard?* That's a new one. I suppose it beats being called 'exile.'

"'It's only'...what?" I prompt him. "You've got my attention. Speak."

Erdahl glances behind him at the other boys, as if for support, but they don't say a word. Facing front once more, he squares his narrow shoulders, looks me in the eye, and says in a rush, "Is it true you can hit a target dead-on with a knife, standing fifty paces away, in a high wind?"

He's so serious, and it's clearly taken him so much nerve to approach me, I ought to respond in kind. But this is so *not* what I'd expected him to say, it takes me off guard. I can't help it: I laugh.

Erdahl's face darkens, and he ducks his head. "It was a foolish question," he says, his voice stiff. "Please pretend I didn't ask."

Something about him reminds me of my old friend Gentian, who was compassionate despite the harsh circumstances of the Commonwealth. Gentian, with his insatiable curiosity and inability to disguise how deeply he cared about people and animals alike. Who I protected with my life, because to do otherwise would be to turn my back on the best part of myself, the part I locked away long ago to become who I needed to be to survive.

Before I think better of it, I reach out and take Erdahl by the shoulder. Beneath the velvet of his crimson tunic, his bones feel light, hollow. "My apologies. There was nothing foolish about your question. And to answer it—yes. Of course I can."

Erdahl's head comes up, his expression eager. "Really? I thought that was just a rumor. Is it true you defeated thirty men almost single-handedly at the pass? And in the battle, in the Great Hall, I saw you run sideways along the wall like a magic trick, with my own eyes. Fade told me—well, he wasn't supposed to, but he did... Anyway, he told me that when you fought Mistress Eva at the training grounds, you bested her, even though she's a skúma and you're a—well, you were a—" His jaw slams shut with a click, and a blush suffuses his face.

"Just a guard?" I say, my voice dry. "A normal human being?"

"I meant no offense. Truly. The fact that you could accomplish such things, without the bond between skúma and familiar...and that despite your lack of training, you were able to bond with Mistress Marteinn...it's more impressive, Master Westergaard, not less." He sounds every bit skúma royalty now, his back straight and his gaze unwavering.

"Well," I say, smiling at him, "thank you for the compliment. As for the pass, thirty men is an exaggeration. We did fight the Bellatorum's Thirty, to be sure, but we didn't take all of them down. Many of them did fall at the pass, but," I say as his face lights up, "I didn't fight them alone. I had help—Eva, of course, but also Jaxon and Camila, who gave her life for the cause." I clear my throat, trying to dispel the memory of that sins-damned bloodbath.

"Now," I say, grinning, "when it comes to besting Eva on the training grounds, yes, that's true. Before I was a guard here, or her familiar, I was Eva's mentor. I trained her in the art of the blade. So you see"—I arch a brow—"I know much of what she'll do and how she'll attack before she knows, herself."

Erdahl and his hangers-on regard me as if I've just told them I scaled their sacred ash tree, lassoed one of their many-headed deities, and dragged it down here for their personal inspection. "By the gods," one of them breathes.

As gratifying as their hero worship is, I feel an obligation to dispel it. "That part's not magic. It's training. There's natural aptitude involved, sure, but most of it's just practice. You have to want it, and you have to work for it. Do that, and you've fought half the battle before you set foot in the arena."

The selkie boy next to Erdahl steps forward. "We were wondering," he says, "if you could maybe...show us."

I glance around the room, at the tables crowded with skúma and familiars and the guards stationed at the doors. It's not the setting I would've chosen for a weapons demonstration. "What did you have in mind? Would you like me to skewer that pig, or shave an inch off Sebastían Pardúr's hair?"

At this, all four of them gasp in unison, and I grin. "I'm joking. I would never impale that pig. It's been through enough."

The boys stare at me in appalled silence. And then they burst into giggles.

"You're funny," the selkie boy says at last. "But you shouldn't say that where Master Pardúr could hear you. He's known for his short temper."

"I'm not afraid of Sebastían's temper." Honestly, I'd welcome an excuse to lose my own. "Here. Let's see if this will suffice."

Motioning them to an empty table, I slide into one of the chairs and draw my dagur. They crowd around me, looking awed, as I show them the best way to grip the blade, how to balance it in your hand. "You should watch us train, if you're interested. Maybe"—I wink at Erdahl, feeling at home for the first time since I stepped into this accursed room—"you'll even get a chance to step into the arena."

"Mother would never allow..." the boy who resembles Eldrina begins, but Erdahl elbows him before he can finish his sentence.

"I would be honored," he tells me, giving a small, regal nod. "When could I—"

His voice breaks off as the boy with the piercing dark eyes

pokes him in the back. "Mother," the boy says again, and when I turn my head, I see Eldrina arrowing toward us. If she were in falcon form, she'd be diving in for the kill.

"What are you doing?" she says as she comes to a halt, voice high with fury. "Is that a *knife?* Are you honestly so foolish—or so brazen—as to bare your blades in front of skúma children...in front of *my* child...for their entertainment?"

The smile fades from my face, along with the brief sense of belonging that suffused me. I stand, palming my dagur. "I don't understand the problem."

"The problem? The *problem?*" Her voice is laced with so much contempt, all four of the boys flinch. "The *problem* is that these are children. Not just children, but our most precious assets. Should they be wounded or killed, you can't replace them the way you would a—a shooting target. There's a time and place for weapons demonstrations, and *this*, Master Westergaard, is. Not. It."

I eye her, incredulous. "Are you insinuating I have so little control over my blades that they'll somehow fly out of my hands and impale one of your children?"

The nostrils of her beak-like nose flare. "I'm *insinuating* that accidents happen. And should such a thing happen here...you wouldn't want to be the one to blame."

I am so sick of this imperious attitude. Every time I turn around, there it is again. "Observe," I say, my tone just as haughty, and raise my throwing arm high.

The blade leaves my hand before she can utter another word, winnowing through the air toward the table where the food sits, a good hundred paces away. It hits the tiny falcon atop the towering chocolate cake and falls straight down, slicing the cake in two. A large slab slides to the floor in a cascade of icing and crumbs.

Eldrina gasps as the room falls silent. I shift my gaze to the left and right; everyone, including the remaining Councilors and Eva, is staring. Well, let them.

"I don't miss. And I don't lose control of my blades. If I wanted to harm these children, or you"—I turn an icy glare on her—"you'd all be dead."

"You insolent brat!"

Just when I'm about to say something I might truly regret, the Panther of the West strolls up behind her. Fantastic. Now my evening is complete.

"Stop giving him a hard time, Eldrina," Sebastían drawls. "The exile doesn't know our ways. He can hardly be expected to behave appropriately."

What a sins-forsaken, obnoxious ass. "I was raised in a Commonwealth, not a barn, Pardúr," I say, giving him my most charming smile. "Perhaps you belong in the latter, hunting rats for sport rather than joining the rest of us in the dining hall. After all, isn't that what cats savor for their supper?"

This must be a bridge too far, because the veneer of civility that's overlaid Sebastían's every move peels away, revealing the beast beneath. His upper lip curls back from his teeth, and he lunges at me, claws out. I step out of the way, channeling my bond with Eva to speed my reflexes. My smile widens as he misses, just catching the edge of my gear. "Is that the best you can do? What a shame, Prince of the Sands. My shirt will never be the same."

"I've had about enough of your disrespect." Sebastían's eyes have shifted to his panther's green. They narrow, and the look in them is all threat. "I'd be pleased to show you *my best*, as you call it, except that my future wife"–he glances across the room at Eva—"depends upon you for your services, more's the pity. I suppose there's no accounting for taste."

"That must be it," I say, my voice honey-sweet. "It couldn't possibly be the fact that you're afraid I might best *you*, and then where would House Satrizona be?"

"Did you just *threaten me?*" He stalks toward me, that now-familiar growl rumbling in his chest. Out of the corner of my eye, I see Eldrina ushering the boys to safety. I half-expect Eva to intervene, but she stays seated. Her face is impassive and the bond is muted, as if she's throttling it at her end, but I don't need our preternatural connection to understand why she's not moving. If she gets between me and Sebastían, it will weaken my position in his eyes and those of everyone else here. She knows I need to be able to defend myself, to stand on my own, or I'll never be anything more than her familiar.

"Why do you ask?" I say to Sebastían, twirling my dagur. "It's not like you're planning to do anything about it. But don't worry; I'll keep my knives to myself. If your head parted ways with your neck and landed in the stew, it might make people lose their appetites."

The growl that rumbles in Sebastían's chest grows louder. "You'll regret this," he snarls, tensing to lunge again. I raise my throwing arm, the blade glinting in the candlelight.

"Leave him." It's Councilor Adelman's voice. "That goes for both of you."

Sebastían's eyes stay fixed on me as the Councilor-in-Chief strides up to us. I stare back, my heart thudding as my grip tightens on my blade. I can't afford to back down first.

Councilor Adelman glances between us. "Step away, Pardúr. Think of the greater cause."

Sebastían snorts, his eyes flicking to my blade. "The exile threatened and insulted me."

"And you did the same to him. Perhaps you could consider it an even exchange."

"I am royalty." Sebastían sounds incredulous. "Were it not for Eva Marteinn, he would be *nothing*."

A laugh rips its way free from my throat. "Oh, Sebastían. Now you're just hurting my feelings."

Through the bond with Eva, I feel her irritation—with him? With me? The idea that she could possibly condone his attitude infuriates me. I curl my lip at Sebastían just as the Councilor-in-Chief says, sounding eerily like Kilían used to, "And you, Westergaard. Stop antagonizing him. You're making it worse."

"I'm sorry," I tell Sebastían. "Tell me, what hit home? Was it my comment about your meal of choice? My critique of your poor aim? Or maybe," I say, tilting my head as if I'm giving the subject serious consideration, "it's the knowledge that Eva chose me, whereas if she accepts your proposal, you'll never know whether it's you she wants or just your title."

That's the blade that sinks deep. I see it in the way his body tenses, the way a growl breaks free from his lips again and his claws slide free. I let my lips rise in a taunting smile as Councilor Adelman steps between us.

"Enough," he says, and his hands go to his robe, parting it. When they come into view again, each of them is holding a gun—one pointed at my chest and the other at Sebastían's.

"I'd hoped it wouldn't come to this," Adelman says, his voice as calm as if we were strolling down City Road rather than on the verge of a shootout. "But I've had enough grandstanding. There have been...developments, and we can ill afford it. The two of you will have to find a way to cooperate, for the sake of our common goal. Do I make myself clear?"

Eva is on her feet now. I can feel her anxiety pulsing through the bond, her desire for this to be over before something worse happens. But I can't afford to be the first one to speak. And that word *developments* tugs at me, fueling my aggravation. What developments? And if what Eva scented in the woods is truly significant, how can they all justify sitting here, gorging themselves?

I stare Sebastían down, ignoring the gun pointed at my chest. The Panther of the West stares back at me. And finally he takes a step away, his claws retracting. "Perhaps," he says, examining his nails as if he's never been so bored, "you can teach Westergaard some manners, Councilor-in-Chief. A little courtesy would go a long way."

I slide my blade back into its holster and mirror Sebastían, stepping away from the panther prince and the muzzle that's leveled at my chest. I don't think Councilor Adelman will shoot me; that doesn't mean I'm arrogant enough to test him. Besides, as Eldrina took such pains to point out, accidents happen. "I appreciate your concern about my manners. However, much as I would like to reassure you by demon-strating my skill with a knife and fork, I've lost my appetite. Excuse me, Councilor."

I stalk through a sea of frozen, horrified faces, to the double doors, and out into the cool, fresh air. Two seconds later, the doors slam again. I don't need the rage that rolls through the bond to know Eva's followed.

Her feet thud on the cobblestones as she stomps over to me. Her dark eyes are dilated, her cheeks flushed. "That," she snaps, "was unnecessary."

"I completely agree. We both know I wasn't going to skewer Erdahl like that poor excuse for a pig. Really, Eldrina has terrible judgment."

She glares up at me. "You're a better strategic thinker than anyone I know. Why bare your blades in the Hall unless you meant to invite trouble? And why continue antagonizing Sebastían?"

I give a rough laugh. "Is that what you think? That I'm the one who antagonized *him*? Whose side are you on, anyway?"

"You insinuated Sebastían was raised in a stable. You threatened to decapitate him!"

I can't help but notice she hasn't answered my question. "Untrue. I specifically remember telling him I planned to keep my knives to myself."

She takes a step closer to me, and the bond sparks at our proximity. Goosebumps prickle over her bare arms. "You have every kind of control. So either you did this on purpose or you've let these people get under your skin. One is disturbing, and the other is dangerous. Which is it?"

In the flickering light of the lamps that line the portico, I can see the pulse hammering at the base of her throat. Even now, when we're fighting, I want to press my lips to it. To pull her against me and claim her for my own. I hate the hold she has on me, even as I would do anything to protect it. How have we wound up in this virtueless mess? "Maybe," I say, my voice gravelly, "it's a bit of both. Or maybe, I don't have as much control as you think."

She shakes her head, tendrils of dark waves coming loose from her braid. A cool breeze curls through the portico, sending her scent toward me: chocolate and spice. I have to grit my teeth to stop from reaching for her as she says, "I don't believe that."

"Then maybe I just need to know. Is it you and me, first and foremost? Or is it *them*?"

"I'm one of them!" Her chest heaves. "That disgust you feel for Sebastían and Eldrina? Admit it. Part of you feels the same about me."

I eye her, incredulous. I bound myself to her, sacrificed my soul. And she thinks I lump her together with that arrogant blowhard and the woman who sought to make a fool out of me? "Of course I don't. How can you say that?"

"Because it's the truth. Every time you look at them, you must see me. How could you do anything else?"

"I love you." My voice breaks. "*That's* the truth, and you

know it. Leave this sins-forsaken nest of vipers behind for the next few hours and I'll show you just how much."

Eva doesn't say she loves me, too. That she'd rather be arguing in the cold with me than sitting by a cozy fire, gorging herself on cinnamon apples with a boy who treats me like the dirt beneath his boots. Instead, she looks me up and down, and when her gaze settles on my face, I can tell that I've been judged and found wanting.

"I'm going to stay here and finish my dinner." Her voice is frigid. "That is, unless you'd prefer me to hunt down rats in the barn."

"Perhaps *you'd* prefer that," I hiss, my anger getting the best of me. "If you cared for me as I do for you, then you'd walk away from that supercilious ass. But you won't do that, Eva. And I know why."

Color burns high in her cheeks. "Because without him, there's no alliance with Satrizona! Don't you think I'd refuse him, if I could?"

"No," I say, biting out each word. "I don't. Because if you wanted to, you could find a way around this alliance. I think part of you is drawn to him, Eva. To the idea of being with someone who's like you, in a way I never can be. Part of you wants him—wants things I can never give you. And there's no way I can compete with that."

"There is no competition!" she retorts, folding her arms across her chest. But an unfamiliar look flits across her face: guilt.

The wind bends the pines, sending an ice-cold blast of air through the portico. I shiver, but Eva doesn't. Of course she doesn't, because she isn't cold. She's not *human*.

I'd thought that no matter what befell us, our feelings for each other would be enough to surmount it. That when we finally bonded, the strength of our love pulling me back from the brink of death, nothing could come between us.

But what if I was wrong? What if we're too different, despite everything?

"I know there isn't," I say, suddenly weary. "Because he's already won."

Eva looks stricken. "Ari," she says, opening the bond wider, trying to sense what's behind my words, to fix this. But I shut my end of it down, hard. She already has enough power over me; I don't need to cede the last bit of my heart, so she can crush it into smithereens.

She reaches for me, but I step back. If she puts her hands on me right now, that will be my undoing. "No," I say, my voice hard. "Don't touch me."

Her teeth sink into her lower lip, white and sharp. "Where are you going?"

"I don't know. Away from here."

"Let me come with you," she pleads. "I'm sorry. We'll talk. We'll work this out."

Two days ago, I would have laid my blades at her feet for the privilege of hearing her say those words. But now, they feel as hollow as my heart. "No," I say again. "You were right the first time. Go back inside, Eva. It's where you belong."

I wait for her to say this isn't true. That she belongs with me, just as I belong with her. But she doesn't say a word, not then and not when I walk away.

CHAPTER 9

ARI

I stalk down Spruce Street and onto Ash, past the barns where I accused Sebastían of belonging, until I find myself outside the training center. At least here, I can channel my anger into something I understand. The center will likely be deserted at the dinner hour, and I can throw knives in peace. Better a target than Sebastían and Eldrina's faces, after all.

I storm through the building, past the empty pool and the weight room, and crack the door that leads to the training yard. And then my eyes go wide.

Kilían paces the gravel in front of the targets, his hands balled into fists. Even from where I stand, in the fading light, I can see the stitches where Sebastían tried to tear out his throat and the bruises that mar his face. He's in no shape for knife-throwing or sparring, so what in the nine hells is he doing here? Perhaps, like me, he's sought comfort in the familiar presence of weapons, something he understands.

I'd welcome a hand-to-hand battle to channel my frustration, the way Kilían and I fought the night he told me about the Brotherhood. But since that's off the table, maybe we can talk in private. I can ask him if he knows anything about Gentian's well-being, though there's no reason he should be familiar with a shy, stuttering vet tech. If he *was*, it would be a poor sign. And, more importantly, I can interrogate him about his connection to Kennett.

Regardless of why he's here, it's a relief to find a kindred spirit, and my mouth opens to hail him. But before I can say a word, I hear another voice, issuing from the shadows, by the side gate the guards rarely use.

My father's.

Shock washes over me as I edge back into the fingers of darkness that curl around the corners of the door, a place where I can observe the two of them, unseen. If this is my chance to get to the bottom of the strange dynamic between them, I'll seize it, and welcome.

"I owe you a great debt," my father says, stepping into Kilían's path. He's wearing a white fitted shirt and linen pants that all but glow in the growing darkness. If someone was out here, hunting him, he'd be hard-pressed to make himself an easier target.

Kilían stops dead. He has to; it's that, or run Kennett down. "What are you doing here?" he says, his eyes scanning Kennett's outfit with disapproval.

"Looking for you. I figured you'd seek this place out. And here you are."

"You think you know me." It's a challenge, but Kennett doesn't rise to meet it.

"Thank you," he says instead, sincerity ringing in every syllable, "for taking care of my son."

"I gave you my word." Kilían's voice is gruff. He looks everywhere but at my father.

"True." Kennett slips his hands into his pockets. It's an uneasy gesture, like he doesn't know what else to do with them. "You did give your word. And I know what that means to you."

Kilían barks a harsh laugh. "Do you, still? It's been nineteen years. For all you know, I could have broken my oath the instant I stepped through that door in the tunnels."

My father shakes his head, lips quirking as if the very concept is absurd. "You're a man of honor, Kilían. Some things will never change."

Kilían swallows hard. Given the stitches in his throat, this must hurt, and when he speaks, his voice is rough. "Honor had nothing to do with it."

Silence falls between the two of them, but it's not easy. It feels heavy with things left unsaid, and when Kilían shatters it, his voice is grittier than ever, as if he's swallowed a handful of gravel. "I know you grieve Miriam," he says, but it doesn't sound like a statement. It sounds like a question he can't bring himself to ask.

"I will always grieve her." Kennett's voice breaks. "She was a part of me. But we both knew the risks we took. Our time together was more than we could ever have hoped for. And she could have asked for no better death, with her last sight our son's face."

For a moment I'm there again, watching my mother run toward me, her face alight, her lips forming my name, a second before the world explodes in a shower of blood and ash. My breath comes short, and a buzzing sound fills my ears, just like it did that day. I breathe in and taste copper, thick on my tongue.

That time is long gone, I tell myself. *And it was not your fault.* But, like I told Jaxon that night on the beam, part of me will always believe otherwise. Part of me will always think that, no matter what choices my mother made, I am the one who took her life.

When my head clears at last, Kennett is still talking. "We owe that to you, Kilían. We—*I*—owe you everything. And I'll never forget."

Kilían starts to give his head a sharp shake, then winces as his stitches pull. "I don't want you to be in my debt," he says, arching one red brow. "Consider it a promise well-kept. As I recall, I made you another."

Bellators don't swear oaths easily; we'll lay down our lives to keep them. Whatever else Kilían promised my father must have been worth such a sacrifice...but why would he make it?

"You did. And here I stand." My father smiles. "Perhaps you're my good-luck charm."

"I don't believe in luck," the Lead Interrogator says. He looks Kennett up and down, and this time I see his brow quirk, as if what he sees entertains him. I used to joke that Kilían could discipline a whole class of recruits using only his eyebrows. Clearly, the skill has not deserted him. "But perhaps you're a little more of a wolf than the last time we met, eh?"

Kennett's smile turns rueful, and he lifts one shoulder, then lets it fall, in that eerie gesture that I recognize as my own. "Sorry to disappoint."

"Ah, well. I'm wolf enough for the both of us, I suppose."

It's strange to hear Kilían and my father speak in what amounts to a code, rooted in their shared history, of which I know next to nothing. Stranger still is the blush that heats Kilían's cheeks, the way he's struggling to meet my father's eyes.

That silence falls again, thick enough to slice with my dagur. Then Kennett says, his voice hesitant, "I've had a lot of time to think since that night in the tunnels and the woods, Kilían. Years and years to think about what passed between us. I didn't have words for it then. But now, I can't help but wonder if you felt...that is, if you..."

His voice trails off, and now it's his turn to blush. Unlike Kilían, whose high color stains his cheekbones, my father's creeps upward from his neck to his brows, a vivid red against the white of his shirt.

Kilían stares at him, not saying a word. He looks every bit the austere warrior, clad in torn black gear and bristling with weapons, and my father's teeth sink into his bottom lip. "Forgive me," he says, turning away. "I don't know what I was thinking. Of course you didn't—I shouldn't have insinuated—"

But Kilían's good hand darts out, quick as a striking snake, and grabs my father's shirt. "Of course I did," he says. "Kennett, I still do."

My eyes widen. What is my father implying? What did Kilían just acknowledge?

Kilían straightens, girding himself. "When we said goodbye in the scholar's room," he says, forcing out each word, "I could've sworn you felt the same. But perhaps I imagined it. For I know Miriam held your heart."

The wind rises, picking up speed. It gusts, so I can hardly hear Kennett's voice when he speaks. "It wasn't your imagination," my father says, his eyes searching Kilían's face. "Another time, another place…"

Kilían takes a startled step back, like my father has hit him. He sets his shoulders, as if for battle. And then, to my consternation, he kneels at Kennett's feet.

My father looks as surprised as I am. "What are you doing?" he says, his voice cracking. "Stand up."

"Let me say this." Kilían pulls his dagur from its holster, laying it flat on his palms. "I swear these words on my blade, so you will know I speak the truth."

"You don't have to—" Kennett begins, but Kilían palms his dagur and holds up his free hand, forestalling whatever my father is about to say.

"I've waited nearly two decades. And with the way things are, who knows when I'll get another chance. Please, Kennett. Listen to me."

I've never heard Kilían say 'please' before, and by the way my father's eyes widen, he's not too familiar with the phenomenon, either. Wordlessly, he nods.

"All these years, my feelings for you have been a flame inside me." Kilían's voice shakes, but his gaze is steady. "When I would have let my empathy for others fade to ashes, when I would have sunk into being no more than an extension of my blade, I saw your face. You are my conscience, Kennett. Any good that's left in me, I owe to you. So you see, the debt is mine. And I swear on my blade that I will repay it. I will protect you from what lies ahead, with all my strength and the last drop of my blood."

In all the years I've known Kilían, I've seen him posture and trick and conceal. I've heard him command and mock and entice. But never, never have I heard this kind of painful honesty from him. It's as if that other version of him is a mask, concealing his true feelings...the way I did, back in the Commonwealth, when I thought Eva could never be mine.

What is happening here?

"No, Kilían." My father takes a step closer to him, his voice vibrating with intensity. "That's not true. You saved my life, and Miriam's. You saved our son. There's been good in you all along."

"You would say that." The bitter laugh rips from Kilían's throat again as he holsters his blade. "But you don't know. Saving you, Kennett—it was selfish. I did it for myself, because I couldn't stand the idea of living in a world without you in it. The things I've done...the people I've hurt...the lives I've taken... if you knew, you wouldn't ever look at me the same way again."

"So tell me," my father whispers. "Wash yourself clean."

Anguish carves lines deep in Kilían's face. "I can't. You're the one unsullied thing I have left. Look at you, all in white, like a sins-forsaken angel. I'll not mark you that way."

"I'm not an angel." For the first time, I hear a hint of anger in my father's voice. "I may not be a wolf, but I've seen terrible things, Kilían. I've sacrificed things I couldn't have imagined, all those years ago. And I've lived my life knowing I loved two people. That I always would. One of them is lost forever, but the other..." He gestures in Kilían's direction. "I never gave up hoping I could see you again. The least you can do is to trust me with the truth."

The words hang in the air, and for a moment, I think Kilían isn't going to reply. But then he whispers, barely audible over the howl of the wind, "'Smooth is the descent.'"

"'And easy is the way,'" my father replies, without the slightest hesitation.

I know this quote—know, too, the first line, which both of them have left unspoken: 'The descent into hell is easy,' from Virgil's *Aeneid*. We were all taught it in the Commonwealth, as soon as we were old enough to understand. But looking between the two of them—like negatives of each other, Kennett in his gleaming white and Kilían in his tattered, dark gear—I can tell it has a greater meaning. Once again, I wonder what passed between them before I was born. Who are they to each other? And why, after all I went through with Eva, did Kilían never tell me?

As soon as the question occurs to me, I know the answer. We were trained to think love would break and destroy us, that it was the key that opened the doors to the nine hells. To confess such a thing to me would mean risking his life. It would mean admitting that beneath his bravado and skilled blade-work, he was no better than the basest sinner.

"The Priests are liars, Kilían," my father says, as if he's read my thoughts. "Love isn't what they would have us believe. It doesn't condemn our souls to an eternity of suffering. It's not a weakness or a flaw. If there's one thing I've learned since I left that damnable place behind me, it's that love will save us all." My father smiles at him, but beneath its surface, I see how much he wants—needs—Kilían to understand.

Kilían sighs, his shoulders slumping as if a weight has been lifted from them. "If you say it, then I suppose I can believe it," he says at last. "Because I have tortured, and killed, and wormed false truths out of innocent men and women using tactics it would shame me to confess. But you, Kennett—you're pure of heart. The furnaces of hell might welcome me, and gladly. But there's no room in such a place for you."

"Get up, please." Kennett rolls his eyes. "Even if nineteen years separate us, I've *seen* the state of your soul. You're good, to the core. You'll not convince me otherwise, no matter how hard you try. And the last place you belong is on your knees before me."

"No." The single syllable breaks loose from Kilían's throat. "No, I—"

"Ego te absolvo." My father grips Kilían's shoulder, as if in benediction. "I, who know you better than the Priests and perhaps even your brethren, absolve you of your sins."

Kilían's gaze sears into him, shock stamped on every feature. But he doesn't pull away.

"You're in pain," Kennett says. "And I'm a healer. So stand, and let me heal you."

When Kilían doesn't move, my father sinks to his knees on the gravel in front of him. His arms wrap around Kilían, holding him close, careful of the Lead Interrogator's wounds. At first, Kilían doesn't respond. I expect him to push my father away. But Kennett just tugs him closer, and I see Kilían draw one deep, shuddering breath, then another. Then, without a word, he surges into my father's touch, gripping the back of Kennett's shirt in his fists.

"Ego te absolvo," Kennett whispers again. "I'm here now. You're not alone."

Kilían grips my father's shirt harder, until the material tears along its seams. But Kennett doesn't break away. From this angle, I can't see his face. But I can see Kilían's. The Bellatorum's fearsome interrogator, ruthless leader of the Thirty—the man who children in the Commonwealth were told would snatch them from their beds if they sinned—is crying.

I don't know what to think. To feel. Part of me believes that if Kilían's love for Kennett could survive all this time untended, like a plant deprived of sun, then anything is possible. That I'm a fool for thinking Sebastían could come between me and Eva. No matter how furious I was, I shouldn't have left. I should have fought for her. But, as I watch Kilían cry silently while Kennett holds him tight, another part of me believes that, for a relationship to thrive, both people must make themselves vulnerable. Both of them must be willing to fight for it. Maybe it's because pride is my besetting sin, but I'm sick and tired of putting my heart on a platter for Eva, only to be rejected. And, like I thought outside the Inn, maybe sometimes love just isn't enough. Maybe *I* will never be enough for her, no matter how hard I try.

The thought guts me. Silently, grief thrumming through every vein and sinew, I ease the door shut and creep back down the hallway, retreating the way I've come.

CHAPTER 10
EVA

The longer I wait for Ari to return to the guards' quarters after dinner, the more agitated I become. Why can't he understand that, no matter what we feel for each other, sacrifices still need to be made, for the greater good? Why can't he keep his head down and his mouth shut until we have what we both want—revenge on the Executor, freedom for my mother, and the destruction of the Commonwealths—instead of throwing a fit and stomping off?

I have so many questions. Why did those exiles attack so close to Vik? And why that lingering scent, like Mei but not? Where is Mei, and what is she plotting? Why did Kilían stare at Kennett that way, when Ari's father appeared in the Council's chambers? And what transpired between Councilor-in-Chief Adelman and my mother? Ari ought to be here with me, helping me discover the answers. And yet, he's nowhere to be found.

The wolf inside me paces closer to the surface, reminding me that I am alpha, that Ari should come to me rather than the other way around. The more she troubles me, the harder it is to sit still. Head high, shoes dangling from one hand, I prowl through the dark, down Ash Avenue and up Spruce Street to the House of Echoes.

The night calls to me, the woods beckoning me to leave the path. To hunt. An image flashes in my mind: letting my panther surface, shredding my crimson dress to bits as she takes her true form. Sinking her claws into the bark of a nearby oak as she climbs, her teeth piercing the neck of one of the many creatures scampering through the trees that border Spruce Street. Feeding until her belly is full, under the light of the waxing moon.

The image is so vivid, I can feel it in every inch of my body. I taste the metallic spurt of blood on my tongue, smell the thousand tiny scents that make up the night, feel the life of my kill wane, flooding me with triumph. The night is *mine,* and it summons me, enticing me with a bone-deep allure that sends a shudder through my entire body.

Come, my panther whispers. *Hunt.*

I don't realize I've ventured into the forest until I feel the dirt crumbling beneath my bare feet. Spruce Street is a thin line, visible through the thicket that conceals me. Branches scrape at my dress and vines twine around my ankles, but not to hold me captive. To welcome me.

Somehow, my panther has taken hold of my body. Her thoughts are mine; mine are hers.

I don't feel in control, not now. I feel...*wild.* And it terrifies me.

Pulse pounding, I push my panther down into the depths and take one step back toward the path, then another, forcing the grasping vines and branches to release me. My panther doesn't want to go; I can feel her resist, can feel the night's siren call tugging at both of us to stay.

At last I reach the road again and stand on the cobblestones, panting. My beautiful velvet dress is ruined, the material rubbed raw in places and torn in others. My stomach twists, churning with the realization of how little I know about what I've become. Of what my body is capable of doing, without my mind's consent. How can I hold onto my love for Ari and fight for Vik if I can't even hold onto myself?

Up ahead, the torches that line the entrance to the House of Echoes flicker. I run toward them, not caring who might see. For the first time, when the white stone building looms in front of me, I feel not crushing obligation, but relief.

The crimson-and-black grandeur of the foyer envelops me, and the guards nod to me as I climb the winding marble staircase to my room, which mercifully escaped the damage that the other skúma's quarters suffered. Two of them follow me at a respectful distance, taking up their posts as I close the door.

I haven't been back here since I told Ari I loved him, since I slit Riis's throat and let Mei flee. Near the fringed hearth rug, the Executor's blood has seeped into the floorboards. I can smell a trace of it—the slightest hint of copper, staining the air.

Someone has kept the fire burning low. Forcing thoughts of the Executor from my mind, I toss on kindling and watch the flames flare. Tendrils of warmth curl through the room as I strip off my dress, remove my weapons, and change into a black tunic and loose-fitting, drawstring pants. Then I climb onto the bed, my gaze traveling between the beasts carved on each post: a plunging selkie, a howling wolf, a prowling panther, a diving falcon. The logs crackle in the fireplace as I close my eyes and breathe deep, seeking sleep.

But sleep doesn't come. I've never been so wide awake, as if the night is alive inside me, humming in my blood. My eyes flicker open, tracking across the room to the fireplace, now cheerily ablaze. The last time a fire burned in that hearth, I'd hurled Karsten into it to save Ari's life. He'd howled as he burned, but all I'd felt was satisfaction. And now, my only regret is that he survived. What kind of monster does that make me?

Yes, I saved Ari's life. But to what end? To break his heart? The devastated expression on his face outside the Inn when he told me Sebastían had already won...the memory of how his voice cracked when he told me to stay with the other skúma, that it's where I belonged...they're engraved in my memory. As angry as I am with him for stomping off like a child, it still makes me ache to think of hurting him that way.

The worst part is, he wasn't entirely wrong. I *am* drawn to Sebastían, despite myself. The way his panther calls to mine is something I can't experience with anyone else. And on a visceral level, even though Ari is the one I love, there's still my beast, urging me to answer Sebastían's call. What am I supposed to do about that? And what happens if it overrides the part of me that's human, taking control of my body like what happened on the path?

I'd hoped that if I surrounded myself with things that reminded me of my humanity—the luxurious crimson-and-black comforter, the finely-crafted stained glass windows, the armoire filled with hand-sewn clothing—the wildness sparking in my blood would settle. I'd feel like myself, like a person, again. But this room doesn't feel like sanctuary; it feels like a trap.

Time tick-tick-ticks and I tick with it, the sparks in my blood flaring brighter. Despite the room's vaulted ceilings, I'm claustrophobic, in desperate need of fresh air.

I can't lie still. I can't stay here.

I just want to be alone. To be myself. To be free.

Before I can overthink it, I stand, strap my discarded sheaths to my thighs, and slip my favorite blades into them. Then I grab a hooded coat from the armoire and climb out the window, down the bare trellis to the ground below. The night is colder than before, the scent of snow-to-come riding the air, but it doesn't trouble me.

In seconds, I've come to a soft landing on the ground, my head twisting left and right to make sure I'm alone. Other than a few intrepid field mice at the treeline, nothing stirs. The falcon within me notes them, but she's drawn to hunt at dawn or dusk, when her prey is most active, not the middle of the night. Besides, she's more interested in the rock pigeons and starlings she smells roosting in the trees, the ones who are hardy enough to brave Minneska's winters.

One route will take me toward the City Road, the other toward the guards' quarters and the stables. I turn my back on them both and face the mountains, looming blue-black against the moonlit sky. Far beyond them lies the place where I was born. And at their base is a thick scrim of forest, stretching out and out until it almost reaches the grass where I stand.

The woods are dark and foreboding at this hour, the wind shaking the bare bones of the oaks and rummaging through the pines. But they're also, I hope, empty.

Making sure to keep to the shadows just in case someone's watching, I venture down the trail that cuts through the forest as the wind gusts once more, this time from the west. For a moment, I feel at peace. And then an unmistakable scent floods my nose, and I freeze.

I came out here to be alone. But it looks like I'm not going to get my wish.

CHAPTER II
ARI

Did Kilían join the Brotherhood because he truly believes in it—or because of what he feels for my father? If things go south and, Virtues forbid, Kennett dies, might he turn on us?

That thought makes me want to stab something. But violence isn't an option, unless I want to charge off into the woods and hurl knives at trees while the-Architect-knows-what is out there gutting people. I may be impulsive, but stupid I am not. So I have to find another way.

Normally, I'd bring my concerns to Eva, but I can't talk to her right now. Honestly, I'm happy to have something else to focus on, other than the sins-forsaken mess of our relationship. Just to make sure she can't talk to me, either, I shut my end of the bond down, so nothing leaks through. That leaves Jaxon, who I meant to check on, anyhow.

I expect to find him irritable and complaining, his natural state. But his room's light in the infirmary is dimmed. He's asleep, his inky hair a sharp contrast with the crisp white pillowcase but his skin nearly as pale. By the moonlight that filters through the window, I see the bruise on his temple where that bastard Karsten smashed his head into the floor. His left shoulder is bandaged, and his arm is in a sling. There's an untouched meal on his bedside table: a bowl of unappetizing stew and a couple of rolls that look like they've seen better days. Apparently, those who've nearly died in defense of the four Houses don't warrant sweet buns with whipped cream and sculpture-topped chocolate cake.

I consider leaving, but someone ought to honor Jaxon's sacrifice. He's all alone here. The least I can do is stay with him. So, padding silently across the floor, I sink into the wooden chair next to the bed, which was designed for a person half my size and wobbles as if it's on the verge of collapse. When I'm confident that it's not going to disintegrate under my weight, I turn my attention to Jaxon. He's sleeping, but not peacefully. His jaw's set as if he's in pain, and his eyes dart back and forth beneath closed lids. As I watch, he mumbles a single word again and again. I lean closer to catch it and realize what he's saying: *Tobias.*

By the Architect. If I didn't feel guilty enough about my mother's death, here's someone else I feel responsible for, whose life was lost in the bombing that killed Miriam: the man Jaxon loved. Part of me wants to run, but the better part of me knows that here is where I belong. If Jaxon has to feel this, then I will bear the burden along with him. And so I force myself to stay.

I shift in the chair, trying to get comfortable. The sins-cursed thing lets out an unholy squeal and tilts, threatening to spill me onto the floor, and I have to grab the side of Jaxon's bed to keep my balance. I right myself, muttering expletives under my breath, and sit back to find him looking right at me.

"What the hell are you doing, exile?" he says, his voice rough with sleep. "A little nighttime stalking? I'm disappointed. You're not very subtle."

I grin, relieved to see him conscious. "I told you that you should've taken up needlepoint, idiot. I wasn't there to look after you this time, and see what happened? A couple of inches to the right, and you would've been dead."

He glances down at his bandage, wincing. "Yeah, but I would've died a hero. Lucky Kennett came along when he did. You met him, huh?"

"I did," I say, refusing to be diverted by the subject of my father—at least, not yet. "Covered in your blood. It wasn't a good look." I level a glare at him. "Ronan told me you took out Jessamine's attacker with a knife, right after you hurled your asinine self between her and a bullet. It was good bladework, just like I taught you. Sounds like I've saved your life again."

Jaxon snorts in amusement, but the sound cuts off when he jars his shoulder. "Ugh, don't make me laugh. What's your arrogant ass really doing here? If you wanted the pleasure of my company, you could've asked. Didn't need to fall off that chair and mangle yourself just to get a bed in the infirmary."

"Very funny." But he's given me an opening, and I intend to take it. I draw a deep breath and tell him what happened in the woods, my voice pitched low to avoid being overheard. I'm hoping he can shed light on Ronan's reaction, but he just shakes his head, puzzled.

"There's something... Can't get a handle on it, though. Maybe if they didn't have me on these wicked meds."

"That's all right," I tell him, trying not to let my disappointment show. "They'll tell us tomorrow, I'm sure. And if not, I'll beat it out of them. Let's just hope it's not too late."

Jaxon gives a pained chuckle. "Well, since you're here, exile...entertain me, why don't you? And I'll keep thinking. Try to make it worth your while."

And so I tell him everything that's happened with Sebastían, first in the Council's chambers and then in the dining hall, though I leave out the fight Eva and I had afterward. That's none of his concern. "I nearly skewered His Majesty like that Architect-forsaken pig," I finish. "You think *I'm* arrogant? At least I can back it up."

"Oh, Sebastard can back it up." He snorts, then winces again. "The guy's a pain. Also, he's got a..." The words catch in his throat, and he coughs to clear it, then shakes his head. "But he's also royalty. Has a pass to do as he pleases."

I could have sworn he was about to say something else, that the cough was a cover-up. But maybe I'm imagining things, being paranoid. "And the rest of us just have to swallow whatever His Royal Cat's Ass says? I don't think so."

Jaxon smirks. "Hold up. Did you just call the Panther of the West *His Royal Cat's Ass?*"

"Do you like 'Sebosstian' better? Because he definitely thinks he's in charge. And I'm sick of it."

Now Jaxon is full-on howling. "By the gods," he gasps, clutching his sling with his free hand, "don't make me laugh, you sadist."

"I don't know what that is. Why are you always calling me things I don't understand? Does it bring joy to your twisted little heart?"

He starts to answer, just as one of the floor's healers pokes her head around the corner of his doorway and admonishes us to be quiet. Jaxon promises he will, looking contrite. But the second she vanishes, he starts chuckling again. "Name-calling aside, something else on your mind? Or did you just show up to watch me sleep?"

I don't want to talk about Eva. So instead, I find myself spilling what I just observed at the training center. With each successive word, Jaxon's dark eyes widen, but he doesn't interrupt.

When I finish, I bury my head in my hands. "What if Kilían

gave me preferential treatment in the Bellatorum because of who my father was? I'm sick of this. Just when I think I've gotten a grip on things, I realize nothing's what I thought it was."

I can't see Jaxon. But when he speaks, his voice is unexpectedly gentle. "You'll do whatever you have to do, Westergaard. You're one of the most resilient people I've ever met. And whatever happened in the Bellatorum, you earned your place. No doubt in my mind." He pauses. "Pains me to admit it, but I'm proud to call you my friend. I wish Tobias could've met you. He would've felt the same."

I sit up, so I can look at him. "You're missing him, yeah? You were saying his name, before. When I came in."

Jaxon drops his gaze to his sheets, as if embarrassed. "Of course I miss him. But..." His head jerks up, the full force of those dark eyes boring into mine. "Before Kennett showed up, I thought I was going to die in the dirt. And for the first time in a long time, I didn't want to. At the pass, on that gods-cursed beam, I would've been happy to go. To be with him. But there in the woods, all I could think was—*I want to live*."

"That sounds like a good thing."

"Is it?" His gaze pins me to the chair. "I wanted to live, Westergaard, even though it meant being without him forever. But now, I wish he was here, telling me it'll be all right. What kind of coward does that make me, when I turned my back on him?"

His tone is bitter, as if the question is rhetorical. But the way his eyes search mine, the hint of vulnerability in their depths, tells me differently.

He turns away, self-disgust pinching his brows, but I reach out and catch him by his good shoulder. "You're no kind of coward," I tell him, "for wanting to live."

Jaxon makes a low, noncommittal sound, and his eyes

flicker shut. Then they open again, finding mine, and I answer the question he can't bring himself to ask, even in his drugged and compromised state. "I'll stay until you fall asleep, to keep the nightmares away, and all that. On one condition: share your food with me." I gesture at his tray. "I'm starving."

"It's disgusting," Jaxon grumbles, but the furrow between his brows smooths. "Your funeral."

I shovel down the stew and the roll anyway, one unpleasant bite at a time, as Jaxon dozes off. But just as I've begun to relax, as much as is possible in the chair-slash-torture device, his eyes fly open again. They fix on mine, wide and alarmed.

"The thing you asked me before. About what Eva scented in the clearing. I think I know what it was."

I lean forward, dropping the remains of the last roll onto the tray. "Start talking."

He does. And by the time he's finished, I'm on my feet, my anger with Eva be damned. "I have to go," I say tersely. "I have to warn her."

He nods, and I sprint from the room.

CHAPTER 12

EVA

"Up here." The voice is soft, but it carries nonetheless.

I raise my eyes and see Sebastían lounging on a limb of one of the great oaks that borders the path, hands linked behind his head. He grins. "Care to join me?"

There's a wealth of innuendo in those four words. I don't care to get tangled up in it. "You're up late."

He lifts his shoulders in a shrug that somehow doesn't dislodge him from the branch. "So are you. Panthers are nocturnal, Eva. We can function just fine in the day if we need to. But night"—he stretches, his entire body undulating—"that's where we truly belong. You'll see, now that you're one of us."

"I'm not like you," I say automatically. But I think of how the night beckoned to me, luring me out here. What if that voice wasn't just calling me to hunt? What if it wasn't just in search of prey, but of *him?*

"Scowl all you like, but I've seen your panther, Eva." He tilts his head, and the moonlight falls full on his face, illuminating those changeable blue-green eyes. "She's beautiful."

Blood heats my cheeks, and he laughs, a low, sultry sound. "Look at you blushing."

Embarrassed, I duck my head, but Sebastían just keeps talking. "That won't help, I'm afraid. I can see just fine in the dark. But don't worry. I won't tell your exile paramour. If there's one thing I know, it's how to keep a secret."

Unbelievable. "Tell him what? That I took a walk and discovered you up in a tree, making inappropriate remarks? Oh, how incriminating that would be."

Sebastían gives me a long, considering look. "Call me crazy, but I don't think Westergaard would care about the details. Knowing you were alone with me while I paid you compliments would be incentive enough for him to make good on his threats."

"Maybe." Or maybe not, after the way Ari stalked off and left me standing outside the dining hall. After he told me not to touch him.

He sits up, scooting back against the trunk of the tree. "Lucky for him, I care enough about my union with you not to let him trigger war between Satrizona and Minneska. Because make no mistake, that's what it will be if he bares his blade to me again."

His voice is mild, but I bristle nonetheless. "There is no union between us."

"Not yet. But there will be." He smiles down at me, a sunny grin that makes him look far younger than his nineteen years, and pats his branch. "Come join me, Eva of the Commonwealth. Tell me why you despise me, even though we've only shared three conversations and a dance. Tell me all the reasons why we'll never be together. And I'll enjoy dispelling every one."

I glare at him. "I don't think so. I'm staying right here."

"Oh, are you? Well, then, I'll just have to do this, and bring your familiar running." He tilts his head skyward, poised to let loose a yowl. In the light of the near-full moon, the column of his throat shines silver. His brown hair, queued back for the meeting, falls loose around his shoulders. He looks feral yet perfectly at home, like a piece of the night set free.

Damn him. "Fine," I say, my tone brusque. "I'm coming up. But only because there's something I want to talk to you about."

Sebastían grins—half-tease, half-threat, all satisfaction. "Color me intrigued. Would you like to share my branch, or get your own? There's plenty of room here for two."

"Very funny." I make short work of clambering up the oak, the rough bark flaking beneath my fingers as I dig my nails in to find purchase. Sebastían leans over to watch, looking more amused than ever. He tilts far enough that most of his weight is in the air rather than on the branch, but it hardly seems to trouble him.

"How are you not falling?" I say, irritated. Even with my superior balance and Bellatorum training, there's no way I could support myself the way he's doing, not at that angle.

Sebastían grins, rights himself, and frees his hand from the tree, holding it up for my inspection. Five razor-sharp claws protrude from his fingertips.

"Show-off," I mutter as I pull myself up onto my branch and lean back against the tree's broad trunk.

His grin widens. "I prefer to think of it as a fringe benefit. One day, you'll be able to do it, too. I can teach you, if you like. Especially now that your trainer's met an unfortunate end."

I shudder at the thought of Sebastían taking Gertrud's place, while Ari takes Jaxon's. "I don't think so. Besides, I'm sure they'll assign me another trainer soon. Trina said they had someone in mind."

Sebastían throws his head back and laughs, a throaty gurgle that reminds me of his panther's growl. "Look at your face. Don't trouble yourself, Eva. I have no intention of instructing you alongside your exile. Such a thing would only end in bloodshed, and we've got more than enough of that to go around. I meant only that I'd teach *you*, on your own."

I'd be foolish not to accept his offer; who better to learn from, where my panther's concerned? At the same time, though, I'm not so naïve as to believe Sebastían doesn't have ulterior motives—or that he wouldn't expect something in return.

"Come now," he coaxes when I hesitate. "Think of what I could do with these claws. Don't you want to be able to defend yourself as well as possible? I can show you how. In dire situations, small shifts like this can save your life."

His voice is reflective, even a little sad, as if he's remembering a time when such an action was necessary. It makes me wonder who Sebastían is, beneath his carefully cultivated surface. Efraím Stinar, the leader of the Thirty, used to quote Sun Tzu to us all the time. *To know your enemy,* he'd say, *you must become your enemy.* What better way to know Sebastían, the boy who wants me to yoke my life to his, than to take advantage of this proposal?

"I'll think about it," I tell him.

"Just don't think too long. Time is, as you know, of the essence." He rubs his back against the tree trunk—an unselfconscious movement, evocative of a cat scratching a place that can't be reached. "So, what was it you wanted to talk to me about?"

"Oh." I tug at the end of my braid, trying to figure out how to ask what I want to know. I half-expect Sebastían to grow impatient with my silence, but he doesn't. Instead, he sits quietly on his branch, regarding me—a cat's assessing stillness, waiting for its prey to divulge its secrets.

Or maybe I'm not being entirely fair to him. Perhaps he's just being polite.

"I was wondering," I say at last, "why Councilor-in-Chief

Adelman is so invested in what happened to Cordelia...my mother."

Sebastían sighs, a heavy exhale that ruffles the loose strands of his hair. The movement sends his scent winging in my direction: bergamot and honey, a blend of spicy sweetness that speaks directly to my beast. Inside me, the panther wakes, uncoiling.

His nostrils flare delicately, the way they did in the Council's chambers when we sensed Councilor Adelman's grief, but all he says is, "It was before my time. But rumor has it they were childhood friends and lovers. You know the Councilor-in-Chief lost his parents in an exile raid, when he was a child?"

Slowly, I nod. "Yes. He murdered the exiles and came back to Vik covered in blood. That's why his hair turned white. Gertrud told me."

"Well," Sebastían says, "back then, he wasn't anything special. His parents owned a bakery on the City Road. It's still there. Adelman's, it's called."

"I've seen it." Ronan loves their strawberry-and-rhubarb confections; he's dragged me there a time or two. My favorites are the cherry puff pastries. "But if his parents are dead—did he have other family?" The more time I've spent in Vik, the more I realize how significant the bonds between parent and child, or brother and sister, can be. I've never heard Councilor Adelman speak of such a person, though, nor have I heard of anyone speak of family ties in association with him. If he isn't in session with the Council, he's always alone.

Sebastían shakes his head. "No. But the bakery was beloved enough that other shop owners decided to take it over. He never goes there, except for once a year—on the anniversary of Cordelia's disappearance. What we all thought to be her death. He always buys the same thing: a bag of cherry puff pastries. He takes them to the footbridge over the Silber. But he only eats half. The other half, he throws into the water, as a sacrifice to Cordelia's spirit."

A shiver ripples through me. "Why those pastries, in particular?"

"They were her favorite," Sebastían says simply.

As they are mine.

When I found out the Executor was my father, the last thing I wanted was to consider the ways we were alike. Perhaps he'd given me my ruthlessness, I'd thought. My ability to manipulate, to kill. Certainly, I never imagined that anything I inherited from him might bring a smile to my face, however bittersweet.

But this—my mother's love of cherry puff pastries, passed down to me—is an unexpected gift. It's a tiny thing, a minuscule connection. But it's a cord that binds us nonetheless, and I have to swallow hard to hold back tears.

"How do you know all this?" I demand.

Sebastían eyes me, puzzled. "Every skúma knows that story, regardless of their House. It's dramatic, despite the difference in their status: she, a skúma, and he, a shopkeeper's son." He snorts, doubtless disparaging such a notion. "Anyway, people who knew him then say he was a trickster, always making Cordelia laugh. That he was a source of sunshine in a life of duty, and that's what drew your mother to him."

I try and fail to reconcile Councilor Adelman, by turns grim and enraged, with the image Sebastían's just conjured. "That," I say, "seems unlikely."

"It baffles me too. But that's what people say." He shrugs again. "At any rate, Cordelia was meant to marry Riley. She was more powerful than Layla, and so he was promised to your mother, instead. But your mother didn't love Riley. Those who knew her then say her heart had long been given to the Councilor...though of course, he wasn't the Councilor back then."

"Who *was* he?" I ask, more than curious, "if he wasn't a baker's son anymore?"

"He was a guard." At my look of surprise, Sebastían smirks. "Don't look so shocked, Eva. I know our society must look very stratified to you, but even among our ranks, there's the potential for upward mobility. The Councilor was orphaned and given to the captain of the guard as an apprentice. After what had happened to his parents...well, let's just say he was especially motivated to learn. Legend has it, he was the best sharpshooter Minneska's ever seen."

"Really," I say, thinking of Councilor Adelman fighting side-by-side with Trina in the Great Hall, firing into the oncoming bellators and hitting one every time. How he pulled the guns from beneath his robe in the dining hall, aiming them in a motion as natural as breathing. "But how did he go from being a guard, however gifted, to the leader of the Council? What happened?"

Sebastían looks away, toward the darkness that shrouds the snow-tipped mountains. "Cordelia happened. They say that when the survivors of her party brought the news of her death, he howled like a mad thing. He disappeared for seventeen days and nights—one for each year of her life. And when he came back, he devoted himself to leading the Houses and bringing the Commonwealths down."

I feel a pang of sadness for the boy that Councilor Adelman once was, wandering Minneska bereft and mad with grief. And for my mother, who loved him, even though she knew he could never be hers. Apparently, we have more in common than an affinity for cherry puff pastries.

"Thoughts are drifting across your face too quickly to track," Sebastían says. "And your scent's changed. What's on your mind?"

The words come in a rush. If I think them through, I'm

afraid they'll never leave my lips. "The Council told me that if I married you, my relationship with Ari could only be that of skúma and guard. They said to do otherwise would be to dishonor you."

Sebastían lies back on the branch, linking his hands behind his head once more—a movement that shows off his lean body to full effect. I'm sure he's doing it on purpose. "Fond as I am of my honor, panthers are polyamorous by nature, Eva. We're not wolves. If you wish to have Westergaard as your consort, that's your business. I wouldn't begrudge it—as long as you realize I don't intend to let my bedsheets get cold, either."

I stare at him, stunned. "You—"

"Let's be realistic, Eva. I feel a responsibility to continue my bloodline. You harbor a desire to murder that snake of an Executor and his slithering accomplices. To do that, you need me and what my House can offer. And I—" He tips his head back, so the moon's gleam falls full on his face. His eyes glint like silver discs, the pupils blown wide to let what remains of the light in. When he speaks, his voice is a note lower than its usual register. "I need you."

The words reverberate inside me: a strange resonance, like the tolling of a bell in my bones. My panther stirs, prowling toward the sound of his voice as if it's an irresistible call. We've crossed the line into dangerous territory, in which my weapons will do me no good. The threat is both without and within, and I have no clue how to defend myself against it.

Sebastían shifts on his branch, looking uneasy. "I feel your panther, Eva. I can smell her." His voice is strained. "I'm trying to behave myself. To respect your wishes. But fair warning: what my human half wants and what my panther craves are two very different things."

He twists, coming to a sitting position, and now I can smell *him*. His bergamot-and-honey scent has sharpened, deepened.

Now he smells like the air just before it rains, like that and like jasmine and deep fertile earth. My human nose can make no sense of the scent, but the cat inside me suffers no such confusion. She doesn't understand rules and strictures, or why my love for Ari should preclude sharing Sebastían's bed. To her, they have nothing to do with each other. She sees another of her kind, a powerful beast, and wants to secure her position at his side. Within me, she rolls over on her back, luxuriating in his admission.

"I've met few others of my kind since my parents died," Sebastían says, sounding half-strangled. "Certainly never a female near my age. My human half understands there are strategic concerns to be weighed, alliances to be formed, contracts to be signed. But my panther, Nyx…" He turns toward me, and I see his cat's eyes in his human face, the iris thinned to a tiny rim, swallowed by the blackness of his pupils. "He just wants you."

The blush is back, heating not just my face now but the rest of me, too. "I—"

"Your panther calls to me, Eva. Behind my eyes, I can see her." He digs his claws deeper into the tree, as if it's an effort not to leap to the branch where I sit. I hear the scrape and bite as they pierce through the bark into the wood. "At least tell me her name."

"She doesn't have one." The words are a choked whisper. "None of my beasts do."

"Let me name her." His voice is soft, tantalizing. "Please."

I want to argue with him, to tell him he has no right to lay claim to a creature tied to my very essence—to give name and shape to my panther before I've done so myself. But the panther within me doesn't agree. She *wants* Sebastían to name her, to claim her. The panther doesn't care that I love Ari, that I'd sooner cut off my right hand than use it to touch Sebastían in the service of her desire for him. Inside me, she scrapes a warning claw down the soft walls of my body, and a hiss escapes my throat. *Allow him this,* she tells me. *Or I will do far worse.*

"Fine," I bite out. "Name her, if you must."

Sebastían smiles—not the open, happy grin he gave me when he told me he'd take pleasure in dispelling all the reasons we couldn't be together, or the flirtatious one he shared when he first invited me to join him in the tree. No, this smile is triumphant, weighted with pride. In the Commonwealth, a smile like that might have gotten him killed. "Ah, Eva," he says, eyes bright with gratification. "This is a great honor. If you will..."

He reaches a hand toward me, retracting his claws. Suspicious, I stare at it, and he chuckles. "I told you before, Eva, I don't bite. Not usually, anyhow. Nor will I this time. A simple touch is all I ask. Surely you'll grant me that."

I stare at his hand, lingering in the air between the branches where we sit, pale against the darkness of the night. He keeps his fingers still, waiting for me to come to him. But when he speaks, his voice holds the edge of his panther's growl. "How are you to decide whether to marry me, if you can't even bring yourself to touch me? You're wounding me, Eva. Surely my touch can't be as repulsive as all that."

Beneath the arrogance of his tone, I hear a note of hurt. It's that, as much as my panther's insistence, that drives me to lean toward him, bridging the gap between us. *It's nothing,* I tell myself. *A simple touch.*

My fingers graze his, and he twines his hand with mine. His skin is flame-hot, searing my palm, and I gasp.

The warmth spreads outward, reaching my panther, wrapping her in it. She flows through me in a way I've never felt before—not trying to shift, but occupying my human form, as if she's reaching for Sebastían within the cage of my flesh. I feel her brush against him. And then she purrs, a deep sound of satisfaction that spills from my throat before I can stop it.

Sebastían's hand tightens on mine. "I name her Carina," he says, the words holding the weight of a vow. "It means 'beloved.'"

I want to jerk my hand away. To tell him that I'm not his beloved, that even if I agree to this alliance, my heart will never be his. But I agreed to let him name her. And now, it's too late to take that promise back. Besides, my panther doesn't want to. She's pleased to have a name. She's thrilled to belong to the Prince of the Sands, the Panther of the West.

I have to get away from him.

Shutting my side of the bond with Ari down hard, I drop my gaze. When I look up again, Sebastían's eyes are wide, his expression filled with wonder. "Eva," he says, "did you feel—"

However he intends to finish that sentence, I want no part of it. "Let go of me." It comes out as more of a plea than a command, but he obeys immediately.

"I'm sorry," he says, sounding humbler than I've ever heard him—like a boy who's uncertain of his welcome, rather than a royal bent on having his way. "Did I hurt you?"

"No." The word squeezes from my throat as Carina settles back into the deepest part of me, warm and safe. "But I can't be alone here with you, like this. It—it's not right."

He wraps his arms around himself, as if trying to demonstrate he is no threat to me. "I would never hurt you, Eva. I'd never force you to do something against your will. Believe that of me, if you believe nothing else."

"I believe you," I say. And, oddly, I do. "But I have to go home now."

He nods, his expression uncharacteristically grave. "That's probably for the best."

"And you?" I say, drawing a deep breath. I smell the edge of a snowfall, the thousand little creatures that call the night home, and Sebastían himself, a scent at once familiar and terrifying. "What will you do?"

"Me?" He gives me a wistful smile. "I'll stay out here. The night speaks to me, especially so close to the full moon. We aren't bound to it, of course, but I can feel its pull."

If he wants to spend three hours up in a tree rather than in the luxury of a warm bed, that's his prerogative. "All right," I say, more desperate than ever for solitude and space—the things I came out here in search of, to begin with. "Goodnight, then."

"Goodnight," he replies as I drop from the branch, landing on the ground in a crouch.

I intend to go back to my room. To lie awake until daylight and figure out how to extract myself from this mess. To remain loyal to Ari while forging this much-needed alliance.

But the moment I step away from the tree, House Minneska's alarms begin to clang.

CHAPTER 13
ARI

I race down Ash Avenue, opening my end of the bond wide. I may be furious with Eva, but not enough to ignore a threat on her life. And if Jaxon's right, she's in terrible danger. I search for her as I run, feeling for the magnetic pull that tells me when she's near. And I find her, beyond the House of Echoes, in the woods.

What in the nine hells is she doing out there? It's treacherous for her to be alone in the forest right now, no matter how powerful she is.

Unless she *isn't* alone.

No sooner does the thought cross my mind than I feel heat surge down the bond. Eva's panther's purr echoes along the same path, the sound somehow hungry and satisfied all at once. Desire curls in my belly, so sharp it's almost painful. But it isn't mine.

It's *hers.*

I skid to a stop, the cold air rasping in my lungs, and double over, hands on my knees. I gasp for breath, but when I inhale, I don't smell the smoke that curls from the stone chimneys of the guards' quarters or the hint of snow that coats the mountain passes. Instead I smell the deep, sticky-sweet scent of honey, mingled with the richness of freshly turned earth and the heavy, expectant weight of the air just before a storm. It assaults my senses, twining around the bond, flooding it until I choke on the flow. But even as I cough, desperate for air, the part of me that is Eva's familiar wants to roll around in the scent, to bathe in it. To let it consume me.

A single word echoes in my mind, spoken in Sebastían's unmistakable voice. But his tone isn't sarcastic and goading, the way it's been every time I've heard it. It's careful, and tender, and threaded with barely constrained want.

Carina, he says. *Beloved.*

By the nine hells. That evocative, all-consuming scent...it's what Sebastían smells like to her. And this feeling—it's what he *does* to her.

I barely have time to stumble to the edge of the path before I fall to my knees and eject the contents of my stomach into the leaves. The roll and the stew tasted bad going down; they're worse coming up. But I don't care.

Here I am, fearing for her life, and she's—where? In the woods, with *him,* letting him give her pet names. Worse still, she *wants* him, just as much as he wants her. She can deny it all she likes, but I've felt it, and I know the truth.

What am I doing, chasing after her like this? She doesn't need me. She doesn't want me. I'm a tool to be used, nothing more. And the last thing *I* want is to be an unwilling audience to whatever's happening in the woods, with *him.*

But as I reach inside myself to close down the bond, Eva's end of it slams shut, hard. She's just...gone, and I don't know if it's because she's shut me out or because something terrible has happened to her.

My heart pounds. My head swims.

And then the discordant, high-pitched clang of bells splinters the air.

THIS IS Vik's alarm system. Adrenaline surges through me, and I don't think: I race for the woods beyond the House of Echoes, toward the place where I sensed Eva before the bond winked out. Over the clamor of the bells, I hear footsteps pounding behind me. I pull my blades and spin, but it's not an attacker. It's Ronan, followed by Adrien, Fade, and a complement of other armed guards.

"What's happening?" I demand as they come even with me.

"I don't know." Ronan scans the path beyond me, searching for a threat. "Where's Eva?"

"In the woods." The words burn like acid. "With Sebastían."

I catch a glimpse of the appalled look on his face before I put on a burst of speed and leave him and the guards behind. As I run, I dig deep for a remnant of the bond, but I feel nothing. It's like a wall's been slammed in my face. Surely I would feel differently if she'd been hurt or...or killed. Surely I would feel pain—

The bells are deafening, reminding me of the sirens that blared the night Eva and I fled the Commonwealth. But this time, the threat is coming from without, not within.

Could Jaxon be right about who's behind this? Could they have breached Vik's barrier?

I can't think about it. Instead I keep running, sprinting up the torch-lit hill that leads to the House of Echoes. My eyes scan the thinning dark, my senses attuned to any sign of distress: shrieks of terror, bodies strewn on the cobblestones, the scent of blood. But there's just the insistent racket of the bells, the labored breath of the guards behind me, and the terrible, horrible nothingness where Eva should be.

Panting, I crest the hill at a dead run. And skid to a stop, blood roaring in my ears.

The grassy meadow is filled with people: Guards milling around. Councilor Adelman, gun in hand. Layla and Riley, pacing and gesticulating, their familiars beside them. And Eva, arguing with Councilor Adelman, Sebastían beside her.

I stride toward her. "Eva." My voice is loud, slicing through the resounding peals, and her head jerks up, eyes wide. Her face lights with relief.

"Ari," she says. "I was so afraid—I thought—"

"*You* were afraid?" I hiss at her as Ronan and the rest finally crest the hill. "You *know* what I felt. And then you shut me out, right before *this* happened." I wave my hand, indicating the chaos. "You actually expect me to believe you were concerned for my well-being?"

"You—you felt..." Her eyes slide toward Sebastían. To his credit, the Panther of the West manages to keep his face impassive, but that doesn't stop my lip from rising in a sneer.

"This is not the time for bickering!" Layla's voice cracks. "My son is gone. The captain of the guard is here. Your familiar is safe," she says to Eva, gesturing to me. "We need to—"

The bells clang again, cutting off whatever she was about to say, as a hand descends on my shoulder. I turn to see Kilían standing there. Beside him is my father, whose gaze flicks to me as if to reassure himself that I'm all right. It's a strange sensation; I'm not used to having anyone other than Eva look out for me.

At last, the bells fall silent. "Erdahl is missing?" I ask. "What about his familiar, Alessandra? Can't you use their bond to track him?"

"He's too young," Layla says impatiently. "The bond's not strong enough, not until after his first shift."

"Well, how do you know he's missing? Maybe he's just

down at the stables, seeing if that foal was born." It would be just like these people to roust everyone from their beds for a child who's used to doing as he pleases. If Eldrina's behavior was any indication, *overprotective* doesn't begin to describe them.

"My son is *royalty*." Layla curls her lip at me. "He wouldn't sneak out of his bed in the dead of night to visit a *barn.*"

I stare at her, incredulous. "You mean to say you sounded this alarm before you canvassed the grounds?"

Kilían gives me the eyebrow. *Point taken, Westergaard,* it means, *but shut your mouth.* "Where is the guard who was at the stables yesterday?" he says to Ronan. "Mateo. Did you dispatch him elsewhere?"

"Mateo should have been asleep in the guards' quarters when the alarm sounded. But he didn't report." Ronan turns toward Adrien and Fade, who flank him. "Have you seen him?"

Adrien scrubs a hand over his blond beard. "Not since last night. He's not been right—ever since Mei..."

"Dispatch a search party," Riley snaps at Ronan before Adrien can finish his sentence. "What are we waiting for? Isn't it obvious the traitor took our son?"

But Ronan is looking at Eva. "Do you smell that same scent you noticed before, in the woods?" he asks, his dark gaze intent on her face.

"No, but—"

"Why do you care about a scent?" I challenge him, not letting her finish. "Are you going to tell us what you know, or were you planning to wait until Eva goes missing, too?"

Eva glares at me. "What are you talking about?"

"Other Mages," I say, suppressing my rage with an effort. "Beyond Vik's borders. Ones that aren't friendly to our cause. And might be in league with our enemies."

Ronan's eyes flash to my face. "I talked to Jaxon," I say,

answering his unspoken question. "What do they want? Why would they kill our scouts? And why now? Is Mateo allied with them?"

The captain of the guard hesitates, and I hold his gaze, refusing to back down.

"I don't know," he says at last. "They haven't posed a threat in a century."

Eva looks stricken. "If there are Mages who wish us ill, then perhaps Mei went to them. Mateo loved her. What if he kidnapped the boy as a favor to Mei?"

In the light of the flickering torches, Layla's face is waxen. "If the Mages have him, my son could be dead!" she shrieks.

"I don't get it." My gaze flicks between Adelman and Ronan. "What would they want with a little kid who can't even shift yet?"

Ronan looks away. "Not now, Westergaard."

Fantastic. More secrets. More lies. I glance at Eva to see if she knows any more than I do, but her brow is crinkled in confusion.

"Come," Adelman says, tone clipped. "The rest of the skúma children are safe in the inn, with their parents and familiars. Ronan's dispatched guards to scout Vik for invaders. If they find the boy, they'll inform us. Let's search the stables before we panic."

"Fine." I turn to Eva. "Are you coming or staying?"

She looks bewildered, then affronted. "I'm coming, of course. Everything Mei's done is because of me."

I'm in no mood to tell her that it isn't, but Sebastían doesn't hesitate. "It's not, Carina," he says, one hand resting lightly on the small of her back. "Mei's choices rest on her and her alone. And if you go, I'm coming with you."

That stupid pet name. Politics be damned, I'd be happy to rip his hand off and then dismember the rest of him. Right after I make sure someone's not doing the same to Erdahl.

THE BOY IS NOT at the stables. Nor is he the only one that's missing.

"Zephyr's gone," Fade says, pointing at one of the empty stalls. "Mateo's favorite stallion."

Layla lets out a choked gasp, and Ronan swears. The rest of us bow our heads. For once, Sebastían is silent.

If Layla and Riley's suspicions are correct, a skúma child has been kidnapped from right under our noses, in the midst of the Brotherhood's stronghold. If Mateo and Mei are in league with these Mages, then who else is? Will they come for Eva next?

A caw breaks the oppressive quiet, and my head jerks up. Perched on top of the half-open door is a raven, soot-black and huge. The bird takes off, spreading its wings wide. It flies straight toward us, a scrap of paper in its beak.

"I recognize this bird." Eva narrows her eyes, regarding it. "I've seen it before. On the cornice outside my room. And in the woods, when we found the bodies. If it was outside my window —and in the woods, where I smelled the Mages—then..."

"Then we have a spy," Ronan concludes, his voice grim. "And a messenger."

The raven's obsidian eyes fix on Eva. It cocks its head, then drops the scrap of paper at Councilor Adelman's feet.

Warily, he picks it up and scans it. "It's from the Executor," he says.

My stomach sinks. "You must be joking. Why would these Mages help him?"

No one replies. Instead, Kilían palms one of his blades, the lines in his face deepening. "Good question. Read it aloud, if you would, Councilor-in-Chief."

Clearing his throat, Councilor Adelman complies. *"Hello, Devereaux. I have something you want: the child Erdahl and the woman you once called Cordelia."* His voice cracks, but he presses onward. *"Lia is mine, I'm afraid, but the child is of no great importance...at least to me."*

Riley gives a growl that makes the building tremble. His eyes have gone to amber, the first hint of his shift to wolf form. "How dare he?"

"But you have something I want as well," Councilor Adelman continues, his bruised hand clenched into a white-knuckled fist. *"Eva Marteinn."*

The raven caws impatiently, as if prodding him to finish. Looking as if he'd like to boot the bird into the rafters, he goes on: *"My daughter comes to me, alone, of her own free will. Then and only then will I release the child. Send your answer back with the bird, and the raven will return to guide you to your destination."*

Councilor Adelman's gaze shifts uneasily between Riley and Layla before he speaks again. *"You have six hours. Then I kill the boy."*

CHAPTER 14
EVA

"I'll go," I say, at the same time as Ari says, "Absolutely not."

I glare at him. Since when does he think he has the right to dictate what I can and cannot do? To my horror, he felt everything I did in the woods with Sebastían before I closed down the bond. Right now, he's just looking for a fight.

"It's a trap," he argues, color burning high on his cheeks, his eyes wild. "*Good hunting, Eva*—this isn't hunting! It's delivering you right into the Executor's hands."

"Fine," I say, folding my arms across my chest. "This time, I won't spare his life."

"You'll be walking right into whatever he has planned for you, in unknown enemy territory! You won't save Erdahl. You won't kill the Executor. Kilían, tell her."

Kilían glances between the two of us, then heaves a sigh. "Westergaard's right, Marteinn. But—"

I interrupt him. "We can't just let the boy die. I have to go."

"Thank you," Layla says icily. "I'm glad someone here is actually thinking about our son. Because make no mistake, Riley and I will go after him if Eva does not. We'll bring him home, or die trying. And if we live, we will never forget this betrayal."

The raven caws as if in agreement and takes flight, soaring upward to land atop the half-door of the pregnant mare's stall. I draw a deep breath, sampling the air in an effort to pinpoint the source of its strange magic, as Councilor Adelman says, "No one's suggesting we abandon your son, Layla. We just need to determine how to approach this wisely."

"Which brings me to what I was about to say." Kilían rubs his bad arm, his mouth tightening. "The Executor must believe he holds an insurmountable advantage, one greater than the threat we pose to him." He runs a hand over his face, the way he does when he's thinking hard. "These rogue Mages must be very powerful indeed if they can heal such a gravely injured man. But why would they help him? What do they have to gain? This doesn't bode well."

His eyes rest on Ronan. "Something larger than a simple kidnapping is afoot. If the decision were mine, I'd say we meet the note's demands, but not without a plan."

"A *plan*?" Ari shoves both hands through his hair, and Kennett makes a troubled sound, concern stamped on the features that are an eerie echo of his son's. "In what plan does it make sense for Eva to walk alone into the den of an enemy whose motives we don't understand? These are the same people who are concealing a man that tortured Eva's mother. The man who wants to use her to bring us all down!"

"All the more reason for me to go after him," I say. By the Architect. I'm a warrior and a shapeshifter four times over. Yet Ari would seal me in a bubble if he could.

"Have you lost your—"

"I'm with Eva and the bellator," Ronan says, ignoring Ari's protest. "We want the boy back. We want the Executor dead. These are simple goals on which we can all agree."

"Death is too good for him," Riley growls. He's pacing, crushing hay beneath his feet. "I'll tear him apart limb by limb, and feed the bits to the crows."

The raven caws again, but this time it doesn't sound like it's agreeing with him. Instead, it sounds like it's...laughing?

I look away from the bewildering bird, fighting a growing sense of violation. Now that I think about it, I remember seeing a raven perched above us in the trees the night I told Ari about Cordelia. What else has it overheard? What have its beady eyes seen?

The odd vibration I felt in the ground beneath our scouts' bodies...was that the magic that made an abomination like this bird possible? Was the exiles' attack so successful because the Mages channeled their magic through them, the same way they're doing with the raven?

"I should have followed the trail of star anise in the woods, when I sensed something was wrong," I say. "Maybe the Mages were right there, concealing themselves somehow. We could have captured one of them, interrogated them. If I'd done that, maybe Erdahl would still be here. I have to make this right."

Ari leans back against the exposed wood that separates the stalls, his jaw tight. "This is reckless, Eva. Foolhardy. There's too much we don't know."

"Be that as it may, I will go wherever I need to go. And when I return, I'll bring with me a living boy and a dead body." I hate the Executor so much, for what he did to me and to my mother, to Ari's parents. There is no way I'll let Riley have him. He is my kill.

Beside me, Sebastían speaks for the first time since the raven dropped the note at Councilor Adelman's feet. "May I speak with you privately, Eva?"

"Now?" I say, confused. "But we—"

"I wouldn't ask if it wasn't important. Outside," he says, jerking his head at the stable's doors, away from the raven.

Ignoring Ari's murderous glare, I follow Sebastían. Alone with him for the first time since our confusing encounter in the woods, I feel vulnerable. On edge. "What do you want?" I say, my tone sharper than I intend. "We're running out of time."

"Don't take this the wrong way, Eva." If possible, Sebastían looks even more uncomfortable than I feel. "Having one beast inside you isn't easy. But having four? I can't even imagine." His throat moves as he swallows. I hate myself for being drawn to the sight. "I would never contradict you in front of others, but as much as I'm loath to admit it, I agree with Westergaard. This plan is suicide."

"Are you serious? You don't know that."

"I know one thing. My panther doesn't always think like I do. He...has cravings my conscious mind denies." A blush heats his cheeks, but he holds my gaze, and I'm the one who looks away. "All I'm saying is, it can be a fight to tell where your panther ends and you begin. Don't let your beasts drive you, Carina."

He reaches out to take my hand, but I jerk away. The very last thing I want right now is a repeat of what happened in the woods. "I don't need your input on how to handle myself," I snap. "Maybe you and Ari should stop dictating how I act and focus on what really matters—getting to the bottom of this mess, killing the Executor, and saving Erdahl."

Sebastían shakes his head. "I'm just trying to help you, Carina."

"Stop calling me that!" I turn on my heel and stomp back inside the barn. After a second, he follows.

Ari doesn't even look up when we come in. I don't need the bond to feel how hurt and furious he is. But right now, his wounded pride isn't my priority. Between him and Sebastían, I've had about enough of boys telling me what to do.

"Now that we're all here," Councilor Adelman says, ignoring the thick-as-mud tension that pervades the room, "I suggest we strategize, out of earshot of...that." He gestures at the raven, which is still perched on top of the door, preening. "There's information you need to know about the rogue Mages before we decide how to handle this, and I'm not sharing it here."

Layla throws her hands in the air, exasperated. "Do what you must, but make it quick. Riley and I will retrieve our son by the deadline in that note, whether or not you accompany us. Either way, we leave at eight of the clock. The bird will show us the way."

The raven caws again. Then it opens its beak, and to my shock, what comes out is an actual voice—raspy and unfamiliar, but unmistakably human.

The four-beast skúma comes alone, it croaks. *Or the boy dies.*

CHAPTER 15
ARI

Adelman fidgets in his chair, jaw clenched, as the Council and the rest of us enter their chambers. Everyone, that is, except Layla and Riley, who are still scouring the grounds for any clues about their son's abduction.

Ignoring protocol, I take a seat as far from Eva as I can get. Right now, I'm having a hard time looking at her, much less sitting beside her like a good little familiar. I keep my end of the bond shut tight, partly so my emotions don't leak over to her and partly because I'm afraid whatever she's feeling might make me overturn the table and storm out of the room before this meeting even gets started.

But that means the seat next to her is empty, and Sebastían is only too happy to fill it. The Architect only knows what the hell he said to her outside the stables. I swear, if he puts a single finger on her or calls her *Carina* one more time...

Tamping down my rage with an effort, I settle back in my chair as Adelman begins to speak. "Our history with the Mages is complicated, but there's little time for details. I'll explain what I can, and I ask that you don't interrupt." His voice is rough, like he'd rather be screaming than giving us a history lesson. From the way his bruised hand is gripping the edge of the table, he'd rather be punching something, too.

His eyes linger on me, as if he thinks I'm going to argue with him. But he's got it wrong this time. I want information badly, and he's the shortest path to it. He's also a lit fuse, waiting for a spark to ignite. When he read the raven's sins-blasted note, his voice breaking on the words *Lia is mine,* I thought he was going to explode right then and there, responsibilities be damned. His robes, his title...all of that is window-dressing. He would burn and bleed and destroy to liberate Cordelia. If that means sacrificing Eva, he won't hesitate. How can she not see that? Is her guilt over Mei's actions blinding her—or is she so driven by her thirst for revenge, she can't see clearly? Or is something else motivating her, something I don't understand?

Adelman's eyes are still fixed on mine. "I'll take questions after, and then we'll move on to strategizing," he says. "Are we clear?"

"Crystal," I reply, holding his gaze.

He turns to face the room, chin held high. "I'll be blunt. There are Mages beyond our borders. They haven't risen against us in years. But Mei's actions, Eva's detection of their characteristic scent at the scene of our guards' murder, and the arrival of that bird...well, it paints a very different picture. It appears that not only are the Mages a direct threat to our city, but they're in league with our greatest enemy."

I want to ask him why *now,* of all times, but I keep my promise, staying silent. The rest of the chamber stares, rapt, as his deep voice echoes off the exposed rafters, unspooling a story of blood and magic, rage and revenge.

Long ago, he tells us, before the Twilight Massacre decimated the skúma and gave rise to the Commonwealths, the Mages were far more powerful than they are now. Now, their gifts center on healing and protecting the Houses' borders. But back then, they could control the elements, raising storms, quakes, and infernos at will. Their gifts were directly tied to the existence of the skúma, so the more skúma, the stronger the Mages' power.

"As long as our two groups were allied, and the Mages acknowledged the skúmas' superior place in the hierarchy," Adelman continues, scanning each attentive face, "this was a good thing. But the more powerful the Mages became, the less they needed the skúma for protection. They came to believe they themselves had the right to rule, with the skúma at their behest as mere magical batteries."

And there goes my promise to keep quiet. "You mean all this time, Mei's family's wanted—"

He shakes his head. "Not them. Be patient, Westergaard. I'm trying to explain."

Fuming, I settle back in my chair. The Mages apparently have a history of wanting to control the Houses. They're fueled by skúma. Now they have a skúma boy, and the Executor's demanded that the most powerful skúma to ever exist be delivered to their doorstep. Isn't it obvious how this is going to end? Surely now, Eva will see sacrificing herself to these monsters is pure idiocy. But when I steal a glance at her, she doesn't meet my eyes, and with the bond closed between us, I can't feel a sins-damned thing.

"Unsurprisingly, the Mages' thirst for power caused a rift to develop between them and the skúma of all four Houses," Adelman goes on. "It isn't commonly known, but during the Twilight Massacre, when the High Priests and villagers rose up against the skúma, some of the Mages sided with the Priests. Though without the skúma to support them, they weren't as powerful."

Eva's head comes up, her dark eyes bright with anger. "The

Mages formed an allegiance with the *Priests?* The very people who would go on to found the Commonwealths?"

Adelman nods, and Kilían pushes back from the table, grunting as the movement jars his wounded arm. "By the Architect," he spits. "No wonder Mei thought the Executor would find safe haven with the Mages' descendants. The Commonwealths and the Mages have a history of collaboration. And you're just mentioning this now?"

A wave of murmurs sweeps the room. I examine each person in turn, trying to figure out who knew this all along and chose to keep it from the rest of us. The other Council members, definitely; I can see the resignation in their eyes. But who else?

A low rumble rises in Sebastían's chest. "I'm the leader of my House," he growls. "Responsible for keeping my people safe. Sure, I've heard rumors about this. Legends. But you didn't think to confirm there was truth to them, Adelman? You hoarded this knowledge, you and your damned Council. And now, you've put us all in danger."

I find myself in the unexpected—and uncomfortable—position of agreeing with him. "Ronan," I say, swiveling to face the captain of the guard. "Did you know about this?"

He toys with his graying braids. "It's as Sebastían said. There were rumors of this alliance. But all of this happened over a century ago, Westergaard. War has a way of destroying records. Politics has a tendency to distort the truth."

I'm too furious to reply, but Sebastían doesn't have the same problem. He turns on Ronan, demanding answers, as my mind spins, churning out possibilities. Did the Executor know about the Priests' old alliance with the Mages? Has he been planning this all along? Because if the Commonwealths, sworn to wipe the world clean of sin, have kept ties to a band of rebellious magic-users, then we are in even deeper trouble than I imagined.

Adelman holds up a hand, demanding silence. "We don't have time to argue amongst ourselves! Cast aspersions and lay blame later. Listen now, or the cost may be all our lives."

Sebastían subsides, giving Ronan one last furious glare, and the Councilor-in-Chief continues. "After the Massacre, the allied skúma killed most of the rogue Mages. The survivors sought refuge with the remaining skúma. They needed each other, in order to rebuild. For a while, there was peace. But as more skúma were born, the Mages' power grew in kind."

He glances around the table, his dark-blue gaze pausing on each of us. "Ultimately, the Mages made another bid for power. The Houses put down the rebellion and this time, they demanded that the Mages leave their territory. Only those who vowed to confine their magic to protecting our borders—like Mei's ancestors—were permitted to stay."

I bite my tongue to keep from speaking, so hard I almost draw blood. Because what in the nine hells did these morons think would happen when they oppressed an entire group of people and tossed them out to wander in the wilderness? Did they imagine the Mages would happily accept their fate? No wonder the Commonwealth's exiles have joined forces with the rogue Mages; they have a lot in common. For the Architect's sake, it's practically predictable. "Do you really not see—" I begin, my voice hot, but Kilían cuts me off.

"The rogue Mages can't enter any of the Houses on their own," he says. "Like the traitor Mei cannot. Correct?"

"Yes," Councilor Elijah tells him, speaking for the first time. The firelight flickers over his ebony skin as he leans forward, steepling his fingers on the table. "The same gifts that allow them to protect our borders forbid them from crossing it once they have betrayed that trust."

"But the Mages who live here," Kilían says, his eyebrows

lowering. "Are they still in communication with those who were forced to leave?"

"It's forbidden for them to meet outside the Houses' borders," Peder says, his good eye roving the room. "And the rogue Mages can't enter. But the use of ravens to communicate was an ability the Mages had long ago. We thought it was lost. It *should* be lost. I don't know..."

His voice trails off, and Eva speaks up. "Just spit it out. The only thing that's changed is *me*. What Mei did, what's happening with the Mages—it's because of how strong I am, how many beasts I hold. I'm fueling this. It's all my fault. It's up to me to fix it."

A low growl rises in Sebastían's throat. In agreement? Argument? I can't tell. If the bastard dragged her outside to reinforce this suicidal idea of hers, I swear I'll provoke him into unsheathing his claws, and then take pleasure in removing each one with a pair of pliers.

"Enough, Marteinn," Kilían says, his voice sharp. "Blaming yourself will accomplish nothing. You didn't know a thing about Mei's intentions, just as I didn't know the Executor held your mother hostage. The thought disgusts me, but there's nothing I can do about it now. Just as there's nothing *you* can do, other than seek revenge and retrieve both your mother and the boy. Acta non verba, eh?" *Actions, not words*, it means. The Bellatorum's motto.

Adelman's eyes narrow at the mention of Cordelia. "Killing our scouts was only a warning," he says. "Sending the bird is a threat. The Mages' hunger for power must have been simmering all this time. Perhaps they've been plotting, waiting for the perfect moment. Now, with Mei's gift of the Executor, they're in a position to act."

"It's not just because of him. It's also because of Eva." I grit my teeth, drawing on all of my training to keep from shouting. "They can sense her power. They crave it. And now..."

Adelman nods grimly. "Now, they have a skúma child."

"They're using Erdahl as a power source to control that damned raven, aren't they? If they can use him to do that, then what will they be able to do when they get their hands on Eva?"

He tries to say something else, but the room erupts. I'm on my feet, hands braced on the table.

"Sit down, Westergaard," Kilían cautions, but I'm not listening. Nor is anyone else. They're all shouting over each other, trying to make themselves heard.

"The Executor's desire for Eva is a means to an end." Trina's voice is pitched above the melée. "The Mages and the Commonwealths have once again found common cause."

"They're working together." Peder points at the window, in the direction of the woods. "The Mages can send ravens to all of their far-flung outposts and summon an army of rogue magic-users. They can't cross our borders, but they can lure us out. Together with the exiles and the Commonwealth's forces, they can unleash hell upon us. This is just the beginning."

"This," Elijah intones, "is war."

Adelman pushes back from the table, the look on his face pure satisfaction. I'm about to protest once again when Sebastían takes the words right out of my mouth.

"How obtuse can you all be?" he thunders, rising to his feet. "This is nothing but a parry—a ruse to draw us out in the open. Have you never heard of military strategy? Perhaps you should consider employing it!"

I never thought I'd find myself aligned with the Panther of the West. But here we are. "I'm with Sebastían. This is impulsive. Reckless. For the Architect's sake, use your heads instead of going off half-cocked."

If looks could kill, the glare Eva levels me with would have me six feet under. "Use their heads?" she hisses at me. "What about their hearts? Erdahl looks up to you. He's too young to defend himself. If we don't act, he'll die. And that's just fine with you?"

Fury boils beneath my skin. "You know that's not what I—"

Adelman pounds a fist on the table. "Enough! I will have silence!"

Sebastían scowls but sinks into his seat, his gaze fixed on Adelman. I grip the back of my chair, too agitated to sit. An uneasy hush falls over the room, and to my surprise, Kennett, who's been sitting silently next to Kilían until now, breaks it. "If the Mages are powered by skúma, and this is an act of war... then why would they agree to release Erdahl?"

It's a sad state of affairs when a medic is the one asking the good questions. "They want to cash him in for a bigger prize," I say, one hand falling to my dagur. "Because whatever he can give them, it's nothing compared to what Eva can do to bolster their power." I glower at her. "How can you just walk into their trap, for the Architect's sake? You'll be handing both the Executor and the Mages the doomsday weapon they need to destroy us!"

My death grip on the bond slips just a little and her anger and frustration pour through, scorching me before I shut it down again. "Stop telling me what to do!" she snarls. "I can make my own choices. And right now, I choose not to let an innocent boy die!"

"They won't kill Erdahl. They need him. Not as much as they need you, but still." I stand and pace the room, unable to contain my agitation. "You think they're prepared to make a trade? Don't make me laugh! Either they'll try to keep you both, or they'll slit his throat and laugh at your gullibility."

Eva twists to face me, her voice lined with her panther's growl. "I'm not a fool, Ari. I can take care of myself."

I come to a halt in front of her, hands on my hips. "So *do* that. They want you. You're in a position of power. State your terms. Negotiate, Eva. Don't commit suicide."

A murmur ripples through the room at this novel idea. I get where Adelman's coming from: he wants Cordelia back at all costs, Eva's life be damned. But are the rest of them just a bunch of mindless sheep? She says *jump,* and they comply—even if she's about to leap right off a cliff to her doom. Idiots.

Kilían leans across the table toward Eva, catching her eye. "Westergaard has a point," he says. "You're in no way obligated to meet their demands."

Thank the Architect, someone here other than myself and Sebastían sees sense. Maybe Eva will respect what the Lead Interrogator has to say, even if she's ignoring both of us. But no. "The idea that they won't kill Erdahl is a theory, not a fact. And I won't stake his life on it. I'm going," she says. "Alone."

Of course she is. "By alone," I say, folding my arms across my chest, "I assume you mean 'with me.'"

"By alone," she says stubbornly, "I mean 'by myself.' Even without you there, I can fight. I'll have Layla and Riley in the woods for backup, since I can't stop them from trying to rescue their son. But I'm not risking you."

Councilor Adelman makes a strangled noise. "You are so much like your mother."

Eva's dark eyes widen, but at this moment, I couldn't care less how she resembles or doesn't resemble Cordelia. "You are taking me," I say, each word measured, "if I have to lash myself to your wrist and walk beside you every step of the way."

"And if the boy dies because of your stubbornness?" she retorts. "What then?"

Silence falls. I want to say, *Then he dies,* but I can't bring myself to say it. Erdahl is innocent. I can't condemn him to death.

"A compromise," I offer at last. "I'll follow you, but at a distance. Like Layla and Riley, assuming they agree to that. I'll stay with them, and we can communicate through the bond."

Eva's nostrils flare, the way they always do when she's exasperated. But at least she stops arguing with me. Instead, she raises her hands, palms-up, in a gesture of surrender. "Fine."

"I'll go too, of course. And when I find Mateo..." Ronan's hands tighten on the edge of the table, his knuckles whitening.

"Is that our decision, then?" Adelman says. "We tell the bird Eva will come alone, and then put together a party to support her?"

"Yes," Trina says. "This was a direct attack, and we must retaliate."

Peder and Elijah nod in agreement as Adelman slams his fist on the table again. "Agreed. If the attack on our scouts and the boy's kidnapping aren't acts of war, what is?" His blue eyes are as dark as a storm-tossed sea. "We fight back, or we die. I know which one I choose."

"And I'm not willing to let a child pay because I was afraid to take a stand." Eva's hands fall to the blades slung at her hips. Her expression fierce, she turns to Sebastían. "What will it be, then? Because if you value politics over a boy's life, then our agreement is at an end."

Sebastían grits his teeth. "You're my future mate. I will support you," he says. "But let me go on record as saying I don't like this. I will not lead the Houses into a foolhardy war." His lips press into a thin line of disapproval. "We're giving our enemy exactly what they want: A skúma who holds all four beasts, who's more powerful than anything they've seen before or dreamed of. I just hope we all survive it."

For once, I couldn't agree with him more.

CHAPTER 16
EVA

The raven leads me on quite a chase. First, down the path we took when we recovered the scouts' bodies, then into the clearing where we found them. It pauses there, as if to give me another look at the exiles' corpses. The crows have been at them, and they smell of rot, despite the deepening cold. It's already snowing in the passes, though not here and in the valley yet. I wish it were. I could do with a blanket of white covering the bodies, so I didn't have to stare at their contorted limbs and eyeless sockets.

"Are you *gloating?*" I say to the raven, which has roosted on a tree limb and is staring down at me. "These are our kills, not yours. Or is the point that your people care so little about these exiles, you abandoned their bodies for the scavengers?" The more I think about it, the more certain I am that this is the message I'm meant to take away. These exiles are just foot soldiers in a larger endeavor, the scope of which I don't understand. But if the Commonwealths and the Mages have aligned —a world dedicated to science and another built on magic— that can only mean dire things.

The bird croaks, as if in agreement. Then it cocks its head, fixing me with one beady eye, and takes flight again. I follow it, uncomfortably aware of other eyes on my back: Ari; Sebastián and Ilsa; Riley, Layla, and their familiars; Kilían; Ronan. They're hanging back, hidden. But I know they're there. Ari's reopened his side of the bond so we can communicate, and I can feel his disapproval and wariness simmering through it. Well, to the nine hells with him, and Sebastían too. I'm free to make my own choices.

The Executor made me to be his weapon. And I will take him down.

I make my way through the woods, brushing aside clinging vines and ducking under branches. The journey seems to take forever, all the more so because I have no idea what I'm going to find when I reach my destination. But at long last, the bird leads me into a clearing, edged by gray standing stones. It roosts on top of one of them and caws at me.

"You could speak before," I say, irritated. "Why be cryptic now?"

It spreads its obsidian wings wide and opens its beak. And then it says, in that same hoarse voice, "Welcome, Eva of the Commonwealth."

Welcome to what? The clearing is empty, nothing here but a bunch of dead grass and those ominous standing stones. I peer more closely at them and see that they're engraved with odd symbols I don't recognize. And here I am, right in the middle of them. Alone.

The first hint of fear rears its ugly head.

I force myself to think. Mei's ability was to prevent outsiders from seeing Vik, unless she chose to allow them in. If this is a Mage stronghold, then it only makes sense that they would do the same. And I can *feel* the weight of eyes on me. Not my companions', hidden in the trees beyond the stones, but close at hand—as if they're inspecting me, looking me over.

"I know you're here," I say, turning in a circle. "You asked me to come. Show yourself."

At first, nothing happens. Then there's a crackling sound that reminds me of the lightning that struck the Bastarour's electric fence, the night I engineered Efraím's death. The air in the clearing flickers, bends. And the next instant, I'm face to face with the Executor, Karsten at his side. Somehow, the bellator has reclaimed his blades. Perhaps Mei brought them to him, before she engineered his escape.

Have the two of them been here this whole time, somehow concealed? Or did they just step between the stones?

I don't like this, Ari's voice sounds in my head. *I don't like this at all.*

"Hello, daughter mine," the Executor says.

The very sound of it makes me want to vomit. I glare at him, somehow upright despite the way I savaged him, then at Karsten, whose burns are bandaged but who is more hale than he has any right to be. "I'm many things. None of them are yours. Where is the boy?"

"Ah. The young wolf prince." The Executor's thin lips rise in a chilly smile. "Patience, Eva. I can't have you here armed, after all. Karsten, take her weapons."

I assumed this was coming. But to put my blades in Karsten's hands, of all people, is unthinkable. "I'll throw them outside the circle," I offer, a compromise.

"I don't think so." The Executor shakes his head. "You're far too fast, when the situation requires it. Karsten will pat you down, and then we'll talk about the child."

The thought of it disgusts me, but I promised to save Erdahl. If this is the worst thing I have to do to make it happen, then I cannot balk. I am my own weapon, after all. "Fine. Let's get this over with."

An obnoxious smirk on his face, Karsten steps away from the Executor and limps toward me. As he searches me for weapons, his movements businesslike but thorough, I can feel Ari's anger. He would be only too pleased to break every one of Karsten's fingers, a sentiment I share. But I stand still, unprotesting. I'll get my blades back soon enough.

Wait, I send to him through the bond. But Ari isn't the one who answers. Instead, my wolf and panther speak as one. *We have waited long enough,* they say. *These pitiful excuses for men will give us what we want. And then they will die.*

I can feel my beasts' eagerness trembling through me. To hell with my blades; they want to sink their teeth into Karsten's neck, to tear his flesh and drink his blood. For a white-hot instant, fear spikes within me again. What if I can't stop them?

I force myself to focus. *Calm,* I tell my beasts. *You'll have your chance. Just not yet. This is a hunt. We have to wait until the time is right.*

To my relief, they subside into silence as Karsten yanks my long blade from its sheath on my back and my smaller blades from their thigh sheaths. Having pulled my last knife from my boot, he gathers them up and stalks back to the Executor's side, where he dumps them into a pile at his feet.

I raise my empty hands to show I'm unarmed. "Well?"

"A deal is a deal, I suppose," the Executor says. "Mateo, bring our young friend."

The air does that disturbing flicker-bend again, and then Mateo steps between the stones, pushing Erdahl in front of him. My skin prickles. Where did they come from? What lies beyond the circle? And how is such magic possible?

The Executor chuckles at the shock that must show on my

face. But when my gaze flicks to him, I can tell *he's* not shocked at all. Whatever's going on here, he understands it.

How long has he understood? Has he always been in league with the Mages?

An even more horrifying thought occurs to me. This whole time, as Ari and I thought we were escaping his clutches, have we just been playing into his twisted strategy? Have we been pawns in a long game that we had no idea existed...one that was always meant to lead to this?

I shove these infuriating thoughts away, focusing instead on the vise-grip that Mateo has on Erdahl's shoulder. The boy's face is white, his arms scratched and bruised. "What did you do to him?" I hiss. In my head, Ari says a single word, heavy with fury: *Traitor.*

"Nothing irreparable," Mateo says, his tone as casual as if we're discussing what will be served for dinner. "Truth be told, he did much of this to himself. I told him fighting back was pointless, but he didn't listen. Alas, this was the consequence."

"I don't have to listen to you," Erdahl says, twisting in Mateo's grip. "You're nothing to me. Kidnapping filth. When my parents get their hands on you—"

"Shut up," Mateo says, and digs his fingers into a fresh bruise on Erdahl's arm. The boy winces, sucking in a sharp breath.

From their vantage point high in the trees, Riley and Layla can see everything. I'm sure they're beside themselves right now. Winging a prayer to the Architect that Ronan, Kilían, and Ari are able to hold them back, I say, "I'm here, as you asked." I gesture at the bird, still perched on that same stone. "Now let him go."

"I don't think so," the Executor muses. "After all, now we have you both. What incentive do we possibly have to let the boy go free?"

"Oh, I don't know." Contempt chokes my voice, and once again, I feel my beasts stirring within me, threatening to break free. "Honor?"

For the first time, I see anger in the depths of the Executor's pitch-dark eyes. "You dare speak to me of honor, Eva Marteinn? You, who betrayed your oath to the Bellatorum? Who slayed the Bastarour, our first line of defense, and killed the leader of the Thirty? You, who murdered your brethren nights ago?"

He must be joking. "They're not my brethren anymore. And of the two of us, you believe yourself to be the honorable one? You, who tampered with my DNA and took my mother against her will? Who engineered the kidnapping of an innocent boy?" I step closer to him, ignoring the way Karsten stiffens and draws his blade. "If that is your definition of honor, I want none of it. Now let...him...go."

The last few words issue between clenched teeth. My wolf's growl rumbles in my chest, and I see Karsten flinch. He always was a coward.

The Executor gives me a cold smile. "Don't worry," he says to Karsten. "She won't hurt me. If she does, Mateo will kill the boy. And she's always been too soft-hearted for her own good."

Rage bubbles within me. Erdahl is of our pack. He is *ours*. This snake of a man has no right to threaten him this way. "Call off your lapdog," I tell him, with a sidelong glance at Karsten. "Or I'll do it for you."

Still smiling, the Executor shakes his head. "Alas, you haven't earned my trust, Eva. You tried to disembowel me, after all." His gaze flicks over me. "But I forgive you. We can accomplish so much together. Change the world. Soon, you'll see."

I want to tell him that he's delusional. That I'd sooner slit my own wrists than cooperate with him. But before I can get out another word, several things happen in quick succession.

Erdahl sinks his teeth into Mateo's arm. The guard backhands him, sending him flying into one of the stones with a sickening crack. Layla howls, an enraged, desperate sound that penetrates the clearing from the forest beyond. The raven takes flight, its wings flapping as it soars toward the sky. And I lose control.

I should have listened to Sebastían when he told me my grip on my beasts was tenuous. That their desires and needs might mesh with my own, entangled beyond recognition. But I was so focused on rescuing Erdahl, so convinced that I couldn't stand by and let an innocent boy suffer, no matter the risks to myself. To us all.

Was I in my right mind when I committed to this mission? Or were my beasts driving me, fueled by their need to take down the prey that escaped us? Did they trick me into believing I was thinking clearly, when all along, they were the ones holding the reins?

Terror strafes through me at the thought. But it's too late to turn back now.

Seeing Erdahl's crumpled body at the foot of one of the standing stones breaks something in me. I don't want to fight my beasts for dominance anymore.

I—we—just want the bastards dead.

I can't shift; the distance from Ari prevents that. Still, my wolf's growl rises in my chest again as she barrels toward the surface of my skin, determined to do injury to the man who hurt our pack's pup.

We will make him pay.

The barrier between my wolf and me disintegrates. I am her. She is me. United in my human body, we charge at Mateo.

There is an instant when I see myself reflected in the dark discs of his eyes. I look as feral as I feel, my teeth bared and my expression empty of anything but the revenge that is my pack's due. I watch as he sees his death on my face. As he turns, far too late, and tries to run.

I am on him before he's gone two steps, the growl that reverberates through me shaking my entire body. He fights, but it is useless. His fate is sealed.

"Look at me," I snarl, and when he does, his terrified brown eyes meeting mine, his mouth forming the words *Please* and *No* and *Don't,* I snap his neck.

My wolf howls in triumph, and, in the forest, Layla and Riley echo me. But as I let Mateo's limp body drop to the ground, the air around the stones flickers again. I hear a high-pitched shriek of rage, followed by the rise of that overwhelming anise scent. The Mages are out there, concealing themselves, Mei probably among them.

Kicking Mateo's body aside, I kneel next to Erdahl. I can hear his heart beating, sluggish and slow—but his head hit the stone so hard. He's alive, yes...but for how long?

Yet another life I can lay at the Executor's feet.

My head comes up and I let the man who has made my life a living hell see exactly what I plan to do to him. To his credit, he doesn't retreat. "I know you're angry," he says, his tone conciliatory, as if trying to gentle a wild animal. "But don't you want to save your mother, Eva? I'm the only one who knows where she is. Kill me, and she'll be trapped forever."

If he thinks reminding me of what he did to Cordelia will cause me to abandon my desire to re-eviscerate him, he doesn't understand me at all. "I'll take my chances."

"You're being shortsighted," he chides me. "Together with the Mages, we can wed science and magic. See how they've healed me, thanks to the presence of the boy? Now that you're here, they'll be more powerful still. When we're victorious, your mother will rule at my side, as will you. And then the world will be ours, Eva, don't you understand? It will be *yours.*"

I stare into his black eyes, gleaming with the intensity of a zealot, and wish I didn't perceive the echo of my own. If I could peel away everything this man bequeathed to me, step out of my own skin, rebraid my DNA, I would. All I can do is prove that I am nothing, *nothing* like him.

I will kill him. I will save my mother and bring her home. I will set the citizens of the Commonwealth free.

"Our deal is off," I tell him, my voice holding the weight of my panther's snarl. "You promised Erdahl would be returned safe and sound, in exchange for me. I came here in good faith, and now there he lies, perhaps hurt beyond repair. A life for a life. It's only fair."

I stalk toward him, intending to finish what I started. But Karsten steps in front of him, blades in hand. His message is obvious: *You'll have to go through me first.*

Fury simmers, narrowing my vision to a red-rimmed tunnel. Karsten's face looms at the end of it, pale and set and determined. He lunges at me, sverd in hand, and I dodge. Once, I dueled him and Riis simultaneously and bested them. Now Riis lies dead, Karsten is wounded, and I hold the strength and skills of four beasts. He doesn't stand a chance.

Through the bond, I hear Ari calling to me, warning me. *Control yourself,* he hisses through the bond. *This isn't what we agreed on.* But I don't listen; why would I? We have our prey in our sights. We're not about to let him get away.

I foot-sweep one of my blades toward me and kneel to grab it. When I glance up, Karsten is standing over me, clutching the hilt of his sverd in both hands, clearly intending to stab me in the back. How fitting.

I push myself to my feet, using momentum and body weight to fuel my strike. My blade goes in beneath his ribs, and I shove harder, fighting bone and gristle, until I feel it pierce his heart.

I raise my bloodied blade to meet my father's eyes. But he isn't there.

What in the name of—

Inside me, there's the strangest sensation: an ache, and then a *tugging*, as if my very essence is rushing outward. No, not rushing. Being *pulled.*

That crackling sound fills the air again. Then the illusion drops and I see what lies beyond the circle: a city built into the forest, with elaborate structures in the trees and bridges strung between them. Under other circumstances, I might find it beautiful. But not now.

Look, my wolf snarls. *There they stand. The ones who sheltered those who splintered our pack.*

From between the trees steps a line of women dressed in red, hair flying out behind them as if in the wake of a wild wind, though the air is still. Their arms are outstretched, channeling their magic.

Mages.

My wolf and my panther speak as one. *Kill them,* they say. *Kill them now.*

The scent of anise fills the air, so strong I choke on it. My pulse trembles through my entire body, fury sparking hot on every inch of my skin. I have my blades. I could move through them in a whirl of silver, mowing them down one by one.

For Erdahl's sake, I *should.*

Eva, Ari sends through the bond, his voice desperate. *Stop. Don't do this—*

But I have no intention of stopping. I wipe my bloodied blade on my pants, grab the rest from the ground, and move toward the edge of the circle, my feet soundless on the grass. But when I reach the stones and try to step through them, I can go no further. Some invisible force holds me back, preventing me from crossing from the circle to the tree-city beyond. Inside me, that tugging sensation intensifies, like something has its hooks in my very soul.

My panther comes forward, lips curled back as she scents the air, trying to understand what this barrier is that holds us. "Let me through," she growls, using my mouth as her vessel.

The phalanx of women in red hold the line, arms extended. Their bodies tremble as if holding me in the stone circle is taking physical effort. And then, from behind them, comes a familiar voice.

"Why would we do that?" it says.

Also clad in red, Mei steps through the ranks of the Mages and strolls toward me. "Hello, Eva," she says, lips lifted in a smile.

At the sight of her, rage breaks over me anew. "I should have let you die when Riis had that blade at your throat," I spit at her. "But there's no time like the present."

I grip a blade in each hand, weighing them. I can't pass the circle. But perhaps my weapons can.

If they can, though...why doesn't Mei look afraid?

Deep inside me, my panther stirs. *Trick,* she whispers. *Trap. Run.*

Inside my head, Ari echoes her. He tells me he's coming. He warns me to flee.

I stand my ground instead and let the first blade fly. It breaches the circle, and I feel a stab of triumph. But as it soars toward Mei, it wobbles, blown off course. I follow its trajectory and see one of the red-clad women waving her hand through the air, directing the knife's path.

How is that possible?

I throw the second blade. It meets the same fate as the first.

Ari's mind-voice sounds, taut with urgency. *Get out of there, Eva. For the Architect's sake, go.*

But I came here to save Erdahl, and failed. Killing the

Executor is still within my grasp. If I can take Mei with me, that will be a bonus.

So instead, I lunge for her, heedless of the invisible barrier in my way.

And the world around me explodes.

CHAPTER 17

ARI

One moment, Eva is standing within that cursed stone circle with two corpses and a battered boy, hurling blades that fail to meet their mark. The next, the air quakes with an explosion so powerful, it knocks all of us out of the trees where we're concealing ourselves. Sebastían manages to catch himself on the way down, the bastard. The rest of us tumble to the ground as smoke begins to fill the woods, billowing from the direction of the circle.

For a terrifying second, I'm back in the Brotherhood's encampment, with the bombing, all over again. My heart thuds against my ribcage, and my ears ring. I can't catch my breath.

Eva! I call through the bond, as loud as I can. *Eva!* But there's nothing.

Coughing, I crawl forward, desperate to reach her. Instead, I slam right into someone who grabs me by the collar. "Stop," Kilían says, close to my ear. "We need a new plan."

"To the Sins with your plans," I snarl, and rip my way free of him. Staying low to avoid the smoke, I belly-crawl in what I hope is the direction of the circle. I can hear Layla shrieking, and pray that Erdahl isn't dead. But he has Layla and Riley to look out for him. Eva has *me,* and by the Virtues, I won't fail her.

The smoke is heavy with anise, the scent Eva smelled so strongly in the clearing where the exiles and scouts lay. My limbs grow heavier the more I crawl, and I wonder whether it has sedative properties. The Mages are healers, after all. And Mei is clear evidence of the fact that they can knock people out when they choose.

Mei, who Eva was trying to kill right before everything went south.

I belly-crawl faster, calling for Eva again—out loud, this time. Concealing our location has dropped right off my list of priorities.

"Behind you," a smoke-raw voice says. Ronan.

I turn my head with an effort, troubled by the way my hearing on the left side is still next to nil, and see him emerge through the smoke, belly-crawling like I am, his gun in his hand. "All right?" he says.

"Fine. Do you know what—"

He shakes his head. "Can you feel her?"

"No." Fear makes my voice tight. "But surely they wouldn't kill her. They need her."

Ronan doesn't reply.

Layla and Riley have stopped calling for Erdahl. Maybe they've shifted to wolf form and are using their superior sense of smell to track him. The alternative—that both of them are dead—is too grim to consider.

A black-furred form streaks past me, low to the ground. Sebastían's panther, determined to retrieve his precious skúma mate. He can claim her all he wants if he can get her back. Because this yawning emptiness where she should be—

Pebbles scrape at my body, my nails ripping as I haul myself forward, fingers digging into the scraggly grass in an effort to anchor myself and stay conscious. The world feels like it's tilting. Every inch feels like a mile. My brain is filled with fog as thick as the smoke.

Then I'm there, in the circle. The smoke is drifting in great clouds, but it dissipates enough for me to see the gray stones standing sentinel. They're engraved with symbols: a loop that folds in upon itself, an eight-pointed star, a moon in all its phases.

The smoke descends again.

Standing up is an impossibility. Not only is the smoke thicker above, but when I try, my limbs won't cooperate. I force myself to keep crawling, stopping only when I encounter a body.

I know right away that whoever it is isn't alive. Their flesh is limp and cooling, with that finality that only death gives. I suck in air and choke as I run my hands over the body, praying with everything in me that it isn't Eva. Or Erdahl.

The body is too big to be a child's, and covered in dirt and grass. My hands tangle in their hair, searching for their face, but I can't find it. I try again and again, each time more of an effort than the last, until I realize what the problem is: their head is on backward.

Mateo, then. I felt Eva's satisfaction when she broke his neck.

With a snort of disgust, I move on, crawling along the perimeter to make sure I don't backtrack. Halfway around, I hear a snuffling noise beside me: Sebastían, coming from the opposite direction. He pauses, and then I feel teeth grab my sleeve, tugging me.

Normally, I'd protest. But this is so far from normal, I don't even have the vocabulary for it. So I let him pull me, until at last he lets go and sits down on his haunches with a chuffing sound.

He's brought me to Karsten's body. I see that much, before

the smoke closes over the circle again. The two of us are alone here. Ronan has vanished. Eva, the Executor, and Erdahl are gone.

It's getting harder to hold up my head. Straining, I grab hold of one of the stones and haul myself to my feet. And then I see Eva, on the other side of the circle, just yards away, in grabbing distance of the red-clad Mages, Mei right behind her. She's on her hands and knees, her face covered with blood, crawling forward, trying to make it back to the stones.

Sebastían growls, a bone-rattling sound so threatening that the hair on the back of my neck rises. I let go of the stone and try to step out of the circle, toward Eva, just as he does the same. But it's as if I've walked into an invisible wall. Both of us bounce off, and I scrape my palm on a stone, barely catching myself in a desperate effort to stay upright.

A fresh wave of smoke sweeps through the circle, and this close to the edge, I can tell it's coming from the direction of the Mages' compound. A compound we could've walked by a thousand times and never seen, because of their gift of concealment.

The smoke can pass through the circle. Eva's blades could pass through, as well, even though the women were able to deflect them. So is it just living things that cannot?

Ronan and Kilían loom up beside me, their heads and shoulders emerging from the smoke. Kilían looks even worse off than I feel. His lips are pressed into a thin line, his jaw set. His good hand grips the top of the stone next to mine to support himself. "You—never listen—" he snaps at me, then dissolves into a fit of coughing.

I ignore him, turning toward Ronan, who's weaving from side to side. It makes me dizzy, and I have to swallow back a wave of nausea. "Bullets," I manage, gesturing at the red-clad women on the other side of the circle. "Shoot them."

"We..." he manages, then doubles over, coughing. "We...

could shoot...Eva. Could shoot...Erdahl...if he's alive. If they... took him."

"Worth," I manage, gripping my stone with both hands to stay on my feet, "the risk."

Ronan's eyes slide to Kilían, who nods. To Sebastían, who's growling steadily. To Mei, who stands behind Eva, watching us, a faint smile on her face.

"All right," he says, and raises his gun.

CHAPTER 18
EVA

The air fills with a thick, cloying smoke as I'm blasted off my feet.

I fly through the air, crashing to the ground with a thud. There's no way to tell where the explosion came from, who set it off. All I know is my ears are ringing, my eyes are stinging, and when I try to move, to get away, my limbs feel weighted with lead. I raise a hand to my cheek, and it comes away slick with blood.

"Eva!" Ari is screaming for me, terror clear in his mind-voice. I try to reach for him, but my mind is fuzzy, refusing to cooperate.

I breathe in again, and this time I taste a hint of the valerian and poppy mixture that Mei mixed with Adrien and Fade's kaffi. Somehow, the Mages have laced whatever that explosive device was with a sedative. I can feel it creeping through my bloodstream, seeping into every cell, luring me into unconsciousness.

I have to find Ari and the rest before I pass out.

I crawl to the left, then to the right, then straight ahead, through the acrid smoke, trying to make my way out of the circle and into the woods. Every time I breathe, it feels like my lungs are on fire. My eyes burn as I fight to peer through the smoke, and tears run down my cheeks, making it even harder to see. But lifting my hand to wipe them away is a mistake: my hands are coated in grit and blood, and now my vision is compromised even further.

I can feel, though, and one thing I know for sure: Karsten's body isn't here. Neither is Mateo's or Erdahl's.

Of course, they could've been thrown out of the circle by the concussive force of the blast. But the stones would surely be here, even chipped or damaged. And I don't feel them anywhere, no matter how far I crawl.

Which means only one thing.

I'm not in the circle anymore.

If that's the case, then by the Sins, where am I? Back the way we came, in the direction of Vik? Or on the other side of the Circle, in the Mages' territory?

I raise my head, straining to see. And then my eyes widen in horror.

To my left are the red-clad Mages, arms still outstretched, palms open. This close, I can hear them chanting under their breath, unaffected by the blast or the smoke. Maybe they placed themselves in a protective bubble; maybe they've swallowed an antidote. Either way, as I crawl forward on hands and knees, coughing so hard I feel like I might shake apart, they're completely unaffected. As for Mei, I have no idea where she is. Nowhere good, that's for sure.

I'd been harboring the hope that perhaps Ronan engineered the blast. That it was part of a plan he hadn't confided, for fear that the Executor or the Mages would torture it out of me. After all, you can't reveal what you don't know. But at the sight of the Mages, unharmed and chanting, I know nothing could be further from the truth. They've done this, and now we're at their mercy.

I cough and cough, struggling to breathe. Finally, the clouds of smoke clear for an instant and I see the stone circle, just a few feet in front of me. The smoke billows through it, too, confirming my worst fear: whatever this airborne weapon is, it's not just targeting me. It's intended for everyone in my party, the party the Mages assumed I would bring with me, no matter what I'd promised their virtueless raven.

Erdahl and the Executor are gone from the circle. In their place stands Ari, gripping one of the granite monoliths to keep himself upright. Next to him is Sebastían in panther form, nosing at the edge of the invisible barrier as if trying to make sense of it. I know the instant when both of them see me: Ari's head comes up, Sebastían's eyes widen, and then the two of them charge the barrier. But it's no use. They ricochet off of it, and Ari nearly falls.

Seeing how weak he is redoubles my determination. Even if they can't get in, maybe I can get out. But first I have to make it to the edge of the circle.

Behind me, the Mages' chanting grows louder. It's not a language I know, but the intensity in their voices is plain. Whatever's happening is coming to its culmination. And I don't want to be here when it does.

My breath rasps as I crawl forward, dragging myself through the grass. The smoke is so thick, I can barely see. But occasionally it clears, and the next time it does, Kilían and Ronan have joined Ari in the stone circle. I see Ari turn and say something to Ronan, see the leader of the Brotherhood's guards pause, considering, before he raises his gun.

I throw myself flat on the ground as he fires. The bullet penetrates the barrier, whistling through the air overhead, and

I wait for the scream of fury that will tell me one of the Mages has fallen.

But nothing comes. And a second later, the bullet thuds into the ground just inches from my face. It kicks up a spray of dirt that threatens to blind me.

The Mages have deflected it, just as they deflected the onslaught of my blades.

Sebastían roars, the sound muted, as if the invisible barrier between us is stuffed with cotton. On the heels of it, I hear Layla wail for Erdahl, sending a stab of fear through me. If he wasn't dead when his head hit the stone, that explosion could have killed him. And what about the Executor? Did it injure him, even take his life? Or is he here, on this side of the circle, protected by the Mages?

Ari calls my name again, this time aloud. His voice sounds fractured, like his throat is full of shards of glass, and I force myself to crawl faster toward the invisible wall. Maybe if I'm close enough to him, we can work the same alchemy we did during the battle in the Great Hall. Maybe we will be enough to overpower the Mages and bring the barrier down.

On hands and knees, spitting out dirt, I finally make it to the edge of the stone circle. Struggling to my feet, I run my hands over the barrier, searching for a weakness, a way out. I find nothing. Ari throws his shoulder against the invisible wall that separates us again and again. Beside him, Sebastían does the same, clawing at the barrier. But it does no good.

Though it's muffled, I can hear Kilían urging them to retreat, hear Ari cursing his name in language more colorful than any I've heard him use. He stabs at the barrier, hacks at it. But it does no good. And the more he tries, the less I can hear what he's saying both inside my head and out, as if someone's got hold of a volume knob for his voice and is turning it down bit by bit. It's getting harder for me to focus. Harder for me to *think,* as if my brain as well as my limbs are filling with molasses.

In desperation, Ari presses his hands flat to the barrier, as if trying to reach through and touch me. On the other side, I do the same. Our palms mirror each other, separated by inches and impossibility. I can tell he's trying to talk to me mind-to-mind, can feel an insistent pressure as he tries again and again. But his words are unintelligible, and when I do the same, his brows knit as he fights to make out what I'm trying to say.

A hand closes on my bicep. Mei.

I fight her, struggling to get away, but I can't twist free. All of my gifts, my abilities, are useless against that insidious smoke. I can feel my strength draining away.

Go, I mouth to Ari. *Save yourself.* But he shakes his head, mouthing something back to me. I narrow my eyes, clinging to consciousness, and finally make it out: *I'm not leaving you.*

Dimly, I hear Mei say, "So romantic, Eva. And yet so hopeless."

Then a needle sinks deep into my arm, Ari's face fades into the murk, and I plunge into unrelenting darkness.

CHAPTER 19

ARI

I wake in the stone circle, my last memory of Mei plunging that sins-cursed needle into Eva's arm. And me, helpless to aid her.

Kilían, Ronan, and Sebastían stir as I struggle to my knees, then to my feet. The smoke has dissipated, just the remnants of it riding the air, and the stone monoliths stand, unaffected by the explosion. Outside the circle, all is empty, quiet. The red-clad Mages have vanished. So has the Executor. And Eva.

Tentatively, I extend a hand between the stones. When the air offers no resistance, I stride through, shouting her name. She doesn't answer me. I can't feel her through the bond.

I've failed her.

Movement catches my eye, and my heart leaps. But it's only Layla and Riley, emerging from between the trees in human form. Behind them come Zion and Noe, their familiars. I half-expect them to be carrying Erdahl's corpse, but their arms are empty.

"They took him," Layla says when she reaches me. "Alive or dead, I don't know. I can't pick up his scent. That smoke…it's made all of us nose-blind. All I know is, he's gone. That bottom-crawler of an Executor isn't here, either."

The agony in her tone is palpable. Riley puts his hands on her shoulders in support, but she slips from his grip. "Where is Eva?"

It takes everything in me not to scream that I told them this would happen. That I warned them this was a trap, and they were so determined to save their son that they've likely doomed him to his death. Now Eva's missing, into the bargain. But that won't help, so all I say instead is, "I don't know." It sounds as bleak as I feel.

Sebastían, Ilsa, Ronan, and Kilían join us beneath the trees, wearing matching grim expressions. Sebastían, thank the Virtues, has also somehow located his pants. Maybe Ilsa brought them to him, like the well-trained little familiar she is.

"Where the hell have they gone?" I say. "What are we going to do?"

Ronan gestures at the house-like structures in the trees. "First, we make sure those are empty. If they are, then we regroup and make a new plan."

"That's the best you've got?" My voice rises. "Those Mages were able to conceal the existence of this entire place from us, when we were standing right next to it. They trapped us in that cursed circle. Erdahl might be dead. Eva's drugged and missing. The Executor's still at large. And all you have to say is, *we need to regroup and make a new plan?*"

"Easy, Westergaard," Kilían cautions, and I round on him, furious.

"Why? As you might recall, I was against this idiotic idea to begin with. But oh no, everyone insisted it was the right thing to do. And now they've taken Eva!"

"Can you feel her?" Sebastían says. "Through the bond?"

Miserable, I shake my head. "No. It doesn't feel...broken. She's just not at the other end of it, if that makes sense. It feels different from when she's shut it down on purpose." I try not to think of the last time she did this, when I heard Sebastían whisper *Carina* to her. Of what else might have happened between them. That won't help me find her.

"It feels like..." I run a hand through my hair, trying to describe it, to put words to something I can only see with my mind's eye. "Like the bond is a rope that connects us, and she's dropped the other end. Or maybe like it's a tunnel, and normally I can call and she'll hear me, but now it's just an empty echo chamber. Maybe both."

"She's not dead, then," Ilsa says, speaking up for the first time. "You'd know. As a familiar, when your skúma dies...it's a terrible thing. Believe me, you'd feel it." Her gaze skitters toward Sebastían, as if she's trying to reassure herself that he's still there.

"What about you?" Ronan says to the Panther of the West. "Not to be indelicate, but...have you bonded with her?"

Sebastían's cheeks redden, but he holds Ronan's gaze, very carefully not looking at me. "Not in the way you mean, no. I named her beast, but...that's all."

Riley's eyebrows rise. "Really. So then, you should be able to sense her panther, if she's close by."

I *hate* not understanding the protocols of this strange world in which I find myself, not knowing what it means that Sebastían named Eva's panther. But in this instance, if it can help him find her, I'm all for it.

To my chagrin, though, he shakes his head. "I've tried. I've been calling for her since I woke up. But...nothing."

"Damn it," Ronan says. "This is the worst possible—"

Another thought occurs to me then. "Do you think they

could be here, watching us, but invisible? That Eva's still here, and we just can't reach her?"

Ronan shakes his head. "It's unlikely that they could maintain a circle of power for that long, not with Erdahl injured and Eva drugged. Not to mention all the energy they expended. Wherever they are now, they're long gone. We'll check their settlement"—he gestures upward—"to be sure, but I'd bet my weapons on it."

I feel sick, my stomach swimming with anxiety and the after-effects of the smoke. "Fine, then," I say, striding toward the ladder at the base of a nearby oak. "We'll sweep their sins-forsaken treehouses, and the Architect help any stragglers we find."

THE TREEHOUSES ARE EMPTY. They're also cleverly made. If they didn't belong to the people who are sheltering the Executor, engineered Erdahl's kidnapping, and have drugged and stolen Eva, I would be inclined to admire them.

Made of reclaimed wood, they're cozy inside, redolent of herbs, with windows cracked open to let in the fresh winter air. There aren't enough of them to constitute an entire village; this must be a waystation of sorts, perhaps connected to that damned circle of standing stones.

That makes sense, of course. Without the Mages to conceal it, this encampment would be visible to anyone who came across it. Wherever their stronghold is, they wouldn't risk leaving it to be overrun or ransacked. There has to be another place, not too far away, where they've been conspiring with the exiles. Where they healed the Executor and Karsten. And where they've likely taken Eva and Erdahl. But how in all the nine hells are we supposed to find what we can't see?

As I step onto a walkway rigged between the trees, feeling the wood give under my weight, my head pounds with frustration. My body's tight, my muscles coiled with the desire to do something, anything. Calling out mentally for Eva again and again, my dagur clutched in my hand in case the Mages materialize out of nowhere, I make my way across to the final dwelling and throw my shoulder against the door. It swings open, revealing yet another tiny structure with a pallet in the corner, a mortar filled with crumbled herbs, and a window overlooking the stone circle. I feel my way around the four walls and across the floor, making sure that no one's concealing themselves. This one is as empty as the rest.

Furious, I kick the door open so hard it almost flies off its hinges and shimmy down the rope ladder attached to the tree. When I reach the ground, I see Ronan doing the same. Sebastían leaps from the treehouse he was assigned to investigate, but not flamboyantly. I think he's as disturbed as I am, and like me, he's seeking a physical outlet for his frustration. That, along with the way he clawed at the barrier separating us from Eva, makes me like him a little bit more than I did before. Of course, *before* I despised him, so the bar is low.

"Great. There's no one up there." I square my shoulders. "So we go back to Vik, tell Councilor Adelman what's happened, and march on the Commonwealth of Ashes. Because that has to be where they're going, at least eventually."

"You can't be sure—" Ronan says, but Kilían interrupts him.

"Westergaard's right. I couldn't hear everything they said in that circle, but one thing I did hear was the Executor's claim about blending science and magic to achieve the greatest power possible. The Mages offer the magic. The Commonwealth of Ashes is a bastion of science, and the Executor is its leader. They're taking him home, so that together, they can accomplish whatever it is they have in mind. Now, before the snow is too high in the passes to navigate."

The wind gusts, as if to punctuate his assertion. It ruffles the remaining leaves in the trees, making the limbs bend before its onslaught. Winter is descending on us, and fast.

"If we don't get to them now," I say, "they'll have all winter and into spring to consolidate what they mean to do. Then *they* will march on *us*, and if what I just witnessed is any indication, we'll be all but defenseless. We have to band together and stage our offense, before it's too late...for Eva, for Erdahl if he lives, and for us."

I expect an argument. But for once, no one says a sins-forsaken word. Sebastían is nodding, his expression determined. Riley and Layla look ready to charge southward themselves, with the backing of the Council or no. And Ronan looks resigned, his shoulders set as if he's bearing the weight of the world atop them.

"Sebastían?" he says.

The Prince of the West straightens his spine. He looks like royalty again, rather than like the bedraggled boy I woke up next to in the circle. "This changes things. House Satrizona supports the invasion."

"As does House Minneska," Layla and Riley say as one.

"That leaves Montyorke and San Fraesco," Kilían says. "How will they vote?"

Sebastían's lip rises in a snarl. "You leave San Fraesco to me. Tristan will do as I say."

In the Council meeting, I was disgusted by his behavior; now, his ruthlessness is an advantage. "And Montyorke?"

Ronan turns, striding back the way we came, eager to be off as soon as possible. "We need the falcons as an advance team. To be able to scout ahead of us, assuming the Mages don't block our way."

"Could they do that?" Noe says. "Now that they have Eva—"

"They'll likely have to keep her sedated," Ronan says, skirting the stone circle and picking up the path again on the other side. "I can't see them taking the risk, otherwise. And I believe they need her conscious in order to be able to draw on that kind of power. So, no. I don't think they could fully entrap us, the way they did today."

"Let's hope not," I say. "But Eldrina can't stand me. Do you think that will influence her call?"

"She despises you," Sebastían concurs, stepping into the trees and retracing our steps back to Vik. "But you're not the one that was taken. A skúma child, my best hope of continuing my family's line, and the most powerful skúma-familiar pair I've ever seen... That's a lot to lose. I'll talk to her. She'll see reason. And if she doesn't...there's always Devereaux."

"Councilor Adelman?" The angle of the sun has changed, and I have to shade my eyes to be able to see Sebastían's face as I wait for his answer. How long were we asleep in that damned stone circle? And what are they doing to Eva, even as we speak? The thought of it sends a fresh wave of fury through me.

"You saw how he was when he found out Cordelia was alive," Sebastían says. "If he had a chance in hell of succeeding, he'd charge down there himself to retrieve her. He'll back us, and with three Houses on our side, Eldrina and the rest of the Council will have to agree."

His tone is deceptively calm, but his fingers drum against his thigh, fast and faster. Kilían gives him a sidelong glance, the Lead Interrogator's eyes meeting mine in a moment of understanding.

Sebastían is as undone as I am.

"So..." I say, "that plan everyone keeps talking about..."

The Panther of the West grabs a low-hanging branch and

snaps it in half to get it out of his way. He hurls it into the forest, where it falls with a crash and a rustling of leaves. When he turns to meet my eyes, his have bled to his panther's green.

"*That* is our gods-damned plan," he growls. "First we parlay. And then, we ride."

CHAPTER 20

EVA

It's dark wherever I am. My arm burns where the needle sank into it. My head lolls, refusing to obey my commands. I reach deep inside myself for Ari, yet where the bond should be is only nothingness. Fear sparks through my body, but when I try to sit up, to flee, my limbs are a heavy, obstinate weight. The air is thick with the scent of the Mages' magic, so cloying I almost choke. A guttural sound escapes my throat, and I struggle to breathe, my chest heaving.

Am I dying? Why would they lure me here, only to kill me?

What has happened to Ari? To Erdahl? To the rest of our party? Are they alive?

Ari was right; this was a trap of the worst kind. But I'd been arrogant, overconfident in my own abilities, in my strength. I'd been determined to save Erdahl, convinced I could survive whatever the Executor and the Mages threw at me. But I'd known nothing, and now we're all paying the price.

I'd ignored Sebastían's warning about losing control of my beasts, but much as it pains me to admit it, he'd been right, too. What if Ari's dead now, and it's my fault? How will I go on?

The drug Mei gave me threads through my veins, beckoning, urging me to give in. Behind my eyes, I can almost see it, an inky, unfathomable blackness. I call to my beasts, but all I hear in return is the weakest sort of echo. Desperate, I thrash, or try to.

Hands press my shoulders down. "Lie still, Eva," Mei says into the darkness. "It's better if you don't fight it."

Has she engineered all of this? Is this her revenge?

I channel all my energy into getting my mouth to open, my sluggish tongue to form words. "Traitor..." I manage to croak. "...kill you..."

Mei laughs, a light, airy sound. "I don't think you'll be killing anyone, Eva. For once, you're at my mercy. Rest."

I want to spit at her, but I can't muster the strength. When I force my eyes open, I see her looming over me, lips curved in a slight smile. Behind her, the world is still swallowed up in smoke. I hear screaming, but it fades in and out. There's only me and Mei.

"Hush, Eva," she croons, even though I don't think I've made a sound.

Her face tilts and flickers, and nausea bubbles up in my throat. I know I'm lying down, but it feels as if I'm tumbling off a cliff like I did at the Trials, falling down and down and down toward the icy water below. My stomach roils. The world swims. I try to fix my gaze on Mei, but it's no use. Her face stretches, her eyes black holes, her mouth a gaping maw.

Her hands still on my shoulders, Mei hums, the melody winding, alluring. It makes its way into every cranny of my mind, permeating my thoughts. *Come,* it says. *Hush. Sleep.* I try to ignore its call, but my lids slip shut again.

The thought of being unconscious and helpless, where these people can do anything they want to me, fills me with fury. That, and a cold terror that seeps through my veins along with the sickening, dizzying sway of the drug. *Ari,* I think desperately, hoping he can hear me. *You were right. I'm so sorry.*

But no one answers. There's only Mei, and her relentless humming, and the scent of roses and anise, flooding my lungs.

I try to open my eyes again, willing myself not to listen. But the combined effect of the song and whatever was in that syringe overwhelms me, and despite my best efforts, I plummet once again into the relentless dark.

CHAPTER 21

ARI

Vik is in an uproar at the news of Eva and Erdahl's disappearances, the entire city vibrating with anxiety. I feel its energy in my bones as I search for Eva through the bond again and again, coming up empty every time.

Where is she? What have they done with her? How is she suffering, even now?

Adelman's called an emergency war council, to determine strategy and next steps. I'm crossing the bridge overlooking the Silber, on my way there, when he comes up beside me. He's wearing black guard's gear. A holster is slung from his waist, weighted with guns.

"Westergaard," he says.

"Councilor." I give him a wary nod. After he backed the plan that led Eva to her doom, I don't trust him further than I can throw my dagur.

The wind blasts, shaking the bridge. On the paved banks of the river, people doing last-minute shopping prior to the curfew we've put in place scurry to and fro, heads bowed against the cold and scarves tied tight around their necks. Adelman shivers before he speaks. "Before we meet with the

Council, I have something to say to you." He clears his throat. "I know what you're going through. And I'm sorry."

Talk about too little, too late. I tug the zipper of my gear jacket up, snorting. "I very much doubt that. I told you this plan was a sins-forsaken disaster. And yet none of you listened to me."

Adelman heaves a frustrated sigh. His eyes are fixed on the river's whitecaps, stirred by the wind. "You're not the only one who's ever lost someone to an ill-conceived plan, Westergaard. I come to this bridge to grieve twice a year. The first, on the anniversary of my parents' murder. And the second, on the anniversary of what I thought was Cordelia's death."

The wind gusts again, and the boats that are moored at the edge of the river knock against their docks with a hollow, clanging sound. Adelman draws a deep breath of the icy air. His hand goes to the chain around his neck, clutching the charm of the wolf. Next to it is nestled a second small charm: an ouroboros. As I watch, his fingers caress it with the familiarity of long habit.

"I loved Cordelia, even though she was promised to Riley from the moment she was born," he says. "After my parents were killed, she was all I had left. I feared what I would become if I lost her. And then...I did. And it almost destroyed me."

"If you've got a point," I say, not bothering to disguise my impatience, "make it."

Adelman lets the charms fall back inside his collar and turns to face me. "My point is this. All this time, she's lived, only to be abused and tortured at the hands of a monster. I could have saved her, had I known. And now I have my chance." His eyes blaze—with grief, with fury, with resolve. "I know you think that I want to take advantage of Eva. To use her. But what I want is the same thing you do. To bring down the system that actually used her in the first place."

I'll believe we want the same things when I see the Executor take up knitting. Which is to say, the eighth day of never. "Oh, sure. We're practically twins, you and me."

He steps closer to me, placing a hand on my arm. "As the head of the Council, it's my job to keep an eye on things. I see how angry you are, Ari. I get it; when I thought Cordelia had died, I wanted to burn down the world. But every pressure cooker must let out steam, or it will eventually erupt. And I don't want you erupting all over this mission."

Seriously? "I'm not the one you need to worry about. I can control myself. But you? I know who you care about retrieving, and it's not Eva." I yank free of his grip and say what I've been thinking since his meltdown in my room. "Part of you has to hate her, right? She's half Cordelia's, but she's half *his*...the monster who forced himself on the woman you love. You can't tell me you're actually concerned for her well-being."

His breath stutters. His heartbeat quickens. And I know that I am right.

"You can hide behind your title all you want," I say, my voice icy. "But let me tell you what I see. I see a man who lost the girl he loved and built a career from his fury. Who sits at the head of the Council not out of a desire for governance or betterment but for one reason only: to get revenge on those who took from him what he loved most. You want to get Cordelia back... well, what will happen if we fail? Do you even care about what becomes of the Houses, or are they just the means to an end? Do you care what will happen to *Eva?*"

The Councilor's jaw sets. He doesn't answer me.

"I see you," I tell him, gripping the hilt of my blade. "To the blackened depths of your soul, I see you. And I tell you now, if you sacrifice Eva to save Cordelia, I will end your life."

He mutters something, makes some excuse about how he

couldn't, would never, et cetera ad nauseum, but I glower at him and he subsides.

We walk the rest of the way to the House of Echoes in silence.

~

"WE RIDE TO WAR," Adelman says five minutes later, glaring around the Council's chambers. If he can't take his anger out on me, his colleagues are the next, best target. "Agreed?"

A low rumble courses throughout the room, dominated by Riley's growl. Beside him, Layla sobs into her hands. Tristan, Eldrina, and Sebastían sit next to each other, backed by their familiars. Across from them are the three surviving members of the Council. Kilían isn't here; in our absence, Vik's Mages were hard at work on a compound that accelerates healing. The Lead Interrogator is back in the infirmary, being doctored. If all goes as planned, he and Jaxon will ride out with us at dawn— assuming we come to an agreement.

I don't care what these fools decide. I'm going anyway.

"I don't see that we have a choice." Across the table from him, Ronan coughs, trying to clear his throat of the smoke's residue. "Mei's family knows nothing. They can't help us, other than to guard our borders and keep Vik safe. It's up to us to retrieve our lost skúma—and defeat our enemies—on our own."

He's right. Maybe going after the Mages like this is exactly what they intend; maybe it's yet another trap, and they're leading us right into the mouth of it. But it's our best option, if we want to save Eva and defend ourselves from whatever they're planning.

Too bad our best option is also a terrible one.

"I agree with Ronan and Deveraux," Tristan says, and Sebastían snorts.

"That's easy for you to say, Tristan of the Waters. You won't be riding to war. You'll be staying right here, safe in Vik, won't you?"

For the first time, I see Tristan's eyes change, morphing from their usual silver to a gleaming black. "I'm no coward, Sebastían Pardúr. Selkies are strategists, as well you know. I'll do more good here than I would elsewhere. And I'll commit San Fraesco's army to the cause. We must find a way to get word to them in time, before the snow makes it impossible to travel."

"I'll send my falcons." Eldrina straightens, resting a hand on Layla's heaving shoulder. "My mate and the two others I brought with me can be dispatched to San Fraesco, Montyorke, and Satrizona, to warn them of the coming offensive. Provided, of course, that House Satrizona supports the invasion."

All eyes turn to Sebastían then. I expect him to agree without hesitation. After all, the last thing he said to me before we came back to Vik was, *First, we parlay. And then, we ride.* But instead, he pauses, his lips rising in an obnoxious smile. "You know my conditions," he says. "I will go to war, and pledge the resources of my House. But if and when we win, I'll ask Eva to marry me once more, and I'll expect all of you to support my claim. Understood?"

Oh, by the bleeding Virtues. "How in the nine hells is she supposed to marry you when she's been kidnapped and taken to the Architect knows where?"

He swivels to look at me, his gaze hard. "We'll find her. When we do, she'll be grateful for the commitment of House Satrizona. And she'll say yes when I ask her to take her rightful place at my side."

"Her rightful—" Enraged, I push to my feet. "You selfish

prick. A boy might be dead. Eva is *gone*. And all you can think about is making a deal about where to stick your..."

"Westergaard!" Ronan snaps, just as Sebastían stands too, mirroring me. His claws have slid out, and he scrapes them over the table, leaving tiny divots in the wood.

"You think I'm selfish?" he growls. "I'm thinking of the future of my House. Of all our Houses. You're the impulsive fool. Of the two of us, I hardly think I'm the one who's thinking with my—"

"Don't you dare finish that sentence." Rage is so thick in my throat, I'm afraid I might choke on it. Instead, I shove my chair back from the table hard enough that it overturns and storm from the room.

THE WHOLE WAY down the hill from the House of Echoes, I alternate between picturing inventive ways to wring Sebastían's neck and trying desperately to reach out to Eva. If I could just talk to her, know she's all right, maybe the ache inside my chest would ease. But there's still nothing at the other end of the bond. Terror ripples through me, and I fight to tamp it down. Fear won't help me find her.

My stomach rumbles, reminding me that the last thing I ate was Jaxon's nasty leftovers. As I turn onto Spruce Street, heading in the direction of one of the restaurants that line the river, I have the unmistakable sense that someone's watching me. I can feel the weight of their gaze on my back, a cold spot between my shoulder blades. My skin prickles with alarm, but when I spin, dagur in hand, there's no one there.

Every sense on high alert, I make my way down Spruce and onto the City Road. This section of it is quiet, the shops closed. Still, with every step, that sense of being watched escalates, until I can't take it anymore. I come to a halt, a blade clutched in each hand, and raise my voice. "I know you're there. Come out. Or are you too much of a coward?"

For a moment, nothing happens. And then a blur of blue hurtles from the roof of the tailor shop, landing on the stones in front of me with a crouch. My breath catches, and I'm halfway to burying my dagur in whatever it is when it speaks. "Surprise."

"Oh, it's you." Aggravation sharpens my voice, blended with relief: at least it isn't an attacker. "What in the nine hells do you want? And why are you stalking me from the rooftops?"

Sebastían straightens, giving me an infuriating grin. "It's faster than walking."

Right. Or maybe he just wants to make the point that his physical capabilities exceed my own, especially now that I can't access my bond with Eva. "I repeat, what do you want? Didn't you say enough in that damn war council?" Sheathing my blade, I narrow my eyes at him. "They must've wrapped up quickly. What did they decide, anyway? To support you?"

"Of course." He shrugs one elegant shoulder. "It's a shit plan, marching right into the jaws of the enemy. You and I both know that. But their options are limited."

It's true: this plan is full of holes. If Eldrina's falcons don't reach the other Houses and summon their guards in time to meet us near the Commonwealth of Ashes, what do we have? Three hundred guards from Minneska. Riley and Layla. Eldrina. Sebastían. Kilían and me. Against a magical force we don't understand and the might of all six Commonwealths, assuming the Executor summons them to fight. "Why are you here, then? To rub it in?"

"No. I wanted to ask…" Shifting his weight, he glances down at the cobblestones. "You truly can't feel her, Westergaard?"

There's a note of vulnerability in his voice, and for a

moment, I wonder if he really does care for Eva as something other than a means to an end. But, surely not. "I can't," I admit. "I've been trying, but...nothing. You, though? When you told Ronan you'd named her panther, what did that mean?"

"It's a bond." The wind riffles through his hair, ripping it loose from its ever-present ribbon, but he doesn't react. Like Eva, he doesn't seem to feel the cold. "Not as strong as yours, of course. And not as intense as it would be if my relationship with her was...consummated." Is it my imagination, or does his voice linger on the last word? "But it's a connection between us."

Much as I hate the idea that this exists, maybe it's something we can leverage. "A connection," I say slowly. "Can you use it to track her?"

"Perhaps." His blue-green eyes bore into mine. "And if so, the gods know it'd be more effective than this hair-brained march on an unknown enemy."

I take a step back, considering him. "You could've brought this up in the Council's chambers. But instead, you tracked me down here to talk about it in private. Why?"

"Think, Westergaard." For once, that obnoxious grin of his is gone. "Both of us want Eva to be safe, more than anything. Our reasons may differ, sure, but our goal is the same. But the rest of them? Think about what Adelman wants. You think Eva's safety is top of mind for him?"

"You're saying you and I are on the same side." By the Virtues, how did this happen? "And you want us to...what? Join forces? Collaborate?"

"I'm saying we have a connection to Eva no one else does. Yours is blunted by distance and whatever's been done to her. Mine isn't as strong, but it's there. We can use that. But we don't have to share everything we discover. If we can extract her without risking all-out war, one we're not positioned to win..." He raises his brows, leaving me to fill in the blanks.

What a damned schemer. I'd like to shove him into the river, but much as I hate to admit it, he has a point. Still, "How can I trust you?"

He smiles at me. "You can trust that I'll work with you as long as it benefits me. Of course, that doesn't mean I'll stop trying to find her on my own. And if I locate her first, with a complement of guards at my back... Well, let the best man win."

I grit my teeth, gauging the distance between the white-capped waters of the Silber and the place where we stand. It's not that far. One good shove, and in he'd go. "You won't find her first."

"Maybe not. But even if I did..." He tilts his head, considering. "You'd want that, right? For her to be safe, no matter what? Even if it was with me?"

He has me there. Much as it tears me up to imagine Eva married to Sebastían, better wedded to him and alive than tortured at the hands of her kidnappers and wielded as the enemy's weapon. "Yes," I say, biting out the word.

"Well then." He extends a hand. "Do we have an agreement?"

I consider what he's asking: to forge my own alliance with him, going behind the Council's back. To align myself with the boy who's hell-bent on marrying the girl I love. Talk about making a deal with the devil.

But if I have to bargain with the devil to save Eva, then I'll do it, and gladly.

And so I take Sebastían's hand, and tell him we have a deal.

CHAPTER 22

EVA

I drift above the ground, buoyed by the wind. This should be impossible, unless I'm in the form of my falcon. But when I manage to open my eyes, what I see confirms my suspicions: I haven't slipped my skin. I'm still in human form, wearing the black-and-magenta gear I had on when I went to meet the Mages. Yet I'm floating, propelled by a force that I can't resist, no matter how hard I try.

Trees glide by me, their leaves coated with snow. I tilt my head back and see the sky above me, a bleak, cold, gray.

"...incredible," an unfamiliar voice says, somewhere close by. "Worth every sacrifice."

"I told you." It's the Executor's voice, gloating, satisfied.

I turn my head and see him beside me, drifting above the ground. If I could move, I could reach out and touch him.

This *has* to be a dream. A nightmare.

His head swivels and his eyes catch mine, dark and fathomless. "Eva," he says. "You are a miracle. *My* miracle. Look what we have done together."

I want to shriek at him. To tell him I'm not his anything,

except his enemy. To demand to know where I am. To be set free.

But my mouth won't move. My eyes slip closed.

I dream of Ari screaming my name. Of teetering on the edge of an abyss, unsure whether to jump or skitter away, to safety. Of a deep, dark forest, and a panther prowling through it, green eyes peering into the shadows, growling, *Carina, where are you?*

I try to answer Ari. To slink from the shadows and tell the panther, *Here. I'm right here.* But my voice doesn't come. Instead Ari's call grows fainter and fainter, and the panther prowls through the shadows, finding nothing, and I'm lost, alone in the dark.

I will have to save myself. But how, when I can't speak or move?

Sweat soaks my body, plastering my hair to my face. I force air through my lungs, but all that escapes is a desperate mewl. My eyelids won't rise. My limbs won't move. Maybe I am still drifting or maybe I lie still. I can't tell.

I focus all my energy on at least trying to open my eyes, to see where I am, but nothing happens. The pull of the drug is too strong.

Come, Eva, a woman's voice whispers, closer than Ari's and the panther's. *You are safe now. It will be all right.*

The voice lies. I may not know who it belongs to or where I am, but I know that much. Deep in the recesses of my mind, I huddle, refusing to respond.

We can help each other, the voice coaxes me. *Many years ago, Mages and skúma worked together. We controlled the elements; you protected us. It can be like that again.*

I don't want to listen. But there is nowhere for me to go. The voice is inside my head, worming its way into all of the crevices. Wherever I try to hide, it finds me. And, I realize, it's oddly familiar.

This is the voice that spoke through the raven, back in Vik. It's devoid of the harsh tones that came from being forced through a bird's throat, yes. But it's unmistakably the same.

We serve the Light, the voice says, soft yet inexorable. *We have always been a force against the Darkness. Once, you were our guardians. The Commonwealths, with their technology and their laws against sin—they seek to replicate what was once our role. Stand with us, and push the Dark into the shadows once more. Fight with us, and save your mother's life.*

Inside my head, I rock, hands pressed to my ears, trying to shut the voice out. But it is me and I am it and there is no escape.

Many years ago, the voice muses, *in a land across the sea, we had another name. Many years ago, you battled by our side, in another form. Now, we are exiled alongside your Commonwealth's refuse. Now, we subsist on roots and rinds of magic; we are ghosts in the woods. We only want what rightly belongs to us. If you will not give it to us, we will take it, Eva. We will take what's ours. Your Executor has shown us the way.*

If this voice is real—if I'm not dreaming—then what is it telling me? That the Mages used to rule over the skúma, and not the other way around? That the Commonwealths' dedication to expunging sin has its origins in something far more ancient... something tied to magic?

I don't know who to believe.

A hand touches my forehead, feather-light, brushing back the hair that clings, sweat-soaked, to my face. *All those years ago,* the voice says, *there was one of us so powerful, she controlled all of the elements, as you control all four beasts. Her gifts have been lost. But now, as you have arisen, so can one such as she. We know it. We feel it. Together, we will rule again.*

I want to tell her I have no intention of ruling alongside

anyone, let alone their pet Mage. That I'm sick and tired of people using me. But to do that, I have to free myself.

With all my might, I fight to peel off the clinging tendrils of darkness that hold me. I crawl out of the shadows, toward her voice. *Let me go,* I snarl. *Let me out.*

For a moment, my eyelids flicker open and I catch sight of her: a tall woman, dressed in red, the same one who deflected the blades I hurled at Mei. Her hair is woven in elaborate braids. Her angular, lined face is inches from mine.

She blinks down at me, surprise in her dark eyes. "So strong," she says, smiling. "That's good, Eva. Your strength is what we need. When we're ready, we will harness it. We will use it to aid your Executor in defeating the Houses, and in turn, he will cede them to us. And then we will take you home again. And the Houses will bow before us."

"I'll never help you," I force out between cracked lips. "I'll... die first."

But maybe I only think it. Because the smile on her face doesn't fade, even as the dreaded needle plunges into my arm. And down I go again.

CHAPTER 23

ARI

We ride out at dawn, many of us on horseback and the rest on foot. Kilían and Jaxon are with us, their wounds mostly healed by the Mages' compounds. Adelman travels with us too, though the rest of the Council of Nine stays behind, along with the selkies and some of the guards, to protect the city and the skúma children. Eldrina and her falcons fly ahead of us, close enough that they can still access their familiars but far enough to scout what lies beyond.

And of course, there's Sebastían, riding silent and watchful by my side. We conferred quickly as we saddled up; neither of us have been able to sense Eva.

It's like she's nowhere. Not accessible through the bond, no matter how hard I try or how loudly I call out for her. Not visible in the tracks the Mages' party left behind, retracing the path we took when we first came to Vik. I can't shake the feeling that something's terribly wrong. That we're not getting any closer to her, no matter how far we travel.

Last night, Sebastían and I briefly considered trying to go it on our own. At least that way, we wouldn't be so conspicuous. If we were able to retrieve Eva, we'd be depriving the Mages of their greatest weapon. Then, we could bring her back to Vik, regroup, and plan the invasion...the right way, this time.

It was a sound plan. But the last thing we needed was for the Brotherhood to split their forces in search of the Panther of the West, which meant bringing our proposal to the Council for their approval. And no matter what reasoning we offered—including the idiocy of leaving the young skúma children unprotected, except for by Vik's wards and a small complement of guards—we couldn't win them over. Adelman was dead-set on riding out to rescue Cordelia, and with Satrizona on board, no one else wanted to be deprived of the glory. So here we are, marching to war against an enemy we can't see and potentially riding right into a trap.

Fantastic.

As I attempted to impress upon the Council, it would be a sound strategy on the Mages' part to leave a false trail in the direction of the Commonwealth, while a complement of forces circles back to invade Vik. Sure, they can't get in without help—but what if Mei's family turns traitor, in an effort to bring her back into the fold? What if they were concealing their true allegiance all along? Ronan left them under guard, but as we saw when the Executor escaped, guards can be drugged. Or killed.

The thought of Eva, unconscious and vulnerable after that bitch Mei injected her with the Architect knows what, being hauled into Vik like an inanimate object, fills me with rage. I imagine the Executor taking Adelman's seat in the Great Hall, those red-clothed women flanking him around the Council's table, the skúma children being caged and exploited, and am hard-pressed not to stab something.

I can tell Kilían shares my misgivings, but he hasn't spoken up. Maybe he thinks it's not his place; maybe he thinks this is a doomed venture no matter what avenue we take. Or maybe his head is so clouded by his feelings for my father that he's not thinking clearly. I want to confront him about what I overheard, to demand to know what he'll do if Kennett falls, but now is not the time. I feel like I'm living in the cautionary tale the Mothers used to tell us, the one about the woman who predicted the future and was ignored again and again. And look what happened to her: raped, enslaved, and murdered in the wake of a war she fought to prevent.

All of which is to say, I'm in a terrible mood as our army canters through the first mountain pass, which is wide enough to accommodate two horses riding side by side. This high up, snow's already begun to fall, dusting our shoulders as we ride along the trail. The ground is a mess, but the trampled earth and disturbed vegetation reveal that a sizable group of people has come this way, moving fast...which would seem to indicate that we're on the right track.

There are no imprints of horses' hooves, though, just footprints, which baffles me: if they're walking, how have we not caught up to them yet? And even the footprints are strange: scattered here and there, uneven and rushed. None of it makes any sense.

I say as much to Sebastían, who reins up and dismounts as the path opens into a valley. Since we're riding at the head of the column, this means everyone behind us has to come to a halt, but for once, I don't mind the Panther of the West's high-handedness.

He bends and sniffs the ground. When he straightens, his brows are knitted. "I smell Mages," he says, lip curling in a snarl. "Including Mei. Others, not Mage or skúma—exiles, perhaps? But I don't smell your Executor. Or Eva, either. And"— his voice catches as his gaze shifts toward Layla, who's come up next to him, leading her horse, "I don't smell Erdahl. Do you?"

She imitates his gesture, black hair sweeping the snow-dusted earth as she inhales. Her shoulders slump, and when she stands, the dark circles under her eyes send a pang through me. I may not be her biggest fan, but the grief that roils off her is palpable. "No," is all she says.

The boy is likely dead. The chilling crack when his head hit those stones will haunt me for the rest of my life. But without a body, we have no proof. And Layla and Riley will never stop hunting for him.

My mind churns, sorting through and discarding possibilities. "You can't detect the Executor or Eva," I say, fighting to keep my voice level. "So...what if neither of them came this way? What if it's what I suggested before: this route is a distraction, with some of the Mages laying a false trail for us to follow while the rest circle back to Vik with their captives?"

Kilían reins up next to me. Snow flecks his red hair and his short beard. It dots his eyelashes, so that he has to blink a couple of times to clear his vision. He looks, I think with faint amusement, like a speckled red owl...if said owl was capable of deadly violence. "Westergaard has a fair point," he says.

I nod, grateful for his support even if I still question where his loyalties will ultimately lie. "Right. I should go on ahead, with Sebastían." It grates on me to say so, but our partnership, however fraught, is Eva's best chance at survival. "We're the ones who have the ability to track Eva. Give us Kilían and a complement of guards; that's all we'll need. But the rest of you —you should turn back to make sure Vik and the children are safe. I don't like the feeling of this."

Layla pales, white as the snow that streaks her cheeks. She remounts her horse, as does Sebastían, but neither of them make a move to ride out. Instead, she turns her gaze on me. It's gone a baleful wolf-amber, like this virtueless situation is all my fault.

"I am not beating a coward's retreat while those monsters might be torturing my son!" she hisses. "Besides, how would the Mages know we'd left the children behind, rather than bringing them along under heavy guard?"

"Because," I say, holding on to my patience and my horse's reins with an effort, "they have spies. Or have you forgotten?"

Ronan, who's ridden ahead with Jaxon, scouting the valley, circles back. "Let's not get ahead of ourselves," he says, making an obvious effort to sound conciliatory, before war erupts right here in the valley. "We have spies of our own, Westergaard: Eldrina's falcons. They would've alerted us if there was the slightest evidence of such a thing."

"Unless the Mages were able to conceal their presence," I argue. "Who knows what they're capable of?" A truly disturbing thought occurs to me then. "What if some of the Mages are coming at us from the rear? What if the ones whose trail we're following are lying in wait, to make us the meat of a very bloody sandwich? Your stubborn posturing is going to get us—"

I'm about to say something truly regrettable when Jaxon, who's come up next to me, places a hand on my arm. "Look," he says.

I shake him off, and my horse whinnies, as if it's absorbed my agitation. "*You* look, idiot. I'm sick and tired of—"

He rolls his eyes at me, then points upward, at the gray sky, scribbled with white. "No, *look.*"

Aggravated, I comply. And then I see what he's indicating, high above, silhouetted against the snow.

That damned raven is back again. And not just one, either.

It's a damned conspiracy of them, coming from behind us— from the direction of Vik. They soar over our party, almost clipping the scrubby trees that are brave enough to take root in the valley's rocky soil.

"What in the sins-forsaken—"

It's all I have time to say before the birds are upon us,

descending even lower with a deafening flap of wings. I say a lot more, then, but it's lost in the melee, and a good thing, too.

They fly low, blocking out our view of the sky. Beneath me, my horse whinnies, tossing his head, and I keep a tight grip on the reins, holding him steady when he threatens to bolt. Next to me, Jaxon is cursing, calling the birds names and describing vividly what he'd like to do to them. Sebastían and Layla cover their heads, pressed almost flat to their horses' backs, as the birds pass over us, a moving, cawing blanket of beaks and talons and feathers. Kilían is yelling and Ronan is hollering and I swear to the Architect I can't take a single solitary second more—

And then, as suddenly as they came, the birds take flight, arrowing toward the pale winter sky in unison. The air falls silent, other than Jaxon's muttered expletives and the horses' disgruntled whinnies. Even Kilían and Ronan have stopped shouting.

I watch the ravens rise, eyes narrowed. And then, my hand making the decision before my mind, I pull my dagur free. Holding my horse steady with the other hand, I aim at the lead bird, the point of the arrow. And I let my blade fly.

It soars true, a flash of silver against the gunmetal-gray sky. And finds its mark.

The bird plummets downward, trying and failing to spread its wings. It falls past its brethren, a smudge tumbling through the whirl of snow. I swing off my horse just in time for the bird to thump, an ungainly heap of coal-black feathers, onto the ground at my feet.

That breaks the silence. Now Sebastían is squawking louder than the damn raven, demanding to know what the hell. Jaxon's cursing again, this time in admiration at my aim. Layla, Ronan, and Adrien and Fade, who were riding behind us, won't shut up: *Why* and *so impulsive* and *how in the name of the many-headed gods?*

Ignoring all of them, I kneel on the snow-dusted ground next to the bird. My blade caught it through the wing, a lucky shot. It's alive, as I intended, though blood pools beneath it, seeping into the earth.

Kilían kneels beside me. One glance, and I know we're thinking the same thing.

The raven's sides heave. Its beak opens, gasping for air. When its beady eyes find mine, sharp with intelligence and calculation, I know for sure this is no ordinary bird.

It flaps feebly, trying to get free, but I grasp the hilt of my blade, pinioning it to the ground. "Tell me what you've done with Eva," I say. "And I will let you live."

CHAPTER 24

EVA

I come to at last with a start, and find myself in the wreckage of an abandoned building, holes blasted in the walls and paint peeling off whatever remains. The air reeks of rot, sulfur, and the now-familiar scent of roses and anise that indicates the presence of Mage magic.

Lifting my head, which seems to weigh a thousand pounds, I look around. I'm sitting on the floor, my arms bound behind me. When I twist my head, I can make out what they're tied to: an exposed support beam that runs from floor to ceiling. I'm propped against the beam, which bites into my back. My legs are stretched out in front of me, my feet bound at the ankles with a rough hemp rope, tied to a metal ring affixed to the floor. I'm immobilized.

I'm also alone.

Through the shattered window across from me, a hint of blue gleams at ground level—maybe a river or a lake. Rumor has it the Empire is bordered by oceans, but I've never seen one. Certainly not in the Commonwealth, and not the only time I've left it, when we journeyed to Vik. Mei told me once that San Fraesco sits on the edge of the westerly ocean, and that the selkies swim through part of the city that's underwater. She said there are ships buried beneath the pavement, relics of an earlier time when explorers sought gold. At the time, it sounded magical to me.

Mei.

The thought of her sends a sick bolt of rage through me. She's got to be here somewhere. If only I could get loose, I could have my revenge.

I strain against my bonds, but they refuse to give. Maybe they're magically influenced. Or maybe I'm just weakened by whatever's in that damn syringe they keep stabbing me with. Pulled taut behind my back, my arms ache, the muscles trembling. How long have I been tied this way?

The room is empty, other than a rolling chair near the window, the floor scattered with trash. There's nothing I could use as a weapon, even if I could reach it. And, with the drugs still in my system and Ari nowhere to be found, I'm not much of a weapon myself. Which means that the only thing I can use, the only way to help myself, is to get information.

"Hello?" My voice cracks, my mouth dry with thirst. I can't remember the last time I ate or drank. Maybe they've been feeding me while I'm unconscious, dripping water down my throat. "Anyone?"

I don't know who I expect. The red-clothed woman, maybe. Or Mei herself. What I get instead is the Executor, who strolls through the doorway as if he's been expecting my call.

He looks...well. His dark eyes are sharp, his skin clear, his carriage upright, as if I never tore into his belly with my teeth at all. "You're awake," he says. "Good. I was beginning to wonder if Dresda had given you too much."

Dresda, I assume, is the red-clad woman. But her name is the least of my problems. "Where am I?" I demand.

"Oh...between." He shrugs, pulling up the lone chair and

taking a seat three feet away from me. The chair's wheels roll over the bits of plaster on the cracked linoleum as he edges a bit closer, making an unpleasant crunching sound that reminds me of the rattling of bones. "Does that matter, Eva? Or would you prefer to know why you're here?"

What I really want to know is where Ari is. If he lives. But if I show him how much the question matters to me, there's no way he'll answer it. Or he'll leverage Ari somehow to hurt me.

"If *Dresda* is the woman who's been speaking in my head, then she made it clear enough. You want to use me to defeat the Houses," I say, straining to keep my head upright against the beam. To meet his eyes and stop my words from slurring. "And you've offered the Mages power in return. They help you; you give them what they want: to control the skúma once more. Which begs the question—did you enlist them to kidnap me for your own benefit, or for theirs?"

He stares at me. And then he starts to laugh. The cackle fills the shattered space, bouncing off the walls. Even in human form and with my senses dulled by the drugs, my hearing is still sensitive. My hands twitch, straining to cover my ears.

"Too smart for your own good," he says when he winds down. "Then again, you always were. My genes at work, no doubt."

At the thought of his blood running through my body, I want to open my veins. "Answer the question."

The Exccutor folds his hands in his lap, prim as a child during story-time with the Mothers. "Both," he says. "Dresda spoke the truth. I will use you, and them, to defeat the Houses. When all is said and done, and the Houses and skúma are no longer a threat, then the Mages can have them, to do as they will. It's no concern of mine."

To do as they will. He means to rule, to reduce the skúma to no more than magical tools. "Except, of course, that your daughter is a skúma," I say, forcing out the words. "I suppose I'll be no concern of yours, then, either?"

"That is a sticky wicket," the Executor muses, steepling his hands beneath his chin. "But you know, Eva, it's not like we've ever been close. I suppose I could visit, if you expect you'll miss me that much."

A growl rips from between my lips as I strain against my bonds, and the Executor rolls backward in his chair. His muscles tense, and I hear his uneven heartbeat pick up speed. The fibers of the rope bite into my ankles and wrists, rubbing my skin raw. But I can't get free, no matter how hard I try.

I slump backward, against the beam, and his body relaxes, his eyes holding a glint of humor. "No?" he says. "Ah, well. A father can dream."

"And my *mother?* Cordelia? You're just going to give her to the Mages, after everything you said to me in Vik's infirmary?"

That glint of humor fades, replaced by icy rage. "She's told me time and time again that she wants only to go home," he bites out. "So...let her."

The thought of meeting the mother I only recently learned existed, only to be condemned into bondage alongside her, sends nausea roiling through me. I draw a deep breath, sucking in sulfur, anise, and the faint scent of salt and brine, from the body of water I can glimpse through the window. Even sedated as she is, my selkie lifts her head, yearning for it. For freedom. There hasn't been much use for her in Vik, and though she's bided her time, I can feel her impatience. *Selkies are strategists,* she whispers, coaxing. *I can help you.*

How far does that river or lake or whatever it is go? If I could get to it, could I swim to safety?

As soon as the idea occurs to me, I dismiss it. Without Ari, I can't shift. I'm a good swimmer even in human form, but there's too much I don't know. Where I am, for starters. How many people have me prisoner, and what their capabilities are. Not to mention, I'm drugged and tied hand and foot.

Plus, I don't trust my own judgment when it comes to taking risks. I was so sure I was right about retrieving Erdahl, but my beasts led me into that circle of standing stones, where the Mages were waiting to ambush me. They led me here: trapped and at a monster's mercy. The lines between us are blurred, and I can't be sure I'm thinking clearly.

I grit my teeth and try to focus on what I *can* do. Which, right now, is limited to dragging intel out of the man I hate the most. And in the end, I can't resist asking about Ari, after all. "You do realize that if you plan to use me to power an epic battle against the Houses and skúma, I'll need my familiar. What have you done with him?"

The Executor raises his dark, arched eyebrows, so like my own. "What have *I* done with him? Why, nothing, Eva. Nothing at all."

My eyes burn. I tell myself it's from the scent of sulfur that pervades the room, not from impending tears. "The Mages, then. Have they hurt him? Do they have him? *Where is he?*"

"Ari Westergaard does me no good if he is damaged," the Executor says mildly. "Surely you realize that."

"Nor do I. But look at *me.*"

"So dramatic, Eva. You're not damaged. Just...temporarily restrained. And can you blame us? The very qualities that make you such an asset make you a threat as well. Think of poor Karsten. And that guard, Mateo." He makes a tsk-ing sound, as if I'm a naughty girl who's been caught sneaking additional turns with the Nursery's communal teddy bear. "So wasteful."

"I owed Karsten. He got what was coming to him. And Mateo hurt a *child*. A child you arranged to have kidnapped." I swallow, an effort given the desiccated state of my mouth, and ask the other question whose answer I've been dreading. "Is Erdahl dead, then?"

The Executor regards me with pity. "This is what you get for becoming attached to people, Eva. Here you are, tied hand and foot. You should be concerned about your own wellbeing. And what are you doing but inquiring after the welfare of a boy and a bellator who's shown that he's perfectly capable of taking care of himself."

Surely Ari isn't dead. Surely I would feel it if he was. So where is he? He must be looking for me. No matter how angry he is with me, he wouldn't just abandon me to my fate.

And Sebastían...he must be searching for me, too. I think of that panther roaming through the woods, calling *Carina.* Was that real, or just a fever dream?

I force my breathing to calm. Force myself to listen, to hear what's beyond this room: the scurrying of feet, the thump of heartbeats, the low murmur of conversation. To *think.*

I have some of the pieces of this puzzle. But others are still missing. And knowledge is power. Unless, of course, he's lying to me.

"I can see you have more questions," the Executor says, giving me the insincere smile I've always hated. *Bees that have honey in their mouths conceal stings in their tails,* as Efraím used to say. "So, ask them, while I'm in an answering kind of mood."

I'd rather bite off his tongue than have to listen to him anymore. But who knows how much time I have before Mei or the red-clad woman come back in with their virtueless syringes. So I look into those flat, obsidian eyes and speak. "The exiles who killed our scouts. What role do they play in all of this?"

He lounges back in his chair, feet crossed at the ankles. Wind blows through the window, stirring the trash that litters the floor: bits of cloth and torn paper and plaster. The gust isn't as cold as I'd expect, which begs the question—are we traveling southward? How far have we gone?

How much time has passed since I've been taken?

"Those poor souls," the Executor says, managing to sound almost compassionate. "All they want, like Cordelia, is to go home again."

I jerk back, the rope digging into my wrists anew, as the meaning of his words breaks over me. "You told them that, if they aligned with the Mages and fought alongside you, you'd grant them permission to return to their Commonwealths. The other Commonwealths' Executors defer to you. If you say so, they'd let these exiles back in. Am I right?"

"Perspicacious as always," he says, smiling at me as if I've passed a particularly challenging Trial. "Unlike you and me, Eva, most people are not shepherds. They are sheep, and all they want is to return to the fold."

Damn him to the nine hells and back again. "I'm not a shep-herd." I bare my teeth, a growl rumbling up from my chest again. "I'm the wolf, and you'd do well to remember it."

His scent changes, sharpening until I can taste the acrid bite of fear. His smile fades. "A wolf in chains," he says, nodding at my bonds. "And you'd do well to remember *that*. Good night, Eva."

He rises from the chair and strides from the room without another word, leaving me alone again. I can hear him muttering to someone outside the door, hear a woman respond. It's *her* voice—Dresda's.

Good night, the Executor said. But it's not night, not in the slightest. Light streams through the shattered window, the sun sparkling on the slice of blue water and illuminating the corners of the room. Which can mean only one thing; she plans to drug me again.

The Executor's voice retreats. Outside the doorway, I hear

the thump of Dresda's heart, fast but even. I focus, committing the pattern to memory. If I hear it again, even with all my other senses compromised, I will recognize it. I will recognize *her*.

The scent of roses and anise sharpens as she stalks into the room, and the breeze stirs once again. The trash on the floor scatters as she advances, as if she's commanded it. Perhaps she has. Inside me, my wolf stirs, the hackles on her neck rising. *Threat*, she warns me. *To us. To our pack. Do not trust her.*

I didn't need my wolf's warning to understand this. *The strength of the pack is the wolf, and the strength of the wolf is the pack*, Gertrud used to say when she was training me. Gertrud, who's gone, just like Efraím. It's from an old book, one written long, long ago. But where is my strength now, if I am without my pack? And where is my pack's strength, without me? What is left of it? Do Riley and Layla live?

Dresda walks closer, until she's standing close enough to touch—that is, if I could move. Her hair is still in that complicated updo, her face as angular as a fox's and her eyes just as cunning. But when she speaks, all she says is, "Hello, Eva. How do you feel?"

"How do you think I feel? Untie me!" I yank against the bonds again. "Dresda, is it? Are you so foolish as to believe whatever the Executor promises you? You've gotten into bed with a snake. You're going to climb out poisoned. Whatever he's told you, it's all lies."

She smiles at me, but it doesn't reach her eyes. "One day, you'll understand, Eva. He may be using us, but we're using him as well. So we dedicate our gifts to his service once; that's a small price to pay for an eternity of strength the likes of which we have only dreamed."

This woman is as deluded and power-hungry as the Executor is. I draw a deep breath, ignoring the way the scent of anise and sulfur scorches my lungs, and try again. "And what about me? What possible motivation do I have to cooperate with you, if you intend to enslave me and all the people I care about?"

One of her long-fingered hands lifts, stroking my hair. I try to jerk away, to bite her, but my head is still so very heavy. It flops to the side, and she sighs, as if exasperated with my failure to understand. "You've got it all wrong, Eva. It's your kind who wants to enslave us. To chain us. You exiled us to the woods. You bound our magic. For centuries we have labored in obscurity. We only want what belongs to us. Our birthright."

"But I didn't do any of that," I protest. "I didn't ask to be what I am." I tilt my head, listening for all I'm worth, but don't hear the Executor's uneven, lolloping heartbeat. Still, I whisper my next words. "If what you say is true, then maybe we can broker an understanding. We can work together. The Houses need me. If I tell them how you feel, then maybe they'll cooperate. They'll let you back in. You don't need to ally yourself with a man like this—"

Dresda reclaims her hand. "This man is your father, no?"

"Only in name! I'm nothing like him. I can't stand him. The way he was hurt when Mei first brought him to you—I did that. I want him dead. Helping him is the worst mistake you could make." I inject all the sincerity I feel into my voice, willing her to believe it.

"You say he is a snake. But so are your precious Houses. You weren't born there, Eva, so perhaps you can be forgiven for your lack of understanding. You are naïve if you believe they will ever help us. You are a fool." Her eyes travel over my body, shining with contempt. "And if you think I believe you will truly ever help us—that your offer is a true one—then you must think I am a fool, too. Just...like...you." Her voice drops, low and mocking. She bends, her next words issuing inches from my ear, so I can't escape them. "Look at you, helpless and at my mercy, thinking you have anything to bargain with. Look how you walked, stupid and blinded by your arrogance and your desire to save that boy, into the trap we set."

I work my mouth, summoning all the saliva I can muster, and spit into her face. She recoils in shock, and then her jaw sets. Her hand carves a swath through the air, etching a complicated pattern, a second before the wind rises, propelling a chunk of plaster upward from the floor. It slams into my cheek, with such force my head rocks back and strikes the beam. Pain radiates from both points of impact, and I grit my teeth, determined not to let it show. I can feel blood trickling down the back of my neck, warm and sticky.

Dresda straightens, wiping her cheek clean with her sleeve. "We have waited for so long to reclaim our full powers. Even with you weakened this way, we are stronger." She raises her hand again, and bits of paper, cloth, and plaster lift, swirling in mid-air. As I watch, they fall to the floor again, this time in the shape of a wolf. "We are made to fight alongside each other, your kind and mine. We don't have to be enemies, Eva."

I glare at her, my cheek stinging and my head aching, and make no effort to reply.

"I see you don't agree. But the fact of the matter is, when we're able to harness your gifts, there will be no limit to what we can do. What we're capable of. And we won't need to ask for your cooperation then. As for now..."

She fishes in the pocket of her red tunic. When she withdraws her hand, it holds another one of those syringes. I fight and twist against my bonds, but it's no use: they hold just as steady as they did before. A wave of her free hand, and they tighten even further, biting into my skin. The scent of anise heightens, a miasma so thick I almost choke.

"Not much longer, Eva," she croons, bending over me again.

I can feel her hot breath on my face, redolent of roses, as if she's swallowed them. "Not much farther now."

Her hand comes down, the silver syringe gleaming in the sunlight. I cling to my surroundings: the brine-laced breeze that washes over my face, sweeping away the reek of magic; the throb of my bruised skull; the trash-wolf on the filthy floor. I will myself to stay. But as the needle pierces my upper arm, as the familiar dizziness threatens to overtake me, I'm fighting a losing battle.

The room fades to gray, its details obscured by a storm of static. Dresda's face recedes, as if disappearing down a long, dark tunnel. I slump against my bonds, welcoming the pain of the rope as it bites into my wrists and ankles, trying desperately to cling to consciousness.

Then, through the haze that fogs my mind, I see Dresda's face go blank, wiped clean of expression. Her hand rises to her throat, and she coughs, falling to her knees atop the rubble-wolf. Her eyes flutter shut. When they open again, they're glazed with pain.

I can't raise my head. It's all I can do to shift my gaze left, then right, to try and locate whatever—*whoever*—might have caused this. But there's no one. And when I drag air into my lungs, I don't smell an intruder.

Am I hallucinating this?

"What do you want?" The words sound like they're being torn from her throat. She isn't talking to me.

There's a long pause. And then, I hear a voice that has no business in this room, coming from everywhere and nowhere at once. *Ari's* voice.

"Answers," he says.

CHAPTER 25

ARI

"What do you want?" the bird croaks, its avid, greedy gaze fixed on my face.

I *knew* it. "Answers," I demand, leaning into the blade.

Ronan gives a snort of disbelief, but I pay him no mind. Next to me, Kilían's silent and still, his attention focused on the raven with the cold ferocity I associate with the Lead Interrogator at his most dangerous. Any lingering animosity I have for him dissipates, replaced with fierce relief. Both of us are out of our depth here, but other than Eva, there's no one I'd rather have by my side.

The sins-forsaken bird doesn't comply. Instead, it caws a harsh, unnerving laugh. Sebastían, who's knelt on my other side, begins to growl, so loudly the vibration shakes the earth beneath us. I swear, if he shifts and eats this damn bird before I get my answers, I'll pull my blade out of the raven's wing and sink it into his heart.

I elbow him in the ribs, a stop-gap measure. "Shut up. I need to listen."

By a miracle, he complies, the growl breaking off. "I smell anise," he says. "And roses. This is that red-robed bitch's work, I'd stake my House on it."

I know which one he means. The one who stood at the apex of the phalanx; the leader. It confirms what I suspected from the moment that damned flock of birds descended on us, flying from the direction of Vik. Mocking us.

"Stop laughing," I tell the raven. "Or..." I lean into the blade, feeling a dim sense of guilt for hurting an animal. After all, it didn't ask to be possessed this way. But I would do far worse, if it meant finding a clue that would lead me to Eva.

The bird gives a squawk of pain, and the pool of blood seeping from beneath it widens. If there's one thing I've learned about magic, it's that unless the relationship is consensual, whoever's utilizing it pays a cost. I'd wager the pain the raven feels is echoed by the Mage who's possessing it. Which is some-thing, at long-godsdamned-last, that I can use.

Its head jerks, its gaze fixing over my shoulder. I turn and look, but there's nothing behind me but Jaxon, Ronan, Layla, and the guards.

"Is this what you want to know?" the bird says, its voice half-scorn, half-agony. "Look, then."

The world around me—gray sky, drifting snow, mountain crags—falls away with an alarming sense of vertigo. Then I am inside the bird somehow, seeing through its eyes. I see an empty, half-built room, scattered with debris. A window, bits of glass clinging to its edges. And then, sitting on the floor, her arms bound behind her and her ankles tied together, I see Eva.

One of her cheeks is bruised, her black hair stuck to the other one with maybe sweat or maybe blood. Her head droops, as if controlling it is an effort. She isn't straining against her bonds, trying to get away; she's sagging in them.

Those bastards still have her drugged.

Rage whips through me, and I speak not to the accursed bird but to the girl I love. "Eva."

CHAPTER 26

EVA

Dresda bursts into harsh, hoarse barks of laughter. Then her head jerks to the side, an unnatural movement, as if wrenched by an external force. Her eyes scan the room, flitting from floor to walls to window, until finally coming to rest on me.

"Is this what you want to know?" she spits to her invisible interlocutor. "Look, then."

Her weight shifts, the bits of the rubble-wolf scattering as her eyes bore into my face. Even if this is a fever-dream, even if I'm still lashed hand and foot, a smile lifts my lips. I like seeing her on her knees. I like it a lot. And if the way my wolf and panther growl in approval at the sight is any indication, they like it just fine, too.

There's a pause. And then Ari's voice comes again, this time threaded with fury. "Eva," he says.

The darkness reaches for me, wrapping inexorable tendrils around my limbs. But I can't go. Not until I discover if this is real.

CHAPTER 27
ARI

Eva's head comes up at the sound of my voice, her gaze sharpens, and for a moment I could swear she hears me. I see her fighting the effects of the drug, her body tensing against her bonds. But then her eyes flutter shut. She blinks them open again, but they're glazed, as if it's taking everything she has to stay awake.

"Where are you?" I demand. "Tell me!"

Her mouth opens. Shuts. A small smile lifts her lips, but she doesn't say a word. I don't think she can.

I'm going to kill these people when I find them. In cold blood, and slowly. Right after I finish disemboweling the Executor. The list is getting longer by the moment.

"Ask about Erdahl," Layla begs me. "Ask the raven if he lives."

I open my mouth to do just that. But the bird, as if programmed to self-destruct, shifts against the blade impaled in its wing, impaling itself further. It coughs once, then twice, and dies in a puddle of blood and feathers.

CHAPTER 28

EVA

Ari's not here. He can't be.

It's just my mind, inventing what I want to hear most as the drugs wreak havoc on my system. As I fight them. It has to be, because the last thing I see before my eyes flutter shut is Dresda on her hands and knees in the rubble, coughing up black feathers coated in blood. And *that* cannot be real.

He may not be here, but he's searching for me. I'd bet my lost sverd on it. And what will happen when he finds me? What price will he pay?

I can't bear to hurt him. Not anymore. Not again.

But if it's not me, then it will be someone. Because if the Executor and the Mages plan to enslave me, they'll hold Ari captive right by my side. I couldn't stand that idea all those months ago, in the scholar's room, when I pulled the pin on the smoke grenade so Ari could go free. It makes me even sicker now, after all we've been through. After he's confessed that he loves me, and I've told him the same.

He's angry, sure. But above all else, he is loyal. He'll come for me, and then they'll use him as leverage to make me do what they want. Refuse, and they'll torture him. Agree, and I'll play right into their hands.

Aut viam inveniam aut faciam, Efraím used to tell us. *I will either find a way or make one.* I may not be able to save myself, but maybe I can still save Ari. Maybe, just like I did before, I can protect him and the cause for which we both fight.

I am the lynchpin on which this awful plan turns. Without me, the Executor loses his bargaining chip. The Mages lose their source of power. But if I become a martyr while Cordelia lives, the Houses will still go to war.

As I spiral down into the cold, beckoning darkness, the knowledge comes to me, cold as ice and just as clear.

I have tried fighting, bargaining, conniving. I have bled and I have begged. Now, much as it guts me, there is only one thing left for me to do.

I need to die.

CHAPTER 29

ARI

We all stand there, staring down at the dead bird. Finally Jaxon says, "Damn, exile. Didn't anyone ever tell you not to shoot the messenger?"

No one ever has. Quite the opposite, in fact. But apparently, this is a joke, because the tense silence breaks. Ronan, Jaxon, Adrien, and Fade all give an uneasy laugh, while Kilían and I share a confused glance. Even Sebastían chuckles, though I've come to notice there's a strange tension between him and Jaxon, something I can't quite put my finger on.

Even though he and I might not get the joke, Kilían taught me the benefit of such things himself: offer people humor in the midst of terror, and they'll endure long past the point where they'd usually fold. But Layla, who didn't get an answer to her question about Erdahl, isn't amused. She stalks forward, pissed off as an angel of vengeance, hands clenched into fists. "You find this *funny*?" she hisses.

Ronan and the rest sober immediately. "Of course not," the captain of the guard says. "Our apologies."

Layla looks mollified, until Kilían opens his mouth. "Granted," he says, prodding the bird's corpse with his foot, "the timing was unfortunate."

With that, Layla detonates. Her eyes go full wolf-amber, she bares teeth that look more like fangs, and when she opens her mouth, what comes out is a shriek of pure rage. "Unfortunate? *Unfortunate?* Is that what you call it? Emotionless Commonwealth scum...!"

She'd probably say a lot more, but Riley emerges from the crowd that's gathered around us and grabs her by the arm. He hauls her off, still spitting curses and invective at Kilían. The Lead Interrogator just stares at Layla, one red eyebrow raised, looking somewhere between bemused and like he's plotting to vivisect her. To say he's not used to people screaming insults at him is an understatement. I'd laugh, if I weren't on the verge of my own explosion. Instead, I kneel, pulling my blade free of the bird and wiping it on the snow-coated grass.

"Where was that building?" I say to Ronan, fighting to keep my voice level. "Did you recognize it?"

He gives me an odd glance. "You mean you saw through her eyes? Is that what she meant when she said, 'Look, then'?"

"You didn't?" I sheath my blade and peer upward to see the flock of ravens still hovering overhead, as if planning our demise.

Ronan shakes his head, and when I glance around at Kilían, Jaxon, and the rest, they look similarly clueless. So, either the Mage granted me the ability to see Eva's surroundings, or it had something to do with our bond. If the latter is the case, then two other things must be true: the bond is still intact enough to connect us, and my tie to her is stronger than Sebastían's. Which means that in our little game of who-can-find-Eva first, odds are I'll win.

The competitive part of me—the bellator trained to best his comrades—gloats over this. So does the part of me that doesn't want to cede any advantage to the Panther of the West. But most of me just wants to rescue Eva from these bastards' clutches, no matter what it takes. With that in mind, I stand and describe everything I saw. By the time I'm done, Sebastían is growling again. Quite frankly, I don't blame him.

"They will pay for this," he says, his claws slipping his skin and his eyes fading from aquamarine to the lucent green of his panther. His pupils blow wide, giving him the unmistakable appearance of a cat hunting in the dead of night.

I huff a bitter laugh. "For the second time, you and I completely agree."

"An abandoned building like the one Ari described..." Ronan says, turning to Jaxon. "Can you think of one within fifty miles?"

"No." Jaxon clears his throat. "Westergaard, you remember when we came this way before. Those buildings are in the ruins of large cities. If that's truly where Eva and the Mages are, then they're moving at a speed that would be impossible to achieve even on horseback."

Kilían looks skyward, where the flock of ravens looms above us. "Maybe that's why Sebastían and Layla can't smell Eva. Because her feet aren't touching the ground."

"Not touching the..." I swallow hard, inspecting the path the Mages took through the valley with fresh eyes. I'd attributed the bent branches and scattering of leaves to the poor weather, but what if the Mages had been able to harness the wind, propelling themselves far faster than they could have traveled otherwise, buoying Eva above the earth?

"I hate this sins-cursed magic," I grit out from between clenched teeth.

Jaxon rolls his eyes at me. "Yeah, well, I don't consider it a party, either. But we know she's alive, exile. We have a vague sense of where she is. It's better than nothing."

"What would be *better* would be if she wasn't tied to a pole, drugged out of her mind," I snap. "I still think we need to check to make sure they haven't split their party to invade Vik. We haven't gone that far; someone could ride back without delaying us that badly."

"All right." Ronan squares his shoulders. I can read his face like a book: *Westergaard was right before. I'm not going to ignore him twice.* It should feel like a victory, but all I feel instead is simmering rage. "I'll send a rider."

"I'll go," Adrien volunteers, patting his horse on the neck. "Flame's faster than most. But keep the army moving; I'll catch you up. I've traveled this way often enough."

Adrien mounts up and rides out of the valley, back into the pass. I watch as he flanks the column of guards, skúma, scouts, and medics that make up our traveling party—some on foot, some on horseback. Councilor Adelman himself is riding in the middle of the column, protected on all sides, too far back to witness our encounter with the raven.

Drawing a deep breath, I let my eyes rove over the valley: snow-dusted crags in the distance, scrubby trees weaving in the wind. It's unforgiving here, no hint of the beauty we saw when we came through these same mountains just a couple of months before. As unforgiving as the foes we face.

Around me, Kilían, Ronan, Jaxon, and Sebastían are remounting their horses. The crowd disperses, falling back into the rhythm of an army on the move. I boost myself onto Tucker, his bulk reassuringly solid beneath me. Ronan and Jaxon take point, and we move out again, cantering through the valley.

But we haven't gone more than five minutes before hoof-beats thud behind us on the packed earth. Adrien and Flame skid to a halt beside us, the horse's hooves sending a spray of pebbles flying in every direction.

"Ronan," he says, panting. "We can't turn around. I didn't

even get all the way down the column before they told me. The message came up from the back of the lines. That invisible barrier you told us about, the one in the stone circle...it's something like that, I think. We have no choice but to go forward. We can't get through."

"You mean we can't get back to Vik," Ronan says slowly.

Adrien nods, his forehead wet with sweat. It mingles with the snow, dripping onto his black jacket. "They're driving us," he manages. "Maybe...maybe the birds..."

I glance up at the ravens, their ink-dark bodies outlined against the snow-bleached sky. As if they can hear us, they re-form in the shape of an arrow, pointing the way out of the valley.

Bastards. "I could shoot them," I offer. "If the Mages are channeling their power through the ravens, then if all the birds were dead..."

Grimly, Ronan shakes his head again. "They'd just find others. No, it's obvious what they intend. They want us to go after Eva, to invade the Commonwealth. They're waiting for us."

"Is it a trap," Kilían muses, "if you walk into it willingly?"

"I don't know," I say. "But there's a reason a group of ravens is called a treachery. And we can't stay here."

Ronan nods grimly, then turns, shouting back along the column, loud enough to be heard over the wind. "If we can't turn back, we must face what lies in front of us. Ride on."

CHAPTER 30

EVA

When I wake, I'm no longer tied to that beam.

I'm in a cage of a different kind. A literal one, this time.

My tongue sticks to the roof of my mouth. My head aches. I feel hollowed out, empty. But I'm awake and unbound, and right now, that's all that matters. To enact the rest of my plan, I need to be conscious.

I struggle to my feet. The world swims as I tug myself upward, and my legs tremble as I peer through the bars.

And then I blink, and blink again. Because nothing I see makes any sense.

I can see through the bars on three sides of the cage, into the room that surrounds me. There's a wheeled partition on the fourth side, outside the bars, blocking me from seeing whatever lies beyond. It doesn't go all the way to the ceiling, but neither does my cage. The barred roof is about eight feet high, leaving another two feet between it and the ceiling above.

The abandoned building is no more. My cell is free-standing inside an opulent chamber, complete with polished wooden furniture. There are bookshelves stuffed with leather-bound volumes, a deep blue velvet couch, lushly patterned rugs, and ornately-carved chairs placed around a gleaming table, which is set for two. In the middle of the table is a cut-crystal decanter filled with burgundy liquid; beside it are two goblets. Next to the couch is a small table, and in the middle of it is a board with alternating white-and-dark squares topped with carved figures. I recognize this, from the library in the House of Echoes: a chessboard.

Am I in Vik? And if so, why am I caged?

Is it possible that the Mages and the exiles broke through Minneska's safeguards so easily? I thought they needed me to be awake in order to draw on the power of my beasts. But maybe not. Maybe they've found another way.

In which case...where is Ari? What have they done with him?

They wouldn't kill him. I need him, which means they do, too. But they would hurt him. They would use him as bait, to get me to do what they wanted.

As if the thought's conjured him, I hear the creaking of chains on the other side of the partition. A low, agonized moan fills the air, as if emanating from an injured animal. There must be another cage, then, inhabited by a prisoner.

It's not Ari's voice. But then, who is it?

Where am I?

I'm getting damned tired of asking this question.

I grip the bars and shake them with all the force I can muster, trying to rip them free from their moorings. But all I succeed in doing is making a lot of noise.

It summons someone, though. From the corner of my eye, I see a shadow cross the threshold, solidifying into the shape of a man as it makes its way into the light, coming at last to a stop outside my cell.

Of course, it's the Executor.

"Hello there," he says. "Finally, you decide to join us."

Finally? "How long have I been here?"

"Oh, a few days, although not in this room. We had to wean you off the sedative, you know. It took a while." He fiddles with the chessboard's rook, rolling it in his fingers before he places it back on its square once again. "Haven't we done this dance before? You were in the dungeons then, of course. The accommodations weren't nearly so...commodious."

"Let me out," I growl at him.

He smiles at me, that cold shark's grin. "I don't think so. You're far too much trouble."

"Where am I? And who's on the other side of that partition?"

He shrugs, crossing to the table, set for two. "You'll both figure that out soon enough. It's much more fun this way, wouldn't you agree?"

"You," I snarl at him, "are delusional."

"Am I?" he muses, filling one of the goblets from the decanter and taking a sip. "On the contrary, I feel my plan is working rather well. Of course, I would have preferred not to lose my precious Thirty; they were of such use. And it would have been far more pleasant had you not gutted me like a fish. But the Mages healed me, after all. It's amazing what can happen when you're willing to give people what they want."

I snort, the sound scraping my too-dry throat like sandpaper. "You can't expect me to believe you're actually going to follow through on your promises."

"Why not?" He lifts his shoulders in an insouciant shrug. "The Houses will fall at last. The nuisance of the Brotherhood will be gone. Far away from my territory, the Mages will carry on with their little fiefdom. Everyone will be happy."

"Not everyone," I point out, my gaze canvassing the room, looking for weapons. I see none. But my eyes fall on the chess set, the austere black-and-white pieces facing off against each other, prepared for battle.

The Executor can't keep me in this cell forever. Sooner or later, if the Mages want to use me to power their offensive, they'll have to let me out. When they do, I will take everyone who's in my way down—starting with him. And ending with myself.

I haven't forgotten the conclusion I came to when I slipped into darkness, tied to the beam. The only way to save Ari and avoid being a pawn in this diabolical game is to remove myself from the board. But first, I need to convince the Executor to unlock this damnable cell.

He takes another sip. When he sets the goblet down, his lips are stained red, as if he's been drinking blood. "Perhaps," he says, "you merely need to adjust your expectations."

"Perhaps," I say right back to him, "if you want to have a prayer of me cooperating, you need to tell me why you have me caged up like an animal."

"If the shoe fits..." he says, licking his lips.

I walked right into that one. "I'm half your blood," I remind him.

"And that," he says, "is why you're still alive."

He strolls closer, though not close enough that I can reach him. I fantasize about grabbing him by the front of his shirt and smashing his skull into the bars. The drug-induced weakness still trembles through me, but it won't be like that forever. Now that they have me caged, maybe they'll find no need to sedate me. And if that's the case, then he's as good as dead.

The Executor chuckles, a low, grinding sound, like gears in need of grease. "Look at you, thinking about how to kill me, when you can barely stand. I'd be insulted, if your savagery wasn't such an asset."

"It's not savagery," I spit at him. "It's common sense. And I do enjoy finishing the things I start."

One of his hands slips to his stomach, lifting his shirt to display the raised scars that cover the damage I did to him. "Half mine," he muses. "Half wild. Half cunning. All dangerous. Everything I ever imagined, when I tampered with your DNA all those years ago."

In his words, I hear an echo of my thoughts about Sebastían: *Half-tease, half-threat, all satisfaction.* The idea that the Executor and I share anything beyond an accident of blood, let alone a way of thinking, makes me want to vomit. I cling to the bars, my grip all that's keeping me upright. "You're sick."

"So you keep telling me. Yet you're the one who can't stand up without assistance. And I'm the one out here"—he gestures at the luxurious room around him—"with all of this."

"Right. A palace, with two cages in it. Who doesn't want one of those?" I suck in a deep breath, wishing desperately for a cool draught of water. But I'll be damned if I'll ask this monster for a thing. He'd probably poison it. Or find some way to hold it over me. "Where are we?" I demand again. "Back in Vik?"

At that, he laughs uproariously. "You are confused, aren't you? Oh, you and I are going to have so much fun."

The moan from the other cell sounds again, louder this time, along with the ominous clank of those chains. The Executor's gaze flits sideways, and a curious expression crosses his face—pain, satisfaction, and pity, all blended for an uncanny instant before it vanishes, replaced with his usual implacable confidence.

A strange suspicion begins to brew inside me. I raise my head, letting the inkling of my wolf come forward. She's still in there, though lulled into complacency by the drug. I can feel her start to wake up, see her raise her head in that imaginary cave that exists inside me. She can't fight, not yet. But she can lend me her sense of smell.

I sniff the air, using not just my human nose but the layered gift of my beast. I smell the rusty scent of old blood. Roses and anise, clinging to my clothes. The crushed-grape-and-jasmine scent of the liquid in the Executor's glass, and the harsh lye of his soap. Beyond these walls, the scent of roasting meat and honey-doused carrots. And something else, something familiar but not, something—

No. No. No.

"Who is that second table setting for?" I say, yanking myself up to my full height. My heart pounds as my gaze scans the room once more, sharpening to vivid clarity. Adrenaline whips through me, burning away the rest of the drug-induced haze.

Half-melted candles on the tables. Books on the walls. A blanket draped over the arm of the velvet couch. Visible through the door the Executor came through, the edge of a four-poster bed.

This is someone's home. A home with two cages, side by side.

"Don't you know?" the Executor says, his smile growing. "Can't you guess?"

A door at the far end of the room opens and a girl scurries through, her brown hair covered by a cap, an apron tied around her waist, and her eyes fixed on the floor. She balances a tray with a metal cup and two covered silver platters, from which the smell of roast pork, cinnamon, and honey emanate. My stomach growls, but I ignore it, my eyes fixed on the girl as she sets the platters and cup on the table and scurries out of the room without a word. Fear bakes off her, acrid and sour, leaving a trail in the air as she shuts the door behind her.

All of my beasts are awake now, my falcon's sharpened vision taking in every detail, the others all warning of the presence of a threat. But from where? The roasted carrots? The man whose insides I carved out a few weeks ago? Whoever is imprisoned in the cell beside mine?

"Dinner time!" the Executor announces cheerily. He isn't talking to me.

As if the words have summoned her, a red-robed woman pushes the door open and walks into the room. Her face is shadowed by her hood, but I can make out her deep-set blue eyes and the rounded curve of her chin. Not Dresda, then. But, if her garb is anything to go by, a Mage.

She holds another tray, but on this one lie multiple syringes rather than what I assume is the Executor's meal. "You called?" Unlike the girl who brought the food, her demeanor holds no subservience: her back is straight, her chin lifted. If she wasn't here to drug me for getting out of line, I'd almost admire her.

"Over there," the Executor says, barely sparing her a glance. He gestures at the far corner of the room, and the Mage strides in the direction he indicated, taking her time.

"Now, you're not going to do anything stupid, are you?" the Executor says.

First I think he's talking to the Mage, but he's not looking at her. He's looking in the direction of the cells. And he's not talking to me, either.

I grip the bars, straining to see, as he presses his thumb to the keypad, unlocking the cell next to mine. The door swings open with a whine and a creak as he steps inside. "Time to eat," he says. "Please join me."

"Do I have a choice?" It's a woman's voice, cracked and weary.

"Not really." The Executor's voice is full of false cheer. "I suppose you could choose to starve, but I would never let that happen. Not to mention, there's someone here I think you'll want to see. She arrived when you were sleeping."

"Oh, is that what you call it?" The scorn in the woman's voice is unmistakable.

"If you would only behave," the Executor says, sighing, "you could spend the night in your comfortable bed. Believe me, it gives me no pleasure to confine you this way. But alas, in my absence, I hear that you were very ill-mannered indeed."

The woman doesn't say a word. I hear the clinking of metal again; the Executor must be unlocking her chains. Then there's the sound of shuffling, and the two of them appear, him pushing her in front of him.

The woman's hands are cuffed, her dark hair a flurry of untamed brown waves and her skin the sort that turns golden-brown in the sun. But this woman looks like she hasn't seen the sun in a long time. The cheek that's visible to me is badly bruised, as if someone's backhanded her. Her eyes are a clear amber.

The amber I have seen in the mirror, in the eyes of my wolf.

No, I think again. *Oh, please, no.*

Her eyes meet mine and take me in, clinging to the bars of my cage. She shakes her head, as if in disbelief.

"Don't you recognize her?" the Executor says. "Granted, she's looked better. But she's not seeing you to best advantage, either." He touches a finger to his lips, as if in thought. "Perhaps I should have given you two the opportunity to clean up, first. You do have so many beautiful clothes, and doubtless they would fit her, too. We could have enjoyed a lovely meal together, if I could trust either of you not to slit my throat. Alas, this is the regrettable situation in which we find ourselves."

"Who is she?" the woman whispers. "Why have you brought her here?"

The Executor drapes an arm over her shoulders, and I see her fight the urge to flinch. "Can't you guess?"

The woman's eyes run over me, again and again. They fix on my face. And then they widen in shock. "Is—is she—"

The Executor doesn't respond.

The woman's expression changes, brows lowering in concentration. A moment later, I feel her voice inside my head. Not her human voice, though. The voice of her wolf, calling to mine.

My wolf tilts back her head and howls, recognizing her pack. The howl finds its way from my own mouth, and across the room, I see the Mage's eyes widen with satisfaction.

The woman takes a step toward me, stumbling from beneath the Executor's arm. Her mouth opens, shuts, opens again.

"Eva?" she whispers.

Speechless, I nod.

Her legs give out, and she crumples to the floor. Tears flood those amber eyes and spill down her bruised cheeks. The sobs that rip from her throat are so violent, they shake her entire body. But through it all, her avid gaze never leaves mine. And I know two things for sure.

This woman is my mother.

And if that's the case, then something else logically follows.

I'm back in the Commonwealth again.

CHAPTER 31

ARI

It's thirty minutes before I'm due to take second watch with Jaxon, and I'm sitting against a pine tree at the edge of camp, reaching out for Eva and failing to find her. Every day since I shot that damned bird down two weeks ago, I've tried. But nothing. Not for me, and not for Sebastían, either... though the bastard's been avoiding me. I'm sure he's hiding something. But what else is new?

He and Jaxon have been avoiding each other, too. They have as little to do with each other as possible, only speaking when it's absolutely necessary, and that odd tension still simmers between them. Maybe it's simple dislike, but I don't think so. I can't help but remember that instant in the infirmary after Jaxon was injured, when we were making fun of Sebastían. *Also, he's got a...* Jaxon started to say, before the rest of his sentence was swallowed up by a cough. I dismissed it as unimportant, but now I can't help but wonder. Maybe tonight, I'll ask— though, given the black mood Jaxon's been in lately, I doubt he'll answer me.

He's not the only one who's unnerved. The ravens are still leading us southward, staying just out of reach of arrows, blades, or bullets. I have to believe that means Eva's still alive. They need her, after all. But accidents happen, and the sight of her, bound and bruised, haunts me. I see it every time I close my eyes.

The last time I drifted off, I heard her voice, cracked and raw as if from screaming. *Aut viam inveniam aut faciam*, she whispered, in the instant before I bolted upright, heart pounding, eyes searching the dim tent for her bloodied face. *I will either find a way or make one.* It's what Efraím used to tell us during a particularly challenging training exercise, one meant to test our mettle. But Eva didn't sound tenacious or triumphant. She sounded...resigned.

I could have just been dreaming, my subconscious feeding my worst fears. By the Architect, I hope so. Because I know Eva. She'd rather sacrifice herself than be used as a pawn. What way would she make for herself if she thought we wouldn't come for her in time? What might she do?

The same thing she did in that damned scholar's room, that's what. Throw herself into the jaws of the beast to save everyone else, and to the Sins with herself.

She heard my voice, damn it. She has to know I'm coming, that no matter how we left things, I'd never give up on her. By the nine hells, she has to wait for me.

But what if she doesn't? What if she does something infernally foolish, something she can't take back?

Losing her to Sebastían is one thing. Losing her for good, out of some misguided sense of nobility, by her own hand or by forcing someone else's, will break me. I have to get to her before that happens. And with every passing second, a little more sand runs through the hourglass.

It's a grim line of thought, but I can't shake it. Nor do I care to close my eyes again, which is why I'm here rather than in my tent, waiting for Kilían to shake me awake.

Even exhausted as I am, adrenaline floods me as footsteps crunch on the leaves. It dials back as I recognize the steps: light and quick, more weight on his left foot than the right. A moment later, my father's voice issues from the darkness beside me. "Can't sleep?"

I shift against the rough bark of the tree, peering back in the direction he came from. The army is mostly asleep, inside the types of tents I first saw when I met Ronan, in the Brotherhood encampment. I can make out the dim, humped shapes of them in the moonlight that filters through the trees, which have become fuller, laden with greenery, as we descend from the mountains into the warmer, southern part of the Empire.

"It's my turn to keep watch next, after Kilían," I say. "Thought I'd get an early start."

"Mind some company?"

"Suit yourself." It comes out harsher than I intend, and I clear my throat. "Sorry, didn't mean it that way. Sure, sit."

He settles himself next to me, leaning back against his own tree. "How are you?"

I sputter a laugh. "Peachy. And yourself?"

"That was a stupid question. I'm sorry." He runs a hand through his hair, mussing it. With a start, I recognize the gesture as one of my own. "I'm a healer, by nature and by trade. I see you suffering, and I want to help, Ari. You're my *son*. I want to be there for you, but I don't know how."

I lean my head back against the tree, listening to the small sounds of the night: the wind stirring the leaves, the guards moving inside their tents, the small creatures hunting in the woods. "You don't owe me anything," I say at last.

"Maybe not. But...I'd like to give you something, if I can."

I stare at him, puzzled. "Like what? A hug?"

"I'm serious, Ari. If there's anything I can give you, all you need to do is ask."

I give his request due consideration, watching the moonlight play on the floor of the clearing. "Tell me about my mother, then," I invite at last. "How did the two of you meet?"

A smile breaks across Kennett's face, lighting his eyes. "She fell off a ladder in the library. Attacked by *The History of the Commonwealth: A Compendium.* Perhaps you've seen it? It's quite a hefty volume."

"Ugh, that book." I sink my head into my hands. "Yeah, I've seen it. Used it as a weapon, actually, when nothing else came to hand. A better purpose for it than as a source of knowledge, in my opinion."

"Miri might have agreed. Then again, she found any source of knowledge worth pursuing. She was brilliant. And beautiful. And brave. Like you."

The wistful tone of his voice penetrates, and I sit up, hungry for more. I never had a chance to speak with Miriam, but maybe he can bring her alive for me this way. "So, you came to her rescue. And then?"

Even in the dim light, I can see Kennett's cheeks coloring. "I asked her to tutor me. So I could understand my patients' minds better. But it was just an excuse. I, um, had an ulterior motive."

Now it's my turn to snort. "I just bet you did."

"It's not what you're thinking. Really, I—I had a sick patient. A little girl, Annalise. I couldn't help her, no matter how hard I tried. She was dying. The more I got to know Miri, the more I could see how much your mother hungered for knowledge, just like I did. And I began to think...maybe I could persuade her to get me into the restricted stacks."

Now he has my attention. The library's off-limits books are inaccessible to everyone in the Commonwealth, scholars included, without special dispensation. To be caught there without permission, with all that the pursuit of such knowledge implies, would be a crime of epic proportions.

I narrow my eyes at Kennett. "Either you're downplaying your own bravery," I say, "or you're an impetuous idiot."

He blinks at me, as if surprised by my bluntness. "I don't think it was either one. I just...I couldn't watch Annalise die."

By the Architect, he reminds me so much of Gentian, who risked everything to save that damned bird. Not that it worked. "And did she? Die, I mean?"

"No." My father's lips curve upward. "The knowledge in those books saved her."

I lean forward, eyes intent on his face. "How in the nine hells did you get in there?"

"Miri and I waited for the eve of the Architect's arrival. We slipped away, while everyone was in the square. She'd stolen a key. And then we...well, we..."

His voice trails off again. I peer at him closely, taking note of the way his eyes shift away from mine, the way his heartbeat speeds. And then my mouth falls open in shock. "By the Architect. You defiled my mother in the *restricted stacks*?"

He doesn't say a word, just blushes furiously. It's as good as an admission of guilt.

I can't help it; I start to laugh. And once I start, I can't stop. Every time I catch sight of his mortified face, I lose control of myself again. But through my hysteria, something else bubbles up: recognition. My father risked death to save a child. He got Jaxon and Jessamine home safely. And he's here with us now.

He has a stronger spine than I originally imagined. And just maybe, we have more in common than a tendency to mess up our hair when we're frustrated. Just maybe, I can trust him.

"And I thought I was trouble," I finally manage to choke out. "Does Kilían know this story?"

At the mention of the Lead Interrogator's name, Kennett's

face darkens. "No," he says. "And I'd appreciate it if you didn't tell him. He and I…well, it's complicated."

"I know exactly how it is." I give him a level stare, my amusement draining away. "In case you were wondering."

"Of course you do." Kennett heaves a sigh. "You're a bellator, after all."

"Former bellator," I correct him. "We tend to be an observant bunch, yeah? It's that, or end up dead."

"Who's ending up dead?" It's Kilían, looming out of the dark. By the Architect, he's as quiet as a sins-forsaken ghost when he wants to be.

"No one. You don't have to sound so enthusiastic about the prospect," my father chastises him. And damn if I don't see an open, sunny smile break across the Lead Interrogator's face. I didn't even know he *could* smile that way.

"I'd welcome the opportunity to put a blade in someone," Kilían says, his face falling back into its familiar harsh lines. "Anything would be an improvement over being herded like a damned sheep."

"You're not kidding," I mumble. We've been traveling for a fortnight, traversing the road through the ruined cities, traveling southward through the plains and then the mountains. I keep expecting an attack, but none has come. Yeah, I should be grateful that nothing's impeding our progress, but like Kilían, I'd feel better if there were an enemy to fight. This absence of an opponent, after the brutal events in the stone circle, is discomfiting.

Kilían claps me on the back. "Be of good cheer, Westergaard. Perhaps tomorrow will bring us someone to impale. And on that note… You and Fjeri have the watch."

He melts into the night, and after a moment, my father follows.

JAXON and I patrol the perimeter of the camp together, our eyes on the darkness between the trees. He's favoring his shoulder a little, which disconcerts me. I'm counting on him to have my back. If he's compromised, I need to know.

"Okay?" I say on our second circuit, as he brushes a branch out of the way and winces when it rebounds to smack him in the arm.

"Fine." He cuts his eyes at me. "Don't need you fussing over me, exile. Your father already poked and prodded me tonight."

"And?"

"I'm *fine*," he says, sounding anything but. "Tell you if I'm not. Think I want to be the reason you get dead?"

I let out an exasperated breath. At least it doesn't puff white in the wintry air, the way it did further north. "What's crawled up your ass? You're even more pleasant than usual."

He stops in his tracks, giving me an aggravated glare. "Nothing. Drop it."

Raising both hands in surrender, I keep walking. The leaves swirl around my feet, the air rich with the smell of firs and the rosemary Ronan used to season the rabbits we caught for dinner. Hard as I listen, I don't hear any indication of humans moving through the woods. Still, I can't shake the sense of being watched. It niggles at me, a cold spot on the back of my neck that I know better than to dismiss.

"Do you think they're out there?" I ask Jaxon.

He flicks his eyes toward the woods. "My honest opinion? They don't need to be. We can't go back. Can't go sideways. Got those damned birds like an arrow pointing the way. We're right where they want us. What would be the point?"

I tend to agree with him. Still, that's no reason to let down our guard. Especially now, when I could swear someone's watching us.

"Listen," I say as we walk side by side at the border of the clearing. "There's something I've been meaning to ask you—"

But I never finish my sentence, because just then, between the trees, a piece of the darkness separates from the rest and prowls toward us, belly low to the ground.

I hiss and palm my dagur, ready to spear whatever it is through the heart, and Jaxon raises his gun. But then there's a rustling sound, and Sebastían's voice sounds from the bushes beyond our perimeter. "Don't shoot. Or stab, exile. It's just me."

I *knew* someone was watching us. I should probably be relieved it's just Sebastían. But he belongs in the camp, not haunting the forest. There's no reason for him to be prowling the woods....unless he's in league with an enemy and sneaking off to meet them. Is *this* what he's been hiding from me?

That bastard. If he's been pretending to be on our side, enlisting me in finding Eva only to turn her over to our enemies, I'll slit his faithless throat.

Jaxon swears, lowering his weapon. "What the hell is he doing out there?"

"I don't know." But I fully intend to find out.

More rustling, and then Sebastían emerges from the treeline in human form, pulling his shirt over his head. "By the Sins," I snap. "I could have killed you."

"That would have made your life easier, no?"

I'd like nothing more than to backhand him. Apparently Jaxon feels the same, because he gets up in Sebastían's face, hissing at him from an inch away. "You think this is *funny*? Look, you entitled little prick—"

Sebastían growls at him, a tearing-fabric sound that rumbles up from his chest and out between his teeth. "Back up." The words barely sound human.

But Jaxon doesn't move. "What were you doing in the woods?"

"That's none of your business."

"Isn't it?" Jaxon grabs the front of Sebastían's shirt, hauling him forward. "I think it's all of our business. Certainly mine and Ari's, here. You out there meeting some kind of informer? Are you a traitor, Sebastard?"

He echoes my thoughts with eerie exactitude, and I watch carefully for any hint of guilt on Sebastían's part: a flick of his eyes, a twitch of his hand. But no: face set in contemptuous lines, the Panther of the West jerks free of his grip. "What did you just call me?"

"You heard me."

Claws sprout from Sebastían's fingertips. He swipes, and they land a solid hit in the upper arm of Jaxon's leather gear jacket, hauling him closer and closer. It's the arm attached to the hand that holds the gun, which falls into the leaves at their feet.

"You are *vox nihili*," Sebastían says, an inch from Jaxon's lips. "The voice of nothing. You speak, and no one listens. You are the wind that blows through the crevices, the space between the shadows. One more word, and you'll become a shadow yourself."

Jaxon throws back his head and laughs, the long column of his throat gleaming in the moonlight. I can see his carotid pulse throbbing, and by the way Sebastían's predatory gaze fixes on it, so can he. It's a near-suicidal move on Jaxon's part, like that night on the beam. Why would he risk this? Does he know something that I don't? Is this the culmination of the tension that's been festering between them since we left Vik?

I'd wager my sverd that something I don't understand is running beneath the surface here. Whatever it is, it's deadly. "Let him go, Sebastían," I say, kneeling to pick up the gun and shoving it into my weapons belt. "We can't afford petty infighting like this."

"He insulted my honor." Sebastían's claws are still embedded in the jacket. He shakes Jaxon, a cat toying with its prey.

I move closer, the cold part of my brain that's trained to defuse conflict analyzing the situation. What will happen if I have to put Sebastían down? Could I move fast enough? And what would it mean to our cause?

Maybe, a small voice inside me says, *it will* save *your cause. If he really is a traitor, then ending him could save Eva. It could save all of you.*

But without proof, I can't kill him, damn it. Or even badly wound him. He can act with impunity, and he knows it. Which means the best I can hope for is to get Jaxon away from him, before Sebastían does permanent damage.

"Fjeri asked a valid question," I counter. "What were you doing in the woods?"

Now Sebastían's gaze flicks over my shoulder, at the place where he emerged from the treeline. For an instant, I entertain the notion that he'll give me an honest reply and let Jaxon go. But when he speaks, his voice is every bit the haughty prince, like we never stood on the streets of Vik and agreed to work together. "I don't answer to you, familiar."

Arrogant sin-loving bastard. I'm tempted to put a blade in his throat. Instead, I force myself to speak calmly. "You don't, no. But you *do* answer to this mission. If you have nothing to hide, then explain yourself."

To my relief, he steps back, disengaging his claws from Jaxon's gear. "The moon is rising. I'm not bound to it, but I do feel its call. I couldn't stay in that camp anymore. It made me claustrophobic. So I was out there, in the forest, in my other form. Happy now?"

Jaxon rocks back on his heels, glaring at Sebastían. "You could have endangered all of us, to have a damned *frolic in the moonlight*. Are you an idiot as well as a power-hungry fool? What the hell's your problem?"

Sebastían bares his teeth, looking like he wishes he'd put his claws into Jaxon's heart instead of his jacket. "Watch what you say, Fjeri, or your next words might well be your last."

Before he can make good on his threat, I step between the two of them, praying that I haven't just signed my death warrant. "Ease down, Jaxon."

He does not. Instead, his hand flashes out, grabbing his gun from my weapons belt. Before he can seal his fate, I grab him, hauling him back against my chest. He's a live wire in my arms, solid muscle and vibrating with fury.

"Let go of me," he snarls, struggling against me.

And take the risk of him shooting Sebastían, one of our strongest assets, less than three days' ride from the Commonwealth? I don't think so. I redouble my grip, but he fights me. Damn his injured shoulder. I could immobilize him easily, but then I'd run the risk of permanently damaging him. I settle for disarming him instead, prying the gun from his grip and tossing it into the bushes.

Nothing daunted, the idiot decides to use his mouth as a weapon. "You think I don't know what you really want?" he taunts Sebastían. "All your high and mighty talk, and you think I don't know how you spend your free time back in Satrizona? I'd bet money you were out there in the woods, brooding about what you're going to tell *her*, if she'll still want you when you've sworn your allegiance to another for the sake of your damn politics. Because you and I both know that's all you care about."

What in the nine hells? "What is he talking about?" I demand of Sebastían.

Maybe I'm *vox nihili*, too, because he ignores me completely.

"You're one to talk," he says, stalking closer to me and Jaxon, until I can feel his hot breath on my face. It makes me want to deck him, but I can't afford to let go. "Moping around, missing your little thieving minstrel. It's too bad he went and got himself blown up. The gods know there's no one else willing to put up with your brand of shit."

Jaxon freezes against me. "What. Did. You. Say?"

"Tobias, wasn't it?" Sebastían croons, prowling around us. "They'd bring him in to entertain us when we visited Vik, him and that viola. Made it sing like an angel, he did. Was that your thing—he was the light to your darkness?" He runs the tip of a claw down Jaxon's cheek in the mockery of a caress, then lower, along the throbbing artery in his neck. "Not all light though, was he, with those sticky fingers? I suppose he thought no one would catch him that night. I kept his little secret, and I thought he kept mine. But it seems he didn't, after all."

I feel Jaxon suck in a breath. "What night?" he spits.

Sebastían gives a mirthless laugh. "He didn't tell you? I suppose he was too ashamed. Or maybe he was protecting you." He taps a finger against his lips. "Come to think of it, maybe he was protecting *himself*. If you knew what he'd done, you'd have been obligated to report it. Off with his head." The finger moves lower, drawing a decisive line across his own throat. "And as for you—well, so much for your glorious military career. Your little viola player and I had a deal, though I shouldn't be surprised he couldn't keep his mouth shut. There's no honor among thieves, after all."

"Stop it." The words emerge in a rasp as a tremor runs through Jaxon, shaking him from head to toe. I redouble my grip on him, as much to hold him together as to restrain him.

Sebastían's lips lift in a taunting smile. "Why should I?"

"Because I *know*," Jaxon hisses. "One word from me, and

your precious reputation goes up in flames. Let's see you marry Eva Marteinn then."

A look of genuine alarm flickers across Sebastían's face, a moment before it's replaced by his usual indifferent mask. "Who would believe you? Maybe you really don't know what I caught Tobias with his greedy hands on that night. But all I'd have to do is say you did, and failed to turn him in. It would be your word against mine—a thief's lover versus a prince. I have your life in my hand, Fjeri, little though you seem to value it."

So this is the source of the enmity between them. A secret that could break Sebastían, something Tobias confided in Jaxon before he died. And a second secret Tobias kept from him, leverage Sebastían holds that can destroy Jaxon's career from beyond the grave.

I want answers. But more than that, I don't want Jaxon to die right here, in this clearing. Because Sebastían's right: Jaxon doesn't value his life. He's damn near inviting the Panther of the West to kill him.

Well, it's not going to happen on my watch. "Enough, Pardúr."

Predictably, Sebastían ignores me. So much for being on the same side. "I don't blame you, Fjeri. You're not good enough to be a familiar," he says, circling us again. "You've lost the only person who could stand you, thief or not. Hell, he probably blew himself up on purpose so he could get away from you."

Jaxon shudders so hard I almost lose my grip, his back heaving against my chest, and my restraint snaps. The hell with our alliance. It's bad enough for Jaxon to use Sebastían to punish himself. It's unforgivable for Sebastían to twist the knife.

"Shut up," I tell Sebastían. "Or I swear to the Architect, I don't care what it costs us, I'll shut your mouth myself."

"Come on, then, if you must." He lifts one clawed hand and

beckons me. "Although—are you sure you want to waste your time defending this pitiful excuse for a warrior? Look at him, baiting me to kill him because he's not brave enough to take his own life. Pathetic." He spits at Jaxon's feet, one insult too many.

I see it coming, but am too late to stop it. Or maybe I just don't want to.

Because with a roar of rage so deep it reverberates through his entire body, Jaxon wrests himself free of me, rears back, and punches the Panther of the West square in the jaw.

CHAPTER 32
EVA

"Lia, meet Eva," the Executor says brightly, pulling my mother to her feet. "Eva, Lia. Welcome to our humble abode."

Is this where the Executor *lives?* All along, while the rest of the Commonwealth existed in ascetic minimalism, while the citizens slept in cots in dormitories, their clothes and food and every thought regulated, he retreated at night to the equivalent of a palace? I didn't think he could be more of a hypocrite, but apparently there's always room for him to live down to my lowest expectations.

Cordelia gasps, and my gaze flicks between the two of them. Her, with her cuffed hands and bruised cheek and tear-filled eyes. Him, with his haughty carriage and firm grip on her upper arm.

My parents, together in front of me for the first time.

Within me, my wolf's head rises, her ears pricked and her nose scenting the air. *Pack,* she growls when she scents my mother's wolf, unmistakable happiness in the sound. *Home.*

But this place is no home of mine. "You bastard," I snarl at him. "Get your hands off her."

"Oh, I don't think so. It's time for dinner, after all." He gestures at the table, set for two, with its silver-domed platters. Cinnamon-and-pork-scented steam seeps from under the lids, curling sinuously into the air. "I'd invite you to join us, but I think we both know how that would end."

"Eva," my mother whispers, like she hasn't heard a word. "How?"

She pulls against the Executor's grip, trying to get to me, and he makes a tsking sound. "I think not. Haven't you missed me, Lia mine?"

That galvanizes my mother. She turns her head, those amber eyes training on his face. "You unmitigated, gods-damned, belly-crawling *worm*. That's my daughter. How dare you bring her here and then keep me from her?"

Pride at her rebellion arcs through me, followed quickly by fear that he'll backhand her and give her a matching bruise on her other cheek. But he just throws back his head and laughs. "Our daughter, Lia mine. And I'm not keeping you from her. She's right there, is she not?"

My mother's eyes narrow, and again, I feel the sense of her wolf calling to mine. It's wordless, but I have the unmistakable sense that she's assessing my well-being, checking to make sure I'm all right. My wolf whines, half in anxiety, half in welcome. It must be enough to satisfy my mother, because her wolf retreats. "Let her out." Her voice is steel.

"And why would I do that? Be grateful she isn't chained. If only you'd behaved in my absence, you wouldn't be, either." He yanks her arm, pulling her in the direction of the table. "I've had a lovely meal prepared for our reunion. Of course, Eva will be appreciating it from the confines of her cell. But they do say it's the thought that counts."

My mother sets her feet, but he drags her anyhow,

depositing her in one of the ornate chairs. "Sit," he commands, and waits until she obeys.

I turn in a circle within my cage, searching the corners of the room for cameras that are meant to surveil us. I'm sure they're here; there's no way the Executor would leave his prize possessions unattended. Sure enough, I find them, winking eyes embedded in the molding between walls and ceiling.

On the one hand, this is unfortunate. On the other, if these cameras are hooked up to the Commonwealth's mainframe, then they can be hacked. If I can get into the system, then I can alter their feed, perhaps long enough for us to escape.

As if he's heard my thoughts, the Executor chuckles. "I see you looking at those cameras, Eva. Which reminds me." He raises his voice. "Traalf!"

The door to the room creaks open, and Bellator Traalf steps inside. He's tall and bulky, with wide shoulders and penetrating dark eyes. Traalf apprenticed with Reykdal Skau, the bellator I bested in the Trials. Needless to say, he doesn't care for me.

"Yes, sir?" he says, standing at attention. He doesn't spare me a glance.

The Executor waves a lazy hand at the cameras. "Unplug them."

Traalf's mouth twitches, the slightest tell of disagreement. "Are you sure, sir? Monitoring these untrustworthy sinners seems wise."

"Are you questioning me?" The Executor's voice is mild, but the threat in it is clear.

"No. Of course not." He straightens, back stiff. "As you wish, sir."

My heart sinks as Traalf rounds the room, unplugging one camera after the other. There's only one reason the Executor would do this: he doesn't want what happens in this room to be seen, even by whoever's monitoring the footage. And that cannot be good.

Traalf unplugs the final camera and exits the room before the Executor speaks again. "I'm going to unlock the cuffs now, Lia mine." His voice is oil on water, a slick, false kindness atop a cold abyss of cruelty. "And you will use your hands only to eat the beautiful meal that's been prepared for us. Should you attempt otherwise..." He gestures at the Mage who stands in the corner of the room, holding that metal tray. "We both know what will happen."

She levels him with a contemptuous look, which he ignores. Instead, he strides to the couch and removes the fabric draped over the arm. What I thought was a blanket is actually a silky garment of deep, rich purple. "I had this made for you in my absence," he says, running his fingers over the smooth surface. "You'll wear it while we eat." It's not a question.

My mother's eyes stay fixed on me as he sets the fabric down on the table, pulls a set of keys from his pocket, and unlocks her cuffs. Humming, he extracts a small tube from the same pocket. The sharp scent of arnica drifts across the space between us as he dabs the ointment on her wrists. "These were too tight," he mutters, a furrow forming between his brows, as if the thought of her being in pain disturbs him. Which is laughable, all things considered.

"I'm sorry, Lia mine," he says, pressing careful kisses to her wrists. My own eyes widen. What kind of man chains and cuffs a woman, then gets upset because her wrists are bruised?

Straightening, the Executor arranges the silk carefully around my mother's shoulders. "Better," he murmurs. "Let me just..."

Scooping up a small brush that sits on a side table, he stands behind Cordelia and brushes her tangled hair. His hands move through her chestnut waves as he hums, his expression transported. In a lifetime of horrors, it's the most terrifying thing I've ever seen.

"Beautiful," he says. "Always so beautiful, Lia mine."

A shudder runs through my mother's body, and I feel the echo of it in my own. But she doesn't say a word.

He sets the brush down and pastes a smile on his face. "And now," he says, rubbing his hands together, "let us eat." With a flourish, he pulls the top off one of the platters. "I've had them make your favorites."

Even from here, I can see the caramelized surface of the pork roast, the cinnamon dusting the carrots, the garnish of parsley that graces the top. I can't remember the last time I actually ate, rather than being force-fed while I was unconscious. My mouth waters.

My mother stares at the food, her lips set in a stubborn line. "I'm not hungry."

"Oh, come, Lia mine. Don't you want to set a good example for our daughter?"

"What I *want*—" my mother begins viciously, but he glares at her in admonition and her mouth snaps shut. When she speaks again, her voice is conciliatory. "What I would like is for you to let Eva out, so she can eat with us. It could be our first meal as a family. Wouldn't that be lovely?"

The Executor's eyes darken. "Oh, yes, very lovely. Right up until she finishes the job she started, and it's my heart being served up on that platter rather than the pork roast." He bends, placing his palms on the table, peering into my mother's face. "Is that what you want, Lia mine? Do you wish me ill?"

It's quite clear to me that nothing would make my mother happier than to strangle the Executor with her bare hands. I can't understand why she doesn't, unless it's the threat of the Mage with the syringes. But surely she could smash the Executor's head into the table. Surely she could lunge for the serving fork that lies on the platter and go for his eyes. It's what I would do, syringes be damned. My hands itch with anticipation, clenching and unclenching on the bars of my cell.

But my mother does none of these things. Instead, her eyes slide to me, and she shakes her head. "Of course not, Armand. But I'm sure Eva would be perfectly behaved. Wouldn't you, Eva?"

Armand. I've never heard anyone call the Executor by his first name before. Honestly, it never occurred to me that he had one.

Her eyes beg me to say yes. But I can't manage it, not even for the sake of strategy. "If your idea of 'perfectly behaved' is breaking one of these chairs over his head and stabbing him with the pieces, then yes," I say, smiling sweetly. "I will behave beyond reproach."

"You see?" The Executor sighs, like I'm trying the last of his patience. "So alas, it will just be you and me, Lia mine. I've had a plate prepared for her, of course. Unlike what you believe, I'm not without sympathy. Besides," he shoots me a calculating glance, "she does me no good if she's weakened."

He whisks a napkin off the second platter, revealing, as promised, a plate of food. The contents are identical to his and my mother's, but the plate itself is made of tin instead of fine china. "Come here, Larisa," he says, crooking a finger at the Mage holding the tray of syringes.

Together they approach my cell. On his signal, she lifts a small, silver object from her tray.

"This is an electric prod, Eva," the Executor says. "Perhaps you're familiar? It's what the vet techs use alongside their tranquilizer darts to subdue the Bastarour. It's strong enough on its own...but with Larisa's gifts behind it, it can call down the power of lightning itself. Perhaps you'd like a demonstration?"

I offer him a stony stare in response, but he just smiles

cheerily at me. "If you would," he says, waving an airy hand at the Mage beside him.

"My pleasure," Larisa says. Her sky-blue eyes find mine. And then I feel it: a strange stirring inside me, the same one I felt in the stone circle just before everything went wrong. It gets stronger, sharper, as Larisa plucks the prod from the tray and carves her free hand through the air, fingers twisting in an intricate gesture. Her lips move, chanting a phrase I don't understand, and the stirring sharpens into a painful tug—like she's pulling on my very essence, commanding it to do her bidding. I press my palms to my stomach, doubling over. Behind the Executor, my mother rises to her feet.

"Stop it!" she hisses from between clenched teeth. "Can't you see you're hurting Eva? If you must do this, do it to me. Not her. Not her, please..."

With a triumphant flick of her hand, Larisa raises the prod high. Lightning explodes from it, sizzling with electricity. The jagged, angry bolt tunnels into the stone floor, which splits in two at the point of impact with a deafening crack. My eyes sting from the glaring light. My ears ring. And deep inside me, that awful tugging deepens until I'm afraid I'm going to split apart—

"That's enough," the Executor announces, clapping Larisa on the shoulder.

Her expression unchanged, Larisa lowers the hand that holds the prod. Instantly, the lightning subsides, taking the pain with it. I straighten, gasping, and glare at both of them, imbuing my gaze with all the hatred I can muster.

"See?" the Executor says with that same sunny smile. "Look how helpful you're being already!" He turns to Cordelia, the smile still in place. "Such a good girl, am I right?"

Fury knots my mother's tear-streaked face. "You bastard," she hisses.

"Now, now. Such language. It's just a little lesson. A taste of what happens when you blend the Mages' gifts with ours. After all, children need to be taught manners. And consequences. Wouldn't you agree?" He winks at me, like we're in on a joke together. "Now, Eva, I'm going to put this plate of food and a glass of water through the slot in your cell door. Any move to damage me, and Larisa here will give us another demonstration of her talents...but this time, the floor won't be her target. Understood?"

My stomach growls, and within me, Carina speaks, her voice peculiarly calm. *Eat, Eva. The food doesn't smell of poison, and refusing it will only hurt us. We need to be strong for what lies ahead.*

"Fine," I bite out.

"Back up, then. Against the far wall of the cell. Don't move."

I do as he asks, wondering why he doesn't have Traalf deal with me. Why he's choosing to do his dirty work himself. But then I see his expression, and I know. He's gloating, reveling in having me at his mercy.

He comes forward, Larisa flanking him. My arms folded across my chest, I watch as the Executor presses his thumb against the wall-mounted pad that he used to unlock my mother's cell. A panel near the bottom of my cell's door slides open, and he pushes the plate and cup through. They clank onto the floor, water splashing onto the stone, as the panel slides shut again.

"Dinner, Eva," the Executor says, and retreats.

Warily, I approach the food. This close, the combined scents of honey, cinnamon, and roasting meat are irresistible. But I go for the water first, desperate to slake my all-consuming thirst. I let my wolf come forward, sniffing it for tampering, and when she finds nothing, I snatch up the cup. It tastes of metal, but I don't care. I drain every drop.

When I'm finished, I set the empty cup down and pick up the plate. It's all I can do not to lower my face and eat directly off it, like a pig from a trough. But I force myself to eat slowly, with my fingers, since he hasn't given me any utensils. This is rich food, and the last thing I need is for my stomach to reject it.

My mother waits until I take my first bite. Then she does the same, wielding her knife and fork with the same exquisite manners Sebastían and Layla possess. Her impeccable etiquette is eerily at odds with the bruise on her face and her chafed wrists.

The meal is interminable, but finally it ends. The Executor re-cuffs my mother and leads her back into her cell. He wheels the partition out of the way, whistling as he does it, and bids us both good night. Then he stalks from the room, Larisa following in his footsteps, leaving the candles guttering on the table.

The moment the door slams behind them, my mother edges as close to the bars as her chain will allow. "Eva," she whispers, even though the Executor is no longer there to hear. "You're real, yes? *This* is real?"

The longing in her voice is unmistakable, as is the doubt. I know, better than most, the drugs that the Commonwealth has at its disposal. How has the Executor tortured her? Has he made her hallucinate? Pity sweeps me. "It's real," I promise.

"I can't believe it. I wish I could hold you. Touch you, just so I could be sure it's not another one of his tricks." She exhales, the sound heavy with frustration. "You're so close and yet... Gods, I'm sorry, Eva. I've waited to see you again for so long. But I never wanted it to happen like this. It's a nightmare to have you locked up beside me. To have to watch him hurt you."

"Where are we? Is this where the Executor lives?"

"It's my quarters. He has another place. I've never seen it." She huffs, dismissing my questions. "Tell me, Eva—I want to know—"

"You've never seen where he lives?" I interrupt. "Have you been trapped in these rooms, for twenty years?"

There's a long silence. Then my mother says, "I've never left this apartment, from the day he brought me here."

The full horror of it breaks over me. "You haven't been outside? Not at all?"

"He would never take such a risk." The scorn in her voice is unmistakable. "But I'm all right, Eva. I've made do. I have books. Clothes. Food. And I'm not always in this cage."

She's so clearly trying to reassure me, it breaks my heart. "How did you get that bruise on your face?"

"It doesn't matter," she says impatiently. "Tell me about you. Are you all right? What has he done to you?" Before I have a chance to say a word, she rushes on. "I have so many questions, Eva. I want to know everything about you, and not through *his* eyes. Who you are. What you love. Why you're here, now. And I need to know—my home—"

Pity rushes through me at the realization that she's been cooped up here for two decades, without sunlight, in the care of a monster. "One thing at a time," I say, my voice as gentle as I can make it. "He's told you about me, you said. How much do you know?"

"I know you became a bellator. That you hold the forms of four beasts, which—oh, Eva. It's miraculous, yes. But what a burden to bear." Her gaze is heavy with sympathy.

"You know I escaped?"

"Of course. Armand was furious. And then he left. And I was so scared..." She breaks off, her head dropping to her chained hands. "Where were you, Eva? Where did you go?"

"To Vik. With the Brotherhood."

My mother's breath speeds up, coming fast and shallow. "Did—did you make it there?"

"I did."

"And it still stands? It hasn't been destroyed?"

"Destroyed? Why would you think—" Then it dawns on me. *I will burn the city you loved, and stand laughing in the ashes.* "He told you Vik was gone, didn't he. That everyone you loved was dead, and the place you fought to protect had been razed to the ground."

The silence that falls is answer enough. "He's vicious," she says at last. "He takes pleasure in hurting me. And what could hurt more than that? But—are you saying it's not true?" Her voice trembles. "That my home...that Dev..." The chains clank, her feet sliding against the stone floor as she strains to get as close to the bars as she can. "Devereaux Adelman. He was a guard. Do you know him? Does he live?" Desperation and hope leak from every word.

At least there's something I can give her, a gift that will hopefully bring her light. "He does. All this time, he's thought you were dead. Once he learned you were alive, he —" I think of Councilor Adelman's face when he crashed into Ari's room, the morning after I learned the truth about Cordelia. About the white-knuckled grip he had on the table in the Great Hall, the scent of grief and rage that baked off him with every word he spoke. "He's the head of the Council of Nine now. And suffice it to say, I'm sure he'll stop at nothing to find you."

Cordelia falls to her knees. "Dev." The syllable is a broken whisper. "Oh, gods, Dev." She presses her chained hands to her face and begins to sob.

Hatred for the Executor flashes through me anew. What better torture than to tell your prisoner that she has nothing left to live for? That everyone she cared for is gone, that she has no home to go back to? To strip away all that she was, all that she hopes to one day return to, and make yourself her whole world? So that, in the absence of an alternative, she may one day turn to you, abandoning her dreams and swallowing your lies whole?

I grip the bars of my cell, wishing I could reach through them and touch her. To offer comfort to this woman who's been tried, tested, and abused but didn't shatter, until she learned that the boy she loved twenty years ago still lived. "He never forgot you. His whole life is dedicated to finishing the work you started. To bringing the Commonwealths down."

My mother's sobs fade to hiccups. Her breath hitches. "Dev is alive," she repeats, clearly fighting to pull herself together. "*Alive*, and the head of the council. That's quite the meteoric rise for a baker's son. Do...do the rest respect him? Do they listen to what he says?"

I draw a deep breath, then tell her everything, hitting the highlights from the moment I left Vik until my arrival in this cage. It takes a long time, and when I'm done, my mouth is bone-dry again.

My mother gives a short, sharp inhale. "I thought perhaps Larisa was...an exception. Someone he'd captured and tricked into doing his bidding. But the Mages have risen? And they're in league with the Commonwealths and the exiles? Oh, by the gods."

"I should have listened when Ari told me meeting them in the woods was a terrible idea. But my beasts..." I sink my head into my hands, unwilling to articulate how my very self has become untrustworthy. "Now Erdahl is probably dead. And any rescue mission they've mounted is walking straight into a trap."

"This is *not* your fault," my mother says firmly. "You wanted to help a child. The fact that you didn't, in fact, manage to save him is beside the point. Your intentions were good."

"You know what they say about the road to hell," I mutter into the dark space between my palms. "And now...now Ari..."

"We'll figure it out," my mother says firmly. "We're together now, and that's all that matters. It's more than I ever dared to hope for."

"Together in *cages*," I point out.

"Together, *alive*." Her voice falls to a whisper, so quiet that a normal human wouldn't be able to hear it. "He's lying to the Mages, Eva. He's using them. It's what he does. We have to find a way to convince them of that and turn them to our side. It's our only chance."

I slide down the bars, hugging my knees to my chest. "I've tried. It didn't work. Their leader just drugged me and knocked me out again." My self-disgust rings in every syllable.

"You're powerful, Eva. But you're not omnipotent. It's one thing to fight the bellators. But magic that you don't understand is something else again." My mother sighs. "I've heard the old stories of what the Mages used to be. If even half of them are true, then you're dealing with a formidable force. You couldn't have anticipated what happened in that stone circle. Nor could you have protected yourself against it."

Lifting my head, I stare through the bars at the luxurious chamber beyond, at the crack in the floor and the candles guttering on the table. The room is windowless. Soon, when the candles die, it will be full dark. "I should have known better than to go. I should have listened to Ari, when he warned me."

"You love him," my mother says softly. "And he feels the same?"

I think of how angry Ari has been with me. How frustrated. He'll come after me, regardless. But just because he'd risk his life for me doesn't mean he still trusts me with his heart. "He loves me," I say, willing this to still be true. Even if I never get another chance to tell him I feel the same, Panther of the West or no. That I regret our last conversations more than I can say.

"I'm glad. When Armand took you from me—when he pried you from my arms—I worried you'd never know love." Her voice breaks on the word. "The Commonwealth is a cold, cold place; I've learned that well enough, even if I've never left these chambers. I feared for you, raised here. I feared what you would become. But despite everything, you and Ari found each other. You escaped this dreadful place. And your love is strong enough to sustain him as your familiar. That, alone, is a miracle. Eva, I'm so proud of you."

After what she's been through—imprisoned, tortured, and forced to bear the child of a predator—it floors me to hear her speak to me with such kindness. "How can you stand to look at me? Why don't you hate me? You have every right to, after what he did to you."

"Oh, Eva." Tears lace my mother's voice again. "You're a gift. Half of you may come from him, but half of you is *mine*. You grew up brave and brilliant and strong. You're all I could have dreamed of. You're a miracle. And I could never hate you."

Tears clog my own throat, and I fight to hold them back. If I start crying, I'm afraid I'll never stop. I draw on the control I was taught as a bellator, slowing my pulse, focusing on the candles' flames until I can speak calmly once more.

"Ari will come here, Cordelia, to the Mages' stronghold. I know it. They'll let him penetrate their defenses. And then, as soon as he's close enough for our bond to work again, they'll use me to power whatever horrific offensive they have in mind. I can't let that happen. I can't let them hurt innocent people."

My heart thuds, steady and sure, as I share the cold conclusion that I came to while I was bound to the beam. "I'm the reason the Mages' power has been awakened. I'm the commodity the Executor is so desperate to get his hands on, he traveled across the Empire, lost the remainder of the Thirty, and nearly died in the process. I am too dangerous to live." Not to mention, I refuse to be responsible for Ari losing his freedom and being forced into servitude.

Her harsh intake of breath resonates in the space between our cells. "Don't say that, Eva. Don't even *think* it. Please. Not when I've just found you again."

I twirl the ends of my battered braid around my fingers, like I used to do as an anxious child in the Nursery, alone in my bed in the dark. "I don't want to be responsible for anyone else's deaths—can't you understand that? And I'm tired of being a pawn. If I take myself out of the game, they'll have to find another game to play."

"You're more than a pawn, Eva. You're a symbol. You represent hope. Take *that* away, and this resistance has nothing." Her voice trembles with intensity. "Why do you think I've survived this long? I believed if I endured, I would find a way to see you again. To escape. And here you are."

"You think I can help you escape? I can't even save myself!" Disgusted, I kick my empty plate. It skitters across the floor and crashes into the bars on the other side.

"But you will." There's not a shred of doubt in her voice.

"How do you know?"

"Because," she says, "you're a survivor. And that is what we do. Don't even consider sacrificing yourself. We'll find another way."

I want to believe this, badly. But— "He'll torture us to hurt each other," I whisper. "Like what he did to me with the prod. I...I can't be used to make you suffer. I *won't.*"

"That wasn't your fault, either. It was his." Her voice is steel. "Don't make yourself into a martyr for the cause, Eva. You're a fighter. So am I. We'll fight, together. We'll bring this whole place down."

Her certainty feels like a lifeline, and within me, a spark of resistance flickers, coaxed into flame. But on its heels comes a choking sense of claustrophobia at the thought of losing my one hope of escape. We're underground here; I can sense it. I'm in a cage inside a room beneath a building within the Commonwealth behind a fence—

"I have to get out of here," I blurt. "I can't be here, not trapped like this. Not again. I fought so hard to escape, and he just dragged me back and now he wants to *use* me and make me watch as he tortures you, and I can't help Ari, I can't help anyone, and I—"

Dimly, I'm aware that my mother is talking, attempting to soothe me, but her words are a meaningless blur. My breath comes shallow, faster and faster. The words tumble over each other as I grip the bars of my cell, shaking them, trying to rend the metal. Within me, my beasts are in chaos, growling and hissing and scratching at the surface of me, desperate for release I can't give them. "I can't be here," I gasp, clawing at the bars. "I have to get out, I—"

"Hush!" my mother snaps, and the urgency in her voice is so strong that I actually comply, shocked into silence.

And then I hear the same thing she must have: footsteps padding down the hall, toward our chamber. They're light and quick, as if the person is in a hurry.

Or as if they don't want to be heard.

I swallow hard, trying to bring my breathing under control, as the door eases open and another red-robed Mage steps through, clutching a silver tray of syringes. She shuts the door behind her and stands in the shadows, regarding both of us from beneath her hood.

"What do you want?" my mother says, her voice brusque. "We're hardly a danger to ourselves or anyone else, locked up like this. Did he send you back down here? Well, you can trot back to him like a good little lackey and report that we're behaving. Go along now. Shoo." She flicks her fingers at the Mage, sounding every bit like the royalty she was born to be.

But the red-robed figure doesn't move.

I peer at it more closely, trying to make out the face beneath the hood. Maybe it's my imagination, but something about the way the figure stands is eerily familiar.

My anxiety is gone now, subsumed by curiosity. Inside me, my wolf raises her head, snuffling the air. *Not pack,* she informs me. *But friend.*

Friend? This makes no sense. No one wearing one of those robes is on my side. "Take off your hood," I demand, a hint of my wolf's growl thickening my voice.

The red-robed figure lifts a finger to her lips, adjuring silence. Then she pushes back the hood and steps out of the shadows, into the wavering candlelight.

And shock reverberates through every fiber of my body.

CHAPTER 33
ARI

Sebastían lands in the fallen leaves and comes up swinging. One look at the way he's going after Jaxon, who's giving as good as he gets, and I know there's no hope of me separating them alone. Putting two fingers in my mouth, I whistle, the high-low-high pitch of the Bellatorum's distress call. Fifteen seconds later, Kilían materializes out of the darkness, Ronan right behind him and Adrien, Fade, and Councilor Adelman on his heels. Kennett follows them, rubbing sleep from his eyes but alert nonetheless. I suppose a medic is trained to wake instantly, just like a soldier.

It takes our combined efforts to pull the two of them apart. Jaxon is hampered by the absence of his gun and his tender shoulder; Sebastían's sole impediment is his unwillingness to kill Jaxon outright. He's pinned Jaxon to the ground and closed his jaws around the latter's throat by the time we drag him off, spitting curses every inch of the way. Disgusted, he shakes us off, growls in Jaxon's direction, and stalks off toward his tent, his back ramrod straight.

So much for getting a good night's sleep, I think as Kennett kneels next to Jaxon, checking him over for damage. Luckily, most of it seems to be to his pride.

"What happened?" Ronan demands.

"*He* happened." Jaxon sits up, gestures at Sebastían, then locks his jaw and refuses to say another word. He looks every bit as wrecked as he did on that damned beam, and my stomach churns. Then, I saved him because he was fated to be Eva's familiar, and because it was the right thing to do. Now, he's my friend. And I protect what's mine.

Getting to my feet, I follow Sebastían through the camp, ignoring the guards who've emerged from their tents, roused by the commotion. Ronan can tell them whatever he wants; my business is Sebastían and the secret he's hiding, along with the nasty sadistic streak he chose to take out on Jaxon. It's clear to me that whatever Tobias got caught trying to steal, Jaxon had no idea about it. And yet, Sebastían didn't hesitate to try to use it as blackmail.

What an unmitigated prick.

One word from me, and your precious reputation goes up in flames. Let's see you marry Eva Marteinn then, Jaxon had said. Well, two can play this game. If I can pry Sebastían's secret out of him, then I'll hold the same leverage. I can use him to find Eva, and then drop the bomb. But if whatever he's hiding has the potential to endanger this mission, that's a different story.

I catch up with him outside his tent, set up at the base of a giant fir. "What," he says without turning. I suppose my scent gives me away.

"We need to talk."

Sebastían turns to look at me. He's covered in mud, his face streaked with it. Those aquamarine eyes peer out of a mask of dirt, making him look even more feral than usual. "You have five minutes," he bites out. "Then I'm going to sleep. Talk fast."

I duck through the doorway of his tent. It's nicer than most:

tall enough to stand up in; plush blankets instead of my plain bedroll; embroidered pillows; a small altar to the many-headed gods set up to the left of the entrance, complete with low-burning candles. It's also got Ilsa, who rises as soon as he comes in, her eyes widening.

"What happened to you?" she says, scanning him from head to toe. "I was so worried when you didn't come back. Are you all right?"

Sebastían's lip curls. "A fool. No need. And yes," he says. "Now get out."

"But what about—" She flaps her hand at a blanket draped over something next to the altar. An odd chittering sound emanates from beneath it, followed by a hiss that ends in a growl.

"Out, I said!" Sebastían snarls, not sparing the blanket a glance.

She must be used to his surly moods, because she obeys without a word. As soon as she ducks through the flap into the night, he pulls his mud-splattered shirt over his head and dumps it in a corner. Then he dips a cloth in a bowl of water and starts dabbing the mud off his face, his back to me.

"Ticktock, exile," he says.

Supercilious ass. It's not like I'm itching to be stuck in here with him. "I won't waste any time with niceties, then. What were you really doing in the woods? And who's the *her* Jaxon was talking about?"

"That's none of your business." His tone is cool, assured, but the hidden thing in the corner takes issue with it anyway, squawking in alarm.

"No? Let's start with something simpler, then. What in the nine hells is underneath that blanket?"

Sebastían turns, his bearing regal and his skin pale in the flickering light of the candles. Even in human form, it's clear he's a formidable opponent, his skin pulled taut over well-defined muscles. A bruise is beginning to darken on his jaw, courtesy of the one good punch Jaxon landed. "I don't have to explain myself to you."

I straighten to my full height, giving me a solid two inches on him. "You said we have five minutes, yeah? So, let's cut the virtueless crap and get to it. We both know I'll get answers one way or another. This is the easy way. I advise you take it."

Sebastían levels his gaze on me, his eyes boring into mine. I stare back, unperturbed. If he thinks he's going to intimidate me like this, he's sorely mistaken. I've engaged in a battle of wills with the best of them, and more often than not, come out on top.

He gives first, sinking down onto his blankets and propping himself up on his hands. "Oh, fine. Sit, if you want," he says, gesturing at the camp chair Ilsa vacated.

Warily, I comply, then wait. Interrogation 101: the one who speaks first, loses.

Sebastían rubs a hand over his face. "I was telling the truth about feeling confined in this camp," he says. "Panthers are nocturnal. We're meant to rove, to prowl at night. Not to be trapped in a place like this." He waves a disgusted hand at the tent. "So I've been swearing Ilsa to secrecy and shifting, once everyone is asleep. It's easy for a panther to slip past guards, no matter how good you are. If we don't want to be seen, we won't be."

"Well," I say, my tone dry, "there's also the small matter that the guards are watching for people trying to get *into* the camp, not out."

"True." He leans back on his hands again, his eyes red-rimmed from lack of sleep and the bruise blooming blue-and-purple beneath his pale skin. "So, yes. I did leave the camp because I wanted to escape. But also—well, you heard what I told Ronan about naming Eva's panther. I thought maybe, if I took the form of my beast, I could call to her more effectively. That Carina would hear me, even if Eva could not."

I sit forward with a start, bracing my hands on my knees. "And could she?"

Sebastían shakes his head. "For a moment, I thought—but no. If she heard me, she didn't reply." His shoulders slump. "It's shameful, to be unable to call your mate's beast-half that way. It's seen as a sign of weakness."

"At the risk of sounding reiterative," I say, iron in my tone, "perhaps that's because she isn't your mate."

"Semantics." Sebastían waves me off wearily. "You can understand why I didn't want to confide this out in the open, to Fjeri, no less. He's always searching for ammunition, that one."

I'm not in the mood to debate whether or not Eva belongs with Sebastían. It's an unwinnable argument, and his belief that they're meant to be mated is, in part, what's convinced him to join this invasion. Besides, I'd be willing to bet that he's just trying to distract me.

"So she hasn't been answering you. And you expect me to believe you didn't try another approach, even though this one hasn't been getting you anywhere?" I stab a finger in the direction of the chittering sound. "I'll ask again. What is that, and why is it so important that Ilsa needed to stay behind to guard it?"

"Oh, for the love of the gods. You're like a terrier with a bone, Westergaard." He heaves himself to his feet. "I suppose you were going to find out anyway. This camp leaks like a sieve."

Stalking over to the blanket, he bends and yanks it off with a flourish. "Behold."

I don't know what I was expecting: some kind of magical

implement? a vicious beast? But as the blanket falls away, I draw a surprised breath.

Beneath it is a cage. And inside the cage is...

"Is that a *ferret*?"

"Very good, exile," he says dryly. "At least they teach the identification of basic animal species in that Commonwealth of yours."

I take another step forward, and the creature in the cage screeches, scuttling away. Its dark eyes are bright with panic, its small ears pricked. The closer I get, the more it puffs out its fur in an attempt to impress me with its size. "Why the hell do you have a ferret in a cage?"

Sebastían arches an eyebrow. "Maybe I wanted a pet. A companion who wouldn't scheme against me or ask annoying questions. Did you ever think of that?"

"And maybe I plan to take up the fine art of basket weaving." I peer more closely at the animal, which seems to have exhausted itself. It's lying on its side now, flanks heaving. "What's wrong with it? Is it sick?"

"It's dying." His voice is flat. "Just like all the others."

"What others? What the hell are you up to?" Hand dropping to the hilt of my dagur, I stare at him, then at the ferret, which has begun to pant.

"I think..." He prods the cage with the toe of his boot. "I think it's a spy."

I glance from the animal, whose show of bravado has subsided into shivering, to the Panther of the West, looming over it. "Have you lost your mind?"

"Think about it, Westergaard. How is this any more peculiar than the Mages using the ravens? This is the fourth one I've caught slinking around our camp, eavesdropping on conversations. They're like you, always where they shouldn't be. But when I try to interrogate them, like you did with that damned bird, they just die." His jaw tightens with frustration. "You want to know where I was tonight? Out in the woods, trying to catch another."

Ignoring the jab, I straighten and glare at him. "We're supposed to be working together. Why keep this a secret?"

"Because." For the first time, I see a hint of embarrassment color his cheeks. "What if I was wrong? You'd mock me, the way you're doing right now."

"So you chose to sneak around behind my back instead? You ever hear the one about how pride goeth before a—"

"Spare me your Commonwealth platitudes." He rattles the cage, heedless of the animal's pathetic whining. Spy or not, I can't help but feel sympathy for it. If Gentian could see this, he'd have a nervous breakdown.

"Let it out, Pardúr."

He shoots me an incredulous look. "Have you heard anything I said?"

"I heard you. But look at it. Does it seem like it's in any condition to go running off?"

Without waiting for his reply, I bend and unlatch the cage. Sebastían huffs, but he doesn't say a word as the ferret gets shakily to all four paws and creeps out. It pauses just beyond the entrance, as if waiting to be shoved back inside. But when that doesn't happen, it sinks to its haunches, still trembling, and looks up at me.

"Fantastic," Sebastían mutters. "You can add another accolade to the list. Ari Westergaard, Commonwealth exile and ferret whisperer."

"Shut it." I kneel in front of the animal, whose jaws have begun to drip with drool. Sebastían's right on one account: it's not well. If I'm going to act, I need to do it now.

Paying no attention to the glowering prince beside me, I close my eyes and draw on my bond with Eva. If Sebastían's right and this poor creature is being used as a spy, then maybe I can see her through its eyes, like I did with the raven. It's a long shot, but better than no shot at all.

Come on, Eva, I think, picturing the cord of our bond, trailing off into blackness. *Give me something. Anything. Please…*

For a moment, nothing happens. I feel beyond foolish, kneeling on the floor of a shapeshifter's tent, holding an imaginary conversation with a dying weasel. "Forget about —" I begin, intending to put the animal out of its misery and get the information I came for: the secret that, if exposed, has the potential to sever Sebastían's claim on Eva once and for all.

And then an image flickers into my mind, fuzzy at first, but sharpening by the moment: Eva, fists gripping the bars of a sins-forsaken cage, dark eyes wide with shock. In them, I see the miniature reflections of a red-robed figure: a Mage.

By the Sins. "What have you done to her?" I say, voice tight with fury. "Let her go!"

Eva's eyes widen even further. "Ari?" she whispers. "But— but how—"

She can hear me, thank the Virtues. "Where are you?" I demand, scanning the room for clues. I don't recognize it: luxurious furniture, cracked stone floor, and of course, that damned cage. "Are you hurt?"

"I'm all right." Her fingers are white-knuckled on the bars of the cage. "But Ari, don't come here. Stay away. It's a trap—"

My mouth goes dry. If she doesn't want me by her side, then I was right: she's decided this is a fight she can't win. *Aut viam inveniam aut faciam* echoes in my head, as clearly as if she's spoken it aloud. "Eva, don't do anything stupid, you hear me? I'm coming. Wait for me."

She shakes her head, her disheveled braid flying. But before she can reply, the red-robed figure speaks. The words issue from the ferret's mouth, hoarse but decipherable nonetheless. "Speak of the wolf," it barks, "and she will come."

"In the name of the gods," Sebastían murmurs, dropping to his knees beside me.

What the hell is a Mage doing, reciting the rebellion's cipher?

Unless, of course, it's not a Mage at all.

I recognize that voice. I would know it anywhere. And now that I take a closer look at the tiny reflections I see in Eva's eyes—

I brace myself for cross-examination. But as the first words leave my lips, the ferret twitches, coughs up a horrifying amount of foamy blood, and dies at my feet.

CHAPTER 34
EVA

The red-robed figure is no Mage. It's Gentian Halverson, Ari's friend.

Though Gentian and I have never spoken, I remember him well. Once, he risked everything to save a bird. Ari took the blame for him...and the whipping.

I was there, that day in Clockverk Square. I saw Gentian watching Ari, his own body flinching with every lash, his eyes welling with tears. I know he was one of the only people in the Commonwealth that Ari respected. The only one, other than Kilían, that Ari missed when he left this place behind.

Ari, whose voice I heard, filled with desperation and pain, before it cut off like a bad transmission. Who has somehow managed to reach out to me a second time.

I tried to warn him, to protect him. But he won't listen. I know he won't.

Wait for me, he'd demanded, the way he used to give me orders when we were still mentor and apprentice. But I know better. Beneath that cool command, he was pleading with me to stay. To still be here when he fights his way to my side.

The problem with understanding someone so well, on a bone-deep level, is that the blade cuts both ways. *Don't do anything stupid* is code for the same thing he said to me when we were alone together in the Brotherhood's tent that first night: *Promise me you'll never do anything like that again. No more of the self-sacrificing games.*

He knows I've been planning to take myself out of the equation, as soon as I can figure out a way. And the agony in his voice, a moment before Gentian spoke and our connection snapped...it shatters me. His pain is my own, even miles apart.

I don't deserve him. But by the Architect, I want the chance to try.

"What just happened?" I whisper, the iron bars biting into my palms as the words spill from my lips. "Have you been talking to Ari? Do you know where he—"

Gentian gives a sharp, vicious shake of his head. Then he digs in the pocket of his robes, coming out with a creased piece of paper and a pencil. Crossing to the table, he smooths the paper on its surface and then scribbles something. A moment later, he holds up the page, and my mother comes forward too, as far as her clanking chains will permit her, to see.

I hoped communicating with him might be possible. But I didn't know for sure, it reads. The paper trembles in his hands, and he irons it out on the table, writes some more, then holds it up again. *The Mages use animals, then discard them like trash. Whatever creature Ari was speaking through is probably dead.* His teeth sink into his lower lip, his expression pained.

I think about the raven that delivered the message to the stables. About hearing Ari's voice, when I was chained to that beam with Dresda looking on. "But you're not a Mage." I speak softly, and Gentian steps forward, straining to hear. "How did you do that?"

Frowning, he turns away and scribbles again. *No one notices a shy, stuttering vet tech. They experiment in my lab. And I listen. One day, I will stop them.*

The expression on his face is fierce, uncompromising. I remember him as a shy, quiet boy, thin and angular, with a headful of curly hair he never managed to tame and gray eyes that always looked a little too big for his pale face. That much hasn't changed. But I also remember him as fearful, hiding his small, animal-rescuing rebellions in the shadows. The boy I recall would never have had the bravery to impersonate a Mage, or to join an insurrection. Yet here he is, uttering the Brotherhood's passphrase—just above a whisper, so the bellators in the hallway can't hear, but clear as day nonetheless. Here he is, spying and declaring revolution.

The hope that faded when the Executor had Traalf unplug the cameras reignites inside me, bright and shining. Maybe my mother and Ari are right. Maybe there's a way out of this, after all, even if I can't see it clearly right now. Maybe I just need to have faith.

If the Commonwealth has taught me anything, though, it's that blind faith is dangerous. I want to believe Gentian's presence here means that victory lies within our grasp. But the conviction of one unskilled boy, no matter how courageous, is not enough to turn the tide.

Gentian holds the page over one of the guttering candles. Fire nibbles at the edges, then devours it. When it's nothing but ash, he lifts his tray once more and approaches our cells. His scent drifts through the bars: lemongrass, with an undercurrent of rubbing alcohol.

When he speaks, the words are barely audible. "What happened after you left the Commonwealth?" His eyes flick toward the door outside which the bellators lurk, then back to me. "How were you and Ari separated? The last time you saw him, was he all right?"

What can I tell him? That Ari risked his life for me over and over, and I repaid him by prioritizing political alliances over his love and loyalty? That when Erdahl was kidnapped and Vik's border alarm went off, I was in the woods, letting Sebastían give my panther a name? That when he cautioned me about meeting with the Mages and Executor alone, I was so convinced I knew best that I ignored his counsel, getting Erdahl killed and delivering myself into the hands of the enemy?

Sebastían would doubtless say it's because my beasts' instincts consumed me. That I wasn't responsible for what happened. But I can't let myself off the hook that easily.

"The last time I saw him, he was trapped inside a stone circle, fighting to get to me," I admit, pain lancing through me at the way Gentian's expression falls. "It was my fault."

He blinks, swallowing hard. "Is it true you hold the forms of four beasts? That he's become your f-familiar, as the Mages call it?"

I nod, and his angular face settles into a determined expression. "Then he'll find you, Eva. It doesn't matter what happened. He c-came back for you once. He'll do so again, like he promised. And we need to be ready when he does."

His voice is so firm, so confident. *He* believes there's a way out of this, that's clear enough. He's placed his faith in me, in Ari, and in his own ability to withstand what awaits us.

I take in the set of his jaw, the glint in his eyes, and feel shame wash over me. Is it the coward's way out to believe that if I manage to escape this cell, the only prayer of foiling the Executor's plans is to do myself in, taking down as many of our enemies as I can until I fall? Is it wrong to play along with Gentian, letting him think we have a shot at true victory, when I'm planning to sacrifice myself at the first opportunity?

When Sun Tzu wrote, "All warfare is based on deception," I don't think this is what he meant. But one thing is certain: If I can't get out of this cage, both defending and eliminating myself are off the table. If I go on a hunger strike, they'll force-feed me. If I bang my head into the bars, someone will come running to stop me. Whether I mean to fight back or die, I have to escape these four walls. And my best hope of doing that is the bright-eyed, steely-jawed vet tech standing in front of me.

Straightening my spine, I meet Gentian's gaze. "All right," I say, imbuing my voice with all the self-possession I can muster. "What do you have in mind?"

He squares his shoulders, then raises the pitch of his voice in an eerie impression of Larisa, speaking loud enough for the bellators guarding the door to hear.

"I've come to give you your nightly injections," he says. "It'll make the evening hours go a little easier. That's what the vet techs told me, anyhow. Right, Cordelia?"

My mother grimaces, and I realize they must drug her overnight. The vet techs are trained to work with the Bastarour. They know how to calibrate doses to sedate and subdue them—and by extension, us. Obviously, so do the Mages, given how they drugged me during our travels. Which begs the question—what are the Mages up to? What have they accomplished, while I've been unconscious and trapped? And how in the nine hells can we put a stop to it?

"D-don't worry," Gentian says, misinterpreting the dismay that must be stamped all over my features. "I'm not going to inject you. Just be sure to act d-drugged, if they come in."

"You're one of us," my mother breathes. There's a note of skepticism in her voice, as if she fears this is too good to be true. "But I've never seen you down here before."

"My specialty is research." His lips purse in distaste. "I'd hoped to slip myself into this rotation. To discover where Bitte and Andersson went each night when they left the vet lab with their little trays. But then the M-mages came, and I learned who the Executor was hiding. What he'd done. Cordelia, I am so sorry." His gaze lingers on her, heavy with sympathy, and my mother swallows hard.

"They whispered about you, too, Eva. Who your m-mother was. Your father. How he corrupted your DNA, to use you as a w-weapon." He closes his eyes, struggling for composure. "I thought my research was meant to help. To heal. But now I know it was always meant to further the Executor's ends." The tray trembles in his hands, but from rage, not nerves. When he speaks again, his voice is low but fierce. "I won't let that happen. I'm done being a tool in the hands of a power-hungry madman."

At the thought of the Executor's research, leveraged to tamper with my DNA and the Architect knows what else, my wolf raises her head and growls. Cordelia does the same, in solidarity. But Gentian doesn't flinch. He looks...reassured, somehow. As if the sound makes him feel at home.

"They intend t-to use Mages in place of the vet techs, now that there are two of you down here. Something about a lightning prod..." He glances down at his tray, jaw tight with disapproval. "Before he left, Bellator Bryndísarson told me that if they c-captured you and brought you back, I should be p-prepared to act. And so here I am, courtesy of an unfortunate accident that befell the Mage who wore these robes." His lips rise in a grim smile.

I try to picture Gentian and Kilían conspiring—the unassuming vet tech and the stern, vicious bellator—and fail utterly. How in the world did such an alliance come to pass? If, by some miracle, we all survive, I would love to find out.

Right now, though, only one thing matters. "Here you are," I echo. "And I'm grateful. But please tell me you have a plan."

"Let's get down to b-business," Gentian says, his smile fading as he squares his thin shoulders. "We don't have much time."

CHAPTER 35

ARI

"What in the nine hells just happened?" I say, staring down at the dead ferret with horror.

"I'll tell you what happened." Sebastían sounds disgusted. "In five minutes, you accomplished more than I've managed in twice as many days." He pokes the corpse with the toe of his boot, then straightens and meets my eyes. "You saw something, didn't you? What was it?"

"Eva. In a cage." My voice is rough with the rage I'm struggling to contain. Maybe it's contagious, because I swear I feel it leap from me to Sebastían, like a spark.

The shadow of his beast swims behind his eyes as the tips of his claws slide from their sheaths. I may not be his familiar, but I can feel the rise of his panther just the same, eager to be set free. "What have they done to her?" he growls.

"I don't know. She...she looked okay." I shove my hands into my pockets to hide the way I'm trembling—with fury, sure, but also terror. The last time Eva was locked up like this, after the bombing that killed my mother, she'd been tortured six ways from Sunday, all because she'd sacrificed herself to save me. And here she is, planning to do the same damned thing again.

250

Stay away, it's a trap, my ass. More like, *Stay away so I can feed myself to the monsters and keep you alive.* Like my life means anything without her in it.

The first time around, I hadn't had faith in her. I'd believed the worst—that she'd been using me—and she'd nearly paid the price.

I'd been so angry with her, so hurt about Sebastían. Maybe if I'd been thinking rather than just feeling, I would've been able to convince her not to enter that damned stone circle.

I hate everything the Commonwealth stands for, but one thing is for sure: attachment does lead to chaos. Or at least, to standing in a tent with a pissed-off panther, with the girl I love planning to martyr herself and the world's most unlikely voice issuing from the mouth of a weasel.

It was distorted, yes. But combined with the tiny reflections I saw in Eva's eyes, I have no doubt. Not a Mage, after all, but a vet tech turned revolutionary.

By the Virtues, what does Gentian think he's doing? He could get himself killed playing spy, and then what?

Keeping a tight leash on what remains of my control, I force myself to speak calmly. "We're supposed to be cooperating, you imbecile. Not turning this into a competition. Yet here you are, capturing creatures behind my back and keeping secrets so substantial, you're willing to kill Jaxon to shut him up. You want to tell me what you're hiding?"

The Panther of the West glares at me in silence, folding his arms across his chest.

"That's what I thought." I glower at him. "And you expect me to trust you?"

It's a rhetorical question, which he doesn't bother answering. And a good thing, too, because I'm not remotely interested in what he has to say. The spark of rage within me ignites into a conflagration, and I have to call on all my Commonwealth training not to lunge at him.

"You've been at this for ten days. All this time, I could've been communicating with Eva. But no. You let your sins-damned pride rule you, and poured our best source of intelligence right down the drain." I clench the hilt of my dagur so hard, my knuckles crack. "You say you want to *marry* Eva. That you're what's best for her. And yet you let her suffer, alone."

Sebastían's mouth opens, then shuts so hard I can hear his teeth slam together. That now-familiar growl simmers in the back of his throat. "I didn't mean—"

"Not another word." I take a step toward him, our faces inches apart, and have the satisfaction of seeing the slightest hint of fear slide through his eyes. "Whatever meager bit of trust you've earned from me? Consider it spent."

His upper lip curls back in a snarl, revealing razor-sharp, elongated canines. "It's not what you think, Westergaard."

Ha. "You have no idea what I think. And you'd better find another messenger. This time, get it to me before it's half-dead."

"I can't guarantee I can—"

"Too bad." I step closer still, the hilt of my dagur pressing into his stomach in an unspoken threat. "Oh, and one more thing. Torture Jaxon like that again, and you'll find yourself dealing with me. I'm stronger than he is. I'm faster. So—you do the math."

Turning, I duck through the tent flap into the darkness. He doesn't try to stop me.

❧

Jaxon is asleep, and after a brief debate, I decide to let him rest. I can shake him down about Sebastían's secret tomorrow. The Lead Interrogator, on the other hand, is another story.

I find Kilían alone in his tent, lying on his bedroll, hands knotted behind his head. He sits up when I step inside. "Fjeri's fine," he says at once. "No thanks to his smart mouth. He's been spending too much time with you, Westergaard."

"Thanks a lot. But that's not why I'm here."

Kilían tenses, his jaw tightening. "Ah," he says, sounding more uncomfortable than I've ever heard him. "If this is about your father, I assure you I meant no—"

"Gentian Halverson," I say, cutting him off. "Really, Kilían? A Brotherhood spy?"

He draws a relieved breath, leaning back to brace himself on his hands. "Yes, since you ask. And a good one. But how did you know—"

Damn it. Gentian was so kind. So gentle. Without me there to protect him, anything could have happened…and clearly, it did. I feel a sudden, sharp pang of guilt for leaving him behind.

"I'll tell you my secrets if you tell me yours." I glare at Kilían. "Did you threaten him? Is that why he's spying for you? Don't even try to tell me you're not behind this."

He raises one red eyebrow. "Threaten him? Hardly. Beneath that boy's submissive exterior beats the heart of a rebel. Believe me, this was his idea."

My temples pound with the onset of a headache, brought on by lack of sleep and an excess of revelations. "What are you talking about?"

He tells me, then. How Gentian came upon me and Eva, kissing in the woods. How he stumbled away, ran straight into Riis, and played the fool, pretending to be lost in order to keep the bellator from discovering us. How, the night we fled the Commonwealth, Gentian stole tranquilizer darts from the veterinary clinic and followed us, taking down three of the Bastarour. How he raced back to the clinic, only for Kilían to catch him red-handed.

With each word he speaks, my eyes grow wider. "Gentian did all that?"

"He did." A grudging smile lifts the corners of Kilían's lips. "And he's become a most useful member of the Brotherhood. As he so rightly pointed out, between his stuttering and his submissive nature, no one would ever suspect him."

Gentian, a gifted espionage agent. Now I've heard everything. "But why did he—"

Kilían shakes his head. "Your turn, Westergaard. Explain yourself."

And so I do, telling him what happened from the moment Sebastían emerged from the woods until the ferret expired at my feet. "It spoke in Gentian's voice," I conclude. "He's there, with her. All this time, we could have been communicating with them, if Sebastían hadn't been..." I wave a hand, indicating all the things that Sebastían is not.

"You don't know that, Westergaard. The timing...our proximity...there are too many unknowns." His eyes flick toward the tent flap, and his voice drops. "Whatever that secretive bastard is hiding, let's hope it's not something that can compromise our mission."

"A little late for that." I sink onto the floor of the tent, arms wrapped around my knees. "Why would Gentian do this? I looked after him, yeah. I tried to protect him, whenever I could. But keeping my secrets, taking down three Bastarour, becoming a traitor...he could have died."

"You took that whipping for him," Kilían points out.

"And got what I wanted from it." The way I stood steady while the Priest lashed my back sealed my fate as a bellator, and both of us know it.

"Be that as it may," Kilían says. "We both know it would have broken him." He runs a hand over his beard, the way he does when he's troubled. "Don't give yourself too much credit, Westergaard. Yes, you stood up for him. Yes, he cared for you. But through that caring, he found a cause greater than himself. Much like I did."

My brows knit. I can think of few people more different than Gentian, who would do anything to help a vulnerable creature, and the ruthless Lead Interrogator. "What are you talking about?"

A red flush stains Kilían's cheekbones. "The boy had...feelings for you. The way I—"

I hold up a hand, interrupting him. I'm in no mood for confessions. "Gentian *what*? How do you know this? Did he tell you?"

"Never mind that," Kilían says impatiently.

"Never *mind*? It's important, don't you think? If he risked his life to save me—"

"Initially, he did." Kilían huffs, as if this doesn't signify. "But the boy is brave. What he's doing now, he's doing for himself. Because of what he wants. What he believes. You were a catalyst, nothing more, so get over yourself and pay attention."

"To what?" I snap, aggravated. "You're not saying anything."

He scrubs a hand over his beard again, and I can hear his heart pick up speed. "By the Sins," he mutters. "Look, Westergaard...I'll just come out with it. I have a favor to ask you."

I lift my pounding head, my interest piqued despite myself. "Don't tell me—you want me to take Gentian on as my new apprentice. Sorry to inform you, but I'm out of the mentoring business. The first time around ended rather poorly, if you recall."

Kilían looks like he wants to strangle me. But instead, he

heaves a sigh, pinching the rough material of his blanket between two fingers, and forges onward. "Just listen, for once in your life. In battle, we have to make difficult choices, eh? There's the mission, and then there's our personal agenda. Our own mission, as it were. You're fortunate that your mission aligns with the larger one. But my own—" The word catches in his throat, and he clears it viciously.

So that's what this is about. "Let me spare you the trouble. I heard you with my father at the training grounds, Kilían. I saw you kneel to him."

The color drains from Kilían's face, but to his credit, he meets my eyes dead-on. "Yet you've said nothing."

"What would I say? I owe my life, such as it is, to you." My hand drops to my weapons belt, gripping the hilt of my dagur in an effort to steady myself. "You could have run with him and Miriam. But you stayed behind. You sacrificed everything to protect me."

"I loved him," Kilían says simply. "And you were his. It was the least I could do."

I draw a breath, so deep it rattles my blades. "You loved him then. And...you still do?"

"I will always love him." His tone is matter-of-fact, like he's stating a fundamental, unalterable truth. "I've loved him since we were children. I loved him even when I thought I would never see him again, and I love him still. I would do anything for him."

"I understand," I say. And I do. It's how I feel about Eva.

"No one cares if Kennett lives or dies, Ari. No one but me." His ice-blue gaze flicks to mine, and in it I see soul-deep pain. "On paper, I'm worth more to this mission. But if you must choose between saving me or Kennett...I'm asking you to save your father. He's *good,* through and through. And my life is worth nothing without his."

The raw honesty in his voice disarms me, and I swallow hard. "You're wrong, Kilían. *I* care for him. And I'm in your debt. If it's in my power to save his life, unless the only alternative is sacrificing Eva, then I'll do it."

Kilían's eyebrows lower, his face shifting into the authoritative expression of the man who once led the Thirty. "Your word," he demands, scanning my face.

Yanking my blade free, I kiss the hilt. "I swear on my dagur, I'll do my best to protect him. And if it comes to a choice between the two of you, I will put him first."

He gives me one last, penetrating look, as if weighing my sincerity. And then he gets to his feet. "Let's hope it doesn't come to that. Right now, we've got another messenger to catch."

He holds the tent flap open for me, and after a moment, I follow.

CHAPTER 36

EVA

Gentian gives us the lay of the land in a hushed whisper. Apparently, there are two bellators guarding the door, and two more at the entrance to the place where we're being held, accessible from the machine shop. There's a secondary entrance from the Executor's quarters, guarded not on our end but his.

"We're under the machine shop?" My eyebrows knit.

"The primary entrance is under the machine shop," Gentian corrects. "It's cleverly disguised. After Bellator Bryndísarson left with the Thirty and I discovered Cordelia's existence, I managed to access the blueprints. This chamber itself lies beneath Clockverk Square."

All this time, my mother has been so close. Every day, when I crossed the square to the dining hall, queueing to recite the Oath of Loyalty and hear the Executor's litany of sinners, she was right there beneath my feet.

But there's no time to dwell on that now. I listen in horror as Gentian goes on.

"The Mages and the Executor are collaborating to create a weapon that blends magic and technology, something strong

258

enough to wipe out the Houses' entire army. I have no idea what it is." His voice is so quiet that if my mother and I couldn't draw on our beasts' augmented hearing, we'd be unable to hear him. "I haven't been able to get c-close enough to learn more. Without Bellator Bryndísarson, my access to intelligence is limited. I've been trying to recruit the natural-born who have access to the Executor, cleaning and serving and such, but they're so t-terrified, it's hard going. Still, I've learned enough to tell you that whatever the weapon is, it's close to completion. And they need Eva's abilities to make it work."

My mother gives a low, warning growl. "Then we need to get her out of here before they have the chance."

"Agreed," Gentian says. "But how?"

The first vestiges of a plan flicker to life in my mind. "We need proof the Executor plans to betray the Mages," I say. "Something actionable, to break their alliance. Have you overheard anything like that? Anything at all?"

"I—"

"You! Mage!" Traalf bellows from outside the door. "What are you doing in there? Not fraternizing with our sins-forsaken prisoners, are you?"

"Of course not, Bellator Traalf. Almost finished," Gentian calls back, raising his voice in that eerie impersonation again. It's alarming how good he is at this, even somehow shedding his stutter when the mission depends on it.

Lowering his voice again, he whispers, the words tumbling over each other in an effort to get them out as quickly as possible, "I did h-hear something I couldn't q-quite make sense of. I was on my way from the vet tech b-building to the Great Hall when I overheard the Executor talking with interim Lead Bellator Rondeau. They said, when the battle was over, that they would d-divide their forces between the Houses. That Rondeau would have to train replacements, and f-fast. And I t-thought...why would they need to do that, if the agreement was for the Mages to rule the Houses?"

"Why indeed," my mother says grimly. "Unless Armand never planned to hold up his side of the agreement. He wants to dominate the Empire—Commonwealths, Houses, and all. Whatever this weapon is, he'll use it to kill every skúma that gets in his way, weaken the Mages, and then keep me and Eva as trophies."

It has the definitive ring of truth, and I open my mouth to say so. But then a wave of dizziness rocks me, and I have to grip the bars to stay upright.

"Eva?" My mother's voice is sharp with concern. "Are you all right?"

Another bout of dizziness sweeps me. My skin tingles, electricity thrumming through me from head to toe. Blood pounds in my ears as my vision blurs. And then the world settles, leaving me with an undeniable sense of wholeness. Behind my eyes, I can see that familiar blue cord—but instead of trailing off into the darkness, it's taut, current flowing toward me from the other end.

"By the Sins," I say, my voice laced with wonder...and more than a hint of terror. Whatever I plan to do, we are running out of time. "I can feel him."

Gentian's jaw drops. The tray falls from his hands, clattering onto the floor. "You can feel Ari? But that must mean—"

"Mage!" Traalf roars. "Is everything all right in there?"

"Yes! Sorry. I just dropped my tray." Gentian stares at me, wide-eyed, as he scoops up the syringes and other paraphernalia. "It's happening, then," he whispers, low-voiced. "We n-need to act fast."

The shreds of my idea come together, shimmering into a plan that just might work, if everything goes right. At least, well enough to free me from this cage. "Have you been able to recruit any of the comp techs into the resistance?"

Gentian shakes his head. "Kilían put out feelers, but no luck. We do have a natural-born embedded in the comp lab, though. She's smart and resourceful. And angry. She'll help us."

"Tell her to disable the bio-ID on that keypad." I gesture at the device that unlocks our cells. "If she's as resourceful as you say, she'll figure out how." Ari was a natural-born, and look what he's capable of. There's a whole host of people that the Executor has been underestimating at his peril. If Gentian is actually able to mobilize them, then—

"Get word to Dresda," I tell him, swallowing down the shards of something that feels a lot like hope. "Fight to convince her of what you heard. And whatever other plans you have in place...activate them now."

"Mage!"

"Coming!" Gentian gives me a firm, determined nod. Then he hunches his shoulders, drops his head, and hurries out the door.

CHAPTER 37

ARI

The wind wails through the mountains as the sun rises, bringing with it a teeth-rattling chill. Or maybe the chill's emanating from within, as I anticipate what today holds.

Our attempts to capture another one of the Mages' messengers were fruitless. Sebastían did make an effort, I'll give him that, and Kilían and I backed him up. But the woods around our camp were empty—suspiciously so. It made me wonder what had actually killed that ferret: the strain of possession by the Mages, or some sort of sequence triggered by its interrogation. Maybe the raven would have died anyway, even if I hadn't stabbed it through the wing.

I wanted to explore this further, to quiz Sebastían about the other creatures he'd gotten his hands on, but when we emerged from the woods, we walked straight into chaos.

Eldrina's falcons had arrived, leading three hundred guards from Montyorke, San Fraesco, and Satrizona, as well as another adult panther pair. So, instead of getting some much-needed sleep, I spent the next few hours strategizing about our strengths and weaknesses, the Commonwealth's security, and our plan of attack.

The falcons flew ahead, taking in an aerial view of the Commonwealth, but they couldn't penetrate it. There's some kind of aerial shield in place, maybe the same forcefield that the Mages used in the stone circle. Which means that our only way in is either through the tunnels Eva and I used to escape, or the forest where the Bastarour prowl.

"The Mages may have herded us here, but I can't imagine they want a full-on battle, one they stand a chance at losing," Adelman said last night. "They'll want to thin our numbers, with an eye on taking the familiars and skúma alive and doing away with the rest of us. Every step from this point on will be rigged."

Like it hasn't been already, I wanted to say, but didn't. Instead, I listened to Kilían's overview of the size, strength, and color-coded gear of each Commonwealth's Bellatorum, all the while trying and failing to reach out for Eva. I wish I'd seen more through the damn ferret's eyes, enough to tell where they're keeping her.

Wait for me, I'd begged her. What if she didn't listen? What if, the closer I get, the more determined she becomes to go through with whatever foolhardy, self-sacrificing plan she's concocted? What if I arrive in the Commonwealth to find her cold and gone?

Try as I might, I can't push the image away. The darkness clings to me as we ride through the pass where we made our stand against the Thirty, on our final approach. I half expect to find corpses, black rags shredding from their bones and birds pecking at their empty eye sockets, but thank the Architect, my imagination has run away with me: though the trees on either side of the path are still shriveled from the fire, the Bellatorum has removed their dead.

I'm lost in a grim tally of the bellators who lost their lives here—Frederik. Mikhael. Erik. Tiberius. Jordan. Noah. Ananias. Simeon. Nathanael. Elias—when Jaxon rides up beside me. I've been trying to get him alone, but no luck. I'm pretty sure he's been avoiding me.

I need to know what he's been keeping to himself about Sebastían. But first, I have to voice what matters most. I'm sick and tired of worrying whether the people I care about are going to stay alive.

"You," I say with finality, fighting to dismiss the vivid image of one of the bellators' corpses wearing Jaxon's face, then Eva's, "are a dumbass."

A surprised expression creeps across his face before his lips rise in a crooked smirk. "Where did you learn that word?"

"Don't deflect. You're lucky you're not dead."

"Am I?" The two syllables are bleak.

"I thought we dealt with this the night I smashed your bottle of ákavíti, you sins-forsaken fool. Tobias would want you to live. And if it's revenge you're after, you're about to get it. Yet you damn near provoked Sebastían into ripping out your throat. What's going on with you?"

Jaxon doesn't answer my question. Instead, he glances at Kilían and my father, cantering down the trail ahead of us. We're too far away for us to hear what they're saying, but I can see the flame of Kilían's head tilted toward my father's dark one. The Lead Interrogator is turned slightly in our direction, revealing his grudging smile.

"They look happy," Jaxon says, guiding his mount over a log that's fallen across the trail. "Don't you think?"

"They've earned happiness," I say with a shrug, doing the same. "In whatever form. So have you. And I won't let you throw it all away because you won't stop punishing yourself."

The smirk is back, but this time it's bitter. "Won't let me, huh? Think you have that much power?"

"I don't care what names you call me. You're my friend. Maybe the only real one I have, unless you count Gentian, who's...well, you'll meet him soon enough." Gentian, who had feelings for me I never understood. Who risked his life to save mine, and has become a hero.

I owe him a debt of gratitude, one I can never repay. But I'll damn sure try.

"Friends look out for each other, as I've come to understand the concept," I say dryly. "And tell each other the truth."

Jaxon jolts in the saddle, as if I've punched him. "I didn't know." The words come slowly, his eyes fixed on the trail ahead. "It's true Tobias had a habit of...taking things that didn't belong to him. Grew up never knowing where his next meal was coming from, but that's no excuse. We fought about it all the time. But whatever Pardúr was talking about, some big heist or whatever —Tobias didn't tell me. Didn't trust me to keep him safe."

I guide my horse around a rock in the trail. "He was protecting you, like Sebastían said. If it had come out that you knew, you would've probably lost your position."

We're riding side by side again, and Jaxon turns his furious, red-rimmed gaze on me. "Oh, yeah? He had no problem telling me what else happened that night. Kept his mouth shut about the fact that Sebastían had leverage over him, and not just the other way around. I always wondered why Pardúr allowed him to walk free after Tobias saw what he did. Now I know."

I brace myself, then ask. "What did he see, Jaxon?"

He shakes his head, lips pressed tight together.

"You were going to tell me, that night in the infirmary," I coax. "Who's the *her* you were talking about, right before the fight? Is he with someone that could compromise our alliance?"

Jaxon stares straight ahead again, eyes fixed on the trail. "Want me to stay on this side of the dirt, exile? More than my life's worth to tell you that."

I try again, letting my urgency bleed into my voice. "Is he with someone that could compromise *Eva*? Or better yet—if I exposed whatever he's up to, could I get her free of him once and for all?"

His jaw twitches. "Pretty thought. But his sort gets what they want. Worry about staying alive and getting Eva back, Westergaard. What happens after that is out of your hands."

"I *am* worried about that. Obviously. But—" I draw a deep breath. "There's something amiss here. You've made that clear enough. And I want to know what it is."

Jaxon barks a harsh laugh. "And I thought I was the one with a death wish."

"You could tell Ronan," I press. "If Sebastían's hiding something that could compromise our military integrity, he'll want to know. Just say you had no idea about whatever it was that Tobias tried to steal. He'll believe you."

His eyes shift to mine, bright with an emotion I can't read. "Maybe he would, maybe he wouldn't. Not all that tempted to test it out. Why besmirch Tobias's memory for something that'll likely go nowhere?" He clenches the reins so hard, his knuckles whiten. "I swore I'd keep his secret. Swore I'd protect him. Already failed at the one. Not about to let him down twice."

By the Sins. "You didn't let him down. The bombing wasn't your fault."

He shakes his head again, this time more vehemently than before. Tears shine in his eyes, and he rubs an angry hand across his face, wiping them away. "Pointless," he mutters, and I'm not sure what he's talking about—this conversation, our invasion, or his existence.

The latter sends a bolt of fear straight through my body. "Forget Pardúr. Let's talk about you. Explain why the hell you goaded Sebastían that way, if you had no intention of telling me or anyone else the truth."

Jaxon frees one hand to stroke his horse's neck. His fingers tremble. "You know why."

If we were on solid ground, I'd shake him. "By the Architect, you can't—" I bite the word off, then try again. "I understand having blood on your hands, believe me. I know what it's like to lose the person you love. But I saved your life, Jaxon, three times over. The way I figure it, at least part of it belongs to me now."

He snorts. "Oh, you do, do you? That's pretty arrogant."

"I take care of what's mine," I say, ignoring the insult. "Which means you're not allowed to sacrifice yourself by jumping off a beam, provoking Sebastían into ending you, or anything else. Got it?"

Jaxon shifts his weight, looking anywhere but at me. "Traveling this route brings shit back," he mutters at last. "Can't sleep, and when I do, I dream of Tobias. Calling me. Then, the bomb. I find him, afterward. In pieces. Can still hear his voice, though. Begging me to save him. Wanting to know why I left him alone."

I suck in air through my teeth. "It's not real, Jaxon. He's at rest."

"You don't know that!" His voice rises, startling Kilían, who turns in the saddle to look at us. I give an infinitesimal shake of my head, and the Lead Interrogator raises one red eyebrow but faces front again.

"He could be wandering," Jaxon says, his voice thick with suppressed tears. "What if the gods turned him back at the gates? What if he needs me, and I'm selfish to stay here? What if Sebastían's right, and there's nothing left for me?"

I square my shoulders and speak the only truth I have. "To

the nine hells with your many-headed gods. If they exist, they would never turn Tobias away. Even Sebastían said he played like an angel, that he was the light to your darkness. Well, this is your darkness speaking, Jaxon, and the darkness lies."

He draws a shuddering breath. I can tell from the set of his body, the tenseness of his muscles, that he's listening. But still, he doesn't look at me. Nor does he speak.

I couldn't stop Eva from being taken. I couldn't save my mother. But Jaxon is still here, and I'll be damned if I'll lose him, too. "Tobias is at peace. The one who isn't at peace is you. You're the one wandering in the darkness, but I won't leave you there alone. I swear it."

Jaxon swallows hard, his jaw clenched tight. "What the hell can you do?"

"You've felt like this before. You've found your way out." I reach across the space between our horses and grasp his good shoulder, letting my touch sink in. "The darkness is a liar. This, right here, is what's real."

Jaxon doesn't say a word. But he doesn't argue with me, either. Heartened, I press on.

"Trust me, until you can trust yourself again, yeah? Because *I* need you, damn you for making me say it. I can count the people I trust on one hand, and you're one of them. The least you can do is return the favor."

There's a long silence, during which I look ahead of us, at the line of skúma and guards on horseback, winding their way through the trail carved through the valley. Then up, at the ravens who still fly above us, pointing the way. And back down, at the man who rides beside me.

A breeze riffles through Jaxon's dark hair, bringing with it the spicy scent of wintersweet. The familiar white-and-red flowers grow along the trail, an uncomfortable reminder of just how close we've come to the place I fought so hard to escape.

Our proximity to the Commonwealth thrums in my bones, a cellular recognition of danger. We are so close, now. Eva is nearly within reach. But a war is on the horizon, and I don't want to face it without him by my side.

I wait. And wait. Wondering if I've miscalculated. If I've lost him. Until finally, Jaxon speaks. His voice is low, barely audible over the rush of wind that eddies between the mountains, but I hear it, just the same.

"Damn you, exile. That's four times now," he says.

THE SUN IS high when we reach the spot in the woods where the grate to the tunnels lies hidden. It's slow going with such a large army, and I itch to break loose from the herd, to go after Eva myself. But such a thing would be suicide, so I content myself with riding at the front of the column, doing my best to dismiss the feeling of being watched that crawls over my skin. I look up, then around, but there's no one there. Still, that means nothing where the Mages are concerned. What if they're stalking us right now? What if they choose this moment to attack?

"All right," Ronan says, tugging the grate free and gesturing to me, Adrien, Fade, and Jaxon. "You four, scope out the tunnels and report back."

Adrien kneels obediently, slipping through the hole. As soon as he hits the ground, the three of us follow suit.

My feet thud onto the gravel, and I blink, adjusting to the dim light that filters from above. I flick my flashlight on, and the other guards do the same. Down the widening tunnel, I can make out the pockmarked walls, beaded with condensation, just as I remember them. The familiar moldering smell fills my lungs.

After everything I went through to escape, here I am again.

The feeling of being watched intensifies. And then it *shifts*, and deep inside me, the bond comes to life. I can't hear Eva, not yet. But I can feel her, that undeniable sense of magnetism drawing me onward. She's alive at the other end of that tether. I haven't lost her, not yet.

"What?" Jaxon says, low-voiced, dark eyes fixed on my face. "You hear someone coming?"

I shake my head, relief surging through me. "No. But Eva—I can feel the bond again. I couldn't before, not until we got into the tunnel. But now..."

He breaks into a grin. "Hold onto that, exile, you get me? See if you can talk to her, let her know we're coming. It'll be tough, dividing your attention. But if anyone can do it, it's you."

"Did you just pay me a compliment?" I whisper, smirking at him.

"Don't let it go to your head. Let's move out."

Elated at the sensation of feeling Eva once more, I pull my dagur from my belt. Next to me, Jaxon, Adrien, and Fade draw their guns. We move in formation down the tunnel, our footsteps echoing—but not the way they should.

Jaxon and I are in the lead. Placing a hand on his shoulder to get his attention, I gesture for him to pause. And then I snap my fingers.

Behind us, Adrien and Fade come to an abrupt halt. They look at me like I've lost my mind, but I hold up a hand, urging forbearance. Then I snap again.

The sound is flat, without the resonance I'd expect. Just like our footsteps.

Indicating for Jaxon and the rest to wait, I palm my blade and ease around the bend up ahead. I don't anticipate an ambush, but you never know.

There's no one lurking around the corner. And when I shine

my flashlight into the murk ahead of me, my suspicions are confirmed.

My beam meets a blank, white wall. I tilt the flashlight upward, following the path of the light along the seam of the wall where it meets the ceiling, then back down to the floor again.

The tunnel has been blocked. There is no getting through.

Which leaves us with just one way into the Commonwealth: through the forest where the Bastarour prowl.

CHAPTER 38

EVA

Gentian's been gone for hours. I don't know if he's been caught, if he succeeded in getting my message to the natural-born in the comp lab or to Dresda. I don't know if he's ever coming back again. What I *do* know is that Cordelia and I are still trapped in these virtueless cells, and with every second, the Mages grow closer to completing their weapon. If he doesn't succeed, Ari, Kilían, and the Houses' army —assuming they're coming for us, too—are marching straight to their doom.

The more minutes tick by, the more I feel like an idiot for letting myself believe we had a prayer of victory, however slim. At this point, it'll take a miracle for us to see the outside of these cells unless it's at the hands of the Executor or the Mages. I'm sure Gentian did his best, but he's one boy, against a tyrant with an army at his disposal and a bunch of powerful magic-users. What if, in trying to help us, he's gotten himself captured or killed? What if he never even made it out of the underground, where we're being held?

I have no answers to these questions. But one thing's for sure: I've never felt so helpless in my life.

"Cordelia," I say, "are you awake?"

There's a rustling from the cell next to mine, and then my mother says, "Of course. Possibly, I'll never sleep again."

"Me neither." I shut my eyes, picturing the bond. It's healthy and gleaming, taut with current that prickles through my veins and over my skin. But I can't hear Ari's voice in my head, and when I call out to him, he doesn't respond.

So, close but not *that* close, then. Thank the Architect for small mercies.

"It's probably daytime, anyhow," Cordelia says. "Not that we can tell down here." She clears her throat. "Eva, you're not still thinking of—"

The lock clicks, interrupting her, and I come to attention, all of my senses straining. But instead of Gentian's lemongrass-and-rubbing-alcohol scent, I smell food: eggs and bacon and cheese. A moment later, the white-capped girl who delivered our dinner comes into view, Traalf by her side and a breakfast tray in her hands. Her clothing and subservient demeanor mark her as a natural-born; if I hadn't been so out of it, I would have likely recognized that from the start.

The tray trembles as the girl approaches our cells, the platters on it rattling. Pursing his lips with disgust, Traalf presses his hand to the identification sensor beside the keypad, and I hold my breath. He tries again and again, but the pad doesn't yield to him. Gratification spikes within me: the natural-born in the comp lab has succeeded in disabling the bio-ID, then.

Gentian came through. He lived long enough to make this happen, at the very least.

Maybe my plan isn't completely doomed, after all.

Huffing with aggravation, Traalf turns to the white-capped girl. "Stand back."

"Y-yes, Bellator Traalf." She obeys, the covered dishes on the tray clattering with anxiety as she retreats. Traalf shoots her a look of disgust before he punches in the code to open the panels on both cells. He's angling his body to conceal the numbers, and were I purely human, he'd manage it. But I'm not, and I let my falcon come forward, her superior vision sharpening my eyesight as I zero in on his fingers.

This saved me once. With luck, it will save me again, at least until I can do what must be done. I have no weapons, no ability to shift. But if I can get out of here, I can disarm Traalf and then plunge his blade into my heart. I may have run out of time to take down the Executor, but I'll be robbing him of his ultimate weapon, and that's the next best thing. When Ari and the rest get here, at least they'll have a chance.

My heart aches at the thought of my mother witnessing this. It breaks at the thought of Ari arriving to find me dead, but I steel myself. He deserves to be free, not imprisoned and enslaved in the name of a vile cause.

I can't let that happen to him. And I have so little time to stop it.

"All right," Traalf says, stepping back as the panels slide open. "You, Marteinn. Back against the bars. You, natural-born —deliver the food to the prisoners and be on your way."

Her head down, the girl scuttles forward, reeking of terror. "F-finish it all," she whispers as the plate slides inside my cell. "You need your strength."

"What are you saying to the prisoner?" Traalf looms up beside her, black brows lowered with suspicion.

"N-nothing. Just t-telling her to eat, as the Executor requested." The girl's face blanches as she scurries away from my cell, delivers my mother's plate of food, and then flees through the door with the empty tray. The bellator's gaze lingers on her back as he follows.

"What did she say to you?" my mother whispers as soon as the door clicks shut behind them.

"She just told me to finish my food." I regard the plate, puzzled. "You don't think—"

"I think that poor girl would never have risked speaking to you unless she had a message to convey. She was terrified. I'm sure you could smell it." My mother heaves a sigh. "This despicable place."

I stare at my plate, steam emanating from the omelet. The girl was scared out of her mind, true. But perhaps she was just afraid of Traalf. Or—

Scooping up my plate, I begin the unpleasant process of digging into my omelet with my bare hands. But this time, I do it more carefully than usual. My efforts are rewarded when, scrambled in with the bits of peppers, ham, and cheese, I encounter something unexpected.

A blade.

"By the Sins," I whisper.

Keep up your strength, she'd said. And slipped me a weapon to defend myself. Which, in turn, means she thinks there's hope for me if I can escape this cell.

I've been hell-bent on my own destruction, so sure it's our only solution. But Gentian, the natural-born in the comp lab, and now this girl believe in me so much that they've risked everything. They've overcome fear and a lifetime of conditioning to disable the keypad and put this blade in my hands.

If the three of them are willing to stake their lives on the slim chance that we can win this war, then how can I do any less? How can I tell them that they put themselves on the line for nothing, that I'm not the fearless warrior they've pinned their hopes on, just a cowed, overwhelmed girl who's set her sights on oblivion? How can I force my mother to watch me die, after she's spent years yearning for a chance to see me again?

I can't. I won't. Ari would never forgive me. And more than that, I wouldn't be able to forgive myself. No matter how poor the odds, I will honor what all of them have sacrificed for me. By the Architect, I can do no less than that.

I draw a deep, shuddering breath, then another. Resolve settles inside me as my gaze falls on my mother, her thin face lit with hope. *I won't give up,* I think, wishing Ari could hear me. *I'll wait for you, like you asked. And then we'll fight and win, or die trying.*

"What is it?" Cordelia says, her voice harsh. "What did you find?"

I don't answer her. Instead I slip the blade into my fist and straighten, pitching my voice loud enough to be heard through the door. "Traalf!"

It takes a moment, but the door cracks open and the dark-eyed bellator strides through, face creased with annoyance. "What is it, Marteinn? Breakfast not to your liking?"

"There was a *rat* in my food," I say, lacing my tone with disgust. "Likely poisoned. That sins-cursed natural-born tried to kill me. Look."

I raise my plate, hoping his distaste for the Common-wealth's lowest rung of society will surpass his caution. Efraím always told us that if we could establish common ground with our enemies, if they saw us as the same, then they would be vulnerable. And sure enough, Traalf approaches, a sneer lifting his lips.

"A rat, eh?" he says. "Looks like the skittish mouse had more courage than I would've given her credit for." He punches in the code to open the panel once more. "Give it over, then, Marteinn. Much as I'd like nothing more than to see a traitor like you part with her head, can't have the girl doing you in before the Executor and the Mages do what they must."

The panel slides open. But this time, Traalf doesn't tell me to retreat. Instead, flush with overconfidence, he reaches for the plate. His hubris is his undoing: I drop the plate on the floor, grab his wrist, and slam him flush against the bars.

"Surprise," I say, inches from his face.

He's still wearing that arrogant sneer when I cut his throat.

CHAPTER 39
ARI

"You say you can feel Eva," Ronan says as we stand in front of the electric fence with Kilían, holding our horses' reins, the army ranged behind us. "Can you communicate with her?"

I shake my head. "I've tried." And I have, again and again. "But...nothing. I can tell she's there, but nothing else." Sebastían and I haven't spoken since our abortive attempt to capture a second messenger. I don't know if he can feel her too, and I don't care. At this point, I wouldn't trust a word he said to me. The skúma are behind us, ready to support our assault, but I'm on guard. If Sebastían turns on us, I'll be the first to stab him through the heart.

"All right." Ronan heaves a sigh. "With luck, the sensation will grow stronger the closer you get. You should be able to use it as a geolocation tool. Assuming we make it through the forest and into the Commonwealth itself, you and Jaxon will go together, along with a detachment of guards. Potentially, she and Cordelia are being held together. Once you've secured the two of them, you'll assess the situation and then rejoin us. Hopefully the two of them will be able to fight by our side."

With luck. Assuming. Potentially. Hopefully. None of these words strike confidence in my heart. "And if they can't?" I say, thinking of how battered Eva was when I saw her through the eyes of the raven. How anything could have happened to her in that cage.

"Then you'll see them safe. You know the Commonwealth inside and out. You'll find somewhere."

"Send Kennett with me," I say impulsively. "He's a medic; they might need care." And that way, I can watch over him, not to mention keep Kilían from getting distracted. Would he hesitate to compromise the mission if Kennett's life was on the line?

I feel Kilían's frosty gaze fix on my face, but I don't dare turn my head to look at him as Ronan considers this. "A good idea," the captain of the guards says at last. "Done."

I hope I haven't just made things worse. After all, separate or together, Cordelia and Eva are likely to be under heavy guard. Have I just brought Kennett into the thick of the fighting? If he dies on my watch, I hate to think of what Kilían will do to me. I'll be watching my back for the rest of my life.

Kilían gives me a long, loaded glare. Then he moves up to take point, eyes narrowed. "Test the fence," he says. "No point in working to disable it if they've done it for us."

Reaching into his bag, Ronan tosses what remains of the rabbit he caught for dinner last night at the fence. I brace myself for the sizzle, but none comes. The fence is off. And, next to it, the keypad flashes green.

"They've rolled out the sins-forsaken welcome mat," I say, peering through the fence into the woods on the other side. Even though the sun is beating down, the trees form a dark, impenetrable thicket. "So, what...we walk right in, only to have the Bastarour eat us and the bellators hurl blades at us from the treetops?"

"I admit, the strategy leaks like a sieve," the Lead Interrogator says. "Like some others that have recently been suggested." His voice is glacial.

"I just thought—" I begin, but he ignores me.

"We'll have to leave the horses, as discussed," he says, turning to Ronan. "They won't be able to navigate through the forest; it's too thick. Not to mention, they'll spook when they see the Bastarour. I know it means ceding an advantage, but we'll be better off on foot."

Ronan grimaces but nods. "Send word through the lines," he says to Adrien, Jaxon, and Fade, standing behind us. "Tie up the horses. Tell the skúma to shift. Then, we go in."

My heart pounds, slow and steady, as Kilían and I grip the gate that once electrocuted Efraím Stinar and tug it open. The gate's heavy, meant to be operated remotely, and we're both breathing hard when it slides the final inch.

No blades come flying out of the trees. No pale eyes regard us from between the leaves. The forest is eerily quiet, and a chill crawls down my spine.

The gate is wide enough to accommodate twenty guards at a time, which means our enemies can work in tandem, picking us off as we enter. Mages aside, the bellators and the Bastarour are predators, skilled in the art of concealment. Just because we don't see them doesn't mean they're not there. But we've committed to this strategy, leaky or otherwise, and it's go time.

I turn to Kilían. "We enter the circle at night and are consumed by fire," I say, the Bellatorum's call to battle.

"With fire and iron," he replies.

Gripping our weapons, we walk through the gate, an army at our backs.

Next to me, Kilían is tense as a bowstring, scanning the shadows. On my other side, Ronan grips his gun two-handed, pointing it left, then dead ahead, then right as he tries to anticipate the direction from which the threat will come.

And come it does, prowling between the trees. Eva killed one Bastarour; the fence electrocuted the other. But four still live, and they step one by one from the treeline, low growls reverberating in their throats.

They look every bit as horrifying as I remember: close to three hundred pounds, with a panther's green eyes and onyx body, the muzzle and ears of a wolf, and the striped face and massive body of a tiger. Sebastían, Layla, Riley, and the mated panther pair that accompanied the guards from Satrizona stalk forward, putting themselves between us and the threat. Ronan and Jaxon raise their guns. Next to them, Kilían and I brace, gripping our sverds.

The Bastarour crouch, about to leap. My fingers tighten on my blade.

And then a familiar figure steps from the trees, raising a hand. At once, the beasts settle, their eyes fixed on his angular, thin face. Obeying him.

"I'll be damned," Kilían mutters under his breath, and then, louder, "Don't shoot! He's on our side."

Ronan and Jaxon lower their guns as the figure turns to look at us, the beasts at his back. His gaze flicks to the skúma, to Ronan, to Jaxon, to Kilían, and, finally, to me, where it lingers. He breaks into a smile, and I return it.

"Hello, Gentian," Kilían says. "Nice work staying alive."

SOMEHOW, Gentian has tamed the Bastarour. "No one ever showed them k-kindness before," he's explaining, a hand resting on one of the horrible beasts' heads. "It took a long time, working with them when I was supposed to be sedating them for examinations, sneaking into the forest with food. I got pretty scratched up in the process, luckily in places I could hide. But in the end, we figured it out together." He strokes the creature's ears.

"I have p-pheromones," he says, digging several small spray bottles out of his pockets and handing one to me. "Pass these back through your l-lines. If you spray yourself, the Bastarour will recognize you as a friend. They won't touch you."

By the Virtues. "What gave you this crazy, brilliant idea?" I say, regarding the rest of the pack warily as I mist my wrists with the contents of the bottle and then hand it to Kilían.

Gentian chuckles. "I'm not a f-fighter. But you know, I'm g-good with animals. And I thought, they're victims, like the rest of us. They never had a c-choice, either. So if they did...what would they choose?"

"Only you," I say, clapping him on the back. I half-expect the beast he's petting to lunge at me, but it stays put. "Who would have thought. Gentian Halverson, rebel."

"It's a far c-cry from that poor bird, no?" he says. "But I wanted to help. I hate it here, especially after what they did to you. I always have."

"You're too good for this place." I want to thank him for what he did to help us escape. To learn how things have been for him. To tell him how much I admire his courage. But now is not the time. "Later, I want to know everything," I tell him. "I hear I may owe you my life. But for now—do you know where Eva is being held?"

I hold my breath as I wait for his reply, but it comes without hesitation. "Of course." He glances at Kilían, who's regarding him with an unmistakable expression of pride. Gentian, I realize, looking between the two of them, has been his protégé. "She sent me to find you."

My mouth falls open, and I start to frame a question. But before I can ask it, "Traitor!" echoes from the space between the trees, and the first blade wings its way out of the shadows.

It's meant for Gentian, but it never reaches him. With a roar, the Bastarour he's been petting rears up, twisting in midair. The beast takes the knife in its shoulder, then charges its assailant, bleeding and snarling. Its companions follow, and our army is right behind them, with the skúma and their familiars in the lead. The air is a blur of bullets and blades as black-clad bellators boil out of the treeline and our guards retaliate.

If the Mages need the skúma, then surely they will want them protected. But I can't tell who's hit and who's not as I run for one of the paths that leads through the forest and into the Commonwealth proper, dragging Gentian along with me.

I'm meant to take Jaxon and Kennett. To take a complement of guards. But there's no time for that. Just me sprinting with my blade in one hand and Gentian's shirt clutched in the other, hacking at whoever looms up in front of me and shoving branches out of my way. Gentian is panting, trying to speak to me, but I can't listen. All my focus is on keeping us alive. Until suddenly we're stumbling out of the forest, unharmed, and into the meadow that lies between here and the training grounds. And by the Sins, I can feel Eva more powerfully now, her presence roaring through the bond.

"Where is she?" I bark at Gentian.

"Under...neath...Clockverk Square..." he gasps, doubling over, his face going red and white and red again. "With... Cordelia. There's an...entrance...beneath the m-machine shop. L-locked. But I stole...the key."

"Good," I tell Gentian, pressing a blade into his hand. He's a vet tech; he'll know where to stab where it hurts. "That's good. Now, run."

We flee across the field toward the city, the pandemonium of the battle in the forest echoing in our ears.

CHAPTER 40
EVA

Traalf manages a single, gurgling scream, thick with blood, before he falls. But it's enough to bring the other bellator stationed on the door running. I recognize him, too: Bellator Gaatlin, who worshipped Efraím Stinar the way the Houses kneel before the many-headed gods. He takes one look at Traalf, bleeding out in front of my cell, and levels me with a glare so filled with hatred, I can feel its weight on my skin.

"What have you done?" he snarls, spinning for the alarm button, on the wall within arm's reach of Cordelia's cell.

I cannot let him reach it. In desperation, I hurl the blade between our cages. It flies true, straight between the bars, skidding across the stones to land at Cordelia's feet. She's still chained, but she has just enough leeway to reach Gaatlin. I'm sure of it.

My mother doesn't hesitate. In one fluid motion, she plucks up the blade, hauls Gaatlin against the bars with her chain around his neck, and plunges it into his carotid. Blood pumps from the wound as he slides down the bars, one hand pressed against his throat in a futile attempt to stem the flow. His body jerks, twitches. Then he is still.

The bellators are dead. The room smells like a slaughterhouse. But we live, one step closer to freedom.

"Can you feel your familiar?" My mother's voice is steady, reminding me once again that she was born to lead alongside an army. That she is trained to fight.

I close my eyes, concentrating. The bond is on fire, filled with a rushing current of electricity that grows stronger by the moment. It prickles over my skin and inside my veins, a sensation almost too intense to contain. "Ari's coming," I tell her, gritting my teeth against it. "We just need to hold on."

My mother's amber eyes darken. "I name your wolf, Eva Marteinn-Navarro, blood of my blood," she says, "I christen her Aelina the Brave."

And then we hear it.

The thud of footsteps, pounding down the hallway outside our prison.

And then, the agonized screams.

CHAPTER 41

ARI

I have to use all of my knowledge of the training grounds to keep to the shadows as bellators march past us, just feet away, en route to aiding their brethren in the forest. Word must've gotten back to them that the Bastarour have switched sides, and who's responsible, because Gentian's name is on all their lips. He's made himself a target, and I'll never forgive myself if it results in his death.

Luckily, there's a basement entrance into the skol that takes us into the tunnel system. After we flee the training grounds, we retreat to the tunnels, taking one fork after another, following the magnetic pull of the bond that ties me to Eva. Thank the Architect for it, because we can't risk using a flashlight, and below ground like this, Gentian has no idea where we're going. Ultimately, though, we have to surface, emerging in the basement of the vet tech building and crawling through the vent system to reach the machine shop, adjacent to Clockverk Square. It's dusty up here, and at one point Gentian has a coughing fit that I think might be the end of us. But by a miracle, we're not overheard, and at last the pull of Eva's presence is so strong, I know we've come to the right place.

I let myself down first, then steady Gentian as he jumps, dragging him away from the arched windows that overlook Clockverk Square, where the bellators patrol. High Priest Erlich, who once made me kneel in the sanctuary all night with a bar of soap between my teeth, is with them, conspicuous in his red robes. As I watch, he disappears into the Great Hall, across the square from the machine shop. It's the largest space in the Commonwealth, built to house all 10,000 citizens. I'm sure they're in there; the windows are boarded up. They must be terrified.

I don't see the Mages or the Executors anywhere.

The bellators' patrol passes, and Gentian tugs at my sleeve, guiding me down a narrow hallway. "Here," he mouths again, pointing at a door labeled 'Hazardous—Keep Closed.' It's marked with a skull and crossbones, a lightning bolt beneath them for good measure. "This is one way down. The other is through the Executor's chambers."

He pulls a small brass key from his pocket and slides it into the lock. The door swings open, revealing an empty chamber, and Gentian tugs me inside. Then he presses a button, and a secondary door slides shut, closing us in.

"What in the—"

"Shhhh," Gentian says, pressing a button embedded in the wall. The chamber jolts, then careens downward. I brace myself, glaring at him.

"You could have warned me," I hiss.

"It's called an elevator," he whispers back, grinning. "I've never seen you c-caught off-guard before. It's entertaining."

As the cursed box continues its freefall, I clear my throat. "Kilían told me all you did for me. You might've saved my life."

Gentian reddens. "That's not—I didn't—"

"Of course you did. It was brave. And I'm grateful." I steal a sideways glance at him. "I want to make sure, though, that you're not risking your life again right now for the sake of our friendship. Or not *just* for it, anyhow."

Gentian straightens as the elevator creaks and slows. "In the beginning," he says, "s-sure, that's all it was. If you spoke to Kilían, then maybe he told you how I used to...well." His cheeks are flame-broiled red, and I shrug, not wanting to embarrass him.

He clears his throat. "I think it was what they called a c-crush, in the Before. One thing hasn't changed, though: I admired you. I still do."

Now it's my turn to blush. He ignores it.

"But Ari, you know I never fit in here, or accepted the Commonwealth's c-cruel methods. I just didn't have a way to fight back, other than saving the odd creature here and there, and even that backfired." He winces, and I'm sure he's thinking of the time I took the whipping for him. "The Brotherhood gave me something I never had before," he says, meeting my eyes. "Power. It gave me a way to fight back, and I will not lay it down."

Pride in who he's become flashes through me. And then the elevator judders to a stop and the door slides open, revealing the two bellators flanking either side.

I recognize them: Johannes and Paulsen, four years ahead of my Choosing. While they weren't good enough to qualify for the Thirty, they're not weak, either.

"Halverson." Johannes frowns. "You're not supposed to be here."

"I know. But I brought a g-guest," Gentian says, one hand gesturing into the elevator and the other stuffed deep in his pocket, where he's stashed the blade I've given him.

Johannes has brows like parentheses, framing his eyes and drawing attention to his dark gaze. As I watch, they lower in puzzlement. "Who?"

"Me," I say cheerfully, stepping out of the infernal box right behind him.

He spins to face me. The look of horror on his face would be comical if I wasn't certain we were about to come to blows.

"Westergaard," Paulsen says, his voice rattling from the barrel chest that made him shine at underwater training. "Always with the bad choices."

I smile at Paulsen, my most irritating grin. "You're here. How bad a choice can it be?"

He lunges at me, which is what I've been waiting for. Control when an opponent comes at you, and you have a much higher chance of controlling *them.* I duck, harnessing the increased speed that comes from being so close to Eva, and slash the tendons behind his bad knee—the one he once took a throwing star to in training. Then I spin my blade, take the butt of the knife, and slam it into his kneecap. He howls, blood spurting, as his leg crumples, and I head-butt him in the stomach, sending him flying into the wall. He hits with a thud that shakes the building, the back of his skull colliding with the plaster, and falls, out cold.

I spin to find Johannes barreling toward me, Gentian clinging to him like a barnacle. He's huge, though, and manages to drag Gentian with him like my companion is no more than an annoyance. "You'll pay for this," Johannes growls, sverd outstretched.

Grabbing his arm with both hands, I slam it against the wall again and again, trying to dislodge his grip on the sverd. He fights me, jabbing an elbow into my gut, making a sins-damned racket that could wake the dead. And then his face goes comically blank and he topples, knocking me to the floor.

I look up to find Gentian grinning at me. "Mnemosyne," he

says, holding up a syringe he must've been concealing in his pocket. "He'll be out for two or three hours, and when he wakes up, he'll have no idea what hit him."

By the Virtues. "What in the nine hells did Kilían *do* to you while I was gone?" I mutter as I roll Johannes's heavy body off me.

"Nothing I didn't ask for. I'm still me," he says in reassurance, giving me a hand up. "I could've killed him, after all."

"True," I say, looking down at their crumpled bodies. Why isn't anyone else coming? If this is the level where Eva and Cordelia are being guarded, where are the rest?

"Come on," I say, disarming the bellators, dividing their weapons between us, and then making my way down the hall, my sverd in one hand and my dagur in the other. Gentian follows, trying to be quiet, but I swear he's as loud as a stampede of Bastarour.

"Down here," he whispers, gesturing for me to take the right fork when the torch-lit hallway divides.

I creep right, hugging the wall. And then I smell it: the unmistakable, coppery tang of blood, followed by the outhouse reek of death. At the end of the hallway, a door's cracked open, and behind me, Gentian gasps.

"That's where they're being held," he says. "Ari, I—"

Whatever he says is lost as I sprint, blades in hand, down the hallway, bursting through the open door. And then I stop short, so suddenly that Gentian smacks into me.

I'm in the luxurious room I recognize from my vision. On the floor lie two dead bellators, blood pooling around their bodies. And in the middle of the room, in cages, are Eva and a tall, amber-eyed woman who can only be Cordelia.

CHAPTER 42
EVA

Ari's filthy, covered in dirt, grass stains, and fresh blood. But his face is the most beautiful sight I've ever seen, just the same. The prickling electricity crests within me, breaking over my skin, a current undammed and free to flow.

I can't stop smiling.

"How—" Gentian says, goggling at the two dead bellators.

"The natural-born gifted me with a blade in my eggs," I say, never taking my eyes off Ari. "From there, it was just a little bit of trickery."

He breaks into a grin. "Lorne came through? I was s-sure she'd be too frightened."

"Time enough for reminiscing later," Ari says, inspecting the keypad. "Eva, tell me you know how to crack this thing."

"I do," I say as Cordelia's eyes widen. "Thanks to Gentian's help, the bio-ID was disabled. Traalf had to input the code, and I memorized it."

I hold my breath as Ari inputs the numbers, hoping I haven't made a mistake. But the locks give way, and the moment they do, Ari leaps for the door to my cell, yanks it open, and envelops me in a fierce hug. His heart pounds against mine, and his burnt-sugar scent fills my lungs. I want to hold onto him forever. To press my lips to his and claim him as my own.

"Ari," I whisper, "I'm so sorry."

He tenses against me, his grip tightening. His head lowers, and for an instant, I think *he's* going to kiss *me*. But instead his grip loosens, and he steps back, letting me go. "I'll tell you one thing, apprentice mine," he says, in the tone he uses to hide what he's really feeling. "I'm getting damned tired of having to break you out of prison. Let's not make a habit of this, yeah?"

My face falls. He came to rescue me, but that doesn't take away from how we left things. I try to tell myself it doesn't matter, that if we survive whatever comes, we'll fix this. Fix *us*. But still, feeling him pull away from me hurts.

Eva, he says through the bond, his mind-voice pained. *Eva, I—*

"Westergaard." My mother's voice is hard, interrupting whatever he was about to say. Gentian must have gotten the keys to her shackles off Gaatlin or Traalf, because she's unchained, standing next to the two bellators' bodies. "How many are with you?"

Through the bond, I feel the warrior's calm settle over Ari, feel him set his emotions aside. He gives a quick rundown of the situation, and I return the favor as my mother kneels, stripping Gaatlin of his weapons and leaving his comrade for me. I am only too happy to relieve Traalf of his blades.

"I g-got the message to Dresda, like you asked," Gentian tells me. "Or at least to one of her minions. But I don't know if she believed me. I had to leave, to wait in the woods with the Bastarour. Otherwise they would've k-killed Ari and the Houses' army."

So the Houses *did* come. I wish we knew whether the Mages were on our side. Whether Gentian succeeded in persuading them. But that's out of our hands now. "You did incredibly well," I say. "If it weren't for you, Ari would be dead and Cordelia and I would still be caged."

Gentian rewards me with a huge smile as my mother straightens. "Was Deveraux Adelman with you when you invaded?" She doesn't bother to disguise the hope in her voice.

"He was," Ari says. "But we split up in the forest, with the Bastarour. I don't know where he is now."

"I'll find him." My mother spits on Gaatlin's corpse, strapping his weapons belt around her waist. "But now, we have to get out of here, before someone comes looking for these brainwashed lackeys and the ones that you killed. Or before the Mages come to collect Eva. If they get their hands on her, the battle's lost."

She heads for the door, leading the way. Sparing a final glance for Ari, I follow.

CHAPTER 43

ARI

As we flee down the hallway past Johannes and Paulsen's fallen bodies, I can feel Eva's wariness, her fear that we're somehow broken. That even though I came for her, I can't forgive her for Sebastían and her stubbornness about meeting the Mages in the woods.

I want to tell her she's wrong. To kiss her until neither of us can breathe, Panther of the West be damned. But we can't afford distractions, and I'm afraid if I start, I might never be able to stop. So instead, I pour all my energy into staying alive. And a good thing, too, because we emerge from the machine shop into chaos.

Clockverk Square is a battlefield, thick with the stench of death. The bellators from all six Commonwealths, alongside the exiles, fight the Houses' guards and the skúma on the stones. Blood courses from the bodies of the fallen, trickling downhill to pool around our feet. The world is a cacophony of clashing blades, growls, and the crack and hiss of bullets, the uproar amplified by the buildings that surround the square.

The Bastarour prowl the stones. Their heads rise as one

when they scent Gentian, and they charge straight for him, surrounding him. It's the best protection he could hope for.

I search for our allies and find Riley and Layla at the edge of the square, eviscerating two bellators. In the midst of the crowd, I glimpse a flash of Sebastían's gleaming teeth as he brings down a third. High overhead, the falcons swoop through the cloudless sky, searching for targets. I don't see Kilían, Jaxon, or my father. Cordelia has disappeared, on the hunt for Councilor Adelman. The battle has swallowed her whole.

The Mages are conspicuously absent. As is the Executor. But I'm sure it's just a matter of time until we have to deal with both.

As I scan our surroundings for cover, footsteps sound behind me, barely discernible above the din. I wheel to confront a bellator, sverd raised and teeth bared, the green stripe across his cuffs marking him as a member of the Commonwealth of Scribes. Palming my dagur, I duck, parry, and plunge my blade into his gut. Blood gushes, staining his gear, as the man falls at my feet. Though he's a stranger—and a murderous one, at that —I feel a pang of guilt as the light fades from his eyes. Bellators are deadly weapons, pointed by the hand of whoever is empowered to wield them. Maybe, if given a choice, this man would have turned to our cause. Now he's bleeding to death, a foot soldier in a battle he was brainwashed to fight.

Forcing the thought from my mind, I wipe my dagur clean, then step over his prone body. Blades in hand, Eva and I flatten ourselves against the rough stone of the dining hall's facade, protecting our backs. Her voice sounds in my mind, clear and urgent: *Where are the Mages?*

This is a diversion. Like the Bastarour in the forest, I say, the realization breaking over me. *Something to thin our numbers, before they unleash the weapon the Executor was talking about. The one they need you to supercharge.* When they discover she's escaped that damnable cage, it's just a matter of time before they track her down here. Whatever victory we hope to wrest from their hands, we have to make it happen before then.

Shift, I tell Eva, swiveling to monitor incoming blades or stray bullets while I wait for the telltale surge of energy to flow through our bond. But nothing happens, and when I spare her a glance, her expression is torn.

I want to. Her mind-voice is filled with doubt. *But what if that makes it easier for them to use me? What if that's what they expect...what they want?*

I'm about to tell her that now is all we have. That we need to use every advantage at our disposal. But before I can speak, my gaze catches a glint of silver atop the Rookery: eight bellators, equipped with crossbows.

Eva sees them at the same time I do. In unison, the bond open and roaring between us, we aim and throw. The blades soar in tandem, clearing the roof and finding their marks in the chest and temple of two of the bellators. But there are still six to go.

We draw another set of blades just as guns go off back-to-back, close enough that the sound is near-deafening. I turn to see Fade and Adrien standing at the edge of the square, firing at the remaining bellators atop the Rookery. Adrien's bullet goes wide, embedding itself harmlessly in the rooftop. But Fade's catches one of the bellators in the gut. The man presses both hands to his stomach, a crimson stain bubbling through his fingers, as one of his fellows sends an arrow winnowing straight for Fade.

Making a harsh kak-kak-kak sound audible even above the fracas, the falcons of House Montyorke dive for the Rookery, wings pressed to their sides. They peck out the eyes of our assailants, who howl in agony. But it's too late for Fade. The arrow impales him in the chest, and his mouth forms an o of shock as he crumples.

Rage consumes me as the falcons take to the air again, their beaks wet with blood. Fade, who's always laughing, who was one of the first people to make me feel like I actually belonged in Vik—

Beside him, Adrien drops to his knees, putting pressure on Fade's chest, desperately trying to stop the blood. It's a human thing to do, but a foolish one, because as soon as he lowers his guard, Bellator Elison materializes behind him, sverd raised. *By the Sins.* I take two steps away from Eva, on the verge of charging into the scrum, when Ronan emerges, takes aim, and fires at Elison, hitting him square in the back. He falls, toppling onto Adrien, both of them landing on Fade's body.

Eva's eyes meet mine, the expression in them fierce. I feel her draw on the bond, readying herself to change form, just as the sun winks off another weapon atop the Rookery. Bellator Rysand has taken the place of his fallen comrades.

He draws back his arm, and the javelin in it hurtles downward. I don't know whether or not we're his intended targets; the day is windy, and perhaps Rysand is aiming for another. It would be beyond foolish, after all, to anger the Executor and the Mages by killing the two of us—and we served beside Rysand. Unlike the bellator from the Commonwealth of Scribes, he recognizes us, without a doubt.

Foolish or not, his weapon flies straight for us. Knocking Eva out of the way, I push her to the ground, shielding her with my body. The javelin hits the packed dirt beside me point-first, embedding itself an inch from my face.

Beneath me, Eva growls, the vibration shaking both our bodies. She rolls me off her, seizes the javelin, and throws it in a single, seamless movement. The weapon soars, embedding itself in Rysand's throat. He topples over the edge of the roof, falling face-first onto the stones of the square, into the midst of the battle.

I rise from my crouch, blade in hand. And find myself looking right into the eyes of one of the Bastarour.

It's injured, badly. Blood pours from its torn shoulder. Still, these beasts are bred to persist through pain, enduring until death, and this one is on the hunt, body coiled as if to strike. I freeze, wondering if the pheromones Gentian gave me have worn off. If the beast is about to close its massive jaws on my throat. But then its gaze shifts to a spot above my head, and it launches itself over me, toward an unknown target.

Spinning, I find Sebastían's panther cornered by five bellators against the machine shop. If I had any doubt that the Executor intended to break his promise to the Mages—that he intended to save the skúma and hand them over—it evaporates the moment I lay eyes on the bellators. They're striking to kill, and though Sebastían knocks the blade out of one warrior's hand and closes his jaws on another, the other three are relentless. One of their knives finds its target just as the Bastarour lands on all fours next to Sebastían. Its brethren prowl from the alleys and join it, their bone-rattling snarls filling the square. They tear the bellators away from Sebastían by the simple expediency of biting his attackers in half, then roar in triumph and launch themselves into the fray.

Through the bond, I feel Eva's horror at the sight of the blade that's embedded in Sebastían's flank. He limps away from the wall, blood coursing from the wound, and she closes the gap between them, yanking the blade free and pressing hard to staunch the bleeding. The panther's eyes widen as he takes her in, but there's no time for reunions: Bellator Thorne slips out of the door to the machine shop, behind Eva, and raises his sverd. It whistles through the air with a single-minded goal: to sever her head from her neck.

"You fool!" the Executor bellows from somewhere close by. From the sound of it, he's watching from inside the Rookery, the coward. "Not her. We need her!"

Thorne freezes mid-strike, but I have no such compunction. I punch him in the face, stab him in the gut, and leave him on the stones to die, robbing him of his sverd as a final indignity.

Eva's satisfaction at his demise thrums through our bond, so potent that at first, I conflate it with the noise that fills my ears: an odd, buzzing hum. But as the bond steadies itself, the sound remains. I try to pinpoint its trajectory, but to no avail: it seems to be coming from everywhere, disorienting me.

Next to me, Eva tenses. *There*, she says, pointing with the hand that's not pressed against Sebastían's wound.

I follow the trajectory of her finger, and bite out a curse. Metal drones crest the slate roofs of the buildings on all four sides of us, heading straight for the square. Whatever they contain, we're sitting ducks for them here.

But the drones are just the beginning. From the alleys between the buildings, the Mages emerge, distinctive in their red robes, their faces painted with the same symbols that adorned the standing stones. They're chanting, their hands raised, palms out, just like in the clearing. Only now, there are far more of them than before.

There's nowhere for us to run; all the alleyways are blocked. The Mages are the spokes of a wheel, and we are at its center. We could try to scale the buildings, but more bellators are doubtless waiting at the top. All I can think to do is to try to fight our way through, but if they throw up the same forcefield as they did in the stone circle, they'll trap us here.

If, if, if. There are too many unknowns, and I can't dwell on them. We have to try to escape. It's that, or die.

But there's no way Sebastían can run. And I know Eva won't leave him.

At least, I think grimly, watching the blood drip from his wounded flank, he doesn't seem to be a traitor to our cause. Whatever secret he's keeping, he hasn't turned on us.

The Mages are still chanting, but the words sound different now, more purposeful. The drones dip, blocking out the sky, and a small compartment at the bottom of each of them opens. A blue stream of gas shoots from the one closest to us, enveloping one of the guards from House Montyorke. His hands go to his throat, and his eyes bug out. Blood spills from his lips. The drone next to that one emits a yellow stream of gas, encasing Noelle, a guard from San Fraesco. Her whole body gleams with it, but the gas doesn't drift anywhere else. It travels with her as she turns, raises her gun, and shoots the guard from Montyorke in the head.

What in the nine hells?

The Mages' chants grow louder as my gaze flicks up, across the square. Everywhere I look, the bellies of the drones open and a different color of gas emerges, targeting only the people on our side. Purple, and they claw desperately at their eyes, blinded and shrieking. Yellow, and they choke on their own blood. Blue, and they attack each other. Orange, and they go up in flames. The falcons dive for the drones, trying to destroy them, but the Mages' forcefield must be in effect here, because Eldrina and the rest can't get close.

The air is a miasma of anise and roses as drone after drone releases their contents, a lethal blend of technology and magic. They attack one member of the resistance after the next, as if the Mages have calibrated them to our intentions. Either that, or maybe they can recognize the biometric imprints of everyone from the Commonwealths, and are targeting everyone else. Eva's the tech genius, not me. All I know is, it's only a matter of time until the entire Brotherhood falls...except, maybe, me and Eva. Because even as I watch guard after guard collapse, and one of the falcons plummets to the earth, its feathers aflame, none of the drones approach us.

Is this our fate, to watch all of our allies, the people we care for, die? And then to be used, at the hands of a mad dictator and a handful of crazed magicians?

The square is full of agonized howls and the smell of burning flesh as members of the Brotherhood turn on each other, claw at their eyes, or burst into flame. A drone hovers above Sebastían, releasing a gust of wind that sends him flying into the stone wall of the Rookery. Eva shrieks, aloud and through the bond, as we run for him and drag him to his feet. Grimly, I point upward, at the drones. "They're not attacking me and Eva," I yell, hoping he can hear. "Stay with us. They won't be able to target you."

He must understand, because he staggers to his feet and leans right up against me, nearly knocking me off my feet. Together, Eva and I grip his ruff and haul him forward, toward the line of Mages, who have emerged from the alleys to circle Clockverk Square. Maybe we can create a distraction, anything that will disrupt the Mages' concentration and their control over the drones so our people can fight back.

Sebastían is heavy as sin. Even with Eva's superior strength, and with the panther lending what aid he can, dragging his bulk is a Herculean effort. We've gotten him within fifteen feet of the Mages when a small figure breaks through the line of red-robed women. His face is streaked with dried blood and his crimson-and-black clothes torn, but I recognize him none-theless.

Erdahl. Alive.

He runs toward us, screaming. I can't make his words out over the buzz of the drones, the agonized shrieking of the guards, and the chanting of the Mages, whose hands are raised to the sky. Again and again, his lips form the same indecipherable sentence as he charges toward us, in the no-man's land between the Square and the Mages, unprotected.

As one, Eva and I relinquish Sebastían and run for Erdahl. But as fast as we are, the drones are faster. One of them zeroes in on him, hovering overhead. Orange gas streams out of its open belly.

Oh, by the Sins, no.

This boy, who looked up to me, who once begged me to show him how to throw knives, is going to die a horrific death right in front of me. I have to do *something*. But what?

I run for him, Eva a blur beside me, knowing neither of us will make it in time. He's sprinting, weaving left and right, but the gas is following him like it's equipped with a damned tracker, and now I can hear Layla howling and oh by the sins-cursed hells *no*—

Then one of the Mages breaks free of the line. Through the multicolored smoke, I make out her familiar features, the narrow set of her shoulders: Mei.

Her painted face a knot of determination, she raises her hands and gestures, a complicated series of twists. The orange gas pauses, then begins to stream in her direction, like an animal called to heel.

"Mei, no! Don't!" The Mage next to her lunges, but Mei sidesteps her. As the orange gas creeps closer and closer, her fellow Mage retreats, eyes wide with terror.

Mei's gaze falls on Eva, regret, shame, anger, loss, and resolve all rippling across her face, before the orange gas swallows her whole and she catches fire. For an instant, she's visible within the column of flame, a red-robed, dark-eyed figure, an inferno of a girl with her hands held high to the drone-filled sky. Her lips form the words *Forgive me*. Then a flash of light fills the square, so bright it nearly blinds me.

When I can see again, there's just a pile of ash where Mei

should be. And a little boy, closing the distance between us, throwing himself into my arms.

I hold Erdahl tight, feeling him shake, feeling his heart pound against me, bearing the weight of Mei's sacrifice. And then I feel it: an undertow in the bond, pulling power from me through Eva, flowing out and out and out, an ocean there's no way to dam.

"Oh," Eva says, a small, surprised sound that's barely audible above the melee.

And then she falls to her knees.

CHAPTER 44

EVA

I can't breathe.

It's like it was in the stone circle, in the cage in Cordelia's chambers, but so much worse this time. I feel like a giant fist has reached into my chest, crushing my lungs. An inexorable current of power flows through the bond and outward, toward the Mages.

They're taking it from me. Taking everything I am, everything I need, not just for my beasts' survival but for my own.

My legs give, and I fall to my knees on the rough-packed dirt beside the pile of ash that was once Mei. My body flickers between forms: wolf, panther, seal, falcon, human again. Ari collapses next to me, panting, and I remember what Ronan once told me: that I'll drain him in an effort to sustain myself. That his job is to fuel me, and the more power I need, the more he'll give, until there's nothing left of him.

I can't let that happen.

Dimly, I hear Layla running for Erdahl, hear her cries of joy as she enfolds him in her arms. The part of me that is Carina feels Sebastían's agony, but it vanishes as I morph into the form of my wolf once more.

"Fight it, Eva," Ari gasps. "Don't let them control you."

I try, picturing the bond and imagining myself sealing it off at both ends. But it's like trying to stem the tide. There are so many Mages and only one of me. The current of energy floods through the blockage I've constructed, bursting it. I fall forward, onto my hands and knees, smelling burnt flesh and the sickly-sweet scent of roses.

The edge of a red robe appears in my field of vision, its hem dragging in the dirt. I struggle to lift my head and see Dresda standing in front of me, her face painted with white runes, eyebrows knitted in concentration.

"Stop," I beg her, my voice a rasp. "Please don't do this."

Dresda doesn't reply. With the last of my strength, I summon determination from the very depths of my being and slam stone walls into place around my power, slicing the bond in half in both directions—to Ari and the Mages. The current smashes against my boundaries, like storm-tossed waves pounding a jetty, but it can't get through.

My entire body shakes as I fight to hold the walls in place. I can feel Dresda and the Mages on the other side, trying to tear at them stone by stone. But as long as I hold, as long as I don't give in, they can't use me this way.

Yet another drone opens up above us, a strange gray gas drifting from it, enshrouding Sebastían. His panther form shrinks, leaving him human, kneeling naked and bleeding in the dirt. Blood streams from the wound in his side as his eyes fix on something only he can see.

"Adeline," he whispers, and starts to crawl, straight toward the Mages. Toward his death. "I should never have left you behind. I should have known you would follow."

Another drone targets him, this one emitting the orange gas. I want to go to him. To save him. But I can't move.

"Adeline," he wails, his blood staining the dirt. "Where are you? I can't see—"

The orange gas flows down and down, and I brace myself for it to light him aflame. But six inches from him, it stops. And then, to my shock, it starts to recede. Untouched by fire, Sebastían collapses face-first into the dirt, one arm outstretched as if to reach for this mysterious Adeline.

"Eva." Dresda is kneeling next to me, her breath warm against my ear. "We're not controlling the drones."

I roll my eyes up, struggling to focus on her face. "Who...is then?"

Her breath comes in harsh pants as she fights to be heard over the shrieks and clash of blades. "That's our magic, yes, but it's residual—what we gave the Executor as part of our trade." She grabs my shoulder, hauling me to a sitting position. "We got the boy's message. I didn't want to believe it, but it's clear the Executor is attacking skúma, that he never intended to keep his word. It's too late for us to stop the drones, but we can shield people, the way we're shielding you and Ari. To do that, though, we need you. Let us in, Eva, please."

There's true desperation in her voice. I want to trust her. To believe that she is on our side at last. But to drop my walls and give her unfettered access to my power... How do I know she's not lying to me?

"Prove...it." The words emerge between gritted teeth.

Dresda turns, lifting her arms toward the circle of Mages. She weaves her hands through the air, and one by one, they do the same. A haze descends over my vision, and when it lifts, I see the forcefield they've created around themselves and the drones, its boundaries illuminated by the multicolor gas. It flares around the edges of my body and Ari's, covering every inch of us. And then, as Dresda chants, her hands still tracing a path through the air, the protective forcefield encases first Sebastían, then Layla, then Erdahl, clutched in her arms.

"We can't sustain it." Sweat beads Dresda's forehead, and her hands shake. "Not to protect so many. Not unless you help us."

"You...tortured me. Why...should I...believe you?"

Her red robes flare in the wind of her magic, the earth quaking with the force it takes to hold the forcefield around the five of us. To protect us from the drones and the blades. "In your Commonwealth, there is a saying, yes? *The enemy of my enemy is my friend.* We share a common enemy, Eva Marteinn. I don't know what will come after. But for now, we will fight beside you."

My gaze falls on Ari, his face and hands streaked with Sebastían's blood. On Sebastían himself, unconscious in the dirt. On so many of the Houses' guards, driven mad or killed by the gas unleashed by the drones.

It can't get much worse than this.

Ari's eyes meet mine, clear and bottomless. He nods, acknowledging our position. Giving me peace of mind to do what must be done.

I make a split-second decision, then, to trust Dresda, in a last-ditch effort to save us all or die trying. "To me!" I scream, as loud as I can. "Guards and skúma, to me!"

With a roar, the guards and skúma that are able charge toward us. I reach out for Ari's hand, gripping it tight in mine, and let the walls I erected around my power crumble to dust.

Before, the Mages had to take it from me. Now, I give it willingly, and that makes all the difference. I feel it flowing out and out and out, cycling through the Mages and out into the crowd, seeking only those whose intentions are aligned with ours. Finding them, it pulls the forcefield from the air, weaving molecules together to form a cloak around the individual guards and skúma as they draw close to us. Once they're within our circle, the forcefield expands like a giant, invisible dome, protecting all of us who are within it, sending tendrils out for those who are beyond its perimeter. The gas trails along the forcefield, seeking a way in, but to no avail. I feel the forcefield repel it, feel my power entwined with the Mages' magic as it cycles back through them and into me again, to be refueled by Ari and begin once more.

We are one, an organism with many parts, cycling and recycling power. It doesn't weaken me; by contrast, I have never felt so strong. I stand, pulling Ari with me. Together with the Mages, we protect what is ours.

I can see Dresda's power, a gold thread intertwined with the red threads of her fellow Mages. They form a web, extending to me and to Ari, power vibrating along each of the silken strands. It flexes, absorbing every molecule we have to give. And then, with a blast so concussive it quakes the ground and crumbles the façade of the Rookery, the web explodes outward, capturing the drones and dashing them to the ground, where they smash to harmless pieces. With a victorious howl, the remaining guards and skúma charge the exiles and the bellators who still stand, Ari and I at their side.

I shift into the form of my panther, a relief after being trapped so long in my human form. There's a freedom in it, in letting my beast come forward, swiping at the bellators, ripping their sverds from their hands. Beside me, Ari is a whirlwind, cutting down everyone in his path. The bellators and exiles attack in return, but the forcefield still holds. Unlike in the stone circle, their blades and bullets clatter off it, falling harmlessly to the ground. The Mages are right: we are so much stronger together. We drive them back and back, until the stones run red with our enemies' blood and the square falls eerily silent.

We've won this battle. But as long as the Executor's still at large, we may still lose the war. What if he's found Cordelia, and taken her? What if he intends to use her as a hostage?

The man is canny as a fox, and like a fox, he doubtless has more than one bolthole to his den. I heard him yelling from the Rookery. Doubtless he's gone out the back, which empties onto an alley that leads to Wunderstrand Square...and from there, through a series of streets that will take him to the gen lab. He knows every inch of that building, I'm sure. If there's a bioweapon he wants to harvest, in order to defend himself, it will be there. And if he plans to escape, that will give him a head start.

I should wait for Ari. But I don't want to waste a minute. Nose pressed to the ground, I prowl through the alley beside the Rookery, then behind it, hunting for the Executor's scent. I don't pick it up. But what I *do* smell is Cordelia, on the heels of another, familiar scent: Councilor Adelman's.

CHAPTER 45
ARI

One moment Eva's beside me, the bond open and roaring with victory as our enemies fall. And the next, while I turn my head to check on our wounded—to see if my father, Kilían, and Jaxon live—she vanishes.

"Where...is she?" It's Sebastían, naked, bloodied, and sides heaving, at my feet. His eyes are unfocused, and I can't tell if he's talking about Eva or the mysterious Adeline, whose name he howled when that gray gas surrounded him. Adeline, who I'm sure is connected to his secret.

I answer him anyway. "I don't know. But I'll find her."

Down the bond, I can feel Eva, a spark of light moving fast in the direction of Wunderkind Square. Tracking someone. Three guesses who, and the first two don't count.

Where the Executor is, Cordelia will be also. I know that in my bones. And wherever she is, I'll find Councilor Adelman. This is a showdown in the making, and I can't let Eva face it alone.

That incredible speed I first accessed in Vik's Great Hall is with me as I chase after her, down the alley that lies between the Rookery and the machine shop. But she is faster still, and I palm my dagur as I run, praying to the Architect and the Houses' many-headed gods that I won't be too late.

CHAPTER 46

EVA

I find my mother and the man she loves on opposite sides of Wunderstrand Square. A smaller skirmish must have happened here; the cobblestones are strewn with bodies, thick with blood. But none of that registers on either of their faces. The years drain from Councilor Adelman's lined visage, his blue eyes lighting with a happiness I've never seen them hold. As for Cordelia, she smiles so widely, it's as if I'm looking at a different person. The woman who the Executor coerced and manipulated and tortured is gone. In her place is someone who's gazing at the person she loves most in all the world. Someone she thought she'd never see again.

Councilor Adelman's lips move, mouthing the word, "Cor."

It's short for my mother's name, sure. But I studied enough Latin to know it also means *heart*.

From the shadows between the buildings, I watch, filled with joy for both of them. After everything, all the loss and bloodshed and devastation, they have found each other again. They will get their happy ending.

It's the last thought I have before the Executor bolts out of the alleyway by the garment factory and lunges for my mother, wrapping an arm around her throat and yanking her back against him. The weapons she took from Gaatlin are strapped around her waist, but the Executor holds a knife, and the blade is pressed against her throat. In his other hand is a syringe.

Concealed in the shadows, my claws dig into the dirt. I could leap for my mother, but am I fast enough to stop him if he decides to slit her throat? Or injects her with whatever is in that syringe?

Across the square, Councilor Adelman's jaw sets. He raises his gun.

"Let her go, or I'll kill you," he says.

His tone is empty, his hand steady. He would have made a great bellator, had he been born in the Commonwealth. But he was born in Vik, into a world that held Cordelia, and it's obvious that, having lost her once, he has no intention of letting it happen again.

The Executor smiles at him, but it's devoid of mirth. "I don't think you will. After all, what if you miss?"

"I don't miss." There's no arrogance in Councilor Adelman's voice, just a simple acknowledgment of the facts. "Do I, Cordelia?"

"No," my mother says. "But Dev—"

"*Dev?*" The single word is vicious, dripping with contempt. "This is the one you cried over, for years after I gave you home and shelter? After I saved you? This is the one you told me would come for you, the one whose name you whisper in your sleep?"

My gaze shifts between my mother and the Executor to Councilor Adelman, who looks like each word has stabbed him in the heart. I lower to my haunches, preparing to spring, as the Councilor says, as if the Executor isn't there at all, "I would have come for you, Cor, if I'd thought there was the slightest chance you'd lived. You have to believe me. I never would have left you here, with *him*."

"I know. Dev, I don't blame you. Go. Get out of here. I'll survive. I always do."

The Councilor-in-Chief's navy-blue eyes darken, until they're nearly black. Even from here, I can smell the rage that emanates from him, deep and visceral as a freshly slaughtered kill. "No," is all he says before he snaps his jaw shut again.

The Executor takes a step backward, dragging my mother with him, the blade still at her throat. "As touching as this little reunion is, I don't intend it to go on for long. Lower your weapon, Devereaux of House Minneska. Lower it and submit to your betters, or the woman you once called Cordelia will pay."

When Councilor Adelman shows no sign of obeying, the Executor tightens his grip on the knife, raising the syringe in his other hand in a clear threat. The Councilor draws one deep breath, then another. And then, slowly, he lowers his gun.

"Put it on the ground."

Never taking his eyes off Cordelia, Adelman sets his gun on the dirt.

"Very good. Now, kick it over to me and back away."

The gun skitters across the cobblestones, coming to rest at the Executor's feet, as Adelman backs away, hands raised. "I'm unarmed. Take me instead. Do what you want to me. Just let her go."

The Executor tilts his head, considering this suggestion. "Beg me for her life," he says, "and maybe I will."

A chill wind blasts through the square as Councilor Adelman falls to his knees without hesitation, his hands open on his thighs. "Please," he says.

Instead, the Executor tightens his grip on my mother, the serrated edge of his blade digging into her throat. She struggles in his grip, trying to break free. But she's been weakened from years of confinement, and he is desperate. A lethal combination.

A thin bead of blood wells up and, from the shadows, I growl, a noise that echoes off the buildings and percolates into the square. Councilor Adelman's eyes slide sideways, finding mine, then focus on the Executor again.

"You told Eva you loved her mother," he says, each word low, careful. "You've taken care of Cordelia all these years. Surely you didn't do all of that for it to end here. If you love her, then you will let her go."

The Executor snorts, dragging Cordelia backward another step. "Loving her was the worst mistake I ever made. Love is a weakness, for fools. She lured me in, with her witch's magic, a spell born of the beast inside her. She tricked me into wanting her, into siring an ungrateful spawn that's been my undoing. Why should I set her free?"

I prowl forward, out of the shadows, as Councilor Adelman says, "I am the head of the Council of Nine. I hold a great deal of power. Drop the knife and the syringe. Send Cordelia over to me. And I will spare your life."

The gust that blasts through the alley behind me is as chilly as the Executor's humorless laugh. "You're more foolish than I thought, if you think I'll believe a lie such as that. I've already lost everything. There is no way you or your Council would let me live. If you didn't kill me, then she"—he gestures at me, prowling toward him—"certainly would."

I coil, preparing to launch myself through the air. I will go for his eyes first, I decide. Then, after my mother is free, I will decimate the rest of him.

"Why give her an excuse?" Councilor Adelman says, not taking his eyes off the Executor. "Everyone will be hunting for you. They'll converge here soon enough. This is your last chance to surrender." His voice drops, as coaxing and persuasive as

Kilían's ever was when he was interrogating a prisoner. "We both know you're not going to kill Cordelia. This charade's gone on long enough, don't you think?"

The Executor's eyes blaze, bright with unholy fervor. "You're right," he says. "I can't kill her, damn her sins-cursed soul. And mine. But I can put an animal down."

He releases my mother, who wrenches away from him, tumbling to the ground. Holding the syringe high, he bares his teeth at me as I charge, trampling over bodies, the cobblestones slick with blood beneath the pads of my paws. My vision narrows until he is all I see: this man who helped make me and wants to destroy me. He is a fool if he thinks a puny dictator with a knife and a needle can stand against an enraged panther hell-bent on putting an end to him.

My mother is shrieking, lunging for him, blade in hand. Councilor Adelman is screaming her name. The Executor stands his ground, and on his face I see nothing but grim acknowledgment. He's accepted the fact that he's going to die. He just wants to take me down with him, as some sort of twisted victory. And because it's what will hurt my mother the most.

Whatever is in that syringe, it means my death.

In my head, I hear Ari's panicked voice, demanding to know what I'm doing. Begging me to wait for him. His footsteps thunder down the passageway to Wunderstrand Square.

I don't slow down.

As I close in on the Executor, in striking distance, a dagur flies out of the shadows, hitting the hand that holds the syringe dead-on. The Executor bellows in pain, dropping the syringe onto the cobblestones. He buckles to his knees.

And lands right next to Councilor Adelman's discarded gun.

CHAPTER 47
ARI

I'm still running when I let the first blade fly.

The Executor shrieks, coward that he is, and crumples. But then he stands again, blood streaming from his wounded hand, and this time he holds a gun. Pointed right at Eva.

The world slows down, revealing itself in a series of freeze-frames. Like in an old-fashioned vid, the shutter clicks.

Me, palming another blade.

Cordelia, screaming *Eva* and *you bastard* and *no*.

Jaxon, skidding to a stop at my side.

Councilor Adelman, jaw set and muscles coiling.

Eva, growling as her paw rises, aiming for the gun.

CHAPTER 48
EVA

I lift my paw to swipe the gun from the Executor's hand, the growl that rips from my chest so violent, it shakes my entire body.

The Executor's eyes are flat, black discs. I see the green eyes and bared white teeth of my panther reflected in them as his finger tightens on the trigger. I smell the rust-rich scent of his blood and the oiled metal of the gun.

Ari steps into view, another blade already palmed, ready to strike.

With fire and iron, I think. The Bellators' call to battle.

My paw comes down. The trigger clicks. And then, in a blur of motion, Councilor Adelman hurtles between us, taking the bullet meant for me in the center of his chest.

CHAPTER 49
ARI

The Executor fires, again and again, his face a rictus of glee and rage. Cordelia is howling and Eva is growling and Jaxon is roaring *No no no no.*

Adelman's body jerks, his eyes roving wildly. They find mine, and before they glaze over with pain, I see the acknowledgment in them: a promise kept, no matter the cost. Through the bond, I feel a rush of horror and fury so strong, it almost knocks me off my feet. And I know, with deadly certainty, what's to come.

The world is nothing but blood.

CHAPTER 50

EVA

I watch in horror as Councilor Adelman falls.

My mother shrieks, "Dev," and runs for him. But there's blood everywhere, pouring from his torn body and even his lips, and though I'm no medic, even I can tell that it's too late. My beasts smell impending death, rotten and thick, riding the air.

My mother's wolf must smell it too. She rounds on the Executor, who's laughing. *Laughing.* "So falls the great defender," he says. "Now what will you do, Lia? When will you realize that you belong to me?"

The air around my mother shimmers, and for the first time I see fear on the Executor's face. He raises his gun, conflict roiling in those pitch-dark eyes.

As much as this vile man is capable of loving anyone, he loves Cordelia. Would he shoot her, to save himself?

My mother doesn't wait to find out. She howls, standing over Councilor Adelman's fallen body, and it isn't a human sound. The air around her shimmers and twists and sparks. And then I feel it—a great rush of energy, blasting past my panther with such force it feels like I should be able to reach out a paw and touch it. It arrows through the air, seeking—and finds its target: Jaxon, standing beside Ari.

Jaxon screams, the way he did the night the remains of the Thirty attacked and I yanked energy through him with all my strength, to take the form of my panther. He falls to his knees, smacking into the dirt so hard I feel the impact. But my mother has what she needs. She shimmies out of her clothes a moment before her body explodes, twisting in midair and transforming into a massive gray wolf by the time her paws hit the ground. She howls again, baring her teeth, and charges for the Executor.

But I am running, too. My paws strike the ground again and again, my panther's tearing-fabric growl ripping from my throat.

He raped my mother. He killed the only man she ever loved. He perverted my DNA.

He is my kill, as surely as he is hers.

We reach him at the same time. His eyes are still filled with fear, warring with disbelief.

"You wouldn't," he says to the wolf that is my mother, as if I'm not there at all. "Lia, I know you love me. I can give you the world—"

A growl erupts from my mother's lips, and she rips the gun from his hands. It lands on the ground and then she's on him, tearing at his throat. Blood arcs from him, spraying onto the dirt, as she shakes him like one of the rag dolls in the Commonwealth's Nursery.

Surely this will kill him. But for me, 'surely' isn't good enough.

I lash out with one great paw, catching him across the chest. His shirt rips open, my claws penetrating his skin. As my mother drops him to the ground, I lower my head and sink my teeth into his body, tasting blood and flesh and sinew. I bite harder, and hear the splintering sound of bone as his ribcage gives way. And then his heart is beating against my tongue, thudding fast as a trapped rabbit's as I close my jaws and put an end to him once and for all.

The Executor is dead.

I raise my head, my jaws dripping with blood, and meet my mother's eyes over his limp body. In hers, I see a grim determination and a terrible, burning grief.

Then her body shimmers once more as she changes shape, taking the form of the woman who shared my prison. She yanks her shirt over her head and pulls her pants on, then runs for Councilor Adelman, her face dead-white and marked with horror.

I spare a brief moment to think about what it means that my mother forced Jaxon into grounding her shift, without asking for his consent. Surely that is a terrible violation. I shift my gaze to him and see him staring at her, an unreadable expression on his face. Next to him is Ari, who is murmuring something in his ear. I catch the words *fatal wound* and *forgivable* before I reach down the bond that ties me to my familiar, feeling the maelstrom of his emotions—shock, vindication, rage—before I send my energy flowing toward him and feel it mingle with his own. Then I'm in my human body again, and Ari is striding toward me, shrugging his gear jacket off and draping it around my shoulders. It's big enough to cover me to mid-thigh.

Together, we watch as my mother drops to her knees next to the Councilor-in-Chief. Her hands roam over him, trying to staunch the flow of blood. But it's useless. He's gut-shot. It's a horrible way to die.

"Dev," my mother says, her voice shaking. "Oh, gods, Dev."

"Cor," he whispers, trying to smile. "I came for you."

Tears stream down my mother's face. "I told you to stay

behind," she says, gripping his hand tight. "You reckless, foolish man. Why don't you ever listen?"

He coughs, blood spraying onto their joined hands. "I listened...for twenty years. Believed...you were dead. But Cor...I never...took it off..."

My mother follows the motion of his hand, leaving a trail of blood as it touches his neck. Her fingers trembling, she tugs his collar aside.

In the hollow of his throat lies the figurine I've seen before —the small, silver wolf. My skin prickles all over as I realize she must have given it to him. It's a symbol of love and belonging. That wolf represents her own. But this time, alongside it hangs something else: a small, golden charm of an ouroboros. A snake swallowing its own tail.

My mother's fingers close around the figurine and the charm. Tears drip from her face onto his. "All this time," she whispers, through her sobs.

His eyes drift close, and he forces them open. With what looks like a tremendous effort, he focuses on her face. When he speaks, it's in a language I don't recognize. "Neshama sheli," he says, the words little more than grit and gravel. "You will always be my soul."

I feel Ari's hand close on my shoulder, hard, as my mother replies, still in that strange language. "Ani ohevet otkha, Dev," she tells him, swallowing so hard, I can see it. "As long as the sun burns in the sky and the oceans lap the land, and longer still, I will always love you."

Councilor Adelman smiles. This time it lights up his fading eyes. It's so bright that, despite the blood staining his cheeks and the lines that pain and a hard life have etched deep, I can see the boy he must have been, back when he and my mother were a girl and a boy who loved each other, against all odds.

"We are a story that never ends," he manages, his chest

heaving as he struggles to draw breath. More blood spills from his lips, and my mother wipes it away.

"Oh, Dev," she says through her tears. "Why did you have to follow me?"

"Tell me a story," Councilor Adelman says. It seems a strange request on your deathbed, but my mother looks unsurprised. Instead she grips his hand harder and nods.

"Once," she says, her voice shaking, "there was a boy who told a girl about the magical city of San Fraesco. There, they say some of the streets are made of water, and everyone travels from one place to the next in boats. And there are tunnels that take you beneath the surface, to the place where the selkies live."

Councilor Adelman draws one shuddering breath, then another. His eyes slip closed.

My mother's teeth sink deep into her lower lip. The air shimmers around her, as if she's on the verge of shifting again. But when she speaks, her voice is as steady as any bellator's blade, full of the steel-core strength that's carried her this far, unbroken, through all she's endured. "Plums and mulberries grow wild, overhanging the canals, so that as you drift by in a boat, you can reach up and pluck as many as you like. And if you're lucky, you can still find veins of gold, the way there used to be centuries ago..."

A terrible, rattling breath escapes Councilor Adelman. His body arches in agony. I want to go to him and my mother, to help, but there's nothing I can do. Ari draws me back against him, offering me his strength, as Adelman's chest heaves and my mother speaks again.

"May the gods be with you on your journey, Dev. This time, there will be no anguish and no pain." Her voice breaks on the word. "You'll come back from San Fraesco rich, with gold bars and plum pits in your pockets, and build yourself a place as grand as the House of Echoes. You'll plant the pits in an orchard, and the trees that grow from them will grant wishes from anyone brave enough to sample their fruit."

She bends, brushing her lips across his, heedless of the taste of blood. "This time, there will be no need to plan a revolution. In this story, the boy and girl are free to love each other, even though she is royalty and he a baker's son. She will be his wolf, and he will bake her cherry puff pastries, and there will be a place for them. A place where they belong."

Councilor Adelman's chest rises with another one of those agonized, shuddering breaths, and my mother's free hand rises to cup his face, holding him still.

"Be easy, Dev," she whispers. "Go with my blessing. I will always be with you."

He dies that way, with my mother taking his last breath for her own, their hands sealed together with his blood.

CHAPTER 51

ARI

Clockverk Square is awash in carnage.

An hour ago, my head echoed with the sound of our enemies' screams. But now, an eerie silence has fallen, broken only by the moans of the wounded and Ronan's orders as the guards prepare to haul prisoners to the dungeons. Bodies, both friend and foe, lie scattered like discarded rag dolls amidst the detritus of the drones. Eldrina stands before two of the falcons' corpses, her tears dripping onto their outstretched wings. Kilían is nowhere to be found, and I'm terrified his body lies somewhere beneath the heaps of bodies strewn across the square. I've been searching, but to no avail. The air is thick with the smell of burning flesh, the dirt and stones stained with blood.

Before the Mages allied themselves with us and turned the tide, the Brotherhood lost over a hundred warriors, and many more were injured. A few of the Mages and our medics, including my father, roam the square, stabilizing the survivors so they can be moved. The rest have retreated to the Commonwealth's infirmary, where medics sheltered in place during the battle. Together with the rest of the Mages, they wait to receive the wounded.

Dresda herself kneels beside Sebastían, slumped on the ground in human form. She weaves her fingers above his body, chanting, and his skin begins to knit together. He grits his teeth, and Ilsa, who'd been separated from him in the fray, grips his shoulder for support.

A few feet away, Gentian tends to one of the Bastarour, his voice low and soothing as he stitches its wounds. When I carried Adelman's body to the Great Hall, I crossed paths with him, leading the charge to liberate the Commonwealth's citizens. Apparently, most of them were ordered to shelter in the Hall, and Gentian figured they'd be less terrified if they saw a familiar face. His, not mine.

Accustomed as they are to obeying orders, they came with him readily enough. But when they learned the Executor was dead and saw the bellators lined up to go to the dungeons, they froze. Their eyes are glazed, their expressions bewildered, as they drag dead bodies from the square under Jaxon's guidance. It will be a long journey to wholeness for them...and for Eva.

Adelman didn't lie to me, there on the bridge over the Silber. He died rather than break Cordelia's heart by losing Eva —and in so doing, broke it anyway. Now he lies in state in the Great Hall, Cordelia keeping vigil beside him. She refuses to leave him, guarding his body in the form of her wolf and growling at anyone who approaches. The Executor's body lies in a separate chamber, awaiting incineration. After appointing a guard to make sure no one troubles Cordelia, Eva and I have returned to Clockverk Square, with Gentian and the liberated citizens in tow.

There's so much I want to say to her. So much I want to ask. But now is not the time.

Now, she stands next to Ronan by the mouth of the

alleyway to the Rookery, preparing to lead the way to the dungeons. Layla and Riley, in wolf form, stalk on either side of the bellators and High Priests who've been taken prisoner, with Adrien bringing up the rear. His face is stoic beneath the blond scruff of his beard, but I know he's grieving Fade.

I watch as they disappear down the alleyway. Then, calling Kilían's name, I pick my way through the carnage once more. I find one mangled corpse after another, but not his.

I'm elbow-deep in bodies when my father looms up beside me, his hands crimson to the wrists and his face white as bone. "Ari. Thank the Architect you're all right. You're searching for Kilían?"

"Yeah," I say, swallowing hard. "With no luck."

"We've stabilized everyone we can. I'll look with you." My father's expression is determined, but I can read the fear in his eyes. He knows as well as I do that if Kilían were able to, he'd be in the thick of things, overseeing the transportation of the prisoners and the organization of the citizens who remain.

Together, Kennett and I embark on the grim task of sorting through the piles of corpses. Our movements are mechanical and silent, except for occasional murmurs when we encounter people we recognize. The bodies of the fallen, still warm, have an echo of life left in them, and I half-expect them to sit up and wrap a hand around my wrist. A throat-clenching odor hangs in the air, the sharp, coppery bite of blood blending with the acrid stench of sweat and the fetid reek of the battlefield. Kennett has wrapped a cloth around his nose and mouth, and I take off my shirt and use it to do the same. My eyes burn with the residue of the smoke, my mouth tastes like ash, and my back aches from hefting one corpse after another. Still, we keep on. Until finally, beneath a pile of tangled, burnt limbs, I see a flash of red hair.

"There!" I let out a triumphant shout, seizing the body atop the pile. My father rushes to help me, tearing through corpses in a mad effort to clear them away. And at last, we uncover him, eyes closed, knife still in hand, black gear smeared with dirt and blood.

"Kilían," my father croaks, collapsing to his knees on the stones. "Can you hear me?"

My own heart stutters as he shifts his fingers, pressing them harder against Kilían's neck, feeling for the Lead Interrogator's pulse. "Is he—" I begin, fearing the worst.

"Alive," my father says, breaking into a smile and sitting back on his heels. "Thank the Virtues. Just passed out from smoke inhalation and getting crushed beneath these poor souls...who he likely killed," he adds, his tone wry.

As if the mention of murder has revived him, Kilían's eyes flutter open, revealing a startled, dazed flash of blue. He blinks, trying to focus on our faces. "Westergaard. Kennett," he says at last, his voice hoarse. "All right?"

"Are *we* all right?" My father barks a mirthless laugh. "We thought you were dead."

"It would take more than that..." Kilían manages, waving at the destruction around us, "to kill me. I took six down with me before I—" His words devolve into a hacking cough.

My father fumbles for his canteen, tipping it to Kilían's lips. "Drink," he admonishes, and to my astonishment, Kilían obeys without complaint, taking one long swallow after another.

"How do you feel?" my father says at last, reclaiming his canteen.

"That depends." The Lead Interrogator scans my father's face, as if the answer is to be found there. "Will you stay?"

Kilían could simply mean *now,* on the battlefield, until he feels well enough to stand. Or he could mean much more than that. But my father doesn't ask. Instead, he gives a small, trembling smile. His voice comes low and steady when he says, "Always."

The dazed expression leaves Kilían's eyes, replaced by joy. He tries to speak, fails, and finally struggles to his knees, pulling Kennett into a blood-stained embrace. I leave them to it, kneeling with their arms around each other in the remains of the place they once both called home.

CHAPTER 52
EVA

Four days have passed since Cordelia and I killed the Executor. Since Councilor Adelman died. But this is the first time I've had a moment to call my own. Right now, in fact, I'm probably needed for something. But here, in the woods, I'm as inaccessible as I can manage.

I'm not alone. But that's by design.

"There you are," I say, coming up behind Sebastían. For most people, tracking him down here, miles from the city center, would have proved challenging. But not for me.

I know what I want. I've done my research. Now, all that's left is to speak.

"Carina," the Panther of the West says in acknowledgment. He doesn't turn.

I sit down next to him, hanging my feet over the edge of the ledge Efraím Stinar once pushed me off, the night of the Trials. Below me, the rapids roil, the cold spray so strong I can feel it against my skin, even so far above.

"You're hiding, I take it," I say, easing my way into the conversation.

He stares down at the waterfall, his gaze fixed on the

tumbling water and jagged rocks. "I've earned it. If I had to sit through one more gods-damned meeting, I was going to lose my mind."

"I know the feeling." And I do. Ever since the battle ended, we've done nothing but burn bodies, argue, and try to figure out next steps. We've made progress: Jaxon accepted Cordelia's apology for leveraging his ability without his consent, given the dire situation. The two have formally bonded as skúma and familiar, minus the usual pomp and circumstance, and my mother was appointed the head of the new Council of Nine, by a unanimous vote. Immediately, she chose a co-leader: Dresda. Yes, the Mages tried to kill us, but they came around in the end. And as Cordelia said at our last strategy session, it's time to end the power struggle between skúma and Mages once and for all. We're still negotiating the terms of a formal peace treaty, but we're doing so as equals.

Even deep in grief, my mother is a formidable leader. No sooner did she bury Councilor Adelman than she stepped into the role he left behind, sending a falcon to the remaining leaders of the Council back in Vik for their approval. The Mages lent the gift of the wind to the falcon's flight, as they had during our journey to the Commonwealth, when the Executor and I floated above the ground. I hadn't been dreaming; my vision of gliding between the snow-coated trees was real. Dresda confirmed it, and delivered a much-needed apology, when she spelled the falcon to fly to Vik. And soon, we had Trina, Elijah, and Peder's answers, accepting Cordelia's leadership and deferring to her decision regarding the Mages. I had my doubts they'd agree, but whatever my mother wrote in the falcon's missive must have persuaded them.

With the Mages' cooperation and Gentian's insistence that the birds not be harmed, my mother sent ravens to the five other Commonwealths, informing them that the Commonwealth of Ashes had fallen and that their bellators had surrendered. She gave the Executors and Priests from each Commonwealth a choice: integrate into the new, democratic order, where citizens are free to live as they choose, exiles can return home, and information is no longer restricted, or face lifetime imprisonment. We're still awaiting their replies, but whatever they decide, I'm not worried. The ravens will tell us whether the remaining Executors are attempting to mount an offensive. Even if the five Commonwealths try to join forces and march against us, they'll be no match for us, united as we are.

After sending the ravens, Cordelia and Dresda put forward a motion to expand the Council, including three additional seats for Mages. It passed by a majority, making the Council of Nine the Council of Twelve. The seats still sit empty: Dresda is choosing carefully among her numbers, eliminating those who didn't fully support her decision to join forces with us. The four remaining seats are intended to be filled by representatives from the Commonwealths, but right now only two individuals hold them: Kennett and Gentian, both of whom have been tirelessly advocating for citizens' rights and rehabilitation. The interim Council gave Kilían the role of Chief Military Advisor for the Empire. He'll stay here for now, with Kennett, helping to rebuild. There's been talk of elevating Kennett's position to bear equal weight with Dresda and Cordelia's; I expect it will happen.

For the two remaining Commonwealth seats, Kennett has suggested implementing a vote so the citizens can choose a representative from amongst themselves—perhaps, even, from two of the other Commonwealths. The democratic process is new here, but I have hopes that once the citizens understand its value, they'll take to it. Even if the citizens of the Commonwealths don't think so right now, I fought not to destroy their world but to free them from its confines. It will be a long struggle for many of them, but I hope in the end, they will come to see that.

Or maybe not. Maybe they'll hate me. The important thing is that they're free to choose.

With hard work, trust, and cooperation, I have hopes that the Empire will pull together—Mages, skúma, and Commonwealth citizens living and working side by side as *people*. But people still have problems, which is why I'm sitting here.

Sebastían gives me a sideways grin, like he can tell what I'm thinking. "I was surprised you and your exile didn't campaign for a seat on the Council."

"Are you joking?" I shudder. "I want to help rebuild, but not like that. Something more...active. I've had enough of politics for a lifetime."

"Speaking of..." he says, turning to face me. "We need to talk. I assume that's why you're here?"

It is. But finding the words to articulate what I need to say isn't easy. I struggle for a way in, and finally settle for what I've been wondering ever since he crawled toward the illusion of her, even gravely wounded. "Who's Adeline?"

Those aquamarine eyes of his narrow. "It figures Westergaard couldn't keep his mouth shut. Fjeri must have told him. I'm surprised they didn't both trot right to the Council."

"What?" Now I am well and truly confused. "Ari hasn't said a word about this. Honestly, we haven't had much of a chance to talk, what with everything that's happened." Ari and I have been avoiding each other since the battle—sad but true. Even when we've both attended open Council sessions, we haven't discussed anything personal. There's too much to be said, and we left things in such a mess before I was taken. It's far easier to occupy ourselves with the details of the battle's aftermath. So, he sleeps in his old room in the Bellatorum's quarters, and I sleep in mine, and we keep our distance, no matter how much it hurts.

Sebastían glares harder. "Fjeri said something to you, then."

"No one told me anything!" I say, impatient. "You said her name yourself, when the drone attacked you. I asked Dresda what that gray gas was meant to do. She said it forced the victim to hallucinate the person they loved most in the world. They'd crawl straight for the hallucination, do anything to reach it...even if it meant their death."

"Gods." He knots his hands behind his head, his sharp teeth sinking into his lower lip. "I don't remember."

I stay silent, my eyes fixed on the spray, waiting him out. And finally he says, "Adeline is...the girl I love. She's a gunsmith's daughter, back home. Her father is the finest smith we have, and she apprenticed with him. I met her on a tour of his facilities to commission new weapons two years ago. And the rest, as they say, is history."

"You love her," I say slowly, remembering what he told me about how panthers aren't monogamous. "But you can't be with her, because she isn't a skúma."

"She can't even be a royal consort." He gives a bitter laugh, ripping grass from between the stones at the edge of the falls. "Our relationship, such as it is, has been built on stolen moments. One of which, unfortunately, Fjeri's lover saw, when I caught him trying to lift a jeweled dagger from the House of Echoes, inherited from the skúma who survived the Twilight Massacre. We caught each other, I suppose." His shoulders heave in a sigh. "I thought the memory had died with him, but apparently not."

"Tobias told Jaxon," I say slowly. "But not anyone else, because..."

"He knew if he tried to implicate me, I'd tell the Council what I'd seen. Tobias was well-known for his sticky fingers.

Who would they believe—the Panther of the West, or a dissolute thief with a good reason to stain my reputation?" Sebastían gives a harsh laugh. "He told Fjeri, though. Not about the dagger, but about her...Adeline." His mouth shapes the word tenderly, as if it's precious. "We fought about it, on our journey to the Commonwealth. And Westergaard overheard. He's been chomping at the bit to figure out what I'm hiding. Probably thinks it's some kind of state secret, instead of a tawdry affair."

His voice sounds pained, and I twist to meet his eyes. "It's not tawdry, is it? You care for her. The only tawdry part is that you can't do so in the open."

"No, it's not." The words are barely audible over the roar of the falls. "I love her, like you said. I would marry her in an instant, if I could. No insult to present company intended."

He rips another handful of grass out by the roots. "Do you feel betrayed, Eva? Angry with me?"

"No." I hold my hands out over the falls, letting the cool spray hit my palms. Within me, my panther luxuriates at Sebastían's closeness, but not in the out-of-control, terrifying way it did before. Over the past few days, Dresda has been teaching me how to calm my beasts, to integrate them into my larger self. Now, I don't worry that Carina will break free and take control of my body. She's just happy to be in the presence of her kind.

"What, then?" Sebastían's voice is wary.

"I feel relieved. And happy for you."

"You would truly wed me, knowing my heart belongs forever to another?"

"*You* were willing to do it," I point out.

He opens his fists, letting the shreds of grass fall. They drift down toward the roiling water, buoyed by the wind. "Ah, but I was raised for such things, Carina. You were not. And you've just finished telling me how sick you are of politics."

Touché. "True," I tell him. "I won't marry you."

His gaze flicks to mine, wide and startled. "Then—"

"I needed you to unite the Houses. You needed me to continue the skúma line," I say. "You kept your end of the deal. Now let me keep mine."

Sebastían's long fingers clench and unclench on the blue linen of his tunic. "I don't understand."

It's now or never. Drawing a deep breath, I meet Sebastían's eyes. "I have a proposal to make to you."

CHAPTER 53

ARI

En route to my second interrogation shift of the day, I find Gentian at the edge of Clockverk Square, deep in conversation with Jaxon. My old friend is fascinated by skúma. Whenever he isn't campaigning for citizens' rights, he's been trying to learn everything he can about shapeshifting and familiars. He's stayed behind to talk to Eva about it after more than one interminable Council meeting.

Once, I would have joined them, thrilled by the novelty of having two people I care about in such close proximity. But now, I could swear Eva's avoiding me. She speaks to me, sure. She's civil enough. But the intimacy I felt when I freed her from that cage, when we fought side by side, is nowhere to be found.

I want to tell her the truth I've discovered about Sebastían, the one Jaxon finally spilled after the final battle, when we were drinking our weight in the High Priests' wine. But I worry she'll think I'm leveraging Adeline's existence to tear down the Panther of the West, so I can get what I want. And there we'll be, right back in the fight we were having before she was taken.

With an effort, I put Eva out of my mind and stride up to Jaxon and Gentian. The former is lounging against the wall of the machine shop, hands in his pockets, looking like he doesn't have a care in the world. Gentian, on the other hand, is bouncing on his toes, as if he can barely contain himself. As I come even with them, he's saying, his voice animated, "So you have a connection with her, is that it? You can f-feel when she's close or far? And when she shifts into animal form, she pulls energy through you?"

"Sort of," Jaxon says, giving Gentian the half-smirk that passes for his smile. "Oh, hello, Westergaard. Perfect timing. I was headed down to give you a hand with the interrogation." He drops Gentian a wink. "Gets a bit cocky, this one. Needs all the help he can get. Catch you later."

He turns to go, and Gentian clears his throat. "I-I um...that is, I was w-wondering..."

"Hmmm?" Jaxon says, that smirk still lifting the corner of his lips. When I first met him, I remember wanting to smack it right off his face.

But apparently, Gentian's seen through Jaxon's obnoxious façade to the decent guy who lurks beneath, because he says, "Would you maybe w-want to discuss the skúma-familiar bond this evening? Over d-dinner? With m-me?"

By the Sins.

Jaxon stares at Gentian, whose face is growing redder by the moment. I'd wager he's thinking about Tobias. If he feels like even considering this offer is disloyal. But as I watch, the smirk fades. And finally he says, "Yeah. All right. I'm off-shift at eight."

Gentian's thin face lights with joy. "G-great," he says. "S-see you then."

Together, Jaxon and I stride off toward the dungeons, where the bellators and High Priests are being held. Sure, we may be able to anticipate and deflect a potential attack, but that doesn't mean we're going to skimp on exploiting all sources of intelligence. These bellators hail from all six Commonwealths. One of them has intel we can use, and we've spent hours doing our utmost to extract it.

"So," I say to Jaxon as we make our way down the steep stairs. "You and Gentian."

"Shut it, Westergaard," he snaps, but I can tell he's trying to suppress a smile.

This is good. He deserves to heal, and Gentian deserves to be with someone worthy. Even if they only become friends, Jaxon will appreciate Gentian's courage, and maybe Gentian's gentleness will ease his sharp edges.

I shove Jaxon's bad shoulder. "Don't hurt him, yeah? He's been through enough."

"Wouldn't dream of it," he mutters, shoving me back. "You, on the other hand..."

We're grinning as we stride down the hall and into the interrogation chamber where Efraím once tried to force Eva to betray our cause.

And find her standing there, waiting for me.

CHAPTER 54

EVA

Sebastían and I walk back from the falls together, parting ways in Wunderstrand Square. Instruktor Bjarki, who the Executor punished the first day I took that tiny pink pill, is stacking debris alongside Valentína, my former dorm-mate in the Rookery. Next to them are two of the natural-born, and I feel a flash of gratitude as I pass them. It was a stroke of brilliance for Gentian to recruit them to the resistance: no one noticed them to begin with, consigned as they were to performing the Commonwealth's most menial tasks. He's told the Council that he's dedicated to continuing the work he began, helping them realize that their lives hold value.

I fully intend to support him. After all, without Lorne slipping me that blade and the natural-born who disabled the bio-ID on my cell's keypad, the battle might well have been lost. But now, it's time for Ari and me to have a conversation that's long overdue.

He's not in his old quarters. Not in the Bellatorum's training grounds, nor the Great Hall, where the Council has been meeting. I could track his scent or open the bond to find him, but that feels wrong, given the delicacy of the conversation we're about to have. So instead I use common sense, making my way down to the dungeons, into the chamber where Efraím tried and failed to get me to confess my secrets.

Ari isn't here. But Kilían and Adrien are, along with a host of others. There are too many bellators and Priests to interrogate one at a time, so they've been bringing them out in small groups. Thirty armed guards line one of the opposite walls, and Layla prowls the perimeter, providing an additional level of security.

Erdahl survived, thanks to Mei's protection, and found his way back to us. But Layla will never forgive the Executor for his role in hurting her child. Since the man himself is dead, threatening the bellators he used to command is the next best thing. She raises her head and gives a low sound of greeting when she sees me, then goes back to her work.

"Marteinn," Kilían says in greeting. "Come to lend a hand?"

"Not exactly. Have you seen—"

I interrupt my own question as Ari's unmistakable footsteps pad down the hallway outside the interrogation chamber. A moment later, he strides into the room, Jaxon at his side. Both of them are smiling, but the grin slides right off Ari's face when he sees me.

"Eva," he says, sounding wary. I can't say I blame him.

"Hi." It's ridiculous, but I feel almost shy in his presence. "Do you suppose Kilían could spare you? There's something I need you to see."

Ari's eyebrows knit, and his eyes rake over the line of waiting bellators. "Now?"

"You've done your part, Westergaard," Kilían says dryly. "Let Fjeri have a chance at the fun."

"You're sure?" Ari says. If I didn't know better, I'd think he was afraid to be alone with me, for fear of what it might yield. "Because if you need me—"

Kilían gives a long-suffering sigh. "One successful revolution, and it goes to your head. I should have known it wouldn't take much to tip that inflated ego of yours over the edge." He lifts an eyebrow, a sardonic tilt. But then he smiles. "I was doing this long before you were born, Westergaard. Believe it or not, the world won't fall apart if you cease to monitor it."

Jaxon, who's pacing the line of bellators, snorts at this. "You heard the man. Go with your princess, exile. These pitiful excuses for soldiers will still be here for you to worm the truth out of when you get back."

Ari gives both of them an obscene gesture that he must have learned from Fade, may his soul rest among the fallen, or maybe from Jaxon himself. "Fine," he says, turning to me. "Let's go."

As we walk away, I hear Jaxon laughing, and Kilían demanding to know what the gesture means. A moment later, I hear him mutter, "Figures. Smart mouth, even when he isn't using it."

Now it's my turn to laugh.

"They get along well," Ari observes as the two of us make our way up the stairs and out into the fresh, cool air, beneath one of the many stone arches on which the Sins and Virtues are engraved.

"They do. It's good, I suppose."

Ari snorts, sounding eerily like Jaxon. "For them. For me... maybe less so."

We cross the square in front of the Hall. The bodies have been cleared away; Ronan took charge of that, employing the Commonwealth's citizens, who were only too happy to have a job to do. They can take orders easily. It's thinking for themselves that's the problem.

Well, there will be time enough for that. It will be a learning curve, but with all of us working together, surely it's possible. It was for me and Ari, after all. For Ronan, who left the Commonwealth of Scribes behind. For Kennett, whose love for Kilían is impossible to hide whenever the two of them are in the same room.

The gentle healer and the scarred, vicious bellator. I suppose there have been stranger things. And if there's one thing I've learned, it is that love sees no logic. The heart wants what it wants, and finally, that's just fine with me.

Whether it will be fine with the boy striding next to me, his black hair tousled by the wind and his jaw set, remains to be seen.

"Where are you taking me, Eva?" he says suspiciously.

"Why?" I give him an innocent smile. "Don't you trust me?"

He mutters something under his breath, but lets me take his hand and pull him into the woods. It's been months since I last set foot here, yet my feet still know the way.

This far to the south, the trees are thick with leaves and the flowering bushes are already in bloom, obscuring the path. I've had to let go of Ari's hand, but I can hear him behind me, his footsteps quick and sure on the packed dirt. I can *feel* him there, his strength feeding mine, his spirit tired but determined. He will go as long as I need him to, do whatever I ask of him. I can feel that through the bond, but I also know it in my heart.

It's training, sure. But it's also love.

The path opens into a clearing, hemmed in by trees. It starts up again on the other side, but I don't go any further. I've reached my destination, and I hear Ari's sharp intake of breath when he takes in where we are.

"The night we trained in the woods," he says, coming to stand beside me. "When you hunted me in the rain..."

"When I caught you," I correct, smiling up at him. "And knocked you out of that tree."

One dark brow rises. "Is that all you remember about that night, apprentice mine?"

I give him the brow right back. Whenever he calls me that, it feels like *before*—when even holding hands felt forbidden, and discovery meant death. It sends a strange thrill through me, one I didn't even have a word for back then. "You know it's not."

"I wanted you so much," he admits, his voice low. "I knew it was a sin. But you were so beautiful, even on top of me with your knife to my throat. I thought if I didn't kiss you, I might actually die." The words are dramatic, but from the matter-of-fact tone of his voice, I can tell he means them.

"What stopped you, then?" I say, tracing the back of his hand with my fingertip.

He sucks in his breath, as if he feels my touch everywhere. "You were my apprentice, yeah? Think about what that would've done to my reputation. Knocked out of a tree and dead on the ground, before you'd done more than prick me with your sverd. Couldn't have that, could I?"

"I guess not." I look up at him, expecting to see the familiar glint of humor in his eyes. But he's staring down at me with a look of such tenderness, his green eyes soft in the light that filters through the leaves, it almost undoes me. "So here we are again, back where it all began. No rain, no knife at your throat. Do you still want me, anyway?"

Ari doesn't justify that with an answer. Instead, his gaze intensifies, but when he speaks, it's as quiet as before. "You think this is where it all began?" he says.

I stare up at him, into those piercing green eyes, and remember the first time I ever saw them. I think about that small girl standing in Clockverk Square, a High Priest's words on her lips and a man's blood pooling around her feet. About a boy who was the only one brave enough to hold her gaze. And I know he's right: that was the day we first found each other, the day everything changed. Not that rainy night in the woods, or the first time we spoke, or even when Efraím made us swear our oaths as mentor and apprentice. Then.

The Executor would say our bond began long before, when the gen techs identified Ari's capability as a familiar, a gift that saved him from a lifetime of servitude as a natural-born. That *he* made us, and everything that followed. But the Executor is dead, and no matter how he tried to twist and warp our lives, our choices are our own.

They always were.

"No," I tell Ari. "I don't. And"—I clear my throat, bracing myself—"I'm sorry, again. For not listening to you when you told me not to go after Erdahl, for making you feel like you weren't enough, for so many things. If I hadn't—"

He holds up a hand, interrupting my rant. "And if I hadn't, yeah?"

"If you hadn't...what?" As far as I can tell, I'm the one to blame here. What can he possibly have to apologize for?

"Let my pride and hurt feelings get the better of my good sense, been blinded by jealousy, the list goes on." He lifts one shoulder and lets it fall. "I'll let it go if you will. I think we've both paid for our sins."

"Consider it done," I say. Too quickly, maybe, because Ari snorts in amusement.

"So what are we doing here, little warrior? Care for a rematch of that night in the woods? Because if so, I never thought I'd say this, but I could use a break from bloodshed."

"So could I. I just...I thought maybe..." By the Architect. Why is this so hard? I've killed enemies, transformed into four beasts, freed my mother from prison. Yet all of it was child's play compared to this.

Ari is staring at me, puzzled. I can feel him poking at the bond, trying to figure out what's giving me so much trouble. Stubbornly, I refuse to let him in.

"I thought maybe," I say, forcing myself to meet his eyes, "that we could try again. Have a rematch of a different kind."

"A rematch of a—"

His eyebrows are knitted. Then both of them rise, and his eyes go wide. "Why, Eva. Are you asking me if I want to finish what we started, that day against the tree?"

A blush heats my cheeks. "What if I were? Would you say yes?"

Ari's gaze sharpens. His heartbeat speeds up; his breath catches. But when he speaks, his voice is deliberately indifferent. "What about Sebastían?"

"That's what I need to talk to you about. We—"

"Wait, Eva. I have something to say, before you go on." The line of his throat moves as he swallows. "Sebastían loves someone else, a girl in House Satrizona."

"I know about her. That's what I—"

"Let me finish." His gaze shifts over my shoulder, following the path of a sparrow that's taken flight, as if looking me in the eye is too painful for him. Or if it would reveal too much. "Even if he married you, I think he always intended to...to keep her. As he expected you to...keep me. If that's what you're thinking...if there's any part of you that believes you still need to be with him, even if in name only, to rebuild..."

His eyes meet mine. They hold a fierce, painful resolve. "I couldn't do it, Eva. I *won't* do it. As much as it would tear me apart to watch you with him, it would kill me a little more every day to be forced to share you the way he means." He folds his arms across his chest, but the gesture doesn't look defensive. Instead, he looks as if he's struggling to hold himself together. "If that's what you came out here to propose to me, then...much as I want to say otherwise, the answer to your question is no."

Through the bond, I feel the pain that pervades every inch of him, the way it hurts when he drags these words from the depths, like they're caught on a barbed fishhook that bleeds him as they rise. I smell his heartbreak, a crumbling, half-lush, half-sweet scent. I feel it, acid dripping into a wound. Abrading his heart with every beat.

I press my hand against my chest, feeling my own heart beat with the agony that echoes within his. His pain is my own. All the worse, because I caused it. Within me, Aelina raises her head, sensing all is not right. *Make this right,* she growls. *Or I will.*

I'm trying, I tell her. *I hope it's not too late.*

"Eva," Ari says, the hint of a tremor in his voice. "Choose what's right for you, and I'll find a way to live with it. But make your choice."

"That's what I'm trying to tell you. I've already chosen." I close the gap between us, and watch him fight not to flinch. "Gentian's a genius, you know."

He blinks at me, startled by my change of topic. "What?"

"I've been talking to him. He says the Executor somehow got access to an ancestral bank of skúma DNA. It's how he made the Bastarour; it's how he made me, with Cordelia's unwilling assistance." I swallow hard, trying not to dwell on what was done to my mother. On how I came to be.

"Um, okay." He shoves a hand through his hair, brows drawn down in puzzlement. "What does this have to do with anything?"

"Everything. Because it means that there's a genetically diverse reserve here. Enough to prevent inbreeding. To rebuild all four species."

Ari's jaw drops. "So what you're saying is..."

"I'm saying that there's no need for me to marry Sebastían to continue the panther line, even if I wanted to...which I don't," I say as his gaze darkens. "If Adeline is willing, the two of them could have children together. We could use the technology that—that changed my DNA to ensure their offspring would be skúma." I pause, letting the impact of my words sink in.

Hope lights Ari's eyes, tempered with wariness. "And Sebastían agreed to this?"

I think of the way Sebastían grabbed me by both shoulders as we sat by the falls, his face aglow with excitement. "Adeline could sit by my side," he said. "Rule Satrizona next to me. No one would dare question her then, not if she gave me an heir." He rose to his feet, pacing. "You really think you can make this happen, Eva? You would do this for us?"

"I would. For you, and for the other Houses, too. With the caveat, of course, that you let me go. I'll be free to make my own choices, no longer tied to yours."

Sebastían stopped in front of me, his expression as serious as I'd ever seen it. "I vow it to you, Eva Marteinn, late of the Commonwealth of Ashes, skúma of House Minneska, and holder of the Four. I swear it on my life and on the honor of my House."

He extended his hand, and I took it. Mist rose from the falls, curling around our interwoven fingers, sinuous as smoke, sealing our deal.

"More than agreed," I tell Ari now. "He's sent a raven to Adeline. All that's left is her acceptance."

"By the Virtues," Ari mutters, staring at me like he's never seen me before.

Anxiety churns in my stomach, but I force myself to speak. "So, to answer your question... I choose you, Ari Westergaard. Now and forever, I choose you. I choose you above Sebastían, above my duty, above the demands of my beasts and the unknowns that life will bring. Because to choose you is to choose myself. We are one, and I was a fool to ever think otherwise."

I wait for him to respond. To say something, anything. But he stands, frozen.

Digging deep, I harness the remains of my courage. "Knowing that, do you want to be with me? Will you trust me, not just with your life, but with your heart?"

I wait for declarations of love, for poetry, for a kiss. But when Ari finally unfreezes, his lips rise in the crooked smile that's driven me out of my mind since the first time I saw it.

"The last time we were here, I told you I'd gladly go to the devil with you, Eva," he muses, slow and sweet as honey. "Though preferably not in a soggy pile of leaves."

"I remember." I sound as breathless as I feel.

"Well," he says, "today is a beautiful day."

His arms come around me then, tight enough that I know he never wants to let me go, gentle enough that I can feel how much I mean to him. He lifts me as if I weigh nothing at all. My legs wrap around his hips, and my mouth comes down on his for the first time since that fateful morning in his room in the guards' quarters, weeks before.

The instant our lips touch, a shudder runs through me. I feel it echoed in his own body, a wave with no beginning and no end. His side of the bond opens wide and I feel *him*: desire so intense it makes my own heartbeat pound even faster, love so profound I wonder how I could ever have doubted it, loyalty so complete, I know I am the alpha and omega for him, the beginning and the end.

My hands tighten in the rough silk of his hair and he gasps into my mouth, his tongue tracing mine. His chest heaves against my body, and he moans, a low, desperate sound that ends in my name. The wind gusts and brings with it his deepening scent, laced with salt and blade oil, sharp with the lust that we both once believed was a sin. An ache builds deep in my belly as he knots a hand in my own hair and takes control of the kiss, nipping at my lips, then letting his tongue delve back inside, licking along mine until it's my turn to moan. His hands are everywhere, roaming feverishly over my body.

When he pulls back, it's only to kneel and look up at me through his lashes. "Come here," he says, his voice husky. Within me, I feel my beasts stir, as if his call is intended for them as well. They raise their heads, scenting him. And then, as one, they prowl forward.

I sink to my knees in front of him. His eyes on mine, he reaches a trembling hand to stroke my hair back from my face. "Show me," he says.

He doesn't have to explain. Taking a deep breath, I open my side of the bond and let everything I'm thinking, everything I'm feeling, show. Baring myself before him.

He draws one shuddering breath, then another, as my emotions hit him. As my desire for him—for *this*—washes over him like a wave. "You really do want me."

Without a word, I pull my shirt over my head. He freezes, his eyes fixed on me. And then, as if I've hypnotized him, he does the same. He looks almost feral, with the bars of sunlight striping his bare chest and his green eyes gone dark with desire.

"I know we never made each other any promises." His bare skin presses against mine, hot and sleek, the muscles beneath it a reminder of his strength. "But you have always been forever for me."

I answer him with a kiss, letting the heat flow between us, making my own promises without words. Through the bond, I know he can feel it.

His hands shake as they tighten on my hips. As he peels each item of my clothing off, asking permission with eyes and hands and voice. Inviting me to do so with his own. Until finally we are naked against each other, his hair falling into my eyes as he leans down to kiss me, his lips tracing a path down my throat to my collarbone, then lower still. I gasp and feel him laugh against me, his breath warm against my skin.

I tremble as he learns every inch of me with mouth and hands. And return the favor, tasting the salt of his sweat, discovering the places that make him shudder and hiss my name, the ones that make his hands tighten in my hair.

"Now?" he whispers, and I answer, "Yes."

I'm not afraid. I was born to be with him.

As he moves over me, I feel everything: the warmth of the sun, the rough caress of his hands, the spark that ignites into wildfire in my blood. I breathe in and taste the life of the forest on my tongue a moment before he covers my mouth with his own. He is heat and light and *home.*

As his body slides against mine, as he trails kisses over all the parts of me that he can reach, as I dig my nails into his back and urge him *closer, faster, more,* I never close my eyes. I stare up through the leaves of the giant oak above us and watch the clouds scud across the sky and think how I dreamed of this—a world that was ours for the taking, a place where loving him like this wasn't a sin. Within me, my beasts rejoice. *Yes,* they whisper. *This.*

Afterward, we lie in each other's arms, panting, wordless. He brushes my hair back from my face, and I rest my head on his chest, content, and there is nothing we need to say.

Later, we'll rebuild. We'll don our mantles as skúma and familiar and do what must be done.

But now, we are together, in our woods under the dappled sunlight.

As we were always meant to be.

Want to be the first to know? Subscribe to Emily's newsletter at emilycolinnews.com for insider updates about the world of the Seven Sins and bonus stories.

WANT MORE SEVEN SINS?

Go deeper into Ari and Eva's world with the FREE prequel, *Sacrifice of the Seven Sins.*

And discover your favorite characters' backstories in the short story collection, *Shadows of the Seven Sins!*

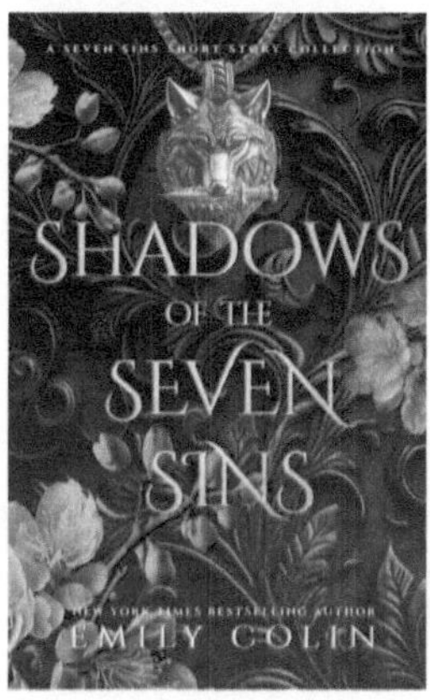

Thank you for loving Ari and Eva as much as I do...and for being the best readers in the world! Sending you love, hugs, and warm chocolate chip cookies.

xoxo,
    Emily

BOOKS BY EMILY COLIN

THE SEVEN SINS SERIES

Sword of the Seven Sins: A Novel

Siege of the Seven Sins: A Novel

Storm of the Seven Sins: A Novel

Sacrifice of the Seven Sins: A Novella

Shadows of the Seven Sins: A Story Collection

YOUNG ADULT ANTHOLOGIES

Wicked South: Secrets and Lies

Unbound: Stories of Transformation, Love, and Monsters

FICTION FOR ADULTS

The Memory Thief

The Dream Keeper's Daughter

Cursed in Love (Serialized Fiction)

NONFICTION

The Long Way Around: How 34 Women Found the Lives they Love

The Secret to Our Success: How 33 Women Made their Dreams Come True

The Changing Face of Justice: A Look at the First 100 Women Attorneys in

ABOUT THE AUTHOR

Emily Colin's debut novel, *The Memory Thief,* was a New York Times bestseller and Target Emerging Authors Pick. She is also the author of *The Dream Keeper's Daughter* and, for YA audiences, the award-winning *Seven Sins* series. Emily is the co-editor of two YA fiction anthologies, including *Unbound: Stories of Transformation, Love, and Monsters,* and the author of the serialized urban fantasy romance, *Cursed in Love.* One of her short stories appeared in the USA Today bestselling romance anthology, *Dissent.*

Emily's life experience includes organizing a Coney Island tattoo and piercing show, hauling fish at a dolphin research center, roaming New York City as a teenage violinist, and working in community arts engagement. Originally from Brooklyn, Emily writes, teaches, edits, and indulges her mocha addiction in a city by the sea in North Carolina, where she lives with her family. Visit her at www.emilycolin.com.

ACKNOWLEDGMENTS

When Ari and Eva's story first came to me, I had no idea that, six years later, it would become a five-book series. All I knew was that, in my mind's eye, I saw a small girl standing in a cobblestone square, her shoulders squared in determination as she fought to hide her trembling. In front of her knelt a man, a black-clad warrior's blade at his throat. From the crowd, I felt someone watching: a dark-haired boy, his green eyes trained on the girl, willing her not to back down. And I heard a single line, as clear as if someone had whispered it in my ear: *The first time I condemned a man to death, I was ten years old.*

And so Eva and Ari were born.

I didn't know much about Eva other than that she was stubborn, smart, and a survivor, a girl who could think for herself and knew when to hedge her bets. I knew a little more about the green-eyed boy: he saw a kindred spirit in Eva, someone worth risking everything for. All his life, he'd felt alone. In that moment on the stones, she stole his heart. And she never gave it back again.

That was the beginning, and since then, we've come so far. Gratitude goes to my sweet parents, Lois and Michael Colin, who've read everything I've ever written; Felicia Eth, my indefatigable agent, who always has my back; and Katie Rose Guest Pryal and Lauren Faulkenberry at Blue Crow Publishing, who gave the series its start.

I've written the entire series with my furry companions by

my side, except alas, now there's one fewer to keep me company. Let us all pour one out for Moo, my sweet doggy. I miss you every day! I'd raise a glass to my puppy, Kaia Rose, but so far she's only contributed by gnawing her way through boxes of my books, trying to bite through my computer cord, and burying my annotated copy of *Siege* under the couch. Ah well, at least she's adorable!

Special thanks to Neil and Lucas Horne, for putting up with me as I disappear into the cave of my mind for hours on end. Neil, thank you in particular for designing my beautiful website, making sure my newsletter reaches actual humans, and always being willing to act out fight scenes with me. I'm so grateful for your support!

This journey would have been far more arduous—and lonely!—without the Fellowship of the Five and my indomitable Sprinters group, who keep me sane. Lisa Amowitz, Ángela Álvarez Vélez, Christy Swift, Marie LeStrange, Sarah Anderson Vivien, Heidi Ayarbe, Madeline Dyer Statham, and John Klekamp, I'm looking at you! Thank you for talking me off the ledge, reading my drafts, and kicking me in the butt when I need it.

Lisa Amowitz, your incredible graphics make me smile every time I see them. You've truly brought the series to life. Those covers! That map! Those images! You're not just the Plot Fairy, you're the Design Diva. I hereby bestow upon you your new title, and bow down to you in awe. Without you, my covers would resemble a bunch of stick figures with little notes that read, "Make this pretty!" "Sword here!" "Like this but better!" May you squirrel away in infamy forever, and may I be so fortunate as to meerkat by your side.

Sarah Anderson Vivien, thank you a thousand times over for helping me create the gorgeous book trailer, designing that incomparable sticker—to love is to die!—spreading the word on Bookstagram, and everything else you've done to help this series shine. Lisa may call you the Design Puppy, but I think of you as the Magnificent Media Maestra of Mayhem. I worship at the feet of your creative genius!

Ángela Álvarez Vélez, where do I even begin? Your insight into human nature, acerbic wit, bottomless creativity, unparalleled compassion, and eerie ability to pierce the heart of the matter (I swear, it's like you have emotional Xray vision) blows me away on a regular basis. I'm supremely lucky to consider you a writing partner and friend.

A special shoutout to Angela's remarkable mother, Olga Lucía Vélez Sierra, my most unexpected Seven Sins fangirl extraordinaire. Thank you for reading—but more importantly, thank you for co-creating one of my favorite people on the planet. Sending you hugs and love.

Everyone needs a Christy Swift, y'all...and when her debut novel hits the shelves in early 2025, you'll all get to find out just how awesome she is! Christy, thank you for making me laugh, sharing my work far and wide, welcoming me into your beautiful home (omg the manatees!) and, of course, reading and sharing Ari and Eva's story. Special thanks to you and your mini-mes, Kira & Ocean Swift, for helping me brainstorm the series' taglines. Christy—when the apocalypse hits, I want you on my side!

Marie LeStrange, thank you for your polymathematical miracle of a mind, for your wickedly creative promo ideas, and for inspiring me! Heidi Ayarbe, Madeline Dyer Statham, and John Klekamp, writer friends extraordinaire...thank you for being there for me, reading my stories, and, in John's case, always being up for delectable mochas. Without my writing community, I would be bereft and probably huddled under a blanket in a corner somewhere. On behalf of blankets and corners everywhere, my deepest appreciation.

Speaking of deepest appreciation, all hail the Seven Sins ARC Team, who have been instrumental in reading and reviewing the series. A thousand halos and garlands of glory go out to the Sin Slingers, my kickass Street Team: Ángela Álvarez Vélez, Lisa Amowitz, Jessica Barton, Raegan Billingsley, Devon Conaway, Amy Condra, Audrey Costruba, Amanda Curry, Tiffany Ewald, Kara French, Krista Hall, Samantha Halpern, Shannon Heck, Whitney Hester, Beverly Hughes, Amelia King, Kristina Marquardt, Jayne Murray, LeeRenee Musgjerd, Pearl Precious, Hunter Sachs, Katie Schiela, Sammy Standing, Christy Swift, Courtney Anne Tarara, and Sarah Anderson Vivien. You entered the circle at night and survived the fire. Love to all of you!

Amanda Curry, Lead Bellator of the Sin Slingers...where do I even begin? Some people come into your life at the perfect time, and turn out to be the greatest gift you ever could have imagined. I don't know what the heck I did to deserve you, but I'm more grateful than I can say. Here's to your generosity of spirit, ridiculous organizational skills, patience with my wild ideas, and willingness to leap right into the fray, dagur in hand. As long as the sun burns in the sky and the oceans lap the land, I will give thanks for you!

I'm also grateful to MTMC Tours and Books Forward, for stellar awareness-raising, as well as The Wandering Bibliofiles. It doesn't get much better than a Seven Sins-themed dinner on a houseboat, y'all!

The worst part of acknowledgments is the terror of leaving someone important out...and over the course of this series, there have been so many people who have made a difference. If I've forgotten someone, I'm truly sorry. Consider this my blanket statement of gratitude!

And, of course, my deepest, undying, eternal flame of appreciation for my readers, without whom Ari and Eva's story would've gone untold. With fire and iron, my friends. I am honored to write by your side.